Spirals of Fate

Tim Holden

2019

1st Edition – Published by Monkey Time Books in 2019
22 Heigham St
Norwich, NR2 4TF, UK

ISBN no: 978-1-9162448-0-1

Copyright © Tim Holden 2019

The right of Tim Holden to be identified as the author of this work has been asserted by him in accordance with the Copyright, Design and Patents Act 1988.

All rights reserved. No part of the publication may be reproduced, stored in or introduced into a retrieval system, or transmitted, inn any form, or by any means (electronic, mechanical, photocopying, recording or otherwise) without the prior written permission of the publisher. Any person who does any unauthorised act in relation to this publication may be liable to criminal prosecution and civil claims for damages.

A CIP catalogue record for this book is available from the British Library.

This book is sold subject to the condition that it shall not, by way of trade or otherwise, be lent, re-sold, hired out, or otherwise circulated without the publisher's prior consent in any form of binding or cover other than that in which it is published and without a similar condition including this condition being imposed on the subsequent purchaser.

For more information on this book, and others
by the same author, visit:
www.timholden.com

*To my father, Anthony,
for his trust and generosity.*

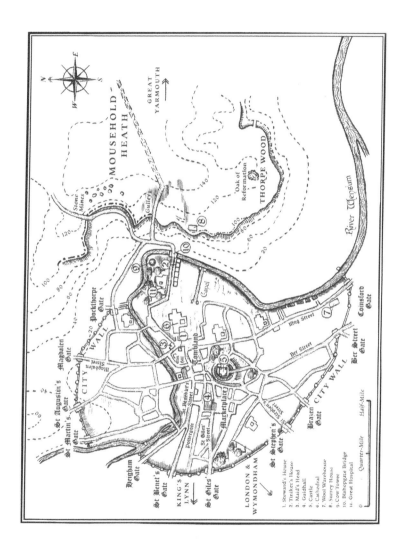

PART 1

1 Corinthians 10:13

[13] No temptation has overtaken you except what is common to mankind. And God is faithful; he will not let you be tempted beyond what you can bear. But when you are tempted, he will also provide a way out so that you can endure it.

1

4th July 1549, Parish of Wymondham, Norfolk

Robert Kett preferred to gamble only what he was willing to lose.

He tipped up his purse and spilt coins onto the dining table, separating out the shillings and setting them in stacks of five. After evensong, he would meet his friends at the alehouse for their weekly game of dice. He selected enough coins to cover his expenses and put the rest back in the purse. This evening's games were an unwelcome distraction; the summer wool clip had finished this week, and Robert needed to cash in his fleece harvest and make certain his speculation had paid off.

He hid the purse under the loose flagstone beneath the table, standing up just as his wife entered the room.

'I'm ready,' Alice declared.

Although her beauty had faded with age and childbirth, she insisted on combing her hair, cleaning her teeth and scenting herself with expensive rose oil before stepping out in public. Everyone dressed up for church, but Alice went to the same lengths whenever she left the house. She had delayed their departure more times than Robert cared to remember, but her devotion to maintaining a good appearance was one of the many things he loved about his companion of thirty years. Many of his peers had mistakenly fallen for the first woman willing to lie with them. One man he knew had prayed for years for his wife to be taken during childbirth, only to spend his later years praying for forgiveness that his wish had been granted.

'Are you going to church like that?' asked Alice, frowning with disapproval as she adjusted her shawl.

'Come along,' said Robert, leaving the room before she could make further observations. 'It won't do to keep the Lord waiting.' Nor could his business at church wait.

Unlike his wife, Robert liked his leather jerkin. He believed it lucky, which made it essential gambling wear, even if it had grown tatty with the passage of time. Robert was past caring about clothes and even took a certain delight in neglecting his appearance. The so-called good and the great might preen like peacocks, but Robert was as comfortable gossiping with commoners as he was rubbing shoulders with the ruling classes. He was never scruffy, but by avoiding bright clothes and expensive fabrics, he felt he never forgot his more humble roots. Not that those roots were truly humble, but they were at least more austere than his current existence. He kept his once black hair, now streaked with grey, in the simple fashion, cut straight across his forehead and long over his ears, and he rarely covered it with a hat, save for the coldest winter days. Today, as so often, he was unshaven, his thick silver stubble neatly covering his sun-tinted face like an even coating of dust. He was missing only two teeth: the top left eyetooth and one from his lower gum. Not bad for a man of fifty-seven.

Alice followed him into the hallway. Mary, their maid, entered the hall a moment later from the direction of the kitchen, but Robert paid no attention as she scurried past, carrying in her arms a copper pot and a horsehair brush.

'Mary,' said Alice, 'before you finish tonight, can you please scrub the floor of the dairy. I noticed a faint smell earlier and we don't want the milk to spoil.'

'Yes, Mrs Kett,' said Mary dutifully, before going on her way to sweep the ashes from the dining-room fireplace.

Robert took his coat from the hook in the porch and folded it over his arm. He stepped aside to let Alice pass, stealing a kiss as she did.

At the end of their track, a slight man on horseback greeted them.

'Mr Kett, just who I was looking for,' he said with some relief.

The man looked familiar, but Robert couldn't place him. Balding with a squashed face, he was no more than fifty. As Robert got older he frequently found he could recognise faces, but names didn't come so easily. He said hello and hoped the man would do or say something to prompt his memory to return.

'It's that time of year again, Mr Kett,' the man said. 'Mayor Codd would like to invite you to discuss your leather goods.'

Robert's relief at discovering the identity of Mayor Codd's messenger was soon replaced by annoyance. Every year Robert was summoned to Norwich under the pretence of selling leather to the mayor. There were at least four tanneries right under the mayor's nose in Norwich, and all of them capable of supplying high-grade leather. Although Mayor Codd might buy a token amount of Robert's leather every third year, his true intention in dragging him the eight miles into the city was to hear first-hand the gossip and goings-on in and around Wymondham. The mayor had been candid enough to explain previously that he never trusted rumours. By the time they reached his ears they were twisted beyond recognition.

'You've come at a busy time, the height of summer. How much does he actually want?' asked Robert, making no attempt to hide his exasperation.

'He'll discuss that with you in person. He maintains your leather is the best around, Mr Kett.' The messenger gave a resigned shrug.

Robert smiled wryly. 'It's the festival this weekend. Tell him I'll come next week.'

'You are a gentleman, Mr Kett.' The messenger nodded his appreciation and acknowledged Alice. 'If you'll excuse me, I'd like to be back before nightfall.'

Robert waved the messenger farewell and wondered to himself what advantage he could recover from next week's ill-timed journey. Over the weekend, he would draw up a list of things that would make his trip to the city worthwhile.

Robert and Alice rode side by side in silence on the short journey to Wymondham Abbey. Its two great towers dominated the flat landscape like giant tombstones, hazy in the bright summer sunshine. Normally they would walk to town, as Robert had grown portly in recent years, and he liked the exercise. He didn't miss the labours of his youth – tanning and farming had taken their toll on his body – but hard work had at least served to keep his belly flat. Now he joked that it was where he kept his money. But this evening they rode to the abbey. Alice would want to be home before dark, and Robert's evenings in the tavern sometimes went on till late.

'Mary asked me for more money this morning, Robert,' said Alice, her body gently swaying to the rhythm of her palfrey.

'Did she?' replied Robert, not wanting to pursue the subject.

'When I said she was looking thin, she told me her family are starving. With the price of things, it's no surprise.'

Robert shook his head. Commenting on their maid's thinness was an invitation for her to ask for more. Robert continued his policy of silence. When money was concerned, everybody wanted more, but rarely did they consider what else they might do to warrant it.

'She's been a good maid,' said Alice. 'I have no wish to see her and her children starve. I said I'd ask you, and now I have. You'll know what to do for the best.'

Robert grunted. This was typical. Alice would introduce a problem then step away, leaving him to resolve it. 'Who will go without then, if Mary is to have more?'

Alice shrugged. 'Perhaps your friends can advise you. Or maybe you can win some of their money.'

Robert felt the gentle reference to his hypocrisy, but what Alice didn't know was all the other demands he'd had to meet over the last seven days. 'Mary has company,' he said. 'Tom the shepherd wants more. Says he's working harder than ever and has been offered more elsewhere.'

'Well, it's true, there's more to be done now you have nearly a thousand sheep.'

'Yes, and half still to be paid for,' he reminded her. Having exceeded the limits of his own capital, he had bought half of his flock on credit. The summer wool clip had come to Wymondham last week, and so his creditors were expecting their money. Not that his labourers or his maid would appreciate the challenges of trying to get ahead under the Tudors. Enormous wealth rested in the hands of so few, and to Robert it sometimes felt as though the deck was stacked against yeomen like himself, who wanted nothing more than to better their lot. But complaining about the hand you've been dealt never won the round. You still had to play the game.

Robert ground his teeth. It was always the same: people saw you investing and assumed you must be knee-deep in money.

He had sunk almost everything into growing his flock. At a thousand head of sheep, it was still some way short of the two thousand four hundred permitted under statute, and a fraction of the flocks held by noble landowners, who as members of parliament, granted themselves exceptions to the restrictions in order to monopolise England's only commodity: wool.

Nonetheless, a thousand sheep was more than Robert had ever owned. After several months, he found himself questioning his bravery in plunging so deep into the wool trade. But he'd seen wool prices continue to rise steadily, and although Robert had responded more slowly than others, he hoped his boldness would help him make up for lost time. He hoped to avoid bad luck, too. With sheep crammed onto every available piece of land, all it would take was one case of rot or scab, and his investment would be slaughtered for meat, which, unlike wool, could only be harvested once. Disease and misfortune never seemed likely before an investment, but once you'd parted with your money – or indeed someone else's – they loomed large.

'It's not just Tom,' Robert continued. 'The shearers, the combers and the winders have all demanded more, saying there are more sheep than they can do. I suggested they have a word with their guild and take in some of the wretched poor to bolster their ranks.'

'What did they say?'

'They shrugged their shoulders, and I paid them what they

wanted. Except for the winders.'

Robert was glad he hadn't contracted his wool to anyone already. He was free to sell it wherever he liked, and to take advantage of the rising prices. All his expenses had risen, so he would need to achieve a good price, but fortunately English wool was much sought after in the cloth-making cities of Antwerp and Bruges. Robert hoped to meet Billy Badcock, the regrater, at the abbey this evening. Billy was the biggest buyer of wool between Norwich and Thetford. He was renowned for sharp practice and was no stranger to forestalling, but Robert felt he had the measure of him and was happy to be patient and agree a last-minute deal for his wool.

Robert's mind was taken off his dealings as they arrived in Wymondham. As their horses drew to a halt outside his tannery, Alice discreetly covered her nose. Robert, oblivious to the foul smell, watched his foreman, Master Peter, lock up the tool house and hang the key around his neck. Master Peter was a good man who had worked for Robert all his life and was now fully responsible for the tannery. His blonde hair looked greasy and his face as serious, as ever, but he smiled when he saw Robert and Alice, and he made his way up the path towards them.

'Peter, when will you prepare some leather so my husband can have a new jerkin?' asked Alice.

Master Peter smiled at Alice and eyed the garment she wanted to replace. 'It looks serviceable to me.'

'Good man, Peter,' said Robert. 'Now, can you ready some of our best samples for me to take to Norwich next week? Don't look too excited – I'm off to see Mayor Codd, so we shouldn't expect much.'

Master Peter nodded. He would have them ready tomorrow morning.

'That apart,' said Robert, 'is all well?'

'An apprentice would be timely. We're due to change the pits tomorrow, and since James Wood died, Mutt and I have been short-handed.'

Robert didn't like to give in to requests too lightly. He found it encouraged more of the same. But the tannery was his oldest enterprise, and the one on which he'd built all his subsequent ventures, so he was keen to see they had what they needed. Besides, there was no debating poor James Wood's fate. He'd been struck down by sickness, one day a fine young man learning his trade, the next bedridden, and the day after that saw him commended to God's care.

'I'll see who I can find. Have a good evening.'

'And you, Mr Kett,' replied Master Peter. 'Good evening, Mrs Kett. Enjoy the service.'

Robert twitched his ankles, and his horse walked on down the narrow street leading to the abbey. It was lined on both sides by small houses, some owned by Robert, others by William, his elder brother. Although William had inherited the lion's share of the family fortune and their late father's butchery, his wealth had been surpassed by that of Robert's. As he rode past their investments, Robert was reminded of the path his life had taken. He had worked hard, provided food and shelter for his wife and children, but his fortunes only really changed when old King Henry VIII sold off the land belonging to the old monasteries. Robert had been able to buy several pockets of land around Wymondham as Cromwell and his cronies rushed to raise funds for the late king. Robert had been sad to see the old order change and didn't like the manner in which it was done, but land was land, and he was unafraid to profit from the church's misfortune. Even now, he had limited sympathy for the church, which would still demand its tithe from the proceeds of the sale of his wool.

The grounds of the abbey were thronged with townsfolk, gossiping in the late afternoon sun. The service was the last before the festival of translation, so the day after next, the surrounding villagers would descend on Wymondham for a weekend's merriment. This would be Robert's only opportunity to do any business before the festival. He slid off his horse and helped Alice down, pressing a coin into the palm of his usual stable boy to mind the horses.

The sight of the abbey sparked mixed emotions in Robert. He had been schooled there, and so knew it better than most, but it was a sorry sight compared to the building he had known. His memories of the monks were not fond, but for all the failings of its inhabitants, the building had at one time inspired awe at man's devotion to God. Now, to Robert's eyes, it stood as testimony to everything that was corruptible and unworthy about man, from sodomising monks to a king who would stop at nothing in his pursuit of a male heir. The second aisle, which at one time ran east beyond the smaller, octagonal tower, was now gone, leaving the abbey with the appearance of a large church conjoined with a tower belonging to another building. The missing nave's materials had been plundered and carted away at the king's pleasure, under the direction of his serjeant-at-law, John Flowerdew. The thought of Flowerdew made Robert bristle.

Arm in arm, he and Alice made their way toward the door at the base of the larger flint tower, exchanging pleasantries and nodding acknowledgements as they went. The conversations around them included the coming festival, the lack of rain, war with Scotland, the rebellion in Cornwall, who would be getting married next, and the scandalous prices of goods at market. Immediately outside the door, gathered in line, were the town's poorest, hands outstretched. As he had become a leading person in the town, so going to church had become a more expensive exercise. Denied the charity of the monasteries, the wretched poor had become the responsibility of those who could afford to help. A girl at the end of the line offered a clumsy curtsey as Robert and Alice approached. She could not have been more than twelve. Her top lip was all but missing, leaving a curved gap under her nostrils, disfiguring what would otherwise have been a pretty face. She was barefoot, and her clothes were ragged.

'Alms for the needy, Mr Kett?' The destitute knew who to address their appeals to.

Robert took a coin from his purse and placed it in her hand. She flashed an unsightly grin and clamped her hand shut.

'Thank you kindly, Mr Kett.'

'Be good and say your prayers,' said Robert, his charity over. The rest of the line would have to make their claims elsewhere. Robert and the other aldermen of Wymondham had agreed that they would each gift one person as they arrived, to stop church becoming too expensive. It didn't stop the other beggars from chancing their arms, though. No sooner had the young girl made good her departure, than a tall boy with broad shoulders confronted Robert. Robert couldn't recall seeing him before: he had the physique of a man but the awkward posture of a boy. His black hair was greasy and uncut, tucked behind his ears and hanging lankly just above his shoulders. His skin bore scars left by pubescent spots. Robert guessed he couldn't be much more than fifteen. Like the girl before him, his hand was outstretched.

'Lad your age should be working,' said Robert.

The boy's gaze turned to Mrs Kett. Finding no purchase, he returned to Robert. 'No work, sir.'

Robert grunted. It wasn't unusual. At one time the

monastery had kept a great many of the townsfolk employed. Since its demise, the demand for stonemasons, lead workers, glaziers, tilers, even carters and casual labourers, had plummeted faster than the Mary Rose. Most of the tradespeople had survived or moved on, but where once they would have taken on apprentices, now they were more cautious. Thatchers, carpenters, and blacksmiths were always in demand, the good ones at least, but it had been the young that had suffered most at the hands of late King Henry's policies. No doubt this boy was no exception.

'Sorry, lad, you'll have to make your case to the next man.'

'Have you any work, sir?'

Alice nudged Robert's arm. 'You need a strong lad to apprentice at the tannery.'

Robert grunted. Why did she put him on the spot like that?

'Surely he would do well?'

'I've not seen you before, lad,' said Robert. 'Who are you, and where are you from?'

'Alfred Carter. Since my parents died, I now live in Hethersett. I'm not afraid of hard work.'

Robert wasn't sure what to make of the lad. He had an honest face, but there was something that gave Robert doubt. As he was trying to work out what that something was, Robert glimpsed Billy Badcock moving swiftly through the crowd. The wool dealer handed a coin to a pauper and entered the abbey. 'You can start tomorrow,' said Robert, his eyes still fixed on Billy. 'At eight o'clock.' Before Alfred could thank him properly, Robert pulled Alice into the abbey in pursuit of Billy.

The pale stone of the abbey's interior shone gold in the glare of the falling sun through the plain glass windows. What once was a riot of coloured glass and golden idols was now a bare, sober offering to God. It was the congregation who brought the abbey to life, exchanging greetings and gossip at the rear of the nave, making enquiries and shaking hands on agreements. Commerce was welcomed in the abbey, and deals struck within its walls were considered unbreakable. God's watchful eye kept all parties honest. Robert located Billy among the worshippers and stepped away from Alice, ready to broach the subject of wool.

Robert waited until Billy had finished a conversation, then guided him to the edge of the crowd so they might talk more privately. Billy was a paunchy man, with stubby fingers and oily skin.

'Billy, good to see you,' Robert said. 'How are you?'

'Not well, Robert. And you?'

That didn't bode well for the discussion that was to follow. 'Well, perhaps I can help you,' replied Robert, eager to talk trade before they were interrupted. 'My wool's in, and I'm ready to sell.'

'Not to me,' said Billy. His face showed no emotion. Robert frowned. Billy wasn't a man to turn his nose up at a deal. 'I'm not buying, Robert.'

'Not buying? Why not?' Robert's mind began to race. Perhaps this was just part of the bargaining process.

'I'm just back from Antwerp, where I sold at a loss. I practically had to give it away.'

'A loss … why?'

'They're not buying English wool.'

'What?'

'It's lost its quality, they say. We're over-farming our animals, and the fleece is thin and coarse. They can't work with it. They want Spanish wool now. It's better, they say, and cheaper.'

'But they've been buying up everything we can send.'

'They say that felt hats are the thing, ever since the old king introduced them, but you can't make a fine hat with worsted wool. You need a broadcloth.'

'Come on, Billy,' prodded Robert, still unwilling to believe what he was hearing. 'You must be in the market for something.'

Billy shook his head and leaned in. 'I'm in trouble, Robert,' he said softly. 'I've contracted to buy early, to avoid the summer prices, but now I'll be lucky to get through this with the shirt on my back.' Robert had never heard Billy Badcock speak like this; it was clear that this was no brinkmanship. 'You'll have to find someone else. I'm sorry.'

Billy left Robert alone with his thoughts: were his plans really unravelling because some nobles in London had decided on a different style of hat? If he couldn't sell his wool, how would he pay his creditors? The flock's value would slump. How would he pay for winter feed? What had once seemed bold, now felt reckless. And if word spread, the scavengers would circle, offering derisory sums for his prize assets.

Robert was relieved to hear the bells toll for the start of the service, sparing him the need to make small talk. He found Alice, and they made their way down the central aisle. They took their usual places in the second pew from the front on the left, just a few feet from the spot where they had been proclaimed husband and wife years before. Behind them, the congregation hurried to their seats. Robert was oblivious to the nod of welcome from the pastor as he took his place at the front of his own flock. Fortunately, Alice, unaware of their change in fortune, smiled and returned the acknowledgement.

William, Robert's brother, appeared at the end of their pew. At sixty-four he was seven years Robert's senior. Their shared lineage was unmistakable; they would have looked almost identical had William not chosen to hide his more deeply-lined face with a beard. Like his younger brother, William had kept his teeth. The wooden pew creaked as he planted himself beside Robert. As usual, William was alone.

They nodded, a greeting that might have seemed dismissive to a stranger, but for brothers who had been close their whole lives, it was more than sufficient. William was a widower, and Robert would sometimes tease William about not having a new woman to accompany him to church. Today, Robert had other things on his mind.

'Where's our friend Flowerdew?' whispered William as the congregation began to settle.

Robert shook his head. When you were as unpopular as Flowerdew, there was little point in arriving at church early. Nobody wanted to be seen talking to the king's extortionist-in-chief.

The pastor welcomed them to evensong and began to recite the general confession in English, one of the many changes of Archbishop Cranmer's recent reforms that Robert thought pragmatic. How could you preach to people in a language they did not understand and expect them to learn? The pastor's introduction was interrupted by the heavy clunk of the main door closing, Robert glanced at William, and a moment later, John Flowerdew swaggered past with his wife and two children. As they took their place in the pew in front of the Ketts, Flowerdew smirked. His pointy nose, short upper lip, freckled cheeks and ginger hair reminded Robert of a fox. He was just as cunning as a fox.

Robert stared at him, emotionless. If ever there was a man who should be on time for the general confession, he thought. How he had the nerve to show his face in this holy building after his actions ten years before, Robert would never understand. Once the monks had been cleared out and the second nave dismantled, the parish had raised the money to secure the building as the town church. Flowerdew, using the full force of his office, seized his opportunity and stripped the adjoining buildings bare. He dragged away the lead, timber and stone of the chapter house, refectory, infirmary and cloisters. The townspeople were outraged, believing that they had purchased the entire abbey. They had looked to Robert to challenge Flowerdew, and he had, but, like the devious lawyer he was, Flowerdew hid behind the trickery of the words in the contract. Robert was no lawyer, but if the material didn't belong to the town, then it could only belong to the crown, so he threatened Flowerdew that he would write to the king. The looting did stop, but Flowerdew kept everything he'd already taken.

The people of Wymondham had long memories, however, and nothing had been forgiven. The episode had served to establish Robert as the leading townsperson in civic matters, and in Flowerdew he had acquired a powerful enemy, one who would seek revenge whenever opportunities arose.

Flowerdew sat down in front of Robert, obscuring his view. The pastor began the absolution.

2

Alfred Carter couldn't believe his luck. Following his chance encounter with Robert Kett, he had work.

'You lucky bastard,' said his older friend, Fulke, as they slipped out of sight around the back of the abbey.

Alfred felt light-headed. He'd been sent to beg in Wymondham by his father-in-law, who was too proud to have him do it in their own village of Hethersett. Everyone in the village shared the same plight, but when you were as unpopular as his father-in-law, it didn't pay to announce it. Alfred had hoped to go home with a penny or two, but would instead be returning as an apprentice tanner. He knew nothing about tanning, but that didn't matter: he would pay attention and learn the trade. For the first time since his brief and unfortunate marriage, he could hold his head high in what now served as his family home. He would be a tradesman. His father-in-law was only a commoner.

'Looks like you'll be buying tonight, Alfred,' quipped Fulke as they sat on the ground, backs against the stone wall of the abbey. Inside, the service was beginning. Fulke thought God a sham and wouldn't shy away from saying so. Alfred went to church because he had to.

Fulke had come into Alfred's life at its lowest point. He'd

offered Alfred a tip at a cockfight, and the bet had paid off. They drank together afterwards, and since then Fulke had taken Alfred under his wing. One thing Alfred had learned was that Fulke tended to do as he pleased and people didn't argue with him. Fulke reminded Alfred of a bulldog: short and squat, with closely-clipped hair. A scar ran down the length of his cheek, and beneath his determined jawline was a vein that looked as though it wanted to escape his neck. Alfred imagined that Fulke was not a man to provoke.

This evening, having decided not to attend church, they had an hour to pass. Being caught at large during a church service was punishable, and there was no shortage of people in Wymondham capable of taking an interest in your affairs: the justice of the peace, the constable, his deputies, the alderman, the watchman, the bailiff, the reeve or the warden. As they waited, Fulke complained about Master Hobart, the lord of his manor, but his grievances were not new, and Alfred paid little attention. As the early evening sky faded from blue to orange he imagined a brighter future for himself. He saw himself tasting wine and buying clothes other than homespun. Extravagances he had never known.

The service ended, and people began to file out of church. 'Come on,' said Fulke. 'I'm thirsty.'

'Fulke, I have no money.'

'I'll pay tonight. You can see me right soon enough, now you've got work.'

'But–'

'No buts. Follow me.'

Alfred heaved himself to his feet. 'All right, just one.'

The door to the Green Dragon was propped open, to let the light in and the smell of its patrons out. It was always full after church. The low wooden ceiling made the crowded alehouse feel dark and small. No fire burned at this time of year, but candles cast a faint glow against the whitewashed walls in the dimmer corners of the room. Rush matting that still looked fresh covered the beaten earth. The Green Dragon was a good deal cleaner than the Rose & Thorn, which Alfred had visited before, but its atmosphere was full of the same heady mix of ale and breath. Alfred followed as Fulke pushed through to the taproom and ordered two ales from the middle-aged innkeeper, who filled two leather tankards. When Fulke complained about the price she invited him to try the Rose & Thorn if he wanted cheap swill to drink. Fulke grimaced, handed over the money, and passed a tankard to Alfred.

'There, don't spill it.'

Alfred took a sip and caught sight of his new employer stepping through the doorway.

*

Robert and William made their way upstairs to the private room made ready for them by Judy, the innkeeper. Their gambling companions followed them up the creaking wooden staircase: Thomas Elmham, Wulfric Smith and Luke Miller were regular players, who met the Kett brothers every Thursday evening for cards or dice, and Anders Marshwell, who occasionally joined them. Set out on the table at the centre of the room were a dozen filled tankards, two bowls of salted fish, a pot for their bets, a deck of cards and an empty tankard containing four dice. The small room was well lit, with windows on either side, and plentiful candles ensured they could play as long as they wished. Judy gave the men every reason to stay late and no cause to go elsewhere.

Robert hung his coat on the pegs behind the door.

'We might be here late tonight, gentlemen,' said Wulfric

with a broad smile. 'Mr Kett has bought his coat!'

Robert ignored Wulfric. After his conversation with Billy, he had little appetite for laughter or games, but after forty years in commerce, he knew how to put on a brave face. He hoped the conversation wouldn't turn to sheep.

They pulled out the benches, sat down, three on each side of the table, and passed out the ale. Each man placed his purse on the table.

Robert looked around the table. 'So, gentlemen, a game of inn-and-inn to start?'

'Your purse looks a little light, Luke?' teased Wulfric.

Luke was thirty-five, and the youngest man present. His hair was mousey brown, his face well-proportioned with tepid brown eyes, his height and build both middling, all of which served to make Luke in every way run of the mill, and so somehow easy to overlook. He'd inherited his father's fortune, but not his father's skill with dice and cards. Each week a little more of his inheritance found its way into the pockets of his friends.

'Not for long,' said Luke. 'I'm feeling lucky tonight.'

Robert and Wulfric exchanged a glance. Young Luke would be leaving empty-handed as usual.

Each man rolled a die to see who would start. Luke rolled a six. 'I warned you, tonight's my night,' he said as they each placed a coin in the pot in the middle of the table. Luke rolled all four dice: a two, a one and two fives. He smiled at rolling a double on his first attempt, put another coin in the pot, and rolled two of the dice again. If he rolled another pair, he would win the pot. Although the pot was still light, winning it on the first attempt would be a good omen. He rolled a one and a five.

Robert took his first taste of the dry and sour ale. He exhaled slowly and began to relax; his worries could wait until the next morning. Problems never seemed as stark after a good night's sleep. He took a second mouthful.

'How's trade?' Wulfric asked Robert. The two men were in the same guild.

Robert turned his mouth down and shook his head. He didn't want to encourage the conversation.

'Mine too,' said Wulfric.

'Trouble is, we're all taxed to the high hilt, and the money is wasted waging war on the Scots. What is there to show for it?' said an indignant Anders.

Although on this occasion Anders was right, Robert never really saw eye to eye with him. He had an air of resignation about him and rarely smiled. He was one of those people who were happiest being unhappy, but he was worth staying close to. Anders was the reeve of Hethersett and acted on behalf of the villagers in any matters that concerned the lord of their manor, John Flowerdew. Given the lingering animosity between Robert and Flowerdew over the abbey, it paid to stay well informed.

'Now the bastards are going to tax our sheep at the end of the year,' Anders went on.

'That's one tax I agree with,' said Luke. 'So much land has been turned over to sheep. Now food is short and prices high. How the poor manage, I don't know.'

Robert grunted. Luke might be right, but it didn't help. Once it came into force, the government's new tax would further depress the value of his flock.

'They can have taxes on half my flock,' Wulfric whispered. 'The other half will temporarily vanish. I refuse to see my hard-earned money wasted on more folly against the Scots.'

Wulfric passed the dice to Robert, who was keen to turn the conversation away from sheep. He rolled the dice – no doubles – and turned to Thomas. 'What news of the rebellion in Cornwall?' he asked.

Thomas had friends in high places throughout the church and was among the first to hear important news, often long before it was altered and distributed for general consumption via the pulpits.

'It rumbles on. Exeter is under siege, surrounded by twenty thousand men.'

'Twenty thousand?' said William. '*Twenty thousand?*'

'It's true,' said Thomas, who was not given to exaggeration. 'I dare say they have any number of grievances, like any of us, but their complaints seem to be principally the young king's religious reforms.'

'What's the lord protector's response?' asked Wulfric.

The young King Edward faced an unenviable predicament, having ascended the throne two-and-a-half years earlier, in 1547, at the age of nine. He had inherited a country at war, with no money and no allies, facing a hostile pope, and still stumbling through religious changes that had divided opinion and split families as people argued over the right way to worship. Robert felt sorry for the boy. His father, Henry VIII, had appointed a regency council to govern the realm until Edward came of age, but Henry's corpse wasn't even cold before the boy's uncle, Edward Seymour, appointed himself lord protector and head of the Privy Council. For now, Seymour was the king in all but name. How readily, Robert wondered, would any man give up that power? And given the state of the country, how readily would a young man accept such a chalice? It rather put his own worries into context.

'The lord protector's tied himself in knots,' said William. 'Since he restricted the nobles' ability to hold armed retainers, they can't nip any rebellions in the bud. The king is safer from the nobles, but the nobles are at the mercy of the peasants.'

'It'll take an army to fight off twenty thousand rebels,' said Anders.

'Aye, and Seymour's army is in Scotland,' said Luke, passing the dice to Wulfric. 'The French must be licking their lips. The pope will back them to reinstate a Catholic on the throne. England is there for the taking.'

'You'd be happier than most with that I'd wager, you old Catholic dog?' said Wulfric.

The room fell silent. Luke's brow furrowed. 'We were all Catholics at one time, Wulfric. Even you.'

'Aye, and some of us still are,' retorted Wulfric.

'I've converted. I was at church tonight, same as you.'

Wulfric grunted. 'Some of us left our conversion to the new faith rather late, and until they had no choice.'

Luke shrugged.

'Now, now, gents,' interrupted Robert. 'Let's not be picking off scabs from old wounds that we want to heal. If Luke here was in church same as us, I aren't worried when he changed his beliefs. Now, if you'd be kind enough to pass me those dice Wulfric?' Robert dropped another coin in the pot and took his turn with the dice. Nothing.

'I hear that Protector Seymour's enclosure enquiry won't now come to Norfolk,' said Thomas, steering the conversation back to less contentious matters as he took the dice. 'By granting copyholders protection from eviction, he believes he can stop landlords enclosing common land for their own sheep. So it seems that those of us who have taken a share of the common land as our own, can continue.' He looked directly at Robert. 'For now.'

'Maybe,' said Robert. Ancient tradition saw pockets of land reserved for the commoners to graze their animals, and he was uneasy at having fenced a parcel of common land for his own use. But too often the local people neglected their commons, and if others were taking commons for themselves, why should he miss out? He had accounts to settle the same as everybody else.

'Did you hear they pulled some enclosures down in Attleborough last month?' asked William.

Robert nodded. He had heard and feared the same might happen to him. Why did this conversation keep coming back to sheep?

'There have been minor uprisings across the country,' said Luke. 'Seymour has been lenient and pardoned them all. So it's no surprise that one more should break out. The lord protector's reaping what he sows.'

'I think he favours the cause of the poor masses,' said Thomas, 'however he's caught betwixt and between. He can't build an army from starving peasants, and he must feed them or face civil war, but he needs the nobles' support and taxes to raise armies, and they will meet new taxes through wool sales, which means land is fenced off and commoners go hungry.'

'When the poor starve, they rebel,' declared Robert. 'They tear down fences, they steal sheep, and they're hung for it. But is it their fault they're hungry?'

'What do you mean to do about it, Robert?' asked Luke.

'The same as you.' Robert drank the last of his ale and slammed his empty tankard down on the table. 'Absolutely nothing! The commission won't stop enclosure. It's a ploy to pacify the peasants which will fizzle out, blocked by men far richer than us. If it ever finally makes a recommendation, it will be ignored. Too many powerful people have too much to lose.'

Robert took the dice and rolled a double two, a five and a

six. 'Look out, gentlemen,' he said, looking around. He put another coin in the pot, which had been growing as they spoke. He rolled a double six and laughed. The others groaned as he emptied the coins from the pot into his pile. He was well ahead. 'Let's get Judy up here with more ale,' Robert said with a flourish. My round.' Together, the men stamped their feet on the floorboards, announcing their needs to the innkeeper below.

'So what happens in the end?' asked Luke, his tone serious. 'When the poor have starved, where will our bread come from?'

'The Lord will decide that, Luke,' said Robert. 'It's not for me to say. Maybe he will punish the sinners with another plague.'

The room below was filling up, and the heat and noise were filtering up between the floorboards.

'Luke, be a gentleman and let in some air,' asked Robert.

The younger man stood and moved to the window, speaking as he did so. 'I don't want to bring down the mood, but you have seen the state of the crops in the field. If you think the poor are angry now, wait till they gather in the harvest and see how little they have for winter. It will be the likes of us they attack.'

'He's right,' said William. 'With nothing to lose, a man has nothing to fear.'

'Why do I come drinking with you lot?' complained Robert. 'My maid wants more pay. No doubt after that every other rascal will be at my door begging for more. The only people buying my leather are rich landowners, but you would deny them their wool income, and me for that matter? I come here to forget these worries.'

'Robert, you have my respect, and I am sure I speak for us all,' said Luke, sitting back at the table. The bench creaked as it took his weight. 'You might be light-hearted about your worries, you might drink and forget them for a while, but they will be waiting for you in the morning. There are few of us who have the influence to do anything, but I put it to you that in this town you are the person who is best placed to resolve matters. I, for one, would follow you and support you.'

Robert looked Luke in the eye. 'Thank you for your opinions, Luke, which are flattering, even though they are unwelcome. You know nothing of my worries, lad, and you must not mistake me for a sheriff. I'm nothing of the sort, so I'll have no more talk of sheep, enclosures, the poor or any related matter in this room tonight. Now roll the blessed dice.'

The next morning Robert sat at his table, suffering only a dry mouth and a mild headache. He usually took a small breakfast early before his main meal at eleven, but these days, after a night in the tavern, Robert liked to sleep longer and take an early lunch. Alice had made him some fried eggs and cold ham. He was feeling better with every bite.

'Am I right to imagine that the evening was a success?' enquired Alice.

'Passable. I at least managed to relieve my companions of their hard-earned money.'

'And spent the rest of the night buying them drinks with their hard-earned money?'

'That's how it works.'

'You're all heart, Robert. Did you give Mary's request any more thought?'

'In truth, no.' Robert mopped up the remainder of the egg yolk with the last of his ham. 'Trade is bad, Alice. I have yet to sell my wool, and I confess I am a little concerned. On top of that, our country is in turmoil. Was it like this when we were young?'

'It's a long time ago, Robert. But no, things were simpler, I think.'

Robert laid down his knife and fork. 'People don't have enough to buy necessities, never mind more. Any rain will be too late to make this harvest a good one. I foresee trouble.'

Alice sat down beside him. 'I think you're right.'

Robert sighed. 'That principled little upstart, Luke Miller suggested I do something about it! Offered me his support.'

'He may have a point,' said Alice.

'How so?'

'Who do you know who understands things the way you do?'

Robert frowned. Alice continued, 'Who in this parish has more experience of sorting out problems, especially to do with money?'

Robert wiped egg yolk from his bristly chin.

'It was you who saved the monastery.'

'You talk about me as though I were a king's official. I'm a merchant.'

'The king's a child, surrounded by his father's cronies – all as trustworthy as a sack of adders. What do they know of the people of Wymondham?'

'With the likes of Flowerdew in the king's pay, I would agree that nobody has our best interest at heart,' Robert conceded.

'I'm worried, too. Not for us, but for our children and grandchildren. They are not going to grow up in the England we knew.'

'Alice, our children are grown men, ready to fight their own battles. Granted, I also fear for the future, but what would you have me do about it?'

'I am not saying you need to solve anything yourself. However, you could make a difference. Who in Wymondham is more capable of that than you?'

'Have you been speaking to Luke Miller?'

Alice laughed. 'No, but think about it. Give that clever head of yours something to wrestle with.'

As if he didn't have enough to think about. 'No. Thank you for breakfast – the food at least was lovely.' Robert was adamant he wasn't getting involved. He got up and announced he was going to take in the air and check his sheep.

Alice called after him, 'What about Mary?'

Robert closed the door behind him.

3

5th July, Hethersett

The shrill sound of a cockerel crowing jolted Alfred into consciousness. He forced his eyes open and found himself lying on the beaten earth floor of his father-in-law's cottage. His mouth was dust-dry, and his head banged like a blacksmith's hammer. A column of grey light shone through the smoke hole in the thatch, and daylight filtered in under the door and through gaps around the windows. On a straw mattress in the corner of the cottage, Lynn, his wife, lay sleeping alongside her parents.

Alfred struggled to remember his journey home. After the Green Dragon they had gone back to the Rose & Thorn. He'd made the mistake of trying to keep pace with Fulke, but he was no match for his older friend.

He managed to swallow and shifted position on the floor. He hadn't planned on drinking last night. How had he been led astray again? Then he remembered: he started at Mr Kett's tannery today. He leapt up, cursing his foolishness. His mother would be berating him from beyond the grave.

Alfred crossed the room, startling the hens that mooched about the floor looking for crumbs. He unwrapped the cheese from its cloth and took a bite. It was dry and hard to chew, so he broke off a corner and tucked it up his sleeve before quickly folding the block back into the cloth. He'd be scolded later, but he didn't care. He had a four-mile walk to the tannery, then a full day's work and four miles home again, so he needed to eat. Alfred checked himself: he'd slept in his clothes, and his boots were still laced. He crept towards the door and carefully lifted the latch.

Outside, he relieved himself on to the dewy grass. The morning sun glowed amber but brought no warmth to his cheeks. He looked down the row of small farmhouses. Nothing stirred. Doors and shutters were closed; no smoke rose from rooftops, and no dogs or cats patrolled the village. Then the cockerel crowed again, and Alfred registered the dawn chorus ringing out from the trees. He sighed with relief: it was still early. He realised how fast his heart was beating. He walked unsteadily to the well outside the neighbouring cottage, pulled up the pail and splashed his face with cool water. His eyes prickled with relief. He washed his hands, then cupped them to drink. The water was heavenly.

Walking up the slope to the church, Alfred retraced his steps passed his father-in-law's cottage at the end of the row. It was a hovel in comparison to the other houses. He should have been grateful for shelter but couldn't help feeling ashamed to be shackled to the Smiths. However, they were his family now. The past month he'd spent married to their daughter Lynn had been among the worst of his life. Sometimes he lay awake at night wishing God would deliver him from them. He longed to see his parents again. Every moment with the Smiths was a brutal reminder of how fast his fortunes had changed. He'd never had wealth, but he had at least had a family and a home, however simple. Then, within the space of a month, his father had died of the sweating sickness, and his mother died an unexpected death that not even the clergy could explain. Forlorn and hopeless, he'd walked to Wymondham to look for work. He'd found none, but had made Fulke's acquaintance. Soon after that Alfred's luck deserted him again, when, unhappy and drunk, he'd found himself in Lynn's arms. She'd ridden him in the churchyard and Alfred, relishing a moment's pleasure, had thought nothing more of it until three weeks later she turned up, accompanied by her father, Richard, claiming to be pregnant. A week later they were married. They couldn't afford wedding rings, and since that day Richard had taken his daughter to task for choosing the poorest man in the parish. Alfred reckoned that Richard wanted to be rid of his daughter, but Alfred had no home to offer, no future, no promise of anything better. Instead, he'd moved into Richard's cottage.

He shook his head to escape the thoughts that plagued him. He should be grateful, he told himself as he ate the rest of Richard's cheese. He was surviving, he had a child on the way, and now he had a job. Whatever was required of him at the tannery, he would work hard and succeed. He might be chained to Lynn, but in time, he would save enough to escape his father-in-law.

As Alfred approached the tall flint church, whose position on a mound gave it a commanding view across the common, he was jolted out of his reverie by an unexpected voice.

'It's the boy, Carter.'

Alfred looked up to see George Newell leaning against the oak tree in front of the church. A sack rested on the floor at his feet. The few times Alfred had met George, he hadn't warmed to him.

'Wouldn't expect to see you at this hour. Unless, to look at you, you've yet to go to bed?'

Alfred checked his clothing and flicked at the dust and debris that remained from his night on the floor.

'Where you headed?' asked George. Villagers needing to travel would often meet at the church so they could walk in groups. You could never be sure who was waiting among the roadside trees.

'Wymondham,' said Alfred. 'You?'

'The other way. Norwich.'

That was good news. Wymondham was only a short walk, but George was a man who didn't keep his thoughts to himself, which made his exchanges with Alfred mostly unpleasant. 'What are you doing in the city?' Alfred asked.

George nodded at his sack. 'Hats. For the market.' George was a milliner with a small workshop in the village. 'Boy like you could use a hat. Keep the sun off you.'

Alfred shook his head.

'What you doing up so early then?'

'I have work in Wymondham.'

'Oh.' George made no attempt to hide his surprise. 'Richard will be pleased.'

Alfred shrugged. He'd never seen Richard happy.

'What sort of work?' George asked a lot of questions, but only ever revealed little about himself.

'Mr Kett's tannery,' replied Alfred, determined to say as little as possible.

'Working for him, are you?' George grunted.

'What do you mean?'

George folded his arms.

'Tell me,' said Alfred.

'Kett likes to think of himself as a good man, but–'

'Morning.'

Alfred and George turned to see who'd interrupted them. It was John Robertson, a bear of a man with tanned skin, black curly hair and a thick beard.

'Either of you going to Wymondham?'

'I am,' replied Alfred.

'Come on then. I need to be getting on.'

Alfred turned back to George who was looking out over the common, dotted with grazing sheep. 'What were you saying … about Mr Kett?'

George half-smiled, taking delight in withholding his knowledge. 'Let's just say I hope he takes better care of his workers than he does the people in his parish.'

Alfred frowned. What did that mean? Surely Mr Kett was a man of good repute. There were stories of men exploiting their workers, even beating them, and apprentices were often the butt of workplace tricks and humiliations. He shivered. He had been so relieved to find work that he'd given no thought to any possible consequences.

John was already walking away, so Alfred followed. The main road ran all the way from Norwich to London but had long since lost the stone surface left by the Romans and was now little more than a dirt track, lined with occasional trees and sunken ditches. Cartwheels had rutted the surface and hoof prints ran down the middle. The dry, sandy earth had cracked under the heat of the summer sun.

As they neared the end of the village common, Alfred asked, 'What do you know of Mr Kett?'

John ground his teeth as he thought. From what Alfred had seen of him, John was slowly spoken and thoughtful, and he wasn't one to talk ill of people. 'I'd say if you have a job with him, you've done well. He looks after his own. Looks after himself too, mind.'

'What do you mean?'

'No different to here,' said John pointing at the sheep to their right. 'That common's ours, yet Flowerdew's sheep are all over it.'

Alfred had listened night after night to his father-in-law's anger at John Flowerdew for erecting a fence across the middle of the common. The half left for the villagers was now overgrazed, and disputes had broken out between neighbours. Animals had vanished. Richard had slaughtered his pig early for fear it would be stolen. He'd since salted it, hoping to make it last through winter. If it didn't, they were in trouble.

'It's wrong,' John continued. 'This land has been there for commoners since God was a boy, but now rich men take it for their own profit, and people are going to starve. Look there.' John pointed to the flat, hundred-acre field on their left, divided up into a stripy patchwork of furlongs so that the farmers of the village each got a share of the fertile land and a share of the less fertile. Acres of barley for beer grew among acres of wheat and rye, oats and peas. 'Them crops are stunted,' sighed John. 'Weak. Not enough rain. Too late for a good harvest now.'

'What's this to do with Mr Kett?' asked Alfred.

John stared at Alfred as though measuring his trustworthiness. 'I won't gossip,' said Alfred.

'Well, it's nothing people don't already know: Kett's done the same as Flowerdew. Stolen our common land for his own gain. I thought he were a better man than that, after all he done for the abbey.'

Alfred stayed silent. Stealing common land was bad, but Mr Kett had given him a job, a chance. That mattered most to Alfred.

Despite being a slow talker, John Robertson proved to be a fast walker. They arrived in Wymondham just as the town was coming to life. Dogs barked as people opened shopfronts and called out greetings. Alfred said farewell to

John and made his way to the tannery. Nobody needed directions to a tannery: you just had to follow your nose.

The tannery was surrounded by a rough, slatted fence to stop people falling into the pits. Looking around, Alfred couldn't see anyone there – he was early, much to his relief. He was tired from the rapid walk and had a full day's work ahead, so he found a spot on the riverbank and watched the murky water flow past. As thirsty as Alfred was, the river water wasn't fit for drinking.

He felt better for the walk, the birdsong and the morning air. His father had always said dawn was the best part of the day. For the past month, Alfred had found solace in ale whenever he could. He woke each morning to another day of helping Richard to farm his acreage, and in return Richard only ever found fault with Alfred's work. Despite its stench, the tannery promised a new start. His parents would have been proud of him, and Alfred decided he would honour their memory by surviving where they hadn't.

The church bells chimed eight.

'Who are you?' called a voice from behind him. Alfred turned to see two men. The one who spoke was tall, with a square jaw and blonde hair, perhaps in his late thirties. The second man, Alfred thought, looked a bit simple.

Alfred stood and introduced himself. 'Alfred Carter. Mr Kett hired me yesterday. At evensong.'

The blond man looked suspicious. 'He never mentioned you.'

Alfred shrugged.

'Well, if you're lying, you won't get paid.'

Alfred smiled. He wasn't lying.

'How old are you?'

'Sixteen.'

'What do you know about tanning?'

Alfred shrugged again but assured the man that he was a fast learner.

'I'm Master Peter.' Alfred held out his hand, but Master Peter didn't shake it. 'When Mr Kett's not here, I'm in charge. This is Mutt.' He inclined his head towards the other man. 'You'll replace young James, who died last week.'

Alfred tried not to show fear as he wondered why the boy had died and whether it happened here at the tannery. Master Peter told him to pay attention while he showed him around.

The tannery consisted of twelve brick-edged pits, each the size of a large table. Arranged neatly in four rows of three, the pits were each four feet deep, filled with a foul-smelling liquid. A wooden-framed canopy sheltered the pits from the sun. There were no walls between the oak posts that supported the canopy, just the low perimeter fence. Mutt went to the far corner, nearest the riverbank, where he unlocked a small shed and picked out the hooks for carrying the hides. Alfred stood next to Master Peter at the edge of one of the pits and made an effort to concentrate while Master Peter explained the craft of tanning. When empty, a pit was filled from the river, then animal hides were laid flat across it, and chips of oak bark were scattered across them. Then more hides were placed on top, covered with more oak bark, and so on until the pit was full. Each pit held liquor of a different strength, according to the quantity of oak bark chips it contained, and each month, the hides were moved to a stronger pit. After a year, the hides were ready to come out and be fashioned into workable leather.

'With me so far?'

Alfred nodded. He sensed that Master Peter resented having to explain how it all worked. He followed Master Peter over to another much larger pit beyond the canopy's shade.

'Right, young Alfred, this is pit thirteen. Unlucky for some.' Master Peter grinned. The pit was full of brown water that made Alfred's stomach turn. 'This pit is very important. All the hides go in here first of all to remove the hairs. We'll be going to see Mr Kett's brother, William, later – he's a butcher and supplies our hides.'

'I know of Mr William Kett,' interrupted Alfred. 'My friend Fulke works for him.'

'En't that lovely,' snapped Master Peter. 'There'll be no time to stand around talking to your mates. Not when you work for Robert Kett. He's a good man, and you're lucky to have a job here. I know lots of folk more worthy than yourself who'd be glad to work here.'

Alfred reminded himself not to speak unless he was spoken to.

'So pay attention, do what I tell you, and don't give Mr Kett any cause to regret being charitable,' continued Master Peter. 'He has a weakness for stray dogs like you.'

Alfred nodded.

'We're emptying pit thirteen today,' Master Peter went on. 'While me and Mutt move the hides, your job is to restock the pit with fresh ingredients. Fetch that sack over in the corner.' Master Peter pointed to an empty hessian sack lying by the tool shed.

As Alfred picked it up, the sack gave off a foul smell. It was filthy and set rigid from never being washed. He gagged and held it at arm's length.

'Now walk round town and pick up every dog shit, cat shit, rat shit, and human shit you can find. If it eats meat, we want its shit. Chicken shit works too, but not cow or horse, so you can leave them.'

Alfred looked at Master Peter, slowly realising that he meant what he said. Now he understood why the water in pit thirteen was so disgusting. Master Peter's expression hardened.

'The shit in the water makes the hair fall out of the hides. Now go and fill the sack. The town will be grateful to you for cleaning up before the festival.'

Alfred gritted his teeth, turned his head away from the sack and walked into town. He'd always been squeamish with farm animals, even his father's grass-eating beasts whose dung was not so repulsive. But he couldn't refuse his first task.

Around noon Alfred returned with his third sack of turds. He was exhausted. It was hot, and his mouth was bone dry. Although he was starving, he was glad he hadn't eaten much, as he'd been sick behind the smithy. His hands stank, and the idea that he was lucky to have this job had disappeared. He'd vowed to work hard for Mr Kett, but not doing this. He couldn't wait to clean up and put this morning behind him. The thought of sinking a tankard of ale had never seemed more appealing.

He tipped the contents of the sack into pit thirteen, which was now emptied of its hides.

'Well done, Alfred,' said Master Peter, patting him on the shoulder, 'It's a horrible job, but credit to you, you didn't complain. The good news is you won't have to do it again for a month.'

Alfred exhaled with relief. Once a month was still too often, but he looked forward to better tasks in the meantime. Master Peter's approval helped, too. He'd found Master Peter unnecessarily frosty at first, but a compliment always meant more from someone like that. Perhaps if Alfred could stay on his good side, keep his head down and not chatter when he should be quiet, then all would be well.

'Alfred, it's time to christen the pit,' said Master Peter. 'It's a tradition. Each time we empty pit thirteen, we top it up with a contribution of our own.'

Alfred looked around, unsure what was meant. Master Peter and Mutt stood either side of him and unfastened their codpieces. Master Peter looked straight ahead. 'You can't make decent leather without a good measure of Wymondham piss,' and unleashed a steady yellow stream.

Alfred stepped up and untied his codpiece. He caught a brief whiff of urine, but it was soon lost in the heady mixture of the tannery stink. Master Peter and Mutt seemed oblivious to the miasmas that surrounded them, so Alfred hoped that he too would get used to it in time.

Alfred avoided touching himself with his filthy hands. He wasn't sure he could go, having urinated earlier in the morning. Mutt was peeing, and Master Peter was almost finished. Alfred began to panic – what if he couldn't go in front of the other men? After a pause that seemed to last an age, he finally managed a feeble dribble into the stinking pit. He exhaled, and just as he relaxed his shoulders, the two men grabbed his arms and threw him forward. Alfred yelled in horror as he hit the stinking brown water. It would have been better to keep his mouth shut.

4

6th July, Hethersett Hall

'Edward, it's time you earned your keep,' said John Flowerdew to his son. 'Put your riding boots on.'

The excited eleven-year-old bounded up the grand wooden staircase, leaving Flowerdew alone in the hall. Unlike its predecessor, the new hall was an impressive brick pile set outside the village of Hethersett, away from its inhabitants. Flowerdew had bought the property, together with farming rights to the surrounding land, ten years earlier.

While he waited for Edward he gazed at the tapestries that adorned the oak-panelled room. He often indulged himself among the impressive things he'd accumulated: marble fireplaces, furniture crafted from exotic woods, oil paintings, even a portrait of himself. He craved a Holbein for his collection but was yet to fulfil that desire. His wife accused him of avarice, but his possessions reminded him of how far he'd come from his humble beginnings.

Flowerdew liked to attribute his success to his own guile. But even he couldn't deny he owed a lot to the dissolution of the monasteries. He'd been in the right place at the right time and seized his opportunity with both hands. In the name of

King Henry VIII, he'd ruthlessly stripped the surrounding monastic communities of their wealth and property, returning the king a handsome profit, as well as lining his own pockets.

He had looked set for further promotion until the king had Thomas Cromwell's head cut off. With his ally executed, his fortunes had plateaued. Flowerdew hoped the change in monarch would afford him new opportunities to gain favour, but in the meantime he focused his energies on accruing more land and wealth. Influence and power did not come cheap.

Flowerdew smiled as he checked himself in the looking glass. He thought he looked impressive in his red robe, no matter that his wife had told him the red clashed with his freckled skin and ginger hair. Over the robe he wore a large gold chain with a ruby pendant. He did not normally wear jewellery when riding, but today he wanted to intimidate. He pulled on suede gloves, then slid gold rings on to his fingers.

He started to pace, the floorboards creaking under his weight. Why was Edward taking so long? His gut was fluttering. He wouldn't admit to apprehension, but today he expected to encounter fear and hostility. His display of finery would remind angry peasants of their place.

Outside in the courtyard the early morning sun cast long shadows. A groom, staring at the floor, held Flowerdew's horse and Edward's pony. His three armed retainers, already mounted, waited with stern faces. The tunics of red and green halves they wore were not formal heraldic arms, but Flowerdew had used the pattern long enough that it was recognisable as his livery. Unofficial or not, his colours made Flowerdew look every inch the man he had become.

Edward ran out of the hall in his riding boots, and the groom interlocked his fingers to create a step for the boy to mount his pony. Edward was Flowerdew's eldest son but was still young to accompany his father on today's duties. Having lost his own father at an early age, Flowerdew was determined that Edward too should leave his childhood behind as early as possible. He needed to become familiar with the harsh realities of Tudor England.

With the aid of the groom, Flowerdew mounted his stallion. It shivered its neck as he settled into the saddle. He and his son rode across the courtyard, the men-at-arms following behind.

'What are we doing today, father?' asked Edward.

'Wait and see,' replied Flowerdew.

'How long need I wait?' Edward was a precocious child.

'When I was your age, the man who adopted me would have beaten me for such a question.'

They passed under the brick archway that formed the entrance to the courtyard and Edward tried again. 'Is it official matters for the king today?'

'No. Not today.' John Flowerdew was now one of only ten serjeants-at-law in the country, and so was often required to manage the king's affairs in the county. 'We're doing Flowerdew work today.'

'What work is it, father?'

Flowerdew told his son to be quiet as they made their way down the track to the village. He reflected on his plans for one last time. Exporting the wool produced by his large flocks of sheep had made him a tidy fortune, all of which he had reinvested into expanding his flock, which had quadrupled in size in the past five years. To sustain this growth he had already turned much of his demesne over to sheep, and then he had taken some of the common land used by the villagers. They had protested, but there was little they could do to stop him. He'd left them enough to survive; he did not want a revolt to quell. Other landowners nearby had been too hasty, taking entire commons for themselves. Faced with starvation, their villagers had had little option but to fight back.

This year's dry weather presented Flowerdew with a problem. Although he had just about enough land, the grass was dry and growing poorly, so it yielded less food for his sheep. Flowerdew's response, to sustain both his flock and the villagers, was to ease the pressure on the commons and free up land already in use. To achieve this outcome, it was necessary to make a sacrifice: to reduce the number of mouths there were to feed.

The early morning sun warmed Flowerdew's cheeks as they rode in silence. The dew would soon dry. The sweet scent, the gentle sway of his horse and the birdsong all distracted from the unpleasantness to come.

In no time they arrived at the edge of the village. He drew his horse to a halt outside a small cottage, which stood next to a line of four small farmhouses, all with mossy thatched roofs. It was too early for cooking fires to be smoking through the smoke holes, and the village was quiet. The inhabitants were still indoors. Early morning was the best part of the day, and yet the peasants slept through it, no doubt sleeping off yesterday's drink. Flowerdew despised their laziness.

It was the cottage on the end that concerned Flowerdew today. He had chosen well. It was on the edge of the village, so they didn't need to ride in full view of the other houses. If they were quick, they could avoid announcing their presence and be gone before doors opened and rumours spread.

Flowerdew looked at his retainers, then Edward, and put his finger to his lips. They dismounted, handing their reins to the youngest of the retainers, leaving him to watch the horses. Flowerdew whispered to Edward, 'Under no circumstances are you to talk or ask questions.'

As they approached, two swallows fled their nest in the thatch. The largest of the two retainers opened the cottage door without knocking. He held it open for Flowerdew, and the party followed him inside.

The room was small and dark. It smelt of peasants. There was no rush matting to cover the earth floor. A mother combed her daughter's hair, and a young man sat on a stool near the hearth, chewing some food. Their faces registered first shock, then fear. It was the older man Flowerdew was looking for. In the gloom at the rear, Flowerdew saw a man's silhouette. Richard Smith stood naked at the end of his straw mattress.

Flowerdew spoke. 'Good morning to you and your family, Mr Smith.'

'Good morning, sir,' they replied in unison, except the young man, whose mouth was still full.

'Who is this young man?' asked Flowerdew. 'I don't recall seeing him before.'

'His name is Alfred Carter, sir,' said Smith, his voice betraying his concern. 'You recently granted him permission to marry our daughter, Lynn.'

Lynn bowed when she heard her name. She was broad-shouldered with a flat chest and wiry, mouse-brown hair. Her unfeminine appearance was not helped by a downturned mouth and a wart on her chin. Altogether she had a sour look. The young man Alfred finally swallowed his mouthful and bowed his head as courtesy demanded. Flowerdew could not recall granting any permission to marry, but he was prone to forget more trivial duties.

Folding his arms, Flowerdew turned to the matter in hand. 'I have called early to be sure to find you before you begin your day's labours. Please sit.'

There was little furniture. Flowerdew waited for Richard to find a stool. He sat down and covered his genitals with his hands, and the women sat on the floor. Flowerdew, his son and his men-at-arms all remained standing.

'The land you farm, which I lease to you, is no longer at your disposal. I am cancelling your lease.'

The two women gasped. Richard Smith, still half-asleep, took a little longer to take the news in. Flowerdew waited for Smith to catch up before he went on. 'If you cannot farm the land, you will most likely not be able to provide me with goods or labour in return for the use of this cottage.'

Smith stood up and started to speak. 'Sit down!' barked Flowerdew. The two men-at-arms unsheathed their weapons with a sharp, rasping sound. Smith sat down, and the women started to cry. The fluttering in Flowerdew's stomach had gone now.

'By compensation, although I am not required to do so, I will afford you thirty days grace to live here whilst you make arrangements for your family. Unless that is, you quarrel with me. Should you do so, I will have you thrown out now with force, as our contract permits me to do.' Flowerdew knew that, like all peasant farmers, Richard Smith could not read or write. He had no idea what he had agreed to when he had taken on the cottage and its acreage.

'Sir, why? What have we done to displease you?' Richard pleaded. His wife and daughter sobbed in disbelief.

'I am entitled to use my land and my property as I see fit. I would advise you not to concern yourself with why. Instead, consider what you do next.' He watched the man's reaction. Smith looked shocked and upset, but not likely to erupt into anger. The offer of the cottage for a month had dampened the flame of his resistance, as Flowerdew had hoped. Instead, in a spectacle Flowerdew found pathetic, Smith fell to his knees and tearfully begged him to reconsider. His wife did the same.

'Despite what people might say, I am a fair man,' said Flowerdew, taking a sovereign from the purse around his waist and tossing it towards Smith. 'This sovereign for your troubles.' The coin hit the earth floor with a dull thud. Smith scrambled from his stool and gripped the coin in his fist. 'May God have mercy on your souls,' said Flowerdew. 'But if you make any mischief for me, now or later, my men will come back and gut you like a fish.'

Flowerdew squinted as he stepped from the darkness of the cottage into the morning light. He exhaled, glad the moment was over and happy to breathe the fresh air. He didn't care two turds what happened to the Smith family, but delivering news that came close to a death sentence was still a disagreeable task. His shoulders softened as he looked around. It had gone well. The Smiths had been quiet, and no blood had been spilt. The rest of the village was still indoors. The only sounds were the dawn chorus and sobbing from inside the cottage.

The five riders mounted their horses and wasted no time in leaving the village.

'Why did you do that, father?' asked Edward.

'Why should I not?' replied Flowerdew, following the lawyerly habit of answering one question with another.

Edward looked puzzled.

'Richard Smith was a copyholder tenant,' Flowerdew explained. 'I let him farm our land. He gave us some of the proceeds, and he kept the rest for himself, but he has no right to that land. We have enough provisions without the surplus generated by his labours, and I have a better use for the land.'

'What will you do with his land?'

Edward was showing no signs of regard for the welfare of

the Smiths and their new son-in-law. That boded well for the day when he would rule the manor. 'Our land, Edward,' said Flowerdew correcting his son. 'For now, we will allow the remaining villagers to harvest it and, after our share, they can divide the rest between them. The extra grain will ensure they don't starve.' Flowerdew cleared his throat. 'Then, after the harvest, we will use the land for our sheep.'

'Do we need more sheep?'

Flowerdew smiled. 'The old rights to land are changing, Edward. Money is more important today, more important than food, and more important than traditions and customs. If we can make more money from harvesting sheep's fleece, that's what we must do.' He'd heard rumours the day before that the price of wool had plummeted. Fortunately, he'd agreed a contract for this season's wool well in advance. His flock had been the first to be sheared, and he'd already been paid. Better yet, farmers holding out for a better price might soon be in trouble, which could present an opportunity for Flowerdew to buy up either sheep or fleeces at knock-down prices. He would keep his ear to the ground.

'What about the commoners?' asked Edward. 'How will they survive?'

'That's the wrong question. Ask yourself, what would they do in our position? These people are lazy and would cheat us if they could. Have you ever heard them complain when our sheep graze their acreage in winter? No. They'll gladly take our manure to sweeten the soil when it suits them. In the past it has suited me to accommodate the commoners, but less so today. Richard Smith doesn't have enough children to farm his acreage. The Smiths are a burden to the village.'

Edward looked puzzled. Flowerdew could see he was thinking hard. 'Will their extra acres make much difference?' he asked.

'All these questions. You'll make a fine lawyer one day.'

'Or a knight in armour!'

Flowerdew did not want his son to dwell on the glory of military service. 'It is only twenty acres, Edward. Not much on its own, but you increase your wealth by adding to what you have. Would you rather it benefit the Smiths or the Flowerdews?'

Edward hesitated. 'The Flowerdews,' he said.

'Good. We'll take the crops this year, and then leave the land fallow for grazing. Better to act now than wait until the food is harvested.'

'What will you do with the money from the wool, father?'

'You can do many things when you have money, Edward.' Flowerdew looked across at his son. 'But looking after it is the first thing to do, whether you're a man, a family, even a country. England has no money. King Henry waged war on France and Scotland, and war is expensive. He had nothing to show for it.' Flowerdew took a coin from his purse and passed it to Edward. 'Look at this. Do you see how bits of silver have been sliced from the edge of the coin?' Edward nodded. 'King Henry couldn't raise any more money with taxes, so he had people clip silver from coins, then they melted it down, blended it with copper and made more coins.'

Edward was struggling to grasp the theory. 'Why not just make more coins?' he asked.

'A pound of silver has to weigh a pound, or it isn't worth a pound. And the silver must come from somewhere. The country can't pay its bills. Not that it matters to a dead king. It's King Edward who has to clear up his father's mess.'

'The king has the same name as me, and we're the same age. Will I have to clear up your mess one day, father?'

Flowerdew laughed. 'No, Edward. When you are older

everybody will respect you. That I promise. You will have money and rank and perhaps even the ear of the young king.'

Edward smiled, imagining himself alongside King Edward.

'But you will have responsibility, too. One day you must do the same for your eldest son, and when he is old enough, he must do it for his eldest. The Flowerdews will be a family that everybody in the land respects.' He reached over and squeezed the boy's shoulder.

They rode a few minutes in silence, then, as they turned into the gates of Hethersett Hall, Edward asked, 'Will King Edward waste his money as well?'

'Who knows,' said his father. 'But a friend in debt is a friend indeed.'

5

Alfred had thought his life couldn't get any worse, but since he started at the tannery he'd believed his fortunes were finally on the rise. Lynn had stopped crying, but her mother was screaming at Richard, who was staring at the floor, gripping his sovereign.

'Richard, we'll starve!' screamed his wife. '*Richard!*'

Richard sat motionless.

'Alfred, you go. Speak to Anders Marshwell. The village must stop this.'

'I can't. I have to go to Wymondham.'

'That's just typical of you, Alfred Carter. Our family won't survive the winter, and you think only of yourself.'

'I'm now the only breadwinner in this house. If I lose my job, what then?'

'You selfish shit,' Lynn snarled. Alfred flinched.

'Do ... do something,' sobbed Lynn's mother.

Lynn stared venomously at Alfred. 'Go on. Sort this out. We have a baby on the way.'

'Which is why I'm going to work. So I can get paid.'

Lynn snatched a pot from the floor and hurled it at Alfred. He ducked, and it hit the wall, causing the hens to skitter across the floor.

'It's not my fault,' snapped Alfred as he got to his feet.

'That's it, run away. Let us starve. And don't come back. You stink of tannery shit.'

Alfred shook his head. Did they think he'd conspired with Flowerdew? He'd just been evicted, too. 'Lynn, you need me now more than ever.' He pulled the door shut behind him, muffling the abuse from his wife. He washed his head and hands in the well – the whiff of pit thirteen had not quite disappeared – then went to the church and waited for the walking party going to Wymondham.

*

Richard Smith was still numb, as though he had fallen through the ice on a frozen pond. He stared blankly at Mrs Marshwell, the village's ale taster. She was on her knees in front of the hearth, scraping glowing embers into a clay pot. She poured a little water on the fire to stop the smoke from filling the hall. Today's brew would need to wait until the farmer's meeting was finished.

It had taken Richard some time to recover from the shock, not helped by the hysteria of his wife and daughter, but once he had regained his composure, he and Lynn had alerted the village to their eviction.

Richard waited for the other farmers in the village to arrive. They were gathering, as always, in the open hall of the Marshwells' farmhouse, around the corner from his cottage. The Marshwell family claimed to have farmed in Hethersett since the time of King William. All Richard's life they had lived in this house, the largest farmhouse in Hethersett and the usual venue for village gatherings. They met every new moon to agree how they would best farm the land. Flowerdew hadn't owned Hethersett long and preferred to distance himself from village affairs, so long as he received his share on time. He had even retired the bailiff. Other than sending a clerk to inspect crops and confirm yields, he left the villagers to their own devices.

Anders Marshwell took his wooden seat on the dais at the end of the hall. His large body filled the chair. A lifetime of outdoor labour had weathered his face and made his hands large and crooked. He owned this building, a hundred acres and twenty beasts, more than anyone else in the village. At fifty he was the oldest of the village commoners and had acted as reeve for the past nine years. He liaised with Flowerdew and presided in judgement over village matters. Anders looked around the room, counting the men present. Women were not involved.

Richard looked at his shoes: worn leather and fraying canvas. He had to gain his fellow men's support this morning. If the majority of the farmers agreed, Anders would attempt to persuade Flowerdew to overturn his decision. At that point Richard's fate would rely on Flowerdew's goodwill and his fear of antagonising the villagers. A few other villages had revolted against their landowners recently, so this was a straw to clutch at, at least.

But if Flowerdew did not reverse his decision, Richard faced the prospect of spending his final years as a homeless vagabond, unable to support his family. He thought of the homeless man who roamed Hethersett and the neighbouring villages begging for bread. He had a large 'V' branded on his forehead. Tears began to well in Richard's eyes. He wiped them with his finger and whispered a prayer to himself.

The last to arrive filed in, muttering and nodding acknowledgements to one another. Richard could feel their eyes on him. Tom Broom, a young farmer, came and sat next to Richard. He was fifteen years old, and the thought that his fate rested in the hands of the likes of Tom scared Richard. The young only ever thought of themselves.

'Your leg's shaking so much we should put it on the footplate of the knife grinder!' joked Tom.

Richard forced his leg to be still. He sat upright and turned away from Tom and, at the same moment, Stuart Marshwell walked in. Anne, the eldest of Richard's three surviving daughters, was married to Stuart, the third son of Anders Marshwell.

Anne had fallen pregnant to Stuart when she was thirteen. Custom demanded they marry, much to the disappointment of Anders Marshwell, who hadn't wanted his family bonded to the poorest in the village. To Anders's credit, other than demanding a large dowry of one cow, he neither persecuted Richard for his son's carelessness nor showed any preference to Richard in village matters. Richard hoped he might rely on his blood tie to Anders today. If not, would the sovereign in the purse hanging from Richard's belt make a difference? Anders was a fair man and not known to be corruptible. Might he be offended? Richard resolved that bribery would be a last resort.

The hall was nearly filled. Forty-two farmers in Hethersett were eligible to attend the meetings, and it seemed that they were all here. Anders curled his finger to call Richard over. He spoke to Richard in his soft and slow manner, as if comforting a sick animal, asking him to relate the events of the morning once again.

When Richard had finished, Anders announced his decision. 'You've had a shock, Richard. By the look of you, you're not fit to represent yourself, so I will appoint John Robertson to represent you.' He signalled John over. 'Richard, explain to John the events as you described them to me, unembellished.'

Richard felt relieved. He didn't relish the task of speaking in front of his peers. John Robertson was known to be a fair man; he was big and had a presence that meant people didn't tend to quarrel with him.

'Who will speak against me?' John asked in his slow, thoughtful manner.

'James Newell,' said Anders.

Richard's heart sank. Not only could James Newell, the older brother of George, the milliner, be cruel in his pursuit of winning an argument, but he also had cause to see Richard suffer. They had been in dispute ever since Richard had borrowed his ploughshare and returned it broken. James claimed he was still owed for the breakage. Richard maintained the plough hadn't been properly sharpened and its fixings were neglected. There was no sense in arguing with Anders's choice, though, as Anders was not a man given to changing his mind.

Richard explained the morning's events to both John and James. He rarely looked at James.

Once Richard had finished, Anders called for silence in the hall. When the conversations had petered out, Anders stayed seated and recounted Flowerdew's actions that morning. Richard confirmed his account was accurate. He returned to his seat on the bench against the wall. The room was quiet. Richard leaned forward, his fingers crossed.

Anders had introduced this new system of decision-making after a fight broke out at a farmers' meeting. Nowadays there were too many present for each one to have his say, and it was easy to speak without thinking and thus upset neighbours. So to stop this – and to avoid hearing the same points made again and again – two people made opposing arguments. The matter in question was then decided by a show of hands. Anders would usually abide by the decision of the majority.

John Robertson stood to Anders's left, facing the farmers. He cleared his throat. 'How would you like it?' he began. 'Being woken by the lord and thrown from your home. Your wife in tears. Knowing that without the charity of your fellow man, you will surely die?' He paused. 'That's what happened to Richard Smith this morning.'

Richard felt numb again. Being at the centre of things felt unreal. While part of him relaxed, knowing there was nothing more he could do, another part was as taut as a bowstring. His stomach rumbled, but even though he hadn't eaten, he couldn't face food until he knew his fate.

John Robertson was speaking, and Richard realised that his thoughts had been drifting. He leaned back against the wall and made an effort to listen.

'… Don't be tempted to think this is the will of God,' said John. 'This is the will of Flowerdew, nothing more, nothing less. Mark my words, whatever he might tempt us with today or tomorrow, this is calculated to return him a greater profit. I wager Smith's acreage will be covered in sheep by this time next year, just as he's covered our common with his sheep, leaving us only barely enough to survive. This man has no knowledge or respect for the customs we live by. He understands and respects only one thing: money.'

This remark drew a cheer from many of the crowd. Richard allowed himself a brief moment of hope. In this very room they had debated Flowerdew's character on repeated occasions. In the time he'd owned Hethersett he'd shown no interest in the welfare of the commoners or their ways. They were sure that if he could farm the manor without them, he would.

'First, it was half our common,' concluded John. 'When he can take no more of that, he takes land from Richard here.

What will he take next? Look at the man next to you: will he be next? Or will it be you?'

Richard looked around the hall. There were nods. Nobody cheered, but he could see they were taken by John's argument. He'd appealed to their self-interest and their survival instinct. Richard squeezed the sovereign in his purse hard.

John Robertson stood down, and James Newell replaced him. James had a lazy eye, and one half of his gaze was directed at the floor. He looked at Richard. Richard looked away.

'I won't deny that what has happened to Richard Smith is unfortunate,' said James. 'It is sad, even, but we must be realistic. This year's crop will be a poor one. Richard's share will be distributed between us, for which we all should be grateful. Flowerdew could keep the excess, but he knows we need more to survive. Despite what John says, Flowerdew hasn't sought profit in this act. We must not reject his charity. It is a fool who rejects a kind gesture and later expects to be offered the same kindness again. I put it to you that Flowerdew, like any of us facing a hard winter, has sacrificed one of his animals to feed his family, in this case, us.'

Richard could see a few heads nodding.

'Tough choices are necessary,' James went on. 'Ask yourself, why would the lord choose Richard Smith ahead of any of us? His family is small. He has only a wife to feed now his daughter is married and therefore the property of her husband, Alfred. If he weren't so often drunk, Alfred, and not Richard, should bear the responsibility to provide for her.'

Richard looked around. Men were nodding. Damn Alfred, he thought.

'In years gone by,' said James, 'at the harvest count we

have seen Richard's yields are often the lowest. Many of us could return from fifteen acres what he produces from twenty. When there is not enough mother's milk to go round, it is the weakest calf that dies.'

Richard returned James's stare. He wanted to speak, to shout back and retaliate, but he didn't. He sat still and waited, numb.

'If we are to challenge our master,' said James, 'let it be for a more worthwhile person.'

The room was absolutely still.

'John, James, thank you for your summaries,' said Anders. 'Are there any questions?'

'What about the king's uncle, Lord Protector Seymour? Should he not stop these abuses?' shouted a voice. The question was met with jeers and derision.

'Don't matter what Seymour says,' said another farmer at the back. 'He can sit in London and say whatever comes into his damn head, it don't make two turds worth of difference. It won't do us no good.'

Another man finished the thought. 'In any case, it's Flowerdew who would be tasked with carrying out Seymour's instructions here, and he won't do anything that don't line his own purse.'

'Right,' interrupted Anders. He never encouraged too many questions or too much talking. 'The day is passing, but I will add one more thing for you to think about. I've had the good fortune to live through more winters than any man here. When I was a boy, and my father held the meetings in this very room, there were less than twenty men farming this land. Hethersett has been blessed. God has spared us his plagues, and there's now twice the number of people living here than when I was the age of some of you. We have many more mouths to feed, yet the manor is unchanged. It troubles me to admit that with every generation we grow a little hungrier—'

'Then how can it be right that the lord of the manor keeps so many sheep for his own needs?' said Stuart Marshwell.

At least he's sticking up for his family, thought Richard, unlike my son-in-law.

'Rich men will always do as they please,' started another man, 'until we—'

'Stuart, you may be my son,' said Anders with some force, 'but you will obey the ways of this hall the same as any man.'

Anders turned his attention back to the gathered men. 'We could talk all day about the lord, his virtues and his failings, but we are here to decide whether we should challenge him for the sake of Richard Smith. If you are willing to lend your name to Richard's cause, raise your arm,' said Anders softly.

This is it, thought Richard. No more waiting. He looked around the room. Would he be condemned to a slow death? He saw hands raised. Several men stood still, hands by their sides. One man wavered, undecided. How many arms were up? Was it enough? Richard couldn't tell by eye alone. It was close. They would have to count.

6

8th July, Wymondham

Under the overcast sky, the marketplace had been cleared of stalls. The triangular space was filled with long tables and benches, along which people passed their empty ale jugs to be refilled from barrels set at the end of each table. It was day two of the town festival.

The previous day, a Sunday, people from the surrounding villages had gathered in Wymondham to commemorate the slaying of Thomas Becket four hundred years before. Each year, the people of the hundred, a collection of parishes forming an administrative division of the county watched as the archbishop's murder was re-enacted, and each year, Becket grew more defenceless, his assailants more savage and the audience's reaction more outraged. It had become customary that the formal Sunday celebrations spilt over into Monday. Men were excused their labours and a day free of civic ceremony gave them a chance to indulge their favourite pastime: drinking.

Alfred burped. He was sitting between Fulke and David Fisher, who took no notice, and although Alfred was drunk, he hoped that by concentrating hard he could overcome the tell-tale signs. The air was warm, and a gentle breeze carried with it the mouth-watering smell of capons spit-roasting over an open fire. As the bells struck twelve, Alfred decided he needed to empty his bladder. He swayed on his feet as he excused himself and made his way across the marketplace, surrounded by laughter, chatter and, in one corner, two neighbours settling their differences with their fists.

The day of outdoor drinking was enlivened by the occasional play, performer or musician, and by gambling: arm wrestling, three-legged races, cockfights, dice, brag, trump or a game of tables. Women were welcome, provided they were willing to drink, be merry and suffer the attentions of the men. Most stayed away on the Monday. The gentry too, were always present on the Sunday, but made their excuses for the Monday.

Alfred emptied himself against the wall of the apothecary, one of the many timber buildings that surrounded the marketplace. While he was enjoying the numbness the alcohol provided, he was afraid of passing out. The last few days had taken their toll: hard physical work at the tannery, followed by despair and self-pity at home. Unable to face his wife's anger, he'd spent the previous night under the stars. In a sheltered space in the churchyard he had been able to avoid the attentions of the town watch, who were ever-vigilant during festival time.

Alfred took his seat on the bench next to Fulke, where a full tankard was waiting for him. Opposite them was Adam Catchpole, a friend of Fulke's, recounting in a lowered voice how he and several others from his village had destroyed Master Hobart's enclosures in Attleborough under cover of darkness, freeing the lord's sheep to wander the Norfolk countryside. Next to Adam sat Geoffrey Lincoln, so called as he hailed from the city of the same name, who added to Adam's tale his delight at witnessing his neighbour's fury on finding some of the stray sheep eating his vegetable crop.

'What has Hobart done?' asked Fulke, keen to hear the whole story.

Adam shrugged. 'What can he do? No one saw anything.'

'He must know.'

'Even if he thinks so, he can't find us guilty without witnesses.' Adam took a swig of ale. He was rosy-cheeked from the drink and clearly enjoying evading capture. His short, curly brown hair was not unlike a shorn fleece.

'Sod 'em,' said Geoffrey, who wore a straw hat pulled down to hide the branding scars he'd acquired in Lincoln. 'All these sheep put me out of work.' He was an unskilled labourer who had earned a living until recently from farmers whose children were too young to work the fields. But as more farmers replaced crops with sheep, which required little in the way of husbandry, labourers such as Geoffrey had found work harder to come by.

'Best we raise a toast,' said Fulke. 'To Hobart – for buying us ale today, for losing his sheep, and for being too stupid to catch the perpetrators!' The men laughed and took mouthfuls of the ale donated by Hobart, the lord of Morley, a neighbouring parish. Alfred carefully returned his tankard to the table. Being around careless talk made him nervous. You only needed to be overheard by one person loyal to Hobart and harsh consequences would follow. The table wobbled as Adam got up to relieve himself.

Alfred turned away from Fulke to talk to David Fisher, someone he felt was more sensible.

'I have work, David,' said Alfred, unable to hide his pride.

'Good for you,' replied David with sincerity. He was a thin man in his late twenties, with dark hair and the manner of someone who liked to get along with others. 'Who for?'

'For Robert Kett. Tanning leather.' Again Alfred sounded boastful.

David nodded. 'You'll need a strong nose.'

Alfred shrugged. There was no denying it.

'The stink of leather and the stench of hypocrisy,' added David.

Alfred frowned. Did David mean Robert Kett, one of the most upright of the town's aldermen? 'What do you–?'

'He owns my house. I refused to pay my rent.'

'Why?'

'Our whole street is united. We won't pay till he gives back the common.'

'Oh, how ... what did he do?' Alfred was amazed at the sheer boldness of the tenants' action. After all, he had done nothing wrong, and yet Flowerdew had evicted him.

'What can he do? We're pleading poverty. Can't throw us all out, or the streets of Wymondham would be littered with his evicted tenants. He'd have to account for his enclosures then. One wrong turn deserves another, in my mind.'

A passing juggler caught Alfred's eye and distracted him for a moment. He took a sip of ale.

'He was a gentleman about it, mind you,' said David. 'Not one to rant and rave, old Kett. If he forces the issue, we'll have to pay, but he won't have it easy.'

Alfred was amazed. At that moment he caught a glimpse of Master Peter across the marketplace. The tannery foreman wore a sombre frown. Their eyes met, then Master Peter's gaze moved to Fulke. Alfred remembered Master Peter's sharp reaction when he'd mentioned Fulke on his first day at the tannery. Perhaps there was ill will between them.

Alfred's thoughts were interrupted by Fulke's laughter. He slammed his ale on the table. 'Bollocks to the lot of them!'

Fulke declared. Alfred assumed he was talking about the gentry, or maybe the church. As the drink took hold, his friend was becoming aggressive.

'Come on, Alfred, that ale won't drink itself.' Fulke slapped him on the back. 'If you're going home to your wife, I think you'll need all the ale you can get!' Fulke laughed at his own joke and was joined by Geoffrey. Alfred did as he was told, but kept it to a single swig.

Big John Robertson walked past and offered a friendly wink. Since Alfred started at the tannery, John had accompanied him on the walk into Wymondham most mornings. John was drinking with a group from Hethersett, but Alfred was happier among the Wymondham men. Not only had his family been the centre of discussion in the village for the past few days he, but the vote at the farmers' meeting had gone against them. The men of Hethersett had offered their sympathies, but they'd voted in favour of Flowerdew's action. The Smiths, and Alfred, were expendable.

As he took another swig, Alfred spotted a commotion at the far corner of the marketplace. Fulke stood up to get a better view, then, as others did the same, he stepped up onto the table.

'Constable Morris has got someone by the pillory. It's Adam!'

Alfred followed Fulke as he dashed around the tables and pushed to the front of the crowd forming around the constable and his three henchmen. The constable, Jacob Morris, wore an orange tunic and a black velvet hat; his thick beard made him look older than his twenty-eight years. Behind him, the deputies held a struggling Adam Catchpole with his arms pinned behind his back. His eyes were wide with fear as they wrestled him toward the pillory. Once there, they held his neck and wrists down against the low oak beam, and the constable swung the heavy upper beam over them and padlocked it in place. Adam wriggled like a rat in a trap.

'What's he done?' Alfred asked Fulke.

Fulke shook his head. His jaw clenched and the vein in his neck throbbed.

Adam shouted a protest as the constable drew two six-inch iron nails from inside his tunic. His deputy passed him a mallet.

As they gathered round, the crowd's mood was uncertain. For the most part, people enjoyed watching the punishment of wrongdoers, but it wasn't clear what misdeed Adam had committed.

'What's this for?' shouted Fulke.

'Quiet!' Morris responded. 'Adam Catchpole is guilty of a crime against his lord, Master Hobart.'

'What crime?' shouted Adam, his face pointed toward the dirt.

'Quiet!' snapped one of the deputies, kicking Adam's feet from under him. Adam choked as he scrambled back to his feet.

Alfred winced. He'd always found Adam a bit cocky, but he wouldn't wish this on him.

Morris held one of the nails to Adam's ear and swung his hammer. Adam tried to stifle his scream, but he soon gave way and let out a rasping squeal. His ear was pinned to the pillory. A trickle of blood ran down the stained wooden block that held him in place.

Fulke stepped forward from the crowd. 'What crime?' he demanded.

'Catchpole was caught fishing Master Hobart's stretch of river.'

'I didn't know it was his,' protested Adam.

'The master bought that stretch of water one week before,

and he doesn't want your sort robbing it of his fish,' said Morris.

'He said he didn't know,' replied Fulke, slurring his words and with his arms outstretched.

'Those waters were restricted, and ignorance is no grounds for wrongdoing,' said Morris. 'If it was, none of you would ever be culpable for your actions.'

A low buzz of discussion rose from the crowd as people debated the justice they were witnessing.

'Don't warrant nailing him to the boards. Wouldn't a fine be enough? It's only fish.'

'The court determined he should be pilloried,' said Morris, raising the second nail to Adam's other ear. The crowd jeered and booed, making clear their disapproval, but no one moved as the hammer swung again and Adam screamed. His tears made dark spots on the dirt beneath.

It was the sound, not the sight, of Adam's suffering that made Alfred feel sick. The ale turned in his empty belly.

'This has nothing to do with fish!' yelled Fulke, angrily pointing a stubby finger at Morris. 'Hobart is taking revenge for his fences being demolished and his sheep escaping.'

Morris's eyebrows rose. 'Well you seem to know about this, so can I take it that Catchpole was involved?'

Fulke spat on the ground in front of the constable. 'When was this court in session?' he asked. Then, turning to the crowd: 'Who here was present when sentence was passed?' There were only shaking heads and angry faces among the onlookers. Fulke turned back to face Morris. 'Why such a harsh punishment?'

'Carry on like this, Fulke, and you'll find yourself in a pillory.'

Fulke ignored the constable. 'Hobart is sending us a message. He's telling us he's above the law and can dish out punishments for crimes we haven't been found guilty of.'

Several in the crowd shouted their support.

Morris smiled. After a moment he said, 'Thank you, Fulke. Now we know Catchpole was involved, we should be able to extract the names of the others.'

'The only crime here is that of the man who puts fences up, not those who pull them down,' shouted John Robertson.

Morris took a step toward the crowd. 'I'm the—' he began, but as he did so, Fulke stepped forward, twisted his foot and stamped it into Morris's knee. The constable buckled forward, and Fulke smashed his block-shaped head into the constables' nose. The constable shrieked in pain as blood began to flow down his face. Fulke grabbed his tunic and threw him to the ground, finding time for one final stamp on the man's fingers before his deputies came to the rescue.

Fulke glared at Morris and his men, ready to take them all on. John Robertson stepped forward, and without thinking, Alfred did the same. Fulke twitched his fingers, beckoning the deputies to come for him. They hesitated, while behind them the crowd shouted obscenities at Morris. Fulke pulled his eating knife from his belt. The deputies took a step back, unsure what a man who had just committed a capital offence might do next.

'Fulke, put the knife down.'

Alfred turned. It was Master Peter.

The deputies retreated, while Morris groaned in pain on the ground. Fulke grinned.

'Put the knife down,' repeated Master Peter.

Fulke turned towards him. He was breathing heavily, nostrils dilated, a wild look in his eyes. 'What's this to do with you? You're Kett's dog, and he's no better than Hobart.'

The two men stared at each other. 'You've gone far enough, Fulke,' said Master Peter, his voice calm but firm.

Fulke spat on the floor, and Alfred stepped back a pace, not wanting to be seen to take Fulke's side against his employer.

The crowd parted as Luke Miller pushed his way to the front. 'What's going on?' he asked.

Alfred retreated another step and in hushed tones explained to Luke what had happened.

John Robertson stooped to pick up the constable's fallen hammer, before he walked between the two men, interrupting the hatred that surged between them. Adam muffled a cry as John grappled to pull out the nails.

Fulke turned to the crowd. 'If Hobart wants to send us a message, I say we send him one back. Who's with me?'

7

Only thirteen people had felt sufficiently roused to follow Fulke on his quest for revenge, but they'd put their anger to good use. There was no clearer way of sticking two fingers up to the lord of Fulke's manor than demolishing his enclosures in broad daylight. At Morley, they'd pulled their shirts up over their heads, dashed to the fence that divided the common, then, in twos and threes, they had wrenched wooden fence posts from the ground. As sections of the fence collapsed, sheep began to seep out like sand in an hourglass.

Fulke's anger felt temporarily quelled as he looked at the fruits of their labour: a common free of Hobart's sheep. The grassland was clear for the commoners to graze their animals on once again, if they hadn't eaten them already. While savouring his victory, Fulke saw a horseman gallop away from the manor house that overlooked the common. It was time to leave.

Fulke led his small band of followers back towards Wymondham, but the town wasn't somewhere he could stop. He'd attacked the constable, a crime for which he could expect his neck to be stretched. Fulke had done worse. He had killed before, but never in broad daylight or with so many witnesses. Whatever the justification for his actions, it would only take the testimony of one trustworthy witness to send him to the gallows, and Master Peter was just such a witness. Fulke's survival depended on turning attention away from his assault on Morris and on to something bigger. The precariousness of his situation made him giddy. Not with fear, but with the thrill of stepping outside the law and putting his life in danger.

Fulke stopped at a marl pit at the side of the road and turned to face his followers. They were jubilant, apparently oblivious to the risk posed by the horseman, and, for the most part, still drunk. They were still drinking, too. Luke Miller had surprised Fulke by buying them a whole firkin of ale for their journey, not that Luke had been willing to join them in person. John Robertson took a swig from the last ale jar and passed it on to Adam Catchpole whose bloody ears had started to scab. Geoffrey Lincoln wiped sweat from his brow. David Fisher peed over the edge of the pit, and Alfred burped.

Fulke reminded them of the injustice Alfred had suffered, being evicted to make way for Flowerdew's sheep. It didn't take him long to persuade them, drunk and elated, to go on to Hethersett to reclaim the common there too. Alfred had looked the most concerned, and big John Robertson, also from Hethersett, was anxious about, as he put it, shitting outside his own door. Fulke knew, though, that neither of them could be seen to put their self-preservation above the fight for the greater good.

The ale was passed around once more before they set off for Hethersett. Fulke set a quick pace as they skirted Wymondham, and with each step his conviction grew. Morris had been long overdue a beating. Fulke had spent time in the stocks because of Morris, and he would never forget the humiliation he'd imposed. But he'd taken his revenge, and now he had to deal with the consequences.

They reached the village well in Hethersett late in the afternoon. Fulke addressed the men as they drank, repeating his instructions to 'do it just like we did in Morley'. He had never had occasion to direct men like this, but it came easily. Show neither fear nor mercy, he'd discovered, and they would follow orders.

As he spoke, Geoffrey Lincoln interrupted by raising an arm to point past Fulke. Fulke looked round to see John Flowerdew approaching on his black stallion, followed by four mounted men-at-arms, stern-faced, hands resting on sword hilts.

'Well,' said Flowerdew. No one spoke for several long seconds. 'What a gathering we have.'

Fulke took a deep breath: they were caught. His instincts told him not to back down, but before he could decide what to do, Flowerdew spoke again: 'Bad news travels fast. I hear a gang of men attacked John Hobart's property a few hours ago. What do you gentlemen know about that?'

No one spoke.

'I've seen no other drunken mobs today, so I can only conclude it must have been your doing. Who is your leader?'

Fulke hesitated. Leaders always faced the harshest retribution, and if he rolled the dice now, there would be no way back. He stared at Flowerdew's pointy, fox-like face, then took a single, deliberate step forward. 'I am. Hobart's fences were illegal.'

'Who are you to decide what's legal?' snapped Flowerdew. 'You are no lawyer.'

Fulke could feel his anger rising. People like Flowerdew believed they could do as they liked simply because of who they were. He shrugged.

'What's your name?'

Fulke smiled defiantly.

Flowerdew laughed and turned to his men-at-arms. 'We have a hero in our midst. A dangerous role indeed.' He turned back to Fulke. 'Heroes die.'

'We all die,' said Fulke, holding Flowerdew's stare. 'Rich and poor, honest and dishonest.'

'Arrest him,' Flowerdew ordered. The men-at-arms drew their swords.

So it would be a fight after all. Fulke had never run from violence, and he wasn't going to flee now. He spread his arms and crouched, ready to defend himself. 'Ready, lads?' he said to his fellow fence-breakers. His willingness to fight was enough to cause the men-at-arms to hesitate. They were outnumbered three to one. The commoners' only weapons were eating knives, but their numbers might give them sufficient advantage to overpower their attackers.

'Your men don't look ready to fight,' said Flowerdew.

Fulke could see that the lord was attempting to defuse the situation and recover an advantage. 'You only need worry about me,' he said, watching Flowerdew's face as he contemplated his next move. Flowerdew's eyes scanned over the men who followed Fulke. He recognised Alfred.

'Are you sure you want to be part of this?' he asked, pointing at Alfred.

Alfred looked down. He had never challenged a person of Flowerdew's rank before, but all he could think of was the morning when the lord had evicted him, his wife and his parents-in-law from their home. He looked up at Flowerdew again.

'What can you do to me that's worse than what you've already done?'

Flowerdew pursed his lips and addressed the gang as a whole. 'You men have committed a crime today, and I would hazard that you were also involved in the assault on Jacob Morris in Wymondham earlier.'

Fulke shrugged.

'You have no just cause to be here,' Flowerdew continued. 'Be gone and take your mayhem elsewhere. Leave now, and I will take no further action.'

Fulke sensed his followers' relief, but he knew that men like Flowerdew had long memories and the means to exact revenge. There was no going back. 'We're here to take back what don't belong to you: our common.'

'Your common? You don't live here.'

'Let's just say it matters to me.'

'And to me,' added John Robertson.

'What's the common worth to you?' Fulke asked Flowerdew. 'What are you prepared to do to keep it?' He spread his arms, inviting a challenge.

Fulke felt strong. His ingrained fear of the hierarchy was forgotten. Under his fancy clothes and ornaments, Flowerdew was just a man, a man whose shit smelled as bad as anyone else's. And for all Flowerdew's money and land, Fulke doubted that he would be willing to risk a violent confrontation. Fulke's advantage, he knew, was that he would risk everything. He already had. Flowerdew had a family and a future, which would make him a coward.

'If you want it back, come and take it.'

Flowerdew snorted, but he stayed where he was. For several moments there was silence.

'Very well,' said Flowerdew. He put his hand to his belt and pulled out his purse, which bulged with coins. He held it for everyone to see. 'Instead of violence, I offer you this, and a promise that I will not relay what I have seen today.'

'Take the money, Fulke,' said David Fisher.

Fulke glared at Fisher. He would decide what happened and would not be undermined.

Flowerdew sensed that he now had the upper hand. 'There is forty pence here. You may leave, and nothing more will be said. Spend the money on what you will: ale, food, gifts for your wives. Or I can have you cut to pieces.'

'Take the money, Fulke,' repeated David Fisher.

'He's right, Fulke,' said Geoffrey. 'You won't get a better offer.'

Fulke could hear a murmur of agreement.

'Our hero is on his own,' said Flowerdew.

Fulke stepped forward and reached up for the purse. As he stretched, Flowerdew moved his arm.

'There is one further condition,' he said. 'This is a large sum of money and entitles me to something further.' His stallion shifted underneath him. 'And I sense that you are still in the mood for violence. If it's common land you want, take this money, and on your way home, destroy Robert Kett's enclosures.'

Fulke didn't like the new condition, but on his own his only option was to fight and die. At least if he took the purse on condition he attacked Robert Kett's property, Flowerdew would also be guilty, and Fulke need not fear any reprisal. Robert Kett was his employer's brother, that was true, but he was also a wealthy man who had enclosed common land for his own gain. And he was an easy target.

'Agreed?'

'Agreed.'

As Fulke reached for the purse, Flowerdew dropped it on to the dry earth. He smirked as he tugged his reins and walked his horse backwards.

Fulke was not going to pick up money in the dirt like a beggar. 'Alfred, pick up our money,' he said. 'We're going to Kett's.'

8

Alfred walked at the back of the gang beside David Fisher. So far it had been a day like no other. Fulke had battered a constable. They'd wrecked a lord's enclosures. He'd been offered a bribe by Flowerdew – a lawyer who'd allowed them to profit from breaking the law. It was dawning on Alfred that things were not as simple as they seemed.

A breeze blew away the dust they kicked up, and the sun poked through the clouds. On either side of the road were large fields, divided into strips. In a corner of the field on their left stood a windmill, its sails still until it was time to grind the harvest into flour. Alfred's father-in-law had complained that it was the only windmill he was allowed to use, and for the privilege he had to pay Flowerdew a fee.

On the right, beyond the other field was a large wood. Flowerdew owned this, too, and the pigs that rooted around in the undergrowth. Alfred had helped Richard Smith collect firewood there on the one day a month when commoners were allowed to gather fallen branches.

Was it right, Alfred wondered, that one man could own so much? His mother had told him that they were working people and they should be happy with their lot. God would reward them in heaven. But it might be years before he got to heaven, or he might endure a lifetime of struggling only to spend eternity wasting in purgatory, if there was such a place, or roasting in hell. For now, he thought it was better to make the most of life, the rest he would worry about later. What good had acceptance and struggle done his parents?

Fulke had promised to distribute Flowerdew's bribe money after they'd destroyed Kett's enclosures – no one would be allowed to take the money and slope off – and Alfred was already imagining the pleasure of spending his share in Wymondham before Richard could demand it for housekeeping.

'What will your family do after the eviction, Alfred?' asked David.

Alfred shook his head. 'No idea. At least I have work.'

'Yes, you do,' David hesitated before continuing, 'you should think carefully about what we're about to do.'

It was a moment before Alfred's thoughts arranged themselves, but then – through the fog of ale and excitement – he saw properly and for the first time exactly what he was about to do. He was about to take part in the destruction of his employer's property. If he were caught, the consequences would be serious.

'There's Kett's house.' David pointed to some ornate brick chimneys that stretched above the treetops. 'If he sees you…'

Alfred nodded. But what would Fulke say? He'd seen a new side to his friend today. Would Fulke understand his predicament?

'Enclosing the commons is wrong,' said David. 'There's no question about that, and we're right to break down the fences, but there's no need for you to be caught up in it.'

'No. Yes, I know,' said Alfred. He didn't know what to say next. He didn't want to be caught by Mr Kett, but he didn't want to be seen to desert his companions. He slowed down and went to the side of the road, partly to relieve himself, but also to give himself time to think. David looked back once, then walked on.

When his bladder was empty, Alfred jumped into the dry ditch beside the road and sat down. If they were spotted ripping down fences, he knew there would be severe reprisals. As the ringleader, Fulke would receive the harshest punishment, but the rest of them would probably suffer at least a flogging, maybe more. Alfred shuddered. How could he distance himself from the gang's actions when Flowerdew had already recognised him?

Suddenly, Alfred knew what he had to do to save himself. Robert Kett was the one person strong enough to oppose Flowerdew, as he had when saving Wymondham church, so Alfred had to get Mr Kett on his side. He'd be betraying his friends, but he was the only one of the group who had been evicted and was facing homelessness. The favour of one rich man was better than that of thirteen paupers.

Alfred jumped to his feet.

As he neared Kett's flint farmhouse, breathless from running, he was confronted by a large sheepdog guarding the door. Its hackles were up, its teeth bared. Alfred slowed down and weighed his choices. People bitten by dogs could die of their wounds. He edged closer, and the dog issued a low, menacing growl. Alfred yelled out for Mr Kett. Finally, the door opened and the dog relaxed as Mrs Kett appeared.

'Mrs Kett, I work for your husband,' said Alfred, still panting.

'You're the boy from the abbey. What brings you here?'

'I need to speak to Mr Kett.'

'He's resting at the moment, but you could wait. He

shouldn't be long.'

'Mrs Kett, please, it concerns his property. It's important he knows as soon as possible.'

Mrs Kett considered Alfred for a moment. 'Very well. Wait here.' She ushered the dog inside and closed the door.

While he waited, Alfred studied the house. It was a big, two-storey house, newly thatched and free from moss. A neat stack of firewood stood by the door. There were no weeds around the house, and on its south-facing side was a large kitchen garden with raised beds and a scarecrow to deter rabbits from eating the vegetables and herbs. Alfred admired the scarecrow's clothes. They were better than his own.

Robert Kett appeared at the door, his feet bare, his hair ruffled from napping.

'What's the meaning of this, Alfred?'

'There's trouble on the common. A mob from the festival is about to destroy your fences.'

'What?' said Kett. 'How do you know?'

'They were in Hethersett, sir, about to tear down Mr Flowerdew's fences, but he paid them to attack yours instead.'

'Flowerdew. The bastard.'

'I came as quick as I could,' said Alfred. 'If you leave now you might still be able to stop them.'

Kett looked steadily at Alfred. 'Are you sure, lad?'

'Yes, Mr Kett.'

'If your tale turns out not to be the truth, you'll be sorry.'

'No, sir, I followed them from Hethersett.'

Mr Kett dismissed him and went back indoors to fetch his shoes.

*

Robert leapt on to his horse with the sprightliness of a younger man. There was no time to put the saddle on, and the common was only a short ride away.

He cantered through a small copse, legs already aching from gripping the horse's ribs, then emerged from the trees at the edge of the marshy common he'd divided up in the spring. Young Alfred had been right. In the middle of the common he could see a party of at least twenty people, pulling the fence posts from the ground. Luckily, the sheep were grazing elsewhere and so were safe for now. Robert slowed to a trot to give himself a moment to regain his composure.

'Who's in charge here?' he barked as he approached the fence.

A short, heavily-built man with a scarred face let go of the fence post he'd been wrestling with. Robert thought he looked familiar.

'I am.'

'What is your name, and what's going on?'

'My name's Fulke, and we are pulling down your fences. What are you going to do about it?'

Robert hesitated. He was unarmed and outnumbered. The short man looked dangerous and was spoiling for trouble. From both directions along the fence, expectant faces stared at him, a mix of mischievous grins and indignation. He had no money to pay them off, so he would have to talk them out of their destructive action. 'When you're finished here,' Robert asked, loud enough for them all to hear, 'what will you do then?'

'Get drunk!' someone shouted.

'Then what?' said Robert. 'I can rebuild my fences. What will you have achieved?'

'We'll pull them down again and again,' said Fulke, 'until

you return this land to the commoners.'

'Your righteousness sounds fine, but that's not why you're here. You're here because you've been bribed.'

Fulke frowned, clearly wondering how Robert knew.

'You are nothing but paid criminals doing Flowerdew's dirty work.'

'That may be, but we're taking back this land all the same.'

Robert had no answer. In the uneasy silence a large man with weathered skin and curly black hair approached. Robert recognised him as John Robertson, a man who had bought leather from him in the past.

'Mr Kett, sir, I know you to be a fair man,' said John in his slow and deliberate manner. 'I have a proposal.'

Robert didn't like negotiating when he was ill-prepared, but he had no choice. He nodded at Robertson.

'I know people who have lived on your land all their lives. This year's harvest will be a poor one, so they need the common to graze their animals. Without their animals they will surely starve.'

Robert nodded.

'I have always found your intentions noble,' Robertson continued, 'so if you can give us a good reason why you need this land more than those who live here, then I will leave your fences where they stand.'

'You can't just go round pulling fences down—'

'Nor should you go round putting them up,' Fulke countered.

'These fences are my property. You are breaking the law.'

'This common is not yours,' said Robertson.

Robert ground his teeth. Their mischievous grins were gone. He thought the vandals would do well to remember his standing in the town, but he kept it to himself. 'Well, two wrongs don't make a right.'

'So you admit you are wrong,' interrupted Fulke.

'No!' protested Robert, cursing his own stupidity.

'Your sort are all the same,' snarled Fulke. 'You think you can do as you please. You go to church, and you think your charity and good deeds overturn your sins. Well, they don't. You don't have the right to take what isn't yours. Flowerdew, Hobart, Kett – you're all the same.'

As he had done earlier in Hethersett, Fulke spread his arms wide in a gesture of challenge. 'You want this common, come and take it.'

'Flowerdew, Hobart … How can you compare me to them?'

'Can you prove you're any different, Mr Kett?' grinned Fulke.

Robert sighed. He had taken some common land, but he was a kinder, more lenient man than Flowerdew and Hobart. Only yesterday, he had given credit to his tenants out of kindness. And if it weren't for him, the town wouldn't have an abbey. The comparisons stung.

Fulke folded his arms. Everyone was silent, expectant.

Robert fought to find an argument. He had a full belly, a stocked pantry, animals, houses, farms and a tannery: everything a man needed and then some. He looked at their staring faces. They were a wretched bunch: poor, helpless folk, uneducated and with no hope of betterment. And they outnumbered him. Robert had been engaged in commerce long enough to know when he was beaten, but there was always something to be gained from even the most hopeless situations.

'Very well,' he said. 'We'll do it your way.' He slid off his horse and walked past them. He was not like Flowerdew, and he was going to prove it. He stopped at the first upright fence post he came to and began to work it back and forth to loosen it. The lattice of branches hanging from it made it too heavy for him to lift out of the ground. He turned and looked at the confused faces of the men who had come to demolish his enclosures. 'This will go a lot quicker if you men help.'

They looked back at him in disbelief. Then one cheered and then another, and a couple of the men came forward to help Robert wrench his fence post out of the ground. Another clapped him on the back, and he smiled to himself at the comments he could hear among the men. The previously unimaginable sight of an alderman demolishing his own property provoked much hilarity.

Once the first post was dealt with, the gang dispersed to destroy the rest of the fence. The one man who hadn't helped Robert, and who remained standing and watching, arms folded, was Fulke.

Robert moved to the next post and helped the man who was struggling with it. He pushed again. Damn Flowerdew, he thought. If he could see me now he'd wet his breeches laughing. But as they worked, Robert had mixed emotions. While his fences were wrong and taking them down felt cathartic, the thought of it being prompted by Flowerdew was sickening. The news would be round all of Wymondham by nightfall, and Robert pictured Flowerdew celebrating with a jug of wine.

When they were done, he surveyed the tangle of posts and branches that had once been his fence. He had proved his difference from Flowerdew and at least partially cleared his conscience. Now it was time to get even. Robert beckoned a nearby man to help him mount his horse. Two men stepped forward with their clasped hands as footholds. Once settled on the horse's bare back, he addressed Fulke's gang.

'I was wrong to take this common.' The men cheered at this admission and Robert waited for them to stop before he continued: 'I thank you for allowing me to put my error right. Now what say you we go one step further?'

The men looked puzzled.

'Who will follow me back to Hethersett and help me tear down Flowerdew's fences?'

No one spoke. The men exchanged glances.

'I will.' It was John Robertson who had broken the silence. Another cheer rippled through the gang. Even Fulke's face wore a brief smile. Robert turned his horse towards Hethersett, and the men fell in behind.

Hours later, as the sun slid beneath the distant horizon, Robert dusted his hands together. John Flowerdew's fences lay in tatters at his feet, and his sheep roamed free. Robert himself had lost one common, but Flowerdew came out of this far worse. He had paid a bribe and lost both a common and a flock. That was a deal Robert could live with.

As he looked up and thanked God for showing him a way, there was a tap on his shoulder. He turned around; the entire gang surrounded him. David Fisher and John Robertson stood too close for his liking. For a second he feared a beating, but before he could find words, they grabbed a leg each and hoisted him on to their shoulders. There was a loud cheer.

Robert's smile masked the relief he felt. From the crowd someone called out, 'If more gentlemen were like Mr Kett, England would be the better for it.' He was surrounded by smiling faces, clapping hands and spirited voices. Robert moved his arms to wipe his eyes and nearly lost his balance. He was lost for words.

Once he had mounted his horse again, Robert addressed the gang. 'You have earned a drink for your efforts. I hope you'll go back to the festival and enjoy Flowerdew's money.'

'Yes,' Fulke replied, calmly but loud enough for all to hear. 'And if anyone brands us criminals, we can say that we are in good company, for the good Mr Kett is one of us.'

Robert gasped at Fulke's brazenness. 'How dare you.'

'We can celebrate, but we might yet face consequences for today's actions. You only need look at Adam Catchpole's ears,' Fulke pointed to a man Robert didn't recognise with wounded ears, 'to know that it's the likes of us who'll pay the price at the hands of Flowerdew and Hobart.'

Hobart again, thought Robert. Then the penny dropped. 'So you damaged Hobart's enclosure as well?' They hadn't told him that.

'Oh, yes,' said Fulke, looking pleased with himself.

'You have tricked me.' Robert's heart sank. Hobart was renowned for acting with a heavy hand. 'I had no part in that.'

'And it won't take Mr Flowerdew long to work out how we ended up back here,' said Fulke. He turned to the men he had led. 'Somebody here will take a beating for today and nobody can blame them for telling tales. But they might go easier on us if they know Mr Kett put us up to it.'

'But nobody need know,' said Robert, who knew the moment the words left his lips that rumours of their actions and his involvement would spread like wildfire.

'As long as we are clear that none of us should escape justice,' said Fulke. 'We're all in it together, aren't we, Mr Kett?'

Robert gritted his teeth. Flowerdew was a lawyer and would revel in making mischief for him for his part in these disturbances. He calmed himself and began to think over the facts. Flowerdew had bribed them, but he could say the bribe was simply to leave him alone, and his word as a gentleman counted for more than the word of illiterate peasants. Worse still, Flowerdew had not taken Robert's fences down himself. By joining in the destruction of Flowerdew's fences, Robert had incriminated himself. He imagined himself in the town pillory, and worse.

Fulke finally broke the silence. 'Well, if you're the big alderman, you can get us off, I reckon. We'll back you up. It will be your word against theirs. If you're as important as you think, it won't be a problem.' He rocked on his feet.

'This is blackmail, and I'll have none of it. Nor will I lie.' Before Fulke could reply, Robert continued: 'It will soon be dark. We must go.'

The gang followed Robert as he rode at walking pace. The silence was tense and sombre. Every so often, Robert drew his horse to a halt to let the tired commoners catch up. He felt calmer but no less uncomfortable. The threat of Flowerdew's revenge gnawed away at him. As they approached Wymondham he could see that the mood of the men had lightened as their thoughts turned to their evening's entertainment, but the confrontation between himself and Fulke was unresolved.

Fulke still looked indignant. He was a strong-willed man, clever too. Robert didn't like him but knew that he had to engage with him.

'Mr Fulke, can we speak?' he said.

Fulke looked up, then moved forward. Together they moved ahead of the group.

'You seem eager to clash with me,' said Robert. 'Have I offended you?'

'No more than any man in your position,' said Fulke.

'Why so?'

'I see through you. You will ride off tonight, back to your big home, your stocked dairy, your barn full of grain, your purse full of coins, but for us nothing has changed. You might reclaim the common, or you might not. But we will wake tomorrow and be no better off.'

Robert frowned. He had worked long and hard for everything he had and was offended by Fulke's attitude, but arguing with him would resolve nothing. 'Then what would you have me do?'

'You must continue what you have started. I fear you will betray what you have promised today.'

'I have promised you nothing, Fulke.'

'I disagree. You've offered these men hope, and I wager they will be denied it. All that awaits them is a flogging.'

Fulke was right, but Robert disagreed all the same. 'On the contrary, I have offered them nothing. It is you who has led them a merry dance, destroying people's property. It is you who has led them astray.'

Fulke was calm. He didn't look up as he walked. 'As have you.'

Robert was about to question Fulke's respect for his authority but checked himself. There was more to Fulke than met the eye. He was sharp and would speak persuasively if given the stand at a trial.

Fulke was thinking along the same lines. 'I'm certain it will all be resolved in the hundred court. Your peers, twelve good men, will judge for themselves.'

A trial was the last thing Robert wanted. As a landowner he would gather no sympathy from a jury. He might bribe his way clear, but his reputation and his family name would be sullied. He had somehow to make sure he didn't end up in court.

As they approached an oak tree, a pigeon fled its nest. Robert watched the bird flap noisily into the fading early evening sky. Robert stopped his horse beneath the tree. 'Fulke, I fear I may have misjudged you. If in the future I can restore some of the hope you say I offered, will you support me?'

Fulke looked up at Robert and, after several seconds, nodded guardedly.

When the others caught up, Robert spoke. 'I am now going to leave you. Tonight you will drink and celebrate, but your problems will be waiting for you in the morning. I thank Mr Fulke here for reminding me that I can do something about the injustices you complain of.'

The men looked expectant.

'Tomorrow I am due to pay the Mayor of Norwich a visit. I will tell him of your grievances and demand that, as one of the most powerful men in the county, he must act to stop this wanton destruction.' If Robert had thought the peasants would be impressed, it didn't show on their faces. 'Mayor Codd is an honest and fair man, with the power to resolve disputes.'

Robert was going to see the mayor anyway, and by relaying the grievances of the men of Wymondham, he hoped he might be able to extricate himself from the dispute. But if things escalated and he did find himself in head-to-head conflict with Flowerdew, then who better to have on his side than the Mayor of Norwich?

He would think it through more clearly overnight, but for now it was important to take the initiative. If he played Flowerdew at his own game, he was beaten before he started. But if he could use his connections to make the conflict more than just a petty local squabble then he might turn the tables in his favour. He might even be able to position himself as the man to resolve such troubles.

'I shall petition the mayor and ask that he puts our complaints to the king if he sees fit. No longer must rich men like myself simply take what they desire.'

There was silence. Robert knew the lord protector was not sympathetic to enclosure. If the complaints could be brought to his attention, perhaps something could be done.

'God bless you, Mr Kett,' said John Robertson. 'This means a lot to me. With your blessing, I'd like to come with you.'

Robert shook his head. 'I don't think the mayor would appreciate uninvited visitors, John.'

'Then how do we know you'll keep your word?' asked Fulke.

'Because I have given it.'

'What is the word of a rich man worth? A fart in an alehouse?'

'I don't–'

'You'll run off to Norwich, and we'll be rounded up,' said Fulke. 'Let us come with you. Let us tell the mayor in our own words. What have you to fear?'

The men surrounding Robert looked at him with expectation. He rubbed his brow. He was tiring of this game. 'It is late, and I have offered to help you,' he said. 'You will have to settle for that for now.'

'You will betray us.' Fulke stared at Robert. 'Help us, or we'll make life difficult for you.'

Robert felt the menace in the man's voice. What was he capable of? Ambushing him? Stealing his sheep? Torching his house? Robert didn't want to find out.

'Very well,' he said. 'Meet me here tomorrow. The mayor will be glad to hear from you himself.' Robert drew some comfort from the smiles and nods of assent around him. The mayor might not appreciate the unexpected visitors, but if their presence made the complaints more real and shifted some of the responsibility from his shoulders, then so be it.

'You swear on your soul you'll be here?' asked Fulke.

Robert nodded. As the men cheered his name, he turned his mare toward home and wondered what he had got himself into.

9

It was approaching early evening. Alfred had walked the short distance from Mr Kett's house to Wymondham and was waiting in the marketplace for Fulke to return. He hoped his absence had gone unnoticed. He would have to see his friend again at some point and, more importantly, he needed to claim his share of Flowerdew's bribe. But why weren't they back yet? Had something gone wrong?

As the sky began to darken, the town watchman lit the beacons at the corners of the marketplace. Then Alfred heard men singing. He watched from behind the market cross as Fulke led his followers into the Rose & Thorn.

A few moments later he followed them in, opening the low wooden door and creeping in like a mouse wary of the cat. The alehouse was packed. Amid the familiar hot, damp smell of beer and sweat, Alfred caught a waft of burning fat from the tallow candles. Over the din of chatter and laughter a solitary musician struggled to make his lute heard.

Across the room he glimpsed David Fisher, in conversation with Luke Miller. Alfred pushed through the crowd. 'David, what happened?'

Luke winked at David and left the conversation.

'Ah, the vanishing man!'

Alfred shivered.

'Mysteriously, Mr Kett came and met us…'

'And?' asked Alfred nervously.

'Relax. It was an extraordinary afternoon. Kett got off his horse and pulled down his own fences.'

Alfred frowned. That made no sense.

'Then he rode with us back to Hethersett, and we pulled down Flowerdew's fences!' David grinned and gulped down a mouthful of ale.

Alfred wondered whether he'd misheard. 'Flowerdew's fences?'

'Flowerdew's fences.'

'He won't like that.'

'No, indeed. As Fulke reminded Mr Kett afterwards.'

As Alfred tried to take in the news, he looked around the dimly lit room. All he could hear was chatter about the day's events. The mood was as good as he had seen it. Then a hand grabbed his shoulder from behind and squeezed hard.

It was Fulke. 'Where the devil have you been?' he demanded.

Alfred wanted to reply, but no words came.

'Tell me, Alfred, how did old man Kett find us, and why were you nowhere to be seen?'

There was nothing Alfred could say that would make it seem different to what it was. He pursed his lips and stayed silent.

'Come outside.'

Fulke pushed Alfred to the back of the room and through a door into an alley. As the door flew open they startled a cat scavenging for scraps.

Fulke pressed Alfred hard against the wall. In the dying light Alfred could see the menace in the older man's eyes.

Fulke jabbed a stumpy finger against Alfred's chest. 'Tell

me why I shouldn't break your nose.'

'Fulke–'

'Listen. We're in trouble for today, but it turns out your disappearing act did us a favour.'

Alfred squirmed.

'Mr Kett come down on our side. With him, we have a chance to show we won't take it any more.'

'But, Fulke–'

'Shut up.' Fulke pressed his finger harder into the top of Alfred's ribs. 'We need to show we won't be pushed around.'

Alfred winced as Fulke's finger dug in harder. 'Why?' he asked.

'Because it will overshadow me roughing up Morris. If everybody gets their common back, our offences are justified and forgotten. If they don't, then Kett is the first to face justice.'

Alfred nodded.

The door to the alehouse creaked open. Luke Miller leant against the doorframe, looking out into the alleyway. 'Lads, let's not have any trouble. No sense in fighting amongst ourselves.'

'We're now coming back in,' said Fulke.

Luke returned indoors, and Alfred breathed a sigh of relief.

'I need to know you are on my side, Alfred, and I swear to God, if you betray me again, I'll gut you. Understand?'

Alfred nodded again.

'Say it,' demanded Fulke.

'I am … on your side.'

'Lucky for you it worked out this way, but from now on, you do what I tell you. Now get inside and help me whip up some trouble.'

Fulke turned and walked back inside, leaving Alfred alone

in the dark alley. He wiped his eyes with his sleeve and gathered his breath. Perhaps he shouldn't have warned Robert Kett after all, he thought. Alfred didn't want a reputation as a man who would tell tales to the gentry.

The door swung open again. Fulke stood in the doorway. 'Get in here.' Alfred followed.

'Fulke,' he said.

'What?' Fulke was looking away from Alfred, scanning the room.

Alfred looked down. 'Can I have my share of Flowerdew's money?'

Fulke's head swung around. 'You've got some cheek.'

Alfred couldn't bring himself to look Fulke in the eye. Fulke took a step closer.

'I came to Morley.'

'We were bribed to pull down Kett's fences, remember? Where were you?'

'Forget it,' said Alfred. He could see Fulke was in no mood to give way.

'No. No, I won't forget it. Where were you?'

'Keep the money. It doesn't matter.'

'It does. It matters that I can trust you, Alfred. Deserters don't get paid.'

'Sorry I asked,' said Alfred. He blinked, worried that he would well up again.

'Best thing you can do, boy, is speak to every man here and see that he turns up to join Mr Kett's rebellion. When the bells sound ten tomorrow, by the oak tree on the Norwich road.'

'Rebellion?'

'Rebellion.' Fulke stared hard at Alfred. 'Don't question it. Just make sure they know.'

Alfred nodded, sensing how dangerous it might be to defy

Fulke. As Fulke moved away, Alfred walked wearily and with heavy limbs to the first table by the door. A group of five men he didn't recognise were leaning in, sharing a hushed conversation. A large man at the end of the table stopped talking when he saw Alfred.

'Tomorrow there is to be a rebellion under the leadership of Robert Kett,' announced Alfred without much conviction. 'We are gathering at the oak tree on the Norwich road.' The man beckoned Alfred to come closer. 'Will you men join us?' asked Alfred, forcing a weak smile.

'I don't know who you are, boy,' said the man, his voice full of hostility, 'and I don't care for you or your poxy rebellion.' Alfred swallowed. The man's companions were all staring at him. 'Now piss off.'

Alfred stepped back, keeping the men in his sight, willing himself not to shed any tears. His hand trembled as he opened the door. He stepped out, sank to his knees and took a deep breath. He hadn't asked for any of this, but now he was unable to step back, and no matter what he did, it would anger someone and land him in a worse situation. He punched the ground with frustration: once, twice, three times. His fist stung. Finally he stood up and dusted himself down. This stupid rebellion was nothing to do with him. He wasn't going to spend the night being abused for his part in something he neither understood nor cared about. If Fulke and the rest wanted to be hung for the benefit of the country, then good luck to them, but Alfred wasn't about to follow them into the devil's care.

The moon hung low in the sky. Alfred was tired, hungry and thirsty, and he had no money. There was only one place to go: home.

He walked the four miles home as fast as he could. There were stories of attacks by outlaws at night, but Alfred was too tired to be frightened. As he walked, he enjoyed the calmness of night-time, broken only by the occasional screech of a fox and the rustle of leaves in the breeze. Problems seemed to fade at night, at least until the sun rose again. He thought about his future. He was going to be a father, and they would soon be homeless. He and his wife were better at fighting than loving one another. He and his father-in-law bore each other little regard. Fulke's anger seemed like the least of his problems. He hoped it would all be easier to understand in the morning.

The cottage was filled with the comforting smell of wood smoke, as the small fire in the centre of the room gave off a soft orange glow. Sitting on his stool beside it was Lynn's father, Richard, who was silently staring at the flickering flames. He didn't look up to acknowledge Alfred, who lay down on the floor next to the hearth, glad to take the weight off his feet.

'Have we any ale?'

Richard shook his head.

'Any food?'

Richard glared at him.

'What?'

'Is that all you care about, Alfred, your belly?'

'No. Just haven't eaten since this morning.'

'Poor you.'

The silence resumed. Eventually, Alfred broke it again. 'How come you lit the fire?'

'What's the point in saving wood for winter?'

'Where's Lynn and her mother?'

'So you care, do you?'

'Only asked.'

Richard grunted.

'What will you do?'

'*Me*? What will *I* do?' snapped Richard. 'You forget that you're part of this family now, Alfred, however much you might regret it.'

'Yes, of course.' Alfred did his best to look offended.

Richard stood up. 'And where've you been? What's so important that you don't come home at night when your family is in peril? Tell me.'

Alfred looked down at the flames. What could he say? He'd been out drinking. He stared into the heart of the fire and hoped that the right words would come to him. But before any words could be uttered, the door to the cottage swung open.

'Father, have you heard?' said Lynn as she flew in. She stopped when she saw Alfred. 'Look at this. Run out of money have you?'

Alfred ignored her. If he argued with Lynn, he never won: she just got angrier until he capitulated.

'What, Lynn?' asked Richard.

'Flowerdew's fences have been destroyed. His precious sheep are roaming free.'

'Good God. Who did it?' asked Richard.

'I don't know.'

'Where did you hear?'

'I was at the Marshwell's with mother when George Newell came in and said he'd seen the flock roaming about, then he'd seen the enclosure torn down.'

'And they don't know who it was?'

'No.' said Lynn. 'Who cares? That evil bastard got what he deserved.'

'And who do you think he'll suspect?'

'How should I know?' said Lynn.

'If there's one family with good reason, it's us,' said Alfred.

'He'll have us killed,' said Richard.

'No! Why? It wasn't us,' protested Lynn.

'He'll need to blame someone, to make an example of them, even if he can't find who really did it,' said Richard. 'It would suit him nicely to blame us.'

'He can't!'

'He's the lord. He can do whatever he chooses. This is his opportunity to get rid of us and show the rest of the village what happens if you cross him.'

'No!' said Lynn.

'I doubt it,' said Alfred.

'What do you know?' Lynn barked back.

'I tell you what I know … I know who tore down those fences.'

'Who?' said Richard. 'Not you, Alfred?'

'No.' Alfred stood up and looked down at Richard on his stool. 'Robert Kett.'

'Ha! You've have been drinking again,' snarled Lynn. 'Why would he of all people do such a thing? He enclosed common land himself. Everyone knows that. You talk such nonsense, Alfred.' Lynn turned her back on him.

Alfred looked Richard in the eye. 'It's true.'

'Were you there?' asked Richard, holding his gaze.

'No. But I came from Wymondham. It was all people were talking about.' Alfred went on to explain the events he knew about, leaving out his own involvement. He could see the relief in Richard's face.

'Nonsense,' repeated Lynn. 'I don't believe a word of it.'

Alfred's jaw clenched.

'It could be true,' said Richard. 'Kett and Flowerdew have been enemies for years.'

'It is true,' said Alfred. 'Mr Kett's leading a march to Norwich tomorrow, to protest against enclosure and other abuses.'

'Robert Kett is leading a march? Why would Mr Kett do that?' said Richard, shaking his head.

'We should go,' said Alfred.

'It's none of our concern,' declared Richard.

'We've been evicted to make room for sheep. It's entirely our concern.'

'Why's he marching?' asked Lynn, more conciliatory now.

'To rebel against the likes of Flowerdew, and to stand up for the likes of us. Everywhere rich men abuse their power, and he wants to put an end to it.'

'The only thing he'll put an end to is his own life,' said Richard.

Alfred cursed his father-in-law. Why did he assume everything would end in failure?

'And that of anyone fool enough to join him,' continued Richard.

The fire quietly crackled in the silence. Alfred thought there was little point continuing this conversation. 'I'm going to bed,' he announced.

'You'll be out of work,' said Richard.

'What do you mean?' replied Alfred.

'When Mr Kett is hung for causing trouble.'

Alfred hadn't thought of that possibility. 'But Mr Kett is one of the gentry. They don't hang their own.'

'He might be well off, but he's far from aristocracy.' Richard shook his head. 'Whatever happens, this family will not be involved.'

'Father, what have we to lose?'

'My head. It's about the only thing I have left.'

Alfred scented a chance to get back into Fulke's favour.

'Richard, you told me after the farmers' meeting that nearly half the people there supported you. Well, what if they joined us and marched with Mr Kett?' Alfred let the question hang in the air.

'It won't get us our cottage back,' said Richard eventually.

'What's your plan then?' Silence. 'To do nothing?'

'What makes you so clever? You're a boy. What do you know?'

Alfred had had enough. 'I'm sixteen, your daughter carries my child, and I have work! I'm more of a fucking man than you are right now.'

Richard glanced up. 'For now, you have work.'

'Well, I'm going. You can't harvest a crop without first planting a seed.'

'If Flowerdew finds out we marched and dirtied his name, he won't take it kindly,' said Richard.

'He can't evict us twice, father,' said Lynn.

'As long as we don't break the law, we have nothing to fear. Flowerdew can't harm us more than he already has,' added Alfred from the corner of the room.

'So you're with us now, Alfred,' said Richard. 'Must be something in this for you.'

'I can't win with you,' snapped Alfred, standing over at Richard. 'I'll be going, and if you're too afraid, you can roll over and die in a ditch.'

'You're calling me a coward?' Richard stood up from the stool and glared at Alfred.

Alfred stood his ground. He folded his arms. 'Yes.' He had wanted to say that for weeks, and it felt good to have finally done it. What could Richard do to him now? He couldn't throw him out, with or without his trollop of a daughter. Richard had no hold over Alfred anymore, and Alfred was going to make the most of it.

Richard spat into the flames. His spittle hissed in the heat.

'You're a spineless turd, Richard.' Alfred stuck out his chin.

Lynn looked open-mouthed at Alfred, unable to believe what she was hearing. 'How dare you speak to him like that!'

'Why shouldn't I?' Alfred turned to face his wife. In the light of the fire her wart cast a faint shadow across her chin.

Richard's feet fidgeted, and he squeezed the purse on his belt. What I wouldn't do for a gold sovereign, thought Alfred.

Richard stood up and pointed at Alfred. 'Tomorrow morning, you and I will see Anders Marshwell, and you'll tell him everything you've told me.'

'Very good,' confirmed Alfred. Finally his father-in-law had grown a spine, and if Alfred could get some Hethersett farmers to join the march, he could save some face with Fulke.

'Don't you be getting my father into trouble, Alfred. You hear me?'

'Shut up, Lynn.'

10

Robert walked in and slumped into his fireside chair, exhausted. It had been the worst of weeks. He still hadn't sold his wool. His tenants had pleaded poverty, claiming they were unable to pay his rents and blaming his enclosures for their hardship. Then, when one of his enclosures was attacked, he had tried to do the right thing but ended up landing himself in a precarious position with his nemesis, Flowerdew. He sighed.

Alice sat opposite, darning a tear in her cloak. Jipp, the sheepdog slept peacefully at her feet. 'No kiss?'

Robert grunted. He wasn't getting up on his feet again. Not for Alice, not for anyone. He stared into the flames for several seconds, then let his eyes close. His face was bathed in the gentle warmth of the fire.

'Go on,' said Alice.

'What?' Robert's eyes remained closed.

'You rush away on horseback and don't return till it's near dark. What happened?'

Robert managed no more than a gentle, 'Mmm,' and slipped into sleep.

The next he knew was a tug on his sleeve. He came to and

saw Alice kneeling in front of him with a tankard of wine.

'How long was I–'

'Not long,' smiled Alice.

Robert groaned and took the tankard. She wouldn't leave him in peace until she knew. He took a sip and recounted the evening's events. Even the taste of the wine seemed tainted by the day's misfortunes.

'Do you think it wise, getting involved in all this?' Alice asked when he had finished.

'Something must be done. You said so yourself.'

'Yes, but leading a march to Norwich? That could be seen as a very aggressive action.'

'Hardly. We'll go and speak to the mayor and come directly home. I doubt it will do much good.'

'Then why do it?'

Robert grimaced. He was too tired for Alice's questions, and he did not want to explain the possible consequences of staying put and facing Flowerdew's retribution. 'You told me to do something, and now I'm doing it, you don't like it?' barked Robert.

Jipp opened his eyes and looked at his master.

'I just don't want any harm to come to you, my love.'

'It won't.'

Alice resumed her seat, and the two sat in silence for half an hour. Robert's eyes were closed, but his jaw was clenched, and he didn't sleep. Alice put a log on the fire.

'I don't like it, Robert, you getting mixed up in this sort of thing, with these sorts of people.'

He ignored her.

'There must be another way.'

Robert thought about the evening again. That Fulke character was as slippery as an eel. What was in it for him? And there was Alfred – if the boy hadn't come to warn him, he would have been angry to discover his fences were destroyed, but that would have been the extent of it. It was strange that somebody could appear from nowhere and have a significant bearing on your actions. He wondered if it was God's doing. Whether it was or not, it had happened, and Robert knew he must have the courage to see it through. This will all be over by tomorrow night, he told himself.

'I don't want you to go,' said Alice, firmly.

Robert banged his fist on the arm of the chair. 'Mrs Kett, I will thank you to cease sharing your opinions on matters you don't understand. What is done is done, and that's all I have to say on the matter.'

He stood up, ready to go to bed. On his way to the door he glanced at Alice, who looked frightened. 'I know what I'm doing,' he said.

Alice looked up. 'I'm not sure I believe that any more than you do, Robert.'

Robert stepped out of the room and closed the door behind him.

11

9th July, the oak tree on the Norwich Road

The land on either side of the Norwich road was flat and unremarkable. A patchwork of feeble crops swayed in the breeze. Big white clouds cast fast-moving shadows on the ground, but still there was no rain. Robert yawned. After a fitful night's sleep, he felt nervous about what lay ahead, but perhaps Fulke and his band of followers would be hung-over or forgetful or simply too idle to turn up. It was a working day: they should all have jobs to do.

While he waited, Robert mulled over what he would say to Mayor Codd, who would be expecting him, but not a dozen others with grievances to voice. His plan was to tell the mayor that rather than simply reporting on matters in Wymondham, he had brought people who would give their own account. Robert knew that the mayor would prefer a quiet conversation with a single trusted voice, but maybe a surprise like this might deter Mayor Codd from issuing future invitations.

Robert felt a twitch in the pit of his stomach as he saw a group of people approaching from the north. So he would have company after all. As they neared, Robert recognised

Anders Marshwell, the reeve of the Hethersett, followed by forty or so villagers: the majority of the village. Robert watched in disbelief. Maybe after years of mistreatment, the people of Hethersett wanted their opinion of Flowerdew to be heard. That was understandable, but it was not what he was here for. His stomach churned. Certainly Anders had made no mention of taking action at their dice game after evensong.

As the group arrived at the tree, Anders came straight up to Robert. 'Your actions yesterday have inspired the village.'

'So I see.'

'It leaves no doubt about the strength of our feelings.'

'No room for doubt at all.'

A scruffy man approached. Robert didn't recognise him, but behind him were a young woman and Alfred, his new apprentice. He should be at work, thought Robert.

'Mr Kett, sir, my name is Richard Smith,' said the man. 'This is my daughter, Lynn, and her husband you know. We're being evicted by Mr Flowerdew.'

'I heard. I'm sorry.'

'I want to thank you for taking up our cause.'

Robert said nothing.

'What is it you have planned?' asked Anders, folding his arms.

The arrivals from Hethersett that were now gathered around Robert, Anders and Richard Smith, fell silent to hear Robert's reply. He was suddenly conscious of having an audience but addressed his answer to Anders. 'I'm simply going to Norwich to speak to the mayor. He should be made aware of the abuses of power taking place.'

Anders nodded. 'What do you expect him to do?'

'That's a matter for him,' said Robert dismissively. Informing the mayor was as far as he would be going.

Lynn called out angrily from among the villagers, 'We want our house back.'

Robert saw the anger on her face. If Flowerdew had made them homeless, then anger was forgivable. 'I'm sure you do,' he said, 'but I can't make any promises about that or anything else.'

'Then why are we going to Norwich?' she snarled. 'I thought it was to see that Flowerdew's injustices are overturned.'

Robert frowned. Events were overtaking him. How had all of Hethersett caught wind of his petition? Their numbers would further undermine Flowerdew's authority, but Robert had envisaged thirteen aggrieved commoners with him, not the whole of Hethersett.

'Are you going to get our house back for us, then?' insisted Lynn.

'I have employed your husband, so I have already done more than most to help your family.'

She grunted, while beside her Alfred looked embarrassed.

John Robertson, who Robert recognised from the previous day, offered his hand. 'I spoke for the Smiths at the farmers' meeting. I'm glad to be doing something to restore some hope.'

Robert turned to Anders, 'You had a farmer's meeting for the Smiths?'

Anders nodded.

'And what was the outcome?' asked Robert.

Anders looked away.

'To do nothing,' said Lynn, making no attempt to hide her bitterness.

'It was put to the vote and they lost,' said Anders.

How typical of Anders, thought Robert. Happy to be brave when somebody else takes the lead.

'Look,' said Richard Smith, pointing to the south.

More people were approaching. Robert's mouth went dry. At first he could only make out the dust they were kicking up, but as they came closer, he estimated that there must be a hundred or more. The situation was spiralling out of control. He had never imagined that this many people would support what he'd offered to do, and for the first time the word 'rebellion' came into his mind. The mayor would never want to hear from a group this large. Worse still, some people were carrying items that could be interpreted as weapons: staffs, hoes, scythes, axes, hammers and bows. What in God's name were they planning?

Robert felt physically sick.

As they neared the tree, there was a welcoming cheer from the people of Hethersett. Caught between the two mobs, Robert felt like a rat in a barrel. He wanted to run away, but how could he? If he deserted, he'd be a laughing stock, the man who offered to speak on behalf of the poor, only to run when the time came. He would never be taken seriously again. Least of all by Flowerdew, who he'd still have to face.

The air crackled with expectation as the two groups merged and fell silent, waiting for Robert to speak. He saw Fulke, sporting a grin. Robert walked across to him.

'A word in private, please, Fulke.' The two men stepped away from the crowd and into the field beyond. 'What in God's name have you done?'

'Nothing,' said Fulke. 'These people are here because of you, and what you've done.'

'Yesterday, there were fourteen of you,' Robert said, trying to keep his voice low and under control. 'Today there are hundreds.'

'Good news travels fast,' said Fulke.

Robert ground his teeth in resentment, Fulke's lips were twitching – he was enjoying this. 'Tell me, why are they carrying tools and weapons? This is a march to lodge a petition.' Then Robert noticed a handle tucked into Fulke's belt. 'Why ... why in God's name have you brought a meat cleaver with you?'

'I'm a butcher. We might need to feed on an animal.'

'Don't insult my intelligence, Fulke. If the mayor sees a meat cleaver, he'll think it's meant for him.'

The two men stared at each other, and Robert noticed that some of the crowd gathered on the road were edging closer to overhear the two men argue. 'I don't know what you've been up to, but I'll have no further part in it,' declared Robert.

'Coward.'

'Coward maybe, but not a fool.'

'Good morning, Mr Kett.'

Robert looked over Fulke's shoulder and saw Master Peter, the tannery foreman, followed by Anders Marshwell and Alfred.

'We've brought nearly all of Hethersett, Fulke!' said Alfred looking pleased with himself. Fulke nodded but said nothing.

Master Peter put a finger to his lips, warning Alfred to be quiet.

'Problem, Robert?' asked Anders.

'This man,' said Robert, pointing at Fulke. 'I don't trust him. Yesterday he was vandalising property. Today he turns up with hundreds of people, and they're armed.'

Anders looked at Fulke. 'Do you intend trouble?'

'Trouble is never far from Fulke,' said Master Peter.

Fulke raised his hands and shook his head. 'No. I merely told people of Mr Kett's great deeds yesterday. They needed no further encouragement.'

There was a pause while they all contemplated Fulke.

'I swear it on my honour,' he continued.

Master Peter snorted.

'It's true,' said Alfred. 'I was in Wymondham last night. There was talk of nothing else. But Fulke said nothing to encourage people. They came on their own.'

'I don't trust this man,' repeated Robert. 'Why do you bring a meat cleaver to see the mayor?'

'You're right not to trust him,' said Master Peter. Fulke glared at him and shook his head.

'I always take it when I journey,' said Fulke, in a tone that suggested disbelief that this was in anyway improper.

'I have attended council meetings, town meetings, guild meetings,' snapped Robert, 'and never once have I seen fit to take a fucking meat cleaver along.'

'Very well. I'll leave it here.' Fulke dropped the heavy blade, turned away and walked slowly and purposefully back to the crowd. As he turned, he looked at Alfred and with his eyes indicated the fallen cleaver.

'I'll keep an eye out for him, sir,' said Master Peter. 'He won't cause no harm while I'm here.'

'Robert, will you address your followers?' asked Anders.

Robert wiped his hand over his eyes and mouth. 'Followers?' he said quietly. 'I can't.'

'Why not?'

'Because this is an army.' Robert gestured to the hundreds of people on the road. Together they produced a hum of greetings, gossip and excitement that allowed Robert to air his concerns without fear of being overheard. 'I never offered to lead an army.'

While the three men looked at the crowd, Alfred picked up Fulke's blade and held it behind his leg. He slid back into the crowd.

From within the crowd, Luke Miller appeared at Robert's side.

'You as well?'

'Well, I said in the alehouse, I'd support you. So here I am. You look worried?'

Robert grunted. Worried didn't cover the half of it.

'Something does need to be done, Robert,' Luke continued, 'I'll keep people in line.'

That was some small crumb of comfort Robert supposed. Many in the crowd were looking – and smiling – at Robert. There were no signs of any anger. He returned their smiles and did his best to look calm. He noticed some women and children among the throng, presumably to support their husbands, or to keep them out of trouble.

The moment was broken by the arrival of a man on horseback: William Kett, Robert's elder brother, wearing a dark green jerkin over a linen shirt. 'Robert, what is this? My stable lad told me all of Wymondham was following you to Norwich? I said nonsense, but he was adamant. Now I see for myself that he was right!'

'I'm not going anywhere,' replied Robert.

'What will you say to these people?' asked Anders.

'To go home.'

William took a breath through his teeth.

'They have come here for you, Robert,' said Anders. 'If you tell them to go home, the mood will change. And not for the better.'

'I agree,' added Luke.

'Sir, it's not my place to advise you, but...' Master Peter stopped himself. It was not fitting to offer his opinion.

'Go on, Peter,' said Robert.

'Very well,' Peter took a deep breath. 'People are angry and fearful, as you know, and their hopes have been aroused.

If you stand down now, well, I would fear for your safety, sir. I would hate to see you become the object of their anger.'

Robert sighed and closed his eyes. He struggled to collect rent from his tenants as it was, and if he backed down now, he would be given the run around for the rest of his life. His family would be mocked.

'The people are right in their grievances, Robert,' said Luke. 'Corruption and abuse are rife. To my knowledge there is no law against seeing the mayor.'

'Seeing the mayor?' said William. 'This looks like a rebellion to me.'

'I, and the people of Hethersett, did not come here to rebel,' insisted Anders. 'I would have no part in a rebellion. If we can maintain order, we should not fear the law.'

Robert looked around, trying to find some sense to cling on to. There was a cheer from the crowd on the road. On horseback, William was the first to see the cause. 'More people. Maybe fifty. From the south. This is going ahead with or without you, brother.'

'I was going to see the mayor,' said Robert. 'I offered to take some people with me to air their grievances. Then I was going straight home.'

'That is still what you're doing, Robert. Just with some extra people,' said Anders.

'Half the county? No. Gentlemen, I thank you for your counsel. I would like a word in private with William.'

Luke, Anders and Master Peter crossed back to the roadside verge, leaving the two Kett brothers in the field, deep in conversation.

A brief gap in the clouds allowed the summer sun to bathe the crowd in its light and warmth. As if prompted by this, the chatter of the hundreds of waiting people started to swell. Someone clapped, then another person, and another.

Then, to the rhythm of the clap, the crowd added a chant: 'Robert Kett, Robert Kett, Robert Kett.'

The brothers stopped their conference, and Robert looked across at the crowd. There was a loud cheer. The chant repeated. The clapping continued.

Robert blew out his cheeks and looked into his brother's eyes before walking to the oak tree. He called Master Peter over and told him to stay close. He tried to push through the crowd, but with so many surrounding him, it was impossible. He gave up and returned to his brother. 'William, I need your horse.'

William gave him a quizzical look but climbed down. Robert hoisted himself into the saddle and looked out at the sea of faces — far too many to count. He ground his teeth. This wasn't going to be easy.

'Good people of Norfolk,' he shouted, his voice cracking and high-pitched. Pull yourself together, he told himself. 'We are going to Norwich!'

A deafening cheer rang out, as hundreds of arms were raised to the sky. Robert winced as he saw tools held aloft by many in the crowd. Now is the time to set the tone, he thought. *Home by sunset*, he'd promised Alice.

'For those who don't know me, my name is Robert Kett, Alderman of Wymondham, loyal subject of King Edward, servant of God.' Robert's mouth was dry. 'If I had any lingering doubts as to the strength of feeling attached to this cause, you have dispelled them. To see so many of you here is a clear demonstration that change is due.'

The crowd cheered.

Robert waited for them to quieten. 'Until yesterday, I had enclosed land myself.' He looked around at the attentive faces, as their silence grew louder. 'But I have seen first-hand the suffering my actions have caused, and to make amends for my misdeeds I vow to do what little I can to end this practice.'

Another cheer, just as loud.

'But my leadership is not without condition, so let me be clear: this is a march, not a rebellion. There will be no fighting, no stealing. God is watching us, and we depend on his blessings if we are to be successful. We depend too on the king's good grace.' He paused, then added with emphasis: 'Any mischief will harm our cause.'

The crowd was largely silent, but Robert took comfort from the heads that nodded in agreement.

'Let me say one more thing. Much of England is protesting the religious changes imposed on us. Whether you are a reformer or a papist, you must respect one another. I shall give no quarter to anyone who seeks to use this march to further their religious convictions. It's for more educated men to determine the right way to worship God, but I do know that it is a subject that brings out the worst in men. We have no use for such divisions and must be united on the matter of enclosure and nothing else. Is that clear?'

After a more muted acknowledgement, he announced that it was time to leave. The crowd cheered again.

It had started.

Robert dismounted and embraced his brother. He felt relief and sickness in equal measure. 'Thank you, William.'

He handed William the reins of his horse.

'What made you change your mind?'

'You did. Just now, in private, once I knew you'd back me. This is fraught with challenges, but with you by my side, it could be possible. Provided we keep the peace, we should be fine.'

William smiled. 'Well, I can't leave you to make a mess of things on your own.'

'Bit late for that!'

'Well, this had better secure us both a place in heaven, brother.'

'Not any time soon, I hope.'

Robert walked towards the front of the crowd. He stomach swirled and his head felt light, as though he'd had a strong drink on an empty stomach. The Lord certainly works in mysterious ways, he thought, as his followers broke into song.

Behind him, the march moved slowly away, a giant snake slithering over the parched countryside. As Robert walked, those near him patted his shoulders and praised his decisiveness. In his mind, meanwhile, he replayed his address. He was pleased it was well-received but cursed himself for not restating more strongly his opposition to violence, and for not asking the marchers to leave their weapons behind.

William rode up to draw level with Robert. 'All the talk back there is of Robert Kett, the hero.'

Robert looked up silently. He felt more like a fool than a hero.

'The eight miles will take some time, Robert. Those at the back haven't started walking yet.'

William was right. Robert needed to plan for his new circumstances. It was already approaching noon, and it was clear that his plan to home again by sunset was unrealistic. It would be after dark; there was no question. His thoughts were interrupted as a young boy, and a small dog ran ahead of him.

A thought flashed into his mind: he could see how he would get everyone home, albeit after dark. They had no supplies, and there were many mouths to feed. Hunger would send them home. Robert could fulfil his obligations: petition Mayor Codd, demonstrate the strength of feeling, then return the marchers to their homes and farms. People would soon tire of the discomfort and hunger, the women and children especially.

'Look!' It was the voice of a child, the boy who had just run in front of him.

The boy pointed farther down the road, where four horsemen had pulled up in the middle of the road. They wore tunics of red and green, the livery of John Flowerdew. As Robert watched, they turned north and quickly broke into a gallop.

He felt his gut tighten and his mind race: If Flowerdew got word to Norwich, there was no telling what he might say, or what the city authorities might do when they hear of an army approaching. Robert shouted at his brother to come over. 'Ride for Norwich as fast as you can and find Mayor Codd. Assure him we come in peace.' He paused to gather his fleeting thoughts. 'Tell him ... to meet us outside the city gates and hear our case. Assure him that if he meets us, we will return home at once. We come in peace. William, as fast as you can.'

'Could a younger man not ride faster?'

'It must be someone credible, someone of substance. If I am to lead this march, then who better than my brother to understand my true intentions? Go!' Robert slapped the horse's hindquarter, and William set off in pursuit of Flowerdew's men.

The people behind sang, talked and joked, blissfully oblivious to the turn of events at the head of the column. The stakes had just been raised.

12

With each passing mile Robert felt more uncomfortable, his anxiety heightened by their snail's-pace progress. He cursed the country people's slow, flat-footed plod, developed over centuries of trudging through mud behind ox and plough. Robert, who travelled regularly to surrounding towns and cities to trade, was accustomed to moving at a faster pace. They were running later than he'd anticipated.

Word of the march was spreading. More people had joined the crowd along the way, some simply curious, some motivated by the cause. In the village of Cringleford, another twenty-five men, women and children joined the ranks. But whether they were four hundred or five hundred strong, it made little difference to Robert. They paused in Cringleford to let the tail end catch up, and Robert learned that a small group had sneaked away to destroy enclosures in the village. Reprisals carried out under his name were not what he wanted, but how could he object, given his own actions the day before? See the mayor, home by midnight, he told himself and set a fast pace.

A mile and a half later they crested the brow of the hill. In front of them lay the city of Norwich, nestled under a grey haze of wood smoke in the afternoon sun. Robert wasn't especially fond of Norwich, but he did normally enjoy this view. Today, though, he was too preoccupied with events to savour the sight.

A flint-curtain wall and towers encircled the city. Behind the gates, the spire of the Norman cathedral and the round tower of the former Blackfriars monastery reached toward the heavens. The limestone castle keep set high on a man-made mound. It had been built to intimidate the conquered subjects of the Norman kings. Today, it certainly intimidated Robert. It was a stark symbol of royal power, planted on the landscape like a stubborn rock in a ploughed field, reminding Robert that many people, seeing the number of followers he had, would argue that he marched in defiance of the king. That was not the case. To ease his nerves he repeated to himself he was here not to fight or defy, but simply to petition.

He waited for his followers and studied the scene in front of him. The city took on a defiant look and felt somehow more imposing than it had during Robert's regular visits to conduct trade. For some, the pull of the city – its smells and sounds, its hustle, bustle and barter, its characters and pageantry – was too much to ignore, but never so for Robert, who had grown up in Wymondham and much preferred to be a big fish in a smaller pool. Norwich's immediate surrounds were bare, the trees harvested for firewood. He caught a whiff of the city in the breeze, a heady mix of dung, livestock and smoke. He crossed his fingers for luck. William should have seen the mayor by now, he thought, and the two men would, with luck, be waiting to receive them outside the gates.

As the marchers made their way down the gentle slope towards the city, a horseman cantered towards them. It was William.

'Did you speak to Mayor Codd?' asked Robert as William drew level.

William was short of breath. 'Yes, but too late. Flowerdew got there first.' William wiped the sweat from his brow with the back of his sleeve. 'When I arrived, he was with the mayor and the high sheriff. He has told them you command a large force and are determined to destroy the city. The sheriff is panicking. He wants to send word to London and is making plans to defend the city.'

Robert gasped, standing motionless at the head of the crowd as he felt the certainties of his old world melting away.

'I spoke to Mayor Codd alone,' continued William. 'He's trying to calm things down, and I explained your aims, but he's powerless to defy the sheriff.'

'Is anyone coming to meet us?' asked Robert.

'No. The gates were being closed as I left. Codd said he would meet you tonight, but in public he must support Sheriff Wyndham.'

Robert's legs shook, but the five-hundred-strong crowd behind him continued to press forward, gently but insistently, towards the city's imposing flint walls. He looked into his brother's face, willing there to be some sort – any sort – of answer.

13

Grazing cattle would have been a common sight on the marshland bordering the river Yare near Bowthorpe, but on hearing news of the approaching commoners, the owner of this stretch of marsh had driven his cattle to safety. The hunger of the horde could easily have ruined him.

Five hundred marchers paced about in between the thick clumps of tall grass and cow pats, pressing their feet hard into the ground. If no water squeezed out, they claimed their spot for the night.

Fulke spat. 'Why is this fool making us camp in the marsh?'

'There's a dry patch there, I think,' said Alfred pointing to a slither of space to his right.

'Is your bit dry?'

'Just about.'

The boy had found a good spot. Fulke toyed with the idea of taking it for himself, then decided against it. Somehow, Alfred had got the whole of Hethersett to turn up this morning. Fulke still didn't know how but was prepared to give him the benefit of the doubt — for now.

'We'll be bitten to hell by morning,' said Fulke to himself, going back to the stretch he'd found a moment earlier. He lay down to test the ground. It was mercifully free of lumps. The grass would attract a heavy dew in the morning, but at least that might quench his dawn thirst.

Fulke stood and looked around. Here the river ran briefly from north to south, marking the camp's western boundary. Less than a mile to the north, beyond the trees, was the road that ran west from Norwich to King's Lynn. To the south, were the rest of the marchers, dotted about on the open marsh. Fulke had another look at the copse the Kett brothers had chosen for their camp. The trees stood on a slight mound, halfway down the camp on the eastern edge, raised a foot or so higher than the surrounding marsh. They'll be nice and dry in there, he thought.

Since the dispute that morning, Fulke had stayed out of Robert's way. It had smarted to back down in front of everyone, but the most important thing was that he was here, clear of Constable Jacob Morris's grasp and under Robert Kett's protection. He consoled himself that he would, somehow, have the last laugh.

The marchers foraged for food, firewood or cowpats dry enough to burn. Behind Fulke, Alfred bickered with Lynn, David Fisher and John Robertson talked conspiratorially together, and Geoffrey Lincoln chatted to Adam Catchpole, whose ears, washed clean of blood, appeared to be healing well. Fulke butted in. 'I reckon I did you a mighty favour yesterday, Adam. If it weren't for me, you'd still be bent double in the pillory, standing in your own manure.'

Adam nodded.

'Let's start with that hood of yours.'

Fulke was unmoved by Adam's disbelieving look.

'Hand it over.'

Adam removed the hood from his neck and gave it to Fulke.

As they settled down for the night, a whiff of fire-roasted meat danced across their nostrils. It was difficult to see where it was coming from. A few people still stood or walked around, but most were sitting down, partly shrouded by the long marsh grass. Against the background hum of chatter it was possible to hear one or two marchers singing, but overall the atmosphere was sombre. In the greying sky, a V-shaped skein of geese flew peacefully over the camp.

Fulke took out the cleaver Alfred had retrieved from the field. As he studied the blade, he reflected on an extraordinary day. When they had finally reached Norwich, the city gates were closed. They'd wasted some time waiting for old man Kett to make a decision. Finally, they continued their slow path around the western edge of the city and Robert decided that they should spend the night in the insect-ridden marsh at Bowthorpe. Other than being close to the river for water, Fulke couldn't see that the area had anything going for it. It was as if Kett wanted the marchers to have the most uncomfortable night possible, Fulke thought. He rubbed his thumb against the blade, testing its sharpness. Good enough to shave with.

He felt a vibration in the ground and heard the sound of hooves.

'There!' said Alfred, pointing towards the King's Lynn road. Fulke sat up. Coming through the trees were five horsemen, slowing to a canter on the small stretch of open ground before halting just ten yards away, at the northern edge of the camp.

In the dusk there was still enough light for Fulke to see that the leader of the five men wore a fine cloak with a fur trim, and around his neck hung a gold chain inset with jewels. His small, puce face sat upon broad shoulders, making his head look too small for his body.

'I am Sir Edmund Wyndham, High Sheriff of Norfolk,' the man called out as Fulke approached.

Somewhere in the grass a marcher wolf-whistled. Several more laughed, and the sheriff's face went a darker shade of red. 'On the king's authority, I command you to disband and return to your homes.'

'Or what?' asked Fulke as he arrived at the sheriff's horse. It was a fine creature. Most of the animals he slaughtered and butchered were in such a state they almost longed for the relief of his knife. Not this one.

Fulke missed the sheriff's reply. 'Say again?'

The sheriff sucked air through his teeth, not accustomed to repeating himself. 'Or I'll have you arrested. Now leave. All of you. Go.'

'Arrested? All five hundred of us?' said Fulke.

'Must be a big gaol in that city,' said Geoffrey Lincoln, walking up behind Fulke.

There was a smattering of laughter and applause as more marchers gathered.

Fulke grinned. He could see the sheriff didn't know what to say next and was close to losing his temper. The stern-faced men in his retinue stood behind, waiting for orders.

'Don't argue with me. If I say go home, you damn well go home.'

'Or what?' asked Fulke.

'Blast you, man. I'll have you strung up and gutted like a swine!'

'See, I'm a butcher by trade, so I know a thing or two about gutting animals.' Fulke held up his meat cleaver and flashed the large blade. Several marchers also drew their knives. Alfred followed suit and pulled out his own eating knife. Fulke stepped back, spreading his arms wide to make clear his advantage.

Twenty paces to the east a voice called out: 'Stop.'

Fulke looked across to see a tall, red-haired man, walking clear of the marshes.

'No need for knives,' continued the red-haired man. 'My bow and arrow will make less mess.' He placed an arrow on the string and pulled back, stretching the yew bow and taking aim. He had the sheriff in his sights.

The marchers retreated, avoiding the archer's line of sight. Fulke did not move.

'Cooper!' shouted the Sheriff.

'That's right, sheriff. Me again.'

'What are you doing here?' The sheriff looked confused.

'You know me, sir. I'll lend my name to anything that'll give you a headache.'

Fulke took a long look at the tall bowman, who had a pox-scarred face and clothes that were of good quality but were unclean.

'Cooper, you'll hang for this. And the rest of you.'

'Goodbye, sheriff.'

The sheriff furiously turned his horse and galloped away, closely followed by his men. The archer loosed his arrow, which hissed through the air and struck the sheriff's horse on its hindquarter. The horse whinnied and stumbled, but had the strength to carry on. The men marchers cheered as the sheriff and his men disappeared into the trees.

'Damn it, lads,' said the archer. 'I thought we might have horse for dinner.'

Any archer worth his salt wouldn't have missed from there, thought Fulke. 'You'll need to shoot better than that if you want dinner,' he said. 'Who are you?'

'John Cooper, though I prefer bows to barrels. Pleased to meet you.' He held out his hand, which Fulke ignored. 'I've come from Norwich with my friends here.' He waved his arms around, indicating a group of men who had walked up to join him as the sheriff rode off. Fulke counted nineteen. 'We heard about your little rebellion and didn't want to miss out.'

'I hope your friends are better shots than you,' said Fulke.

Cooper's expression hardened. 'Let's find out. I'll give you a head start to the count of twenty.

'I've a better idea. Put down your poxy bow and see if you can take me with your hands.' Fulke paused. 'Like a man would.'

Geoffrey glanced at Adam and Alfred, who looked concerned. 'Fulke, there are nineteen of them,' said Geoffrey.

'There's only one of him. Come on, pox-face.'

The two men stood motionless, each waiting for the other to move. Then, from the corner of his eye, Fulke noticed heads among the onlookers begin to turn.

'Fulke, careful, look,' said Adam.

'What's going on?' Robert Kett hobbled through the long grasses of the marsh. Ten paces behind him came his brother, William.

'Who was that?' said Kett. 'What is going on?'

Fulke quietly put his meat cleaver down on the ground. Kett scanned the faces, his eyes coming to rest on Fulke. 'You! I might have known you'd be near any trouble.' Kett strode towards Fulke, 'What have you done now? I told you to go home.'

Fulke's glare remained directed at Cooper. 'It was him.'

'Him? What?' demanded Kett.

'Fulke? What's going on?' asked William, catching up with his brother.

'I was causing no trouble, sir,' said Fulke, addressing William, his employer. 'This fool here' – he nodded at Cooper – 'is the one who should answer for his actions.'

'It's true, Mr Kett,' said Alfred, addressing his employer. 'We came over to see what was going on. This man shot the sheriff's horse.'

'He did what?' yelled Kett, his cheeks turning red.

Cooper said nothing.

'You shot at the sheriff?'

'Only his horse.'

Kett cupped his forehead with his hand.

'I told you,' said Fulke.

'Fulke,' Kett gave him a look of such menace that even Fulke twitched. 'The whole time … every time there's trouble, you're there, in the mix.'

'Easy, Robert,' said William, putting his hand on his brother's arm.

'Mr Kett, sir, really he did nothing wrong. It was this man here.'

'Shut up, Alfred. I don't want to hear it.'

'Robert, stop,' said William. 'Let me deal with this.'

'These men will get us killed! We came to petition the mayor, and these fools – this man – has shot the sheriff's horse! What the … how do we explain that, William?'

Fulke allowed himself a sly smile. The old man's losing his grip, he thought.

'Robert, enough. Go,' said William. Robert Kett turned and stormed off. His temper frayed beyond the point of usefulness. William turned his attentions to Cooper, the rogue archer, but his problem was immediately apparent: Cooper's men had slowly formed up behind him.

'Where are you from?'

'Norwich,' replied Cooper.

'This is a peaceful march of country folk. We have no need for city-dwellers.'

'Our commons are enclosed, just as yours are,' replied

Cooper. 'In fact, we broke down the enclosure at Town Close on our way here. That's the idea, ain't it?'

'I have four witnesses here,' said William, indicating Fulke, Alfred, Adam and Geoffrey, 'who will testify to what they saw.'

Fulke grinned at Cooper.

'There are too many of you to take on here, now, but while you may be twenty strong, I have over a hundred from Wymondham alone. Any more trouble or antics to impress your mates, and you'll pay with your lives. Understood?'

Cooper nodded slowly.

'Then be gone.'

William turned to Fulke as Cooper and his companions drifted back into the marsh. 'Come here. I don't know what you've done, but it's plain that my brother doesn't care for your help.' Fulke was about to protest his innocence, but William carried on. 'Listen, if you value your work with me, you behave. Don't bring shame on me or yourself.'

'But–'

'No buts, Fulke. And you watch that man Cooper like a hawk for me. Understood?'

Fulke nodded.

'Good, then we'll say no more.'

At that moment, Robert Kett returned, calmer now. 'Listen to me, Fulke,' he said. 'If anything happens, anything at all, you come and tell me. Nothing happens without my knowing. Next time somebody important arrives and wants to talk, send him directly to me.'

'He didn't want to talk, sir. He just wanted us to leave,' said Alfred.

'I don't care!' Kett snapped back. 'Send them to me. That man's actions have likely compromised our entire purpose. William, we must report him to the authorities. He and his men must answer for their crime.'

William nodded.

Robert looked at Fulke. 'Stay out of trouble.' Then, turning to Alfred, he said, 'Anything happens, anything at all, you are to fetch me immediately.'

Alfred nodded.

'Enough. Back to your...' Robert paused, trying to think of the right word.

'Marsh?' offered Fulke.

*

As darkness enveloped the marsh, the Kett brothers returned to their copse. Fulke, Alfred, Geoffrey and Adam went back to their patches of dry ground and prepared for sleep. It would be a cold, damp night, but Fulke was relieved. He'd done enough to distract anyone who was interested in his misdemeanour with the constable in Wymondham. What came next didn't really matter to Fulke, but he knew it mattered a lot to the Ketts, and he knew he would find some advantage for himself. He smiled and drifted into sleep.

Fulke woke to the noise of a horse snorting. He wasn't sure but didn't think he'd been asleep long. With all the excitement he'd neglected to empty his bladder before he went to sleep, so he searched for a nearby clump of grass that didn't have a sleeping marcher beside it and relieved himself. The air was cool, and the three-quarter moon gave enough light to see by. It was then that a brief movement caught his eye – it came from the mound where the Kett brothers were sleeping.

Fulke peered into the dark. He saw it again. Just a horse flicking its tail. He finished his business, retied his codpiece, and went back to the spot he'd been sleeping on. What had seemed flat before now felt like a ploughed field. As he tried to settle, he thought about the horse he'd just seen. It was white, but William Kett's horse was chestnut. Somebody must be paying them a visit.

Fulke got up and tiptoed through the marsh, taking care not to tread on his fellow marchers. Nearer the copse, he crouched down, using the tall grass for cover. All was quiet, but he could hear the faint whispers of a conversation from under the trees. He slowed as he got closer and moved carefully like a cat stalking a bird. He crawled as close as he could, inching forward, knowing that a single snapped stick could give him away. He looked up: twenty feet from him, a stranger, presumably the rider of the white horse, had his back to Fulke, but still he could not make out their words. He dropped to his belly and crawled again. He was now just six feet from the tethered horses and could go no closer. Fulke lay still, his head raised. The Ketts' fire smouldered, casting just enough light for him to make out their faces. William Kett had been speaking, and now the visitor replied.

'Since the imprisonment of the duke and the execution of his son, the administration of Norfolk has been dire.' The man cleared his throat and continued, 'Nobody is in charge. The county is in chaos. Those left with any authority spend their time jostling for personal gain, and trying to prevent the advancement of others.'

Fulke could see Robert Kett's face in the glow of the fire. He was shaking his head. The visitor continued, 'The affairs of the county are being neglected. I confess that I have become disillusioned, and I would gladly resign the office, but I cannot think of a single man I would trust to take it on. However, I fear my problems are nothing compared to yours, Robert.'

'What is happening?' asked Kett.

'The enclosures at Town Close, the city common, were wrecked this evening, and I believe those responsible have joined your number.'

'People have been arriving in small groups all day. In truth, Thomas, I am powerless to stop people joining.'

Thomas? Fulke reckoned this must be Thomas Codd, Mayor of Norwich. The man Kett had set out to meet. The authorities, including the mayor, had refused to meet the marchers and yet here they were, the mayor and the Ketts, gathered in secret in the dead of night. Fulke's belief that Robert Kett and his brother were not to be trusted was confirmed.

'That's what the city fears,' said Codd, 'events taking hold of themselves and chaos descending. The sheriff is worried not only for his position, but, if this goes badly, for his head. Flowerdew visited to warn us and made a show of impressing on the sheriff his responsibilities to execute the rule of law, and the consequences for him personally for failing to do so.'

'Blasted Flowerdew,' said Robert, looking at his brother.

'In spite of Flowerdew's meddling, having a rebellion occur on your watch is something Sheriff Wyndham could do without. He's prone to rash judgements at the best of times, but after today he's really panicking.'

'He visited tonight,' said William, 'and he threatened us. Did you know?'

'No, but it's well within his gift to make matters worse. He wanted to send a message to the king.'

'The king?' gasped Robert. 'We are on a peaceful march!'

The mayor shook his head. 'I can keep London out, but only for a day, two days at most. You must stand down and send the rebels home.'

In the brief silence that followed, Fulke shifted to get more comfortable. He hoped that this might be the moment when Robert Kett showed his true colours.

Kett scratched his cheek.

'If you do,' continued the mayor, 'I think you will escape with only a gaol sentence. For inciting trouble, most likely five years, if you give a decent bribe. Otherwise ten.'

'Thomas, I'm nearly sixty years old. I wouldn't survive five years in prison.'

'Robert, keep your voice down,' whispered William.

'These people are desperate and rightly so,' said Kett, following his brother's advice. 'If I told them to go home tomorrow, they'd murder me themselves, and I can't say I'd blame them.'

Fulke raised his eyebrows.

'What if Robert stood down and renounced the rebels?' asked William.

Robert Kett answered before the mayor could speak. 'We're not rebels, William. Calling the marchers that, and renouncing them, would only incite them to riot and destruction, and I would still get the blame.'

'In which case you would face the executioner's axe for sure,' confirmed the mayor.

In the undergrowth, Fulke allowed himself a wry grin.

'We only came to present you a petition,' explained Robert.

'Mm, yes, but your arrival has, unfortunately, stirred up grievances in Norwich that were dormant. Once word of your 'march' spreads, I dare say there will be more uprisings.'

'Then the quicker you give us some assurances and send us home, the better for everyone.'

Another silence. From behind the trees, Fulke could see Robert Kett's expectant face, staring at the mayor. When no answer was forthcoming, he tried again. 'We need a fruitful outcome for all. If the sheriff could agree to end enclosure within the county, I give you my word, we would all go home tomorrow.'

'It's not that simple, Robert. The sheriff enforces the law. He doesn't create it.'

'But enclosure isn't legal.'

'No, but strictly speaking it isn't illegal either.'

'He has power to do whatever maintains the rule of law, does he not? So get him to end enclosure, and we'll go home, and the rule of law will be restored.'

'I'll try, Robert. I'll talk to him in the morning, but he won't like having to back down. Like any man of authority, he doesn't bend easily to the whims of others. Nor will he want the gentry baying for his blood.'

'Reason with him, Thomas. This is not a whim. It's about our future. Seymour, The Lord Protector, is sympathetic to our cause. He has commissioned parliament to revoke enclosure.'

The mayor nodded. 'He has, but so far without success. Robert, I will do everything I can, but the sheriff must not know that I have been here. If he suspects I have betrayed him, I'll face gaol myself. I have to be seen to support him.'

'Understood.'

'For the sheriff,' said William, 'saying that he'll end enclosure and actually doing so are two separate things. The first would be enough to send us home.'

'You have a head for politics, William,' said the mayor.

Robert Kett shook his head. 'Then all this would have been for nothing.'

'No,' said William. 'Not necessarily. People would half expect the authorities to betray them anyway. If the sheriff says he will ban enclosure, we can go home having served your original aims. Then the authorities can drag their heels and life will return to normal.'

There was a pause while the men considered William's suggestion.

'Look,' said the mayor, 'if you won't go home, at least keep your army out of Norwich. Set foot in the city and you are as good as dead.'

'I give you my word,' said Robert. 'We don't want trouble.'

The mayor stood up and embraced the Kett brothers in turn.

'God bless you for coming here in the dead of night. A safe journey home,' said Robert Kett.

The mayor left the cover of the trees and walked towards his horse. Fulke lowered his head into the cover of the grass and cursed himself for not foreseeing the possibility that somebody might leave.

Just a few feet from Fulke, the mayor grappled in the dark with his horse's tether. Fulke heard William Kett's voice: 'Mayor, let me help you see your way clear of the marsh.' Fulke could hear the old man's footsteps as he too stumbled about. Fulke pressed his cheek into the earth, his heart pounding.

'Got it,' said the mayor.

'Here, let me help.'

Fulke heard a grunt as the mayor heaved himself onto his horse, then he felt the vibrations of the horse's hooves in the ground as it shifted position. After they had turned away from the dying fire, William led the horse in Fulke's direction. Being trodden on by a horse's hoof was like being struck by a blunt axe. Fulke lay motionless, bracing himself for the impact. He could smell the beast and hear its breathing. Its front feet stepped over his ankles, the white bulk of its body passed over him, and he felt a rear hoof brush his foot. Fulke breathed a silent sigh of relief.

'There, Thomas, you are clear from here,' whispered William, patting the horse's rump as it passed him. He watched the mayor ride away, then turned back towards his brother, but he took a slightly different path, and his toe caught Fulke's heel. William stumbled, took another step, then fell to the ground. He groaned as he landed on his hands.

Fulke lay stone-still.

'Are you all right?' Robert Kett called out softly.

William grunted again. 'Yes. No harm done. I just tripped over…' He stood up and half-turned to see what had caught him.

Fulke clenched his fist, ready to strike.

William studied the still, dark undergrowth beneath the trees. 'I'm too old to be wandering about in the dark,' he said to himself.

He dusted off his hands and, stepping carefully, walked back to the fire.

Fulke lay still, his heart thumping against the ground. He listened quietly as the brothers planned their actions for the next day. They spoke too faintly for Fulke to be able to hear it all, but he heard enough to give him some ideas of his own.

Like a snake, he crawled back to where he had come from.

14

11th July, Hellesdon, outside Norwich

'Alfred, I'm hungry.'

Alfred was hungry too. He hadn't eaten all day. He shifted against the tree that provided some refuge from the midday sun. To his left and right, a line of poplar trees stood tall, with weary marchers competing for resting space in the narrow shade the trees cast across the track.

'Alfred, I have your baby in here,' said Lynn rubbing her stomach as she lay on the ground. 'Get me some food, or do you want your child to die?'

Alfred wondered for a brief moment whether Lynn herself might die during birth. He glanced at her tummy. It hadn't grown any bigger yet. She returned his stare, and Alfred thought about moving, but there was no space left in the shade, and clear of the shadow, there was only the sweltering sun. Alfred had a headache – he needed a drink. In the three days since they had left Wymondham, he'd had a little of Adam's cheese, some raw peas, a few herbs scavenged from the undergrowth and part of a loaf of bread stolen from a market trader on his way home. All washed down with river water.

He looked down the tree-lined dirt track. Under the next tree was his neighbour, George Newell, lying on the ground holding his belly. If Alfred's own smell was anything to go by, George Newell's clothes would want burning after three days under the sun's heat. George had his eyes closed, and his face wore an expression of permanent strain. Maybe the river water disagreed with him. But it wasn't only George: the dismal conditions were beginning to exhaust all the marchers' patience.

Alfred swallowed. His mouth was dry. He closed his eyes and dreamed of a river, its cool water washing over his hot skin…

'Say something,' said Lynn. 'Do something, Alfred.'

'Do what?' His eyes were still closed.

'Other men's wives have food.'

Your father's the one hoarding a sovereign somewhere on his person, thought Alfred. Plague him, not me.

'Alfre-e-e-d,' said Geoffrey Lincoln in a whiny, mocking voice, 'my arse is itching!' He laughed at his own joke as he played cards with Adam Catchpole.

Alfred shook his head, too tired to respond, even though Adam and Geoffrey's jokes were wearing thin. He heaved himself up before they could continue, and to get out of earshot of Lynn. Twenty paces away, in the undergrowth beneath the trees, stood Master Peter, arms folded and exhibiting his usual stern expression. Alfred followed Master Peter's line of sight: he was watching Fulke again. Perhaps Fulke's suspicion that he was being spied on was right.

Master Peter nodded to acknowledge Alfred, but his gaze stayed fixed on Fulke.

'What's happening?' asked Alfred.

'We're resting,' said Master Peter.

Alfred ground the ball of his foot against the earth, tearing at a nettle root. 'I thought you might know what Mr Kett has planned next?'

Master Peter's blonde stubble was getting long after three days. He stayed silent, staring at Fulke.

'Now the Mayor refuses to see us, and we're locked out of Norwich, are we going home?' If Master Peter did know Mr Kett's intentions, he was staying tight-lipped. Alfred gave up and walked over to speak with the object of Master Peter's attention.

Fulke was leaning against a tree, whispering to John Cooper, the man who'd shot the sheriff's horse. Alfred was surprised that the two of them were talking. At the marsh, Fulke had seemed more interested in fighting. Mr Kett's brother had told Fulke to keep a watch on Cooper, but now it seemed the two men were becoming friends. Fulke looked over his shoulder, but when he saw it was only Alfred, he carried on. 'Honestly,' he said, 'I overheard them with the mayor the other night, at the marshes.'

Cooper, standing two feet above Fulke, pursed his lips. He held his bow stave, unstrung, as a simple staff. 'You're sure? The mayor was at the marshes?'

'I swear it. On my life.'

Leaning on his bow stave, Cooper rolled his head from side to side.

'The Ketts are worried for their own skins,' said Fulke. 'We won't be going into Norwich, and we won't be seeing the mayor. Mark my words.'

'So what are we still doing here?' Alfred asked, keen to be included. Neither Cooper nor Fulke showed any sign of having heard him.

'What do you think then?' Cooper asked Fulke.

'My bet is they're waiting for us to get exhausted and give up,' said Fulke.

Cooper shook his head.

'So we have to make it clear to them,' Fulke continued, 'that we aren't going home.'

'Why doesn't Mr Kett just go home, then?' asked Alfred.

They ignored him again. 'What you got planned, Fulke?' asked Cooper, scratching at the pox scars on his cheeks.

Fulke shook his head. 'I've grown a tail.' He nodded in the direction of Master Peter.

Cooper looked over. Alfred already knew who Fulke was referring to.

'Kett's man. Works at his tannery. He hasn't taken his eyes off me since your run-in with the sheriff. I am getting the blame for you shooting the sheriff's horse.'

Cooper grinned, exposing the gaps in his teeth.

'We need more than words,' said Fulke. 'We need to act, to prove to Kett we're not going home. The sooner he realises he's in shit up to his eyeballs, the sooner we can take the fight to the bastards who steal the commoners' land.'

'I'm not sure I trust you, Fulke.'

'Fine. If you're happy to march round in circles all summer, I'll find someone with bigger balls.'

Cooper didn't rise to the insult. There was a stirring noise as marchers nearby stood up. To the north, the marchers were stepping out of the shade.

'Looks like we're on the move again,' said Fulke, shifting his weight away from the tree.

Alfred sighed but decided to stay with Fulke and Cooper for a stretch. Better to be ignored by them than mocked by Adam and Geoffrey. Lynn had been testing his temper all morning, too, so the farther away from her, the better. She would find other villagers from Hethersett to walk with.

One by one, the marchers shuffled off. The pace was slow. Alfred held out his hand to brush across the tall grass stems beside the track. The gentle strokes across his palm helped take his mind off the gnawing hunger. He picked a seed head and crumbled it in his fingers. He wanted to know where they were going and what the Ketts had planned. The day before they'd left the marshes and walked back in the direction they had come from, to the south of Norwich. They'd stopped at the city's main gate, and Robert Kett had shouted to the archers manning the gate that he wanted to meet with the sheriff and the mayor. Then they had waited for hours in the hot sun.

Alfred had wanted to buy some food. He stayed close to Richard in case he tried to spend his sovereign, but the gates were locked all day. A few pedlars had come out to sell their wares, and Alfred heard that one had been beaten and robbed of his food. Since then, the traders were too scared to come out.

Alfred yawned as he walked clear of the poplar trees.

In front of Alfred, Fulke and Cooper walked in silence. Everyone was silent. On the first day there had been singing, children laughing and playing, and people had shared whatever they had. Yesterday had been a day of rumours and gossip and opinions about what Mr Kett ought to do. Today, it was just weary silence. Even so, as word of the march spread, more people had been drawn in from surrounding towns and villages.

Alfred's enthusiasm, though, was rapidly giving way to the cravings of his belly. Ahead, a smaller, more overgrown track from the west joined the one they were on. On either side of it was the usual patchwork of ridges and furrows in the large fields, and shimmering in the afternoon heat about a quarter of a mile away, were some old barns. Alfred wondered what they might they offer up. It was worth a look. No sooner had he left the main column of marchers than he was followed by

Adam and Geoffrey. As they neared the buildings, though, Alfred could see that they were more derelict than they had appeared from a distance. They searched them anyway but left empty-handed.

'Wishful thinking,' said Geoffrey as they retraced their steps to meet the tail end of the column.

'Hunger gives you false hope,' said Adam.

'Mm,' said Alfred, 'Bit like this march.'

'Lads, look, behind us,' said Geoffrey pointing back, beyond the derelict barn, to three fully laden carts, each pulled by a single horse, coming towards them along the track. On each cart, large barrels and wooden crates were stacked high behind the driver. Ahead of the three carts was a solitary rider.

'Food?' said Alfred.

Geoffrey nodded. 'But I count four men, and we are only three. Adam, run ahead and tell Fulke our dinner is here. Alfred and I will slow them up. We don't want them to catch up with the marchers before we've taken our share.'

Adam ran on to find the column of marchers. Alfred and Geoffrey stayed on the track and waited for the carts. The man on the lead horse was well to do. He wore fine clothes and a velvet hat, and his clean-shaven face looked unaccustomed to the heat of the sun. His skin reminded Alfred of uncooked pastry, dull and smooth. Also, his animal, unlike the cart horses, was well fed and in good condition. He started to speak, in the accent of the gentry: 'Good day to you all. I come in search of Robert Kett.'

Geoffrey delayed them with small talk before offering to lead them to Kett. Alfred eyed the carts, laden with food and what he assumed was a hogshead of ale on each. His stomach rumbled at the sight of it all. He and Geoffrey walked side by side on the track as slowly as they could to hinder the progress of the convoy.

Soon Alfred saw two men running towards them from the direction of the marchers. One was Adam, and the other had ginger hair: John Cooper, the archer. Alfred wondered why Fulke hadn't come. Cooper stood, holding his bow stave, at the junction where the overgrown track re-joined the larger one. His feet were planted wide apart. The rider and carts drew to a halt in front of him. Alfred wiped a little sweat from his brow and made his way to the side of the first cart, salivating at the sight of loaves of bread and rounds of cheese in the crates.

'Get back,' ordered the cart driver.

Alfred stepped back and smiled at him. He was a giant of a man, more than six feet tall.

At the front, Cooper was addressing the gentleman rider. 'I could take you to see Kett if you could spare us something to eat?'

'I'd sooner turn around than barter with you,' said the pastry-faced man. 'Now take me to Kett.'

'Very well,' said Cooper.

He'd given up rather easily, thought Alfred?

Cooper took hold of the horse's reins and led the group back towards the marchers. The wooden carts creaked and squeaked as they rolled over the track's hard, rutted surface. Alfred walked alongside the first cart, unsure why they were returning to the rest of the marchers before securing their own share. The cart was old, with a dry, brittle wooden frame topped by new planks. Every few yards Alfred had to take an extra step to keep up with the horses. Even pulling fully laden carts, on hard ground they still travelled faster than a man's normal walking pace. Behind Alfred, Adam and Geoffrey walked on either side of the second cart.

They soon caught up with the slow-moving column. As

they approached, the rearmost marchers turned to look. When they were twenty yards away, Alfred saw some of the marchers point at the ale barrels, their faces alive with the prospect of food and drink. Once the carts were in among the crowd the food would soon disappear, so if he wanted some food to himself, he had to act now. He stepped in close, reached over and grabbed a loaf of bread.

'Hey! Put that back!'

Alfred glanced behind. The shout came from the driver of the following cart, who now yelled to his companion on the lead cart, but Alfred was too hungry to care and sank his teeth into the bread's soft crust. The smell filled his nostrils. He ripped a chunk free with his teeth and started to chew.

The giant driver turned to look back. 'That ain't for you! Put it back right now, or I'll tear your arms out.'

Alfred continued to chew, savouring the taste of the thick wheat dough.

Now Adam and Geoffrey leapt up and grabbed a loaf and a cheese each. All three cart drivers shouted to their master, who turned his horse. Without hesitation, he ordered the drivers to put the stolen food back.

The giant halted his horse and jumped from his seat, grabbing Alfred with one huge hand. They fell to the ground, with Alfred crushed under the man's weight. The bread in Alfred's mouth made it hard for him to breath. He tried to spit it out, but he had taken too big a bite. The giant pushed himself up, using one hand to grip and twist Alfred's shirt just below his neck. His other hand was clenched into a fist, which he drove hard into Alfred's face, his oversized knuckles landing square in Alfred's left eye. Alfred's shriek was muffled by the doughy ball of bread still in his mouth. He tensed his body ready for the next blow, turning his head away and squeezing closed his eyes shut, waiting for the pain.

But the driver's weight shifted as Adam Catchpole hurled himself into him. Alfred was smothered as the two men collapsed on top of him. The force of them landing on him, winded him. His chest crushed, his mouth blocked, he tried to breathe through his nose, but his breath wouldn't come. As he tried to wriggle free of their weight, he saw Geoffrey run up and kick the driver viciously in the ribs. The blow forced the huge man to roll over, but just as air was flooding into Alfred's lungs he felt Geoffrey's misdirected next kick smash into his ribs.

Alfred rolled onto his knees, gasping for air, clear of the melee. He spat the dough into the dirt and looked up, searching for the loaf he had dropped. Then, while still on hands and knees, he took another sharp kick to the ribs, this time from the second cart driver. The pain shot through his torso. Before another blow could land, he instinctively rolled away under the cart, fighting to regain control of his breathing.

To his side, Adam and Geoffrey were wrestling the two drivers, while their pastry-faced master barked at them to stop and stand aside. Cooper held the reins of his horse, laughing at the spectacle. Alfred watched as Pastry Face swung a leg at Cooper and missed. Cooper stepped around the side of the horse, jumped up, and with one hand, grabbed the gentleman's tunic and yanked him clean from his saddle. He hit the ground, face first.

'I am Sir Roger Wodehouse,' he protested. 'Stop this—'

Cooper straddled the fallen knight and delivered a sharp blow to the chest. 'See, my lord, I reckon that under these fancy clothes, you're just the same as me.'

As Wodehouse writhed and gasped for air on the ground, Cooper ripped at his expensive-looking breeches, pulling them down as far as his boots, where they stuck fast. Then, paying no heed to Wodehouse's protests and flailing limbs, Cooper turned him over, tore off his cloak, and pulled him out of his tunic.

Sir Roger Wodehouse was now naked from the ankles up. Alfred, holding his swollen eye, managed a laugh from under the cart. To his left, one cart driver was down, but the giant had bested both Adam and Geoffrey, who lay collapsed on the verge. The giant heaved himself up and lumbered over to save his lord. He shoulder-barged Cooper, and the two men crashed to the ground. Sir Roger scrambled to his feet and hoisted his breeches. Cooper rolled over back on to his feet, and the giant stood and swung a punch in the same movement. Cooper swayed out of the way.

By now the marchers were cheering the fight, and Cooper, the giant and Sir Roger Wodehouse were surrounded. The giant stepped closer to his master to protect him.

Alfred got to his feet, clambered onto the cart and helped himself to a second loaf of bread.

Wodehouse glared at Cooper. 'Stop this. Take me to Kett.'

'I'll take you to meet Mr Kett,' said Cooper. 'But you are coming as my prisoner.' The onlookers cheered.

The giant took a step forward, but his master raised his hand to stop him. 'I will dress again first.'

Meanwhile, the jubilant marchers were stripping the carts of their loads. As word spread, more and more of them ran back towards them, eager to claim their share. Among them, moments later, were the breathless Kett brothers. Robert Kett's face dropped as he recognised Wodehouse. Immediately behind the Ketts – to Alfred's surprise – came Fulke, looking pleased with himself, and Master Peter.

'What the devil is going on?' demanded Kett, regaining his breath.

Cooper stood tall and defiant next to Wodehouse. 'Mr Kett, I have taken this man prisoner for our cause.'

Robert Kett's mouth fell open as he struggled to find the words he needed. 'Sir Roger? What? How–'

'Robert, I came to talk you out of this madness,' said Wodehouse, still dishevelled after his encounter with Cooper. 'Then this man attacked me.'

Kett looked at Cooper, then at Fulke, who nodded knowingly. It dawned on Alfred that after Adam ran back, Fulke must have betrayed Cooper and alerted Mr Kett. Before he could understand why, Kett was speaking again. 'You? By what right do you take this man prisoner? Who do you think you are?'

A long silence followed. 'You need a prisoner, Mr Kett,' said Cooper. 'If you want the authorities' attention, that is.'

Kett's forehead furrowed. 'I decide what I need, and how I do things, not you.'

'Then please be kind enough to tell us what it is we're doing. You have us walking back and forth with neither food nor drink.'

'We are waiting to see the mayor, as you damn well know.'

'I don't think he's coming, Mr Kett,' said Fulke.

'Oh, I'm not so sure,' said Cooper with a knowing look at Fulke, then Kett. 'You never know when the mayor might drop by.'

Kett looked away.

'Robert, I pray, return to Wymondham and send these men home,' said Sir Roger. 'I have brought you food and ale if you will only stop this foolish rebellion.'

'A bribe?' said Fulke.

'Sir Roger, this is not a rebellion,' said Kett. 'I'm sorry for what has happened to you. You will be released at once, together with your goods.'

There was a groan from the watching crowd, and a woman of thirty-five or so, accompanied by two sickly-looking young children, spoke up. 'Mr Kett, we are hungry. If we go home, there is little to eat, and we can't afford what precious little there is. I cannot feed my children. You have to change that, Mr Kett.'

'I cannot make the authorities meet us,' snapped Kett. 'Do you not understand that?'

'You can now you have a prisoner – we've captured one of their own,' Fulke pointed out with a sly grin. 'Now they'll to listen to us.'

'I said no violence! Was I not clear?' shouted Kett.

Fulke's cheeks reddened.

'Yes. Indeed, I was the one who brought these misdeeds to your attention. But you do now have a prisoner, Mr Kett, and you promised us justice.' Fulke spoke forcefully but stopped short of shouting. Alfred realised what Fulke's plan had been: to get Cooper to do the dirty work so Mr Kett couldn't accuse him of interfering, and for Fulke to prove his loyalty by informing Mr Kett.

'So far you've taken us for a long walk,' said Fulke. 'You claim nobody will speak to you, but we have waited three days. Then this man arrives, bribing us to go home…'

'And so you should,' said Wodehouse.

The crowd booed. Somebody at the front of the mob spat at Wodehouse. The spittle landed in the dirt at his feet.

'Stop that,' shouted Kett, looking for the perpetrator.

'No more from you,' barked Cooper, slapping Wodehouse across the chest. The knight's face went red as his fists clenched, but he suppressed his fury at being taunted.

'Have some blasted respect for a gentleman,' demanded Kett.

'You have got the stomach for this cause, haven't you, Mr

Kett?' asked Cooper.

'Of course I have. How dare you accuse me of...'

Kett's words petered out. David Fisher, one of the original group who attacked Mr Kett's fences, stepped forward from the crowd to fill the silence. 'Pray, Mr Kett, tell us what is our plan? If we go home we will lose our chance. We will perish this winter.'

The crowd shouted their agreement.

Kett exchanged a look with his brother. 'We are not going home,' he conceded, 'but we are not taking prisoners. I have said all along, no violence. Now release this man.'

Cooper looked steadily at Kett. 'No,' he said.

There was an awkward silence.

'Please, Mr Kett,' said another marcher. 'I just want my land back for my animals.' The crowd cheered. 'I want my lord to treat me fair, that's all. It's not much to ask.'

'Yes,' said Kett, 'but we did not come here to take prisoners.'

The crowd began to shout and jeer.

William Kett raised his arms 'Enough!' he shouted. 'We will keep Sir Roger in our custody, but there is no gain to be had by treating him like a thief.'

While the crowd cheered, Robert Kett frowned at his brother. William's expression in reply was a clear appeal for his brother to trust him.

'Robert, I beg you, return to your senses,' said Wodehouse, at which Cooper cuffed him on the back of the head.

Kett looked around the crowd. Alfred followed his gaze and couldn't see a soul who agreed that Sir Roger Wodehouse should be released. Sensing his defeat, Kett spoke up: 'Master Peter, you are responsible for this man's welfare. Put him on the cart and see that the food is kept secure. We will distribute it fairly tonight.' Master Peter nodded. Fulke smiled.

Now Kett pointed at Cooper. 'You are a troublemaker, and you are not welcome on this march. You will return to whatever stone you crawled out from under.'

Cooper opened his mouth to protest, but Kett was too fast: 'No!' he bellowed. 'Fulke, see to it this man is removed from our number.'

Fulke flashed a malevolent smile at Cooper. 'My pleasure, Mr Kett.'

'We camp tonight at Drayton Woods. Tomorrow, we'll force the city's hand,' said Kett, to loud cheers. 'You have my word.'

*

As the march resumed, the two brothers held back until all their followers had passed them. 'What the hell did you do that for?' said Robert Kett, his voice flat and quiet. 'Now we have a blasted prisoner to add to our problems.'

'Robert, you were moments away from being mauled.'

Robert shook his head and started to walk. His legs felt heavy, and his feet weak as if they might give way without warning. Ahead, he could see the marchers swarming all over the moving carts, passing and throwing the cargo down to marchers on the track. His plan had been to rely on their hunger to send them home, but now some of them at least would be well fed and watered. His own stomach gurgled.

'We've been stalling for days, Robert,' said William. 'If you want to change your mind, time has run out.'

'I know, I know. What in God's name are we going to do?' Robert Kett went to bite his thumbnail, but there was no nail left to bite. He looked at his brother. 'We could slip away later, into the night?'

'The thought had crossed my mind.'

'I wouldn't put it past them to put a guard on us, to see we don't.'

'Did you get the impression that that blasted creature Cooper knew about the mayor's visit?'

Kett shrugged. 'He's a real snake in the grass, that one. I'm glad he's gone.'

At least, Robert consoled himself, he'd finally found a use for Fulke.

The brothers walked side by side behind the six hundred people who marched in their name. Six hundred people, who demanded their leadership, but would not reciprocate with their obedience. William lifted his hands and tapped them against his chin as if offering a prayer. 'We have two choices, Robert. We stand down, or we see it through. You're a gambling man, stick or twist?'

Kett looked around. It was hard to think clearly when he was so hungry and tired. On either side of the path were more parched crops, a reminder of the commoners' predicament.

'Stick, and we definitely lose, all of us,' said Robert. 'Although we will bear that cost more than most.'

'We will lose this hand,' said William, 'but we live to play another day.'

'At our age, we don't have time to play many more hands. Not if we lose this one.'

They walked in silence for a while, and Robert looked away from the track, across the fields. On his left, an imposing oak tree caught his eye. It stood alone in the middle of a field, dominating its surrounds. It reminded him of the oak tree under which this journey had started. If I only knew then what I know now, he thought. He wondered what he might do and why he had chosen to lead these people in a bid to end enclosure. Above him the sky was a clear, bright blue. Finally he spoke. 'I don't want my last years to be years of failure, William.'

William nodded. 'I agree. I think back to times in my life, and yours, when everything seemed forlorn. When I had staked a fortune and lost it. When I was owed money I knew would never get back. When I didn't have enough to see me through winter. When I was sick. When my crops failed, or my livestock perished. Whatever it was, it seemed at the time that all was lost. Yet in hindsight, every time, whatever the problem was, it led me to a better place eventually. I learned a lesson which served me well and helped me become stronger. Or maybe things just unexpectedly turned out for the best. You can never see it at the time, and I can't see a way out of this right now, but there will be a way, somehow.'

'I hope you're right.'

'There's something else, though. I'm widowed, but you must consider Alice.'

Robert sighed. He went to bite his nail and failed a second time. 'We both have children,' he said. 'And grandchildren. My loss would be no greater than your own.'

He looked again at the oak tree, alone under the blue sky. 'If we could strike a blow against enclosure, or even end it, what better legacy could we leave? People have risen elsewhere, and we know they've been pardoned by the lord protector. We are not the only ones, and he is sympathetic to our cause. If there was ever a time to make a stand, it is now.'

'So this is a rebellion after all, then?'

Robert nodded slowly. 'It's starting to feel like one.'

'Well,' said William, 'nothing of value is accomplished without some risk of failure. With Protector Seymour's support we should be safe.' He looked around and smiled wryly. 'Besides, it's a lovely day to make a stand.'

'And we might just win. We're six hundred strong now and no doubt, more will come. That is a fearful prospect for the city.' Robert stopped and waited for his brother, his hand outstretched. 'Twist?' he asked.

William shook his brother's hand. 'Twist.'

Their minds made up, they embraced. At that moment, Robert was sure their decision was the right one and that together it would be possible to see it through. At the same time, he felt a knot tighten in the pit of his stomach.

PART 2

Hebrews 11:6
⁶ And without faith it is impossible to please God, because anyone who comes to him must believe that he exists and that he rewards those who earnestly seek him.

15

11th July, Palace of Whitehall, London.

Edward Seymour was slumped in his chair at the head of the table. His eyes glazed over. He resembled a tailor's mannequin in his brightly coloured finery, thought Dudley, looking on from his usual place at the far end of the table, next to Archbishop Cranmer.

For God's sake man, stand up and lead, thought Dudley of Seymour.

Between them sat the Regency Council, willing Seymour to speak with their pursed brows. Outside, beyond the diamond-shaped panes of glass, the bells of London tolled noon. The council had been sitting in chamber for an hour with nothing to show for their attendance. It was stiflingly hot with the windows closed to keep out the noise and stench of the city. The painted roses of the Tudors that adorned the wooden ceiling did nothing to lift the mood.

Dudley twisted his gold wedding ring round his finger, as was his habit. He glanced in the direction of the slumped figure at the head of the table. Careful what you wish for Seymour, thought Dudley.

When old King Henry became ill, Edward Seymour

coveted the role he now occupied: Lord Protector. Forced to execute his own brother in March, Seymour had since become half the man he once was. Unfortunately, England needed him to be twice the man, for the kingdom was out of sorts. As the king's uncle, Seymour had coerced enough of the council to support his appointment as Lord Protector before Henry VIII was even stiff. Now, he was in charge of the kingdom until such time as the boy, King Edward VI, was old enough to take over.

Now he's got it, I'd wager he wished he hadn't, reflected Dudley.

It was two years since the forty-nine-year-old Seymour had snatched the throne of England. He'd aged in that time. His brown beard had greyed, creases like cracks in porcelain lined his face, and now his characteristic indecisiveness had returned with a vengeance. Seymour changed his mind as easily as the wind changed direction.

The eleven-year-old boy would have done a better job, rued Dudley.

'Regretfully,' Seymour broke the silence, 'it appears once again I am left with no alternative but to resort to the use of force.' Seymour turned to Lord Grey. 'You will take your soldiers to Oxfordshire and quell the rebellion quickly. Then you will ride west and reinforce Lord Russell to recover the city of Exeter.'

'Your orders for the treatment of the rebels, sire?' enquired Grey.

'Confiscate their lands in the name of the crown,' said Seymour.

'Sire, if I may?' said Grey. 'Our repeated failure to severely punish the rebels only encourages them further.'

'You would have me hang my own people because they cannot eat, when the likes of you all take their land and starve them. There is not a man around this table that has not helped in some way to agitate my people.' His voice trembled. He stared blankly ahead and continued his limp tirade. 'We are at war with Scotland. France threatens invasion. Calais and Boulogne are under garrisoned. How can I raise an army to defend us when the populace would rather fight *against* me than for me?'

Dudley sat back in his chair. He commended the lord protector for being so concerned with the peasant's stomachs, but Seymour was in need of the noble men and their money if he were to prove victorious. Dudley had not yet forgiven Seymour for making an example of him with his agrarian reforms. Seymour's enclosure commission, which had singled out Dudley's land, had damaged his hedges and ploughed a furrow through his parkland, only serving to encourage the commoners to revolt, believing they had the support of 'The Good Duke'. To Dudley's mind 'The Reckless Duke' was more apt. Left to manage the fall out from Seymour's policy, he'd narrowly avoided having to hang his own tenants, managing instead to quell their anger with threats.

No matter how noble the intention, Seymour's cavalier approach to reform was dangerous, and it was costing him allies on the council. Dudley stroked his beard, luxuriant with lavender oil. It made up for his bald pate. The forty-five-year-old former commander of the navy glanced over at the portrait of King Henry VIII beneath whose all-seeing gaze they sat.

What would he make of this shambles?

Seymour's propensity to govern by committee was naïve.

Men needed a leader.

Grey continued to speak.

Dudley knew what was needed. Take back Exeter, hang

everybody involved, send a message to the whole country that rebellion would not be tolerated. That alone would scare Oxford quiet. The Scots could wait. Whatever towns they captured, they proved incapable of holding. You couldn't tackle Scotland until you had England under control. Not that he was offering his advice. Better to watch Seymour flounder like a cat in a water barrel. Drowning slowly. Deservedly so.

A loud knock at the door interrupted them.

Without invitation, the household chamberlain walked in, adorned in white robes, a look of consternation on his face.

'Your grace, my apologies for the intrusion, but I bring you urgent news.'

'Go on,' replied Seymour, sounding hopeful, perhaps for a turn of good fortune.

'Gentlemen, we have received a messenger from the Sheriff of Norfolk. There is a rebellion in East Anglia. A large force has assembled at the gates of Norwich. A thousand men, maybe more.'

Seymour slumped into his chair with a groan. Around the table, eyes widened, and expressions of alarm were shared.

Dudley sighed. More insurrection.

'When? Who leads them? Why? What are their intentions?' said Seymour at last.

The grey-haired chamberlain didn't reply.

That settles it then, thought Dudley. War on two fronts. As the most experienced military man here, it must fall on him to act and save the realm for the king. Rising from his seat to address the room, he spoke with authority.

'Sire, let me crush the Norfolk rebels.'

There was a long silence.

'No. Not until we understand their intentions.' Seymour looked to the chamberlain.

Dudley resented this. The time to quash a rebellion was *now*, at its outset. Quickly and ruthlessly. Was this fool really going to sit here and let the country tear itself apart?

Members of the council shifted uncomfortably in their chairs. They exchanged knowing glances.

'We must tell the king,' declared Seymour finally.

'To what end?' Dudley spoke; challenging him once more.

Seymour shrunk into his chair. It was painful to watch. Dudley resolved he could no longer waste time. He would canvass support amongst the nobles this evening. They had to act and remove Seymour. It was treason, he knew, but it was for the sake of the country. It was a gamble: his own head the stake, but the prize was equally valuable: command of the realm. The thought came to him: If I could I seek an audience with the king, perhaps I could receive his blessing in advance?

He would have to do it without raising suspicions. Would the king betray his uncle? If he knew his throne was at risk, maybe.

Dudley locked eyes with William Parr sitting opposite, the young Marquis of Northampton. He assumed from Parr's raised eyebrows that he was thinking something similar.

'We will send an educated man, a preacher, to Norwich,' began Seymour. 'He must meet with the rebels and attempt to reason with them, such that they are encouraged to disperse.'

Dudley nearly choked. Another rebellion has started, and he intends to send a preacher? The wide-eyed counsellors sat in mute disbelief.

'Sir, a delay in our response will only encourage them,' Sir William Paget, the council's secretary spoke in a muffled voice as if to avoid embarrassing the lord protector.

'What encourages them is the sharp practice of their

landlords,' Seymour insisted. 'Archbishop Cranmer, please attend to it. A man of persuasion and reason.' Cranmer nodded dutifully.

'If it is successful, your grace, maybe we should try this new tactic against the French. Nothing like a good sermon to deter the enemy!' said Dudley, making no attempt to conceal his contempt.

Seymour banged his fist on the table.

'If that is the only contribution the Earl of Warwick is willing to make, I would prefer that he refrain from interfering.'

Dudley bowed his head, and Seymour continued, 'Would you have me murder every man on this isle, just so that they may no longer rebel? How can I deal with a situation until I understand its cause and its aim?' His voice trembled before he recovered his composure. 'We must protect London at all costs. I am declaring martial law in the capital. Curfew at sunset, double the watch, have artillery placed at the gates. When word spreads that London is impregnable, these rebels will be deterred from attempting an assault.'

'Sire, those measures will unsettle people. If it looks like we've lost control, you will cause panic…'

'Enough, Dudley,' interrupted Seymour.

Dudley gritted his teeth. The only word Seymour would spread with these actions was that he was vulnerable. The taverns and inns would be rife with gossip following these draconian measures.

'Once we have recovered Exeter then we'll have more options. Gentleman, that is all for today,' said Seymour, dismissing them from the chamber.

Dudley caught Parr's contemptuous smirk beneath his wispy ginger beard. Parr was another one, like Seymour, only here because the old king rutted his sister. It was no qualification for exercising governance. One by one, the councillors stood up and filed out.

Alone, Seymour moved to the window, which looked south across the Thames as it sparkled peacefully in the afternoon sun.

He began to cry.

16

12th July, Mousehold Heath, outside Norwich.

Alfred hurled a handful of stones from the collection cradled in his shirt into the bush. 'Ger on,' Alfred shouted at the sheep. Daft inquisitive creatures; their inclination was to peel off the track into the undergrowth. His job was to walk at the rear of the flock of sheep and keep them together. So far, he hadn't lost any. It would have been easier without his left eye being shut, now fully swollen from the cart driver's punch, or the pain in his ribs where he'd been kicked.

At the front, leading their sortie to round up the nearest available sheep, was a young man named Luke Miller. Evidently he had inherited a fortune from his father and was known to Mr Kett. With him, walked his companions from Wymondham: David Fisher, Geoffrey Lincoln in his straw hat and Adam Catchpole who stood at either flank of the flock. Alfred's mouth watered at the thought of eating mutton tonight.

Today had passed quickly since arriving at the high ground, at the top of an escarpment known as Mousehold Heath. It had a commanding position over the impressive city, but there had been no time to admire the view. Mr Kett had declared it their camp and those who hadn't volunteered to fetch supplies had stayed to gather wood and build makeshift shelters. Alfred had left Lynn in charge of gathering the wood for their shelter and had placated her protests by promising he would help build it when he returned.

Two sheep peeled off into the trees. Alfred launched an attack of stones.

The trees either side of the track gave way to reveal two windmills that marked the heath's northern edge. On the right was the high flint wall that enclosed Norwich. Along the wall, its gates and towers were quiet. There was no one in sight. It looked deserted.

They drove the sheep up the wide gully that parted the heath. Since their departure hours earlier, a great camp now covered the heath. In all directions it was covered with hundreds of small shelters and crowds of animated people. A child of about ten-years-of-age staggered past, struggling beneath the weight of the long branches in his arms.

'Oi, lad, watch where you're going,' said Alfred.

The little lad took no notice and struggled on.

Behind them, more people were turning up. A gathering of twenty men, carrying sacks, looked unsure where they should be.

A sheep made a break for it, and Alfred threw a stone to no avail. One of the men dropped his sack and headed the animal off. His arms spread wide to drive it back to the flock.

Alfred thanked him.

At the top of the gully, they managed to get the sheep into the crude, hastily-erected pen. It was already filling up with hundreds of sheep, raided from the surrounding countryside. Around its edges, men leant on the fence, eyeing their dinner and discussing the merits of this almighty endeavour.

Alfred felt a sense of pride in having made a contribution to filling the larder, but there was no time to celebrate. He needed to find Lynn and build their shelter. He was tired and thirsty, but if he stopped now, he knew he'd never get started again.

Adam Catchpole joined him as they made their way through the camp.

He was hard pushed to find the spot he and Lynn had marked for themselves. He tried to get his bearings but was disorientated by the hammering, shouting, laughter, wood snapping, and a woman appearing with a large clay pot under her arm. 'Honey for sale, my love?' Alfred shook his head. Where was Lynn? He thought he had left her vaguely level with the trees. He stood in a small clearing in between tents. It must be close.

He spotted Fulke putting the finishing touches to his and Adam's shelter. Just in front was his father-in-law Richard.

'You're back,' said Richard, patting turf onto the roof of a small wooden shelter. 'Should keep the rain out.'

'Looks good,' said Alfred, relieved to be in the right place. 'Where's Lynn?'

'She went down to the river to bathe her feet.'

'Where's she put our wood then?'

Richard shrugged his shoulders.

Alfred struggled to contain his anger.

'Most of the good stuff has probably gone by now. You'll have to scavenge at the back of the woods.'

Alfred cursed his wife. She had *one* job to do. As much as he wanted to complain about her to anyone who would listen, it wouldn't get the shelter built. He'd have it out with her later, when she'd finally finished washing her feet. Alfred charted a course through the tents and headed the short distance to Thorpe wood, which covered the eastern rise to the heath. He hoped to find whatever the previous scavengers had left behind.

'Surely you don't expect me to sleep in that, Alfred Carter?' complained Lynn when she returned from the river to find Alfred lying on his side, adjusting the sticks that formed the canopy.

He'd made three return journeys to the woods, and unaided, had nearly finished their shelter. The sound of his wife's disapproval at the end of that was too much to bear.

'What did you expect? A four-poster bed with silk sheets?'

She stood defiant, her hands pressed into her hips.

'Well, you're going to have to do better than that. It's a boy's effort,' she said scornfully.

'Why don't you do something for once?' shouted Alfred. Only she had the gall to come on a rebellion and complain about her accommodation.

She stamped on his foot, which was poking out of the entrance to their abode, prompting Alfred to sit bolt upright. He hit his head on the main beam of his wooden tent. The beam slid off its support at the far end and fell, collapsing his construction.

'Told you,' said Lynn, turning her back to him.

Alfred emerged from the pile of wood. He picked up a branch that had previously been part of his roof and swung it at Lynn, catching her full on the shoulder. She cried out in pain and fell to the ground. Enraged, Alfred stood above her, raised the branch over his head, and with both hands, swung it down. He aimed for the wort on her chin and struck her square in the face. She screamed in pain.

Alfred, blushing with anger, brought the branch down again, clubbing Lynn for a second time as she tried to wriggle to safety. Weeks of pent up frustration were coursing through his veins, directed at the women he blamed for falling pregnant and turning his life into a waking misery.

Fulke fell about laughing.

Next to him, Catchpole roared.

'Stop, Alfred. I'm going to piss myself,' said Fulke, struggling to get his words out.

'Oi, stop that!' shouted Lynn's father, Richard as he ran towards them.

Alfred raised the branch again. This time he swung it to the side like a giant pendulum, and Lynn cried as the stroke thumped into her neck. Richard cannoned into Alfred. He was three quarters the size of his son-in-law but hit him with all the fury of a father protecting his daughter. The two of them tumbled to the ground.

'Go on, Alfred,' shouted Fulke, 'show the old man what you're made of.'

Hearing the disturbance, people began to gather round, forming a circle. Lynn crawled away, leaving the two men on the ground before Richard emerged on top. He threw a punch and hit Alfred on his swollen eye. Alfred howled in pain, swung his fist and missed.

The onlookers cheered and clapped.

'Stop this nonsense now!' Master Peter walked into the circle and yanked Richard off his son-in-law, dumping him on the ground.

'Alfred, what in the blazes are you doing?' shouted Master Peter.

Alfred held his hand over his injured eye, which throbbed with pain. He knew he was in trouble. Mr Kett had warned them this morning that he wanted no disturbances at their camp.

'What's this about?' Master Peter asked.

'He was beating my daughter,' said Richard pointing to Lynn.

'Alfred, is this true?'

Alfred spluttered, failing to come up with his explanation.

'Alfred, why is that woman's face red and marked? Did you do that?' pressed Master Peter.

'I think it's an improvement,' said Fulke, who laughed at his own joke.

'Alfred, I'm not going to ask you again.'

'Yes. She started it. She stamped on my foot.'

'You cowardly weasel, beating your wife, she's pregnant,' protested her father.

The crowd fell silent.

'Get up, Alfred. You'll be spending the night at Mr Kett's pleasure.' Master Peter turned to the onlookers. 'The rest of you, get lost. Go back to your duties. We'll have no more of this.'

Alfred stood up, and Master Peter grabbed him by the arm. Alfred took one last look at Lynn as she lay, crying on the ground. He felt a strange mix of guilt and relief.

She'd had that coming for weeks.

'You were warned. You'll spend tonight locked up.'

'But she...' Alfred protested.

'I'll hear nothing of it, Alfred,' Master Peter interrupted him. You of all people, working for Mr Kett, should be leading by example. He was very clear. He expects decency and discipline in the camp.'

Master Peter walked him through the camp and didn't release him until they arrived at a half-flint, half-timber building. Despite looking like the residence of a gentleman, its garden was overgrown, windows dirty and adorned with cobwebs, and the perishing timber gave it a neglected appearance. It perched on the edge of the heath at the top of the escarpment, overlooking a steep slope dotted with spindly trees, and the city beneath.

'In you go,' said Master Peter, pointing to the door.

'What is this place?'

'Surrey House. It was once a priory, and then it was the home of the Duke of Norfolk's son, The Earl of Surrey. It has lain empty since his execution, so now it's Mr Kett's headquarters, and your home for the night.'

Alfred felt strangely hopeful as he walked through the large wooden door onto the terracotta tiles of the hallway, but there were no paintings or embroideries, only cobwebs and pigeon droppings. Despite that, it was markedly better than his shelter.

On the right of the main wooden staircase was a metal gate. Master Peter stepped forward and took a large key from his belt. He wrestled with the lock, and then the gates clunked as they swung open. 'Down there,' said Master Peter pointing to the stone steps.

It was dark, and Alfred inhaled the damp air as he trod carefully, waiting for his one good eye to adjust to the light. He heard the cage door swing closed and lock behind him.

'You'll face trial in the morning, Alfred,' said Master Peter at the gate.

'Hello?' said Alfred as he entered the cellar.

In front of him, in the dim light of the stairway, he saw a silhouette of a man sat on the floor. Alfred shivered, it was cold, and there was a foul smell.

'Who's there?'

'I'm Sir Roger Wodehouse.'

He was the rich gentlemen whose carts they'd pilfered yesterday. Alfred didn't say anything but flopped down in despair. The sharp flints in the cellar walls dug into his back.

That evening when the last of the light had faded, Alfred could hear the faint hum of music. People were dancing.

There was singing and laughter. He caught the occasional whiff of roast mutton. They're getting fat out there.

Indoors, the rank odour of faeces lurking in the corner of the room took his mind off his hunger.

This was all Lynn's fault. If I could just be free of her, I could give my heart and soul to this rebellion, he thought.

He lay down and tried to sleep. The stone floor was as cold, and he went over and over the events of recent months. Lynn had ruined his life. She didn't love him, nor he, her. Yet now he'd been told he would go on trial in public for beating her. Mr Kett had explained when they arrived that he would hold a court to dispense justice in the camp. She would claim to be pregnant. Alfred knew he faced punishment.

He would likely miss the rest of the rebellion.

He'd probably end up pilloried. What had he done to deserve this? If only he could talk to his father, but he was dead, and nothing would bring him back. Since his parents' deaths, his life had fallen apart. Alfred's face contorted with self-pity. He rolled onto his side and curled into a ball. He began to cry, as his body shook, and his heart ached with a pain so deep he couldn't control his sobs.

17

13th July, Surrey House, Mousehold Heath.

Robert felt the gentle rise and fall of his brother William's body lying next to him. It had been many years since he'd slept in a bed other than his own, but it was a big improvement on the woods and marshes of the previous nights. The curtains that must have once adorned every window in the house were missing, either reclaimed or looted Robert assumed. Dawn was rising, bathing the room in a faint grey light, sufficient to see the carved gargoyles around the edge of the wooden ceiling. Robert found their snarling faces disconcerting. He thought of Alice: her smile, her laughter, her silver hair. In the dead of night his heart ached to see her. By now she would have heard that Robert's march had escalated into something much bigger. He hadn't returned home by sunset as he'd promised. She'd have worked out he was not coming back. She must be worried. He resolved he would send word to her today.

The gentle patter of the first rain in weeks fell on the roof tiles. Too late for this year's harvest; the crops had stopped growing and were starting to flower. Nonetheless, the rain was a good omen. It wouldn't be enough to fill up the water butts, but Robert might get enough for a small drink. He cleared his dry throat and offered God a silent prayer of thanks and asked for his wisdom and guidance.

He looked at his brother again. 'You awake?'

William grunted.

The bed creaked as Robert stood up. The floorboards did likewise as he walked to the sideboard and picked up the chamber jug. It was nearly full, so Robert opened the window and poured out the contents before refilling it himself. Once finished, he rubbed his eyes and looked out of the window at the heath littered with shelters like hundreds of molehills, blurred by the summer rain. The air smelt clean and sweet from the rain, and the camp was quiet. A shadowy figure bolted through the drizzle to relieve himself against a large oak tree.

We must organise latrines, thought Robert, or we'll be ravaged by disease.

Since they'd arrived, his mind hadn't stopped. He'd called a camp meeting for this morning. Terrified of chaos breaking out, he was determined to impose some order at the outset. It was essential to find out how many they numbered; well over a thousand was his estimate. With every new arrival, his responsibilities increased, and the burden on his shoulders grew heavier. If he had any doubts as to the strength of feeling that ran through the common folk, it had long since vanished. The authorities couldn't ignore this protest now. Crucially, any spat between him and Flowerdew was forgotten. That was one worry he was able to shed.

I have to ensure this stays peaceful, he told himself for the umpteenth time.

A few hours later, all the occupants of Surrey House were up and crammed around the dining table. Robert sat at the head, with William to his right, straddling the table leg. The table was large enough for sixteen. Crammed shoulder to shoulder, Robert did a quick count, there were thirty men altogether. Extra chairs had been scavenged from other rooms.

Despite the dark wood panelling, the room was well lit through the large leaded windows, a few of which were broken.

'Such a window must have cost a small fortune for the lead and glass alone,' he'd remarked yesterday.

What a shame to see such a room coated in dust and mouse droppings. The absence of women's work was evident in the filth and squalor: dirty plates from last night's mutton, mud from the morning's rain on the tiled floor, the unswept fireplace. He would need to appoint a housekeeper. Living amongst such filth, they would soon risk falling ill to malodorous vapours.

The men tucked into the remains of three sheep carcasses for breakfast.

Robert had decided to use the same system of governance here as was used throughout the county. The men of every hundred, an administrative division of the county, were to elect two men to represent the people of that hundred. This way Robert could ensure his instructions could be relayed consistently to all his followers. By concentrating the concerns of the camp through a smaller number of elected representatives, it would save Robert from having to listen to the opinions of every Tom, Dick or Harry, allowing him to concentrate on maintaining order. A general loss of law and order was Robert's biggest concern. It would undermine all their best endeavours.

Robert looked on in silence as the men around the table talked and joked as men do in the absence of their wives. He envied their carefree enjoyment of an experience more familiar to soldiers than to laymen. Robert had never been soldier, nor fought a battle. His interests had only ever been commercial. This required a different leadership because unlike a general of an army, he could not have his men killed for disobedience. He needed to reason with them, appealing to their self-interest, though with this many men, it may not be possible. Discipline had to be maintained.

At least I am relieved of the responsibility of returning a profit, he thought.

He took a swig of ale. It was dry and sour, not like Alice's ale.

'William.' He tapped his brother's arm to get his attention. 'I've been thinking. This camp must stand as an example of government administration done well. We must behave with legitimacy if we are to avoid accusation of rebellion.'

'It's a little late for that!' interrupted John Bossell, a short piggy man with a nose to match.

Bossell was the representative for Holt. The reason for the man's self-confidence was a mystery to Robert. He disliked earwigging and grimaced as Bossell waved his mutton-greased fingers about.

'I am consulting with my brother, Mr Bossell.' Robert turned his back on him, making it clear he didn't welcome further interruptions.

'Agreed, protest not rebellion' confirmed William with a morsel of sheep fat hanging from his bearded chin. 'We must avoid conflict with the city. I would suggest nobody enters Norwich without both express permission and good reason.'

'You're right. Any violence in Norwich will condemn us. Our followers won't like that though.' Robert nodded. 'What if they want to visit church?'

'I would forbid it. It's large groups we must be cautious of. Men are brave together. Send them in twos and threes, and they'll keep their noses clean.'

'Then we should make some provision for their spiritual needs in camp,' said Robert, eyeing the food still nesting in his brother's beard. 'Only the king's religion. Catholic worship will risk his reprisals.'

William leant in and whispered, 'Man's other need was being catered for in camp last night. As I walked about to take in the evening air, I saw a band of prostitutes coming from the city, making their way up the gulley to camp.'

Robert stroked his chin. 'Our plan had been to walk to Norwich and return that night. It is now four days since we left. I fancy some of the women who at first accompanied us have had to return home. There are animals to feed, milk and muck to remove.' Robert's thoughts again turned to Alice alone at home.

William brought Robert's mind back to the present. 'Whores will corrupt the camp.'

Robert took another swig of ale. Along the table, men were becoming boisterous. The composition of their force had changed. What at first had been almost a family affair was now a male army.

'The whores stay, William.' Robert announced, putting his tankard back on the table. 'Let the men spill their seed, and we quell their aggression.'

Chastened, his brother disagreed. 'What sort of example is that? You talk about acting legitimately like a government, and you would have the camp turn into a bawdy house?'

'It's the lesser of evils. Besides, I defy you to tell me there isn't a member of our government who isn't dipping his wick in London's bathhouses.'

William turned to face his brother. 'God will punish us. They'll call you a pimp.'

'I dare say they'll call me many things by the time this is over. If pimp is the worst of them, then I'd settle for that now. The whores are welcome, and that's an end to the matter.'

Robert knew there was little to be gained from debating with William, the more you argued, the more he dug his heels in. Robert stood up and reached over to grab another handful of last night's mutton.

'Nothing like a young wench to settle a man!' said Bossell slapping Robert's back with his greasy hands.

Robert ignored Bossell. The man was infuriating, but Robert had bigger battles to settle. As the ale settled in his belly Robert reflected that he felt settled at their camp. No doubt sleeping indoors again and fresh food had helped, but something else had changed. Sitting in the filthy dining room, Robert realised that the indecision of the first four days had passed. No longer was his mind wrestling with the do-we-don't-we of committing to something, which was altogether larger and more serious than that which he had originally intended. For better or for worse, he and William had made the choice, and now it was time to get on with it.

With that, Robert stood up and left the table.

The rain had stopped. The distant church bells sounded eight as the dining table was dragged outside and positioned under the boughs of the large oak tree. Around it now gathered the people from the camp as Robert clambered up with all the vigour his fifty-seven-year-old limbs would allow. Any worries he had were quickly dispelled by the cheers and applause that rang out across the heath. He was humbled. He reckoned there must be at least a thousand faces staring back at him. Behind them the tip of the cathedral spire poked up above the treeline that separated the rebels from the city.

Robert cleared his throat.

'If there be any doubt to the justice of our cause then it must be gone now that the Lord has seen fit to send us rain,' he bellowed the words, as loudly as he could.

More cheers. The mood was merry. They had full bellies, and he had their full attention.

Once the cheers subsided he continued. 'I pronounce this fine oak tree to be our Oak of Reformation. It will symbolise our strength, our resourcefulness and the purity of our cause. From this spot, all camp administration will be enacted.'

Going on to explain how food supplies would be acquired, Robert noticed a gang of mud-splattered boys who had pushed their way to the front. Between eight and twelve years of age, with tatty clothing and knives in their belts, they were delinquents one and all. Robert detailed how every day parties would leave the camp bearing a written warrant from himself demanding the supply of provisions so that the occupants of this camp could restore the king's honour. All local landowners would be obliged to surrender their produce. Food would be distributed orderly and fairly under the oak tree to everyone in attendance. Anyone caught stealing food would face trial here under the Oak of Reformation.

'Ay ay.' This declaration was met by nodding heads and gentle murmurs of approval.

Next, he ordered latrines to be dug, and punishments issued for anyone caught defecating in the camp.

'We could use the abandoned flint quarry on the eastern slope. It's up-wind,' somebody suggested.

Now the rub: 'During our stay, no man will be allowed into Norwich without a permit. I will be making contact with the city officials and asking them to close the gates to us.'

As expected, this prompted open dissent from the onlookers. He was met with a volley of disapproving comments and questions.

'I understand your concerns, but we must retain good relations with the city at all costs. The alderman will be scared by our presence here. If trouble breaks out, our cause is lost, and you shall starve this winter.' He paused. 'I will establish a clerk's post at this tree.' He gestured towards his brother. 'My brother, William will serve as the clerk. Any of you needing permission to enter Norwich must explain your reasons to the clerk, and if acceptable, you will be issued a permit to enter.'

William didn't look best pleased with his new role.

People were starting to fidget.

Robert knew from his days acting in the Wymondham stage plays you could only maintain an audience's interest so long. Nonetheless, it was essential they heard his next point, as their only chance of success was if they forged a unified and legal protest. Robert raised his arms and in his loudest voice, demanded that they behave with courtesy and respect to one another whilst in camp. Anyone found causing affray would be put on trial, under the oak. If found guilty, Robert would pass sentence and whilst in camp, his word was that of the king's.

'Mr Kett.' A tall man in the front row spoke up. 'Sir, I congratulate you on your thorough preparations, but you leave the most important matter of all unattended.'

'I do?' Robert queried him.

'I, like many, if not all here, should be at home mending my barn in this weather. But I came because we want change. Behaving honourably is fine, but how do you propose we achieve our aims?'

There were nodding heads in the front rows. Another man shouted, 'We must end enclosure of our land.' Then another voice, 'We must take prisoners.' 'Burn the city.' Followed by more. Too many to hear. People started to turn to one another, discussing matters between themselves.

Robert was losing them.

'Quiet please,' he demanded. 'We came here to petition the mayor.'

'That's not going to cut it,' replied the tall man. 'A paper petition will be put on a fire and turned to ashes. We need action.'

'What if we are attacked?' shouted another man.

'Silence!' shouted Robert. His cheeks flushed with anger. 'I decide what happens in this camp, and if you don't like it, you can leave.' He took sense of himself. 'If you will let me finish, we came to petition the mayor. Our pleas have so far fallen on deaf ears, but I will be inviting the city authorities to parley with us. We will resolve our differences peacefully.'

People started to murmur.

'If that is not possible, then we will escalate our tactics in a controlled manner. I repeat my warning: anybody found guilty of violence or disturbing the peace will face trial.'

'How?' It was John Bossell's voice. 'How will we escalate our cause? People are angry, and they should know what you have planned?'

The tall man spoke again. 'It should not be us who faces trial. We are not guilty of any crime. It is the rich and powerful who should face justice.'

He had a point.

Thinking on his feet, Robert responded in kind. 'If our talks are not successful, then we will assume the responsibility of executing the king's law. We will seek to bring to justice those members of the gentry that have corrupted our fine county. They will be afforded a fair trial, the type denied to many of us, and if guilty, will be imprisoned.'

A cheer ran through the crowd, and Robert sighed with relief. He was angry with himself. He been so preoccupied with attending to the basic needs of the camp that he'd neglected to consider how he would deliver the political change people demanded. It had been rash to promise to try the gentry, but it had pacified the crowd. He was especially angry with Bossell for undermining him. They were supposed to be on the same side. Robert dismissed the crowd. A meeting of the hundreds' representatives in Surrey house was now due.

*

A short while later the Ketts and the representatives of the hundreds were reunited in the dining room.

'Robert, you should organise raiding parties for food.' The suggestion came from Anders Marshwell nominated as the representative for Hethersett. 'The people are restless. If you keep them fed it will buy you time,' continued Anders, his large frame filling his wooden chair.

'Thank you, Anders, we'll come to that in a moment,' snapped Robert. He had a more pressing matter to clear up first: 'Let me be very clear, and I am looking directly at you, Bossell. As part of my committee, don't ever question my leadership in front of our followers. Is that clear?'

Bossell nodded reluctantly.

'That goes for the rest of you too. Outside we are as one. Our arguments take place in here and nowhere else.' Robert looked each man in the eyes. 'Now to business. Anders made a good suggestion, please kindly see to it. Arrange for warrants for the food parties.'

It was Anders turn to nod.

'Without delay,' insisted Robert.

Robert was not going to be dictated to by his own lieutenants.

'William, issue permits to send parties to Norwich. We need ale and bread.'

'We have no funds, Robert.'

Robert threw him a look that suggested his brother solve that problem on his own.

'Then ask for donations. We are here on behalf of everybody. Encourage them in their duty to contribute.' Robert turned his attention to young Luke Miller. 'Luke, have a food party sent to Wymondham. Fetch my entire flock of sheep and bring them here.'

There was a gentle intake of breath around the room.

'Send word to Alice, tell her I am well, and she is to stay at home.'

Luke smiled, then nodded his understanding.

'Thomas, my apologies, I forget your surname,' said Robert addressing the representative from the borough of Taverham.

'Garrod, Thomas Garrod.'

'Thank you. Go to Norwich, invite the mayor or any alderman to meet and talk with us here. Assure them of their safety.'

'Should I say we are prepared to take prisoners?'

Robert paused. He wanted justice, and he feared others were out for revenge, but they had to be appeased. He needed the city authorities to be seen here in camp, bending to Robert's will. It might take the threat of prisoners to do that.

'If they don't come willingly, then yes.'

As the words left his lips, Robert knew he had taken

another step down a road he wanted to avoid. As if reading his mind, Thomas Garrod spoke: 'We have Sir Roger Wodehouse in captivity. The crowd may appreciate an early display of justice?'

Robert had forgotten about Wodehouse. He'd planned to release him. If the camp got wind he'd been let out, they might mutiny. He had no choice but to put Wodehouse on trial. It would show the crowd and the authorities he meant business.

Robert agreed. 'Yes, let's start as we mean to go on. He'll face trial tomorrow. There's too much to do today. He must be treated with dignity and unharmed.'

Robert's mind was beginning to tire. He needed time to gather himself.

'Gentlemen, that will be all. Please meet with your hundreds. Remind them of their obligations and our rules. Whatever concerns they have, bring the important ones to me in private. I have no wish to found wanting in public again.'

The assembled men stood up and navigated paths through the discarded plates, knives and bones that littered the floor.

As they filed away, Robert called out, 'I want our table back, have somebody build a dais under the tree with some steps for me to climb up.'

Robert looked up at the large portrait above the fireplace of the former owner of the house. The late Earl of Surrey, on horseback surrounded by his dogs. He'd been executed by the old king.

'By the grace of God, I ask for better luck than you,' said Robert.

Thomas Garrod was last to leave the room, as he reached the doorway, he turned to look at Robert.

'What do you want to do with our other prisoner in the cellar?'

'Another prisoner? Who's that?'

'A young lad. Goes by the name of Alfred Carter.'

18

13th July, Norwich Guildhall.

Mayor Codd rarely took wine before noon. Returning his beaker to the dresser in his private chamber, he felt the wine fortify his resolve. From behind the closed door he heard the hallway fall quiet as the councillors filed into the council chamber. They were waiting for him. Codd double-checked his beaker was empty before making his way to join them. The council that controlled Norwich was more accustomed to debating the accuracy of weights and measures than hostile rebels camped on their doorstep. Merchants and politicians, none had military experience. They would need to pool their negotiating prowess to talk their way out of harm's reach. Despite having seen Robert Kett in person, Mayor Codd didn't believe the man he knew as an alderman of Wymondham could truly be the head of the venomous snake that had coiled around their fine city. In the four days since their clandestine meeting at the marsh, much had changed. London had been informed of the uprising, and they awaited the lord protector's response. With every day that passed, the stakes piled higher as yet more men flocked to join Robert's camp.

The church bells rung three. The chamberlain held the carved oak door open for the mayor who entered the chamber.

The door closed with a thud and brought the assembled councillors to a silence.

All turned to Mayor Codd who cleared his throat as he took the chair at the head of the table. It wasn't his usual seat. Mayor Codd had received a messenger last night. Owing to a sudden illness, the high sheriff was bedridden. He would be unavailable for the foreseeable future. With the Duke of Norfolk still languishing in prison at the king's pleasure, Mayor Codd had found himself the foremost authority in the county.

His acquaintance's rebellion was now on his watch.

He scoured the faces at the table. All were present despite the threat at their gates. John Flowerdew wasn't an alderman, but it was he who had alerted them to the rebel advance and had since taken a personal interest in developments.

As the king's man in Norfolk, he may prove useful.

'I also regret to confirm,' Mayor Codd began. 'If you hadn't already heard, other rebel camps have sprung up on the outskirts of King's Lynn and Bury St Edmunds.'

'There is talk of men gathering in Suffolk to threaten Ipswich,' added Thomas Aldrich, the eldest and wealthiest man in the room.

Mayor Codd knew Robert's intentions were peaceful, and yet the region was falling prey to copycat movements. He clenched his fists to stop his hands from shaking. Short of words, he willed somebody else to talk.

It was his deputy, Augustine Steward, who broke the silence.

Steward purred and leant back in his chair. He was a tall man with a swallow face. Tiny red veins interrupted his otherwise grey complexion. His eyes may have once been blue, but they too had faded grey.

'Well, that puts you in charge, mayor. What have you planned?'

As Mayor Codd knew only too well, despite Steward's hawkish appearance, there was nothing dull about his mind, which was as sharp as a knife and equally as menacing. Steward made an arch of his hands and pressed his fingertips against his lips.

To Mayor Codd's ear, Steward's exaggeratedly slow speech was plainly cynical. Perhaps today, Steward could afford to be cynical, as the mayor didn't have a plan and in truth didn't want one. He enjoyed the ceremony of his office, not the responsibility. However, with all eyes trained on him, he began. 'I understand the men camped on Mousehold don't want violence.'

'And how would you know that?' snapped Steward.

Mayor Codd hesitated, not wanting to disclose that it was because Robert Kett had told him so.

None of his colleagues in the council were aware of his visit to Bowthorpe marsh, which could be interpreted as fraternizing with the enemy. The council had refused to grant Kett an audience, which rather than driving the rebels away, had instead caused them to set up camp.

'You certainly seem well informed, mayor,' continued Steward. 'But their number grows stronger every day. If your grace favours a military response, the sooner he orders it, the better.'

Mayor Codd was used to Steward's traps, but this was blatant even by his standards. Attack the rebels and lose, and his career was finished. Steward was a former mayor and coveted the chair again.

'I have prepared an inventory of our munitions and our

fighting strength.' Steward recounted the weaponry and manpower at their disposal, making mention of pikes, muskets and cannons.

'I'm no fighting man, but it seems to me,' said the elderly Aldrich, 'the rebels hold the high ground. They would see the city's men coming a mile off.'

'If we raise the militia, we outnumber them, and would be better armed,' countered Steward.

'Some in the city are sympathetic to their cause. Don't make the mistake of thinking this is just about enclosure. They live in fear of our justice, our institutions, our wealth.'

'Gentlemen,' interrupted Mayor Codd. 'If we establish a good relationship with them, then cooperation is not beyond the wits of man.'

'Is that cowardice or treason, Mayor?' Steward bolted upright from his chair.

Treason made the mayor squirm.

'I simply seek to stop them destroying our city,' he countered. 'I am confident that if we invite violence, it will find us and pay us in kind.'

Steward grunted. 'And if the rebels attack us first?'

An uneasy silence gripped the chamber.

'If I may?' Flowerdew piped up from the end of the table.

The mayor nodded.

'It would be treason to form an army without the king's permission, strictly from a legal perspective, you understand, and if I may be forthright, you gentlemen, skilled as you are, don't strike me as a formidable opposition.'

There was uncomfortable acknowledgement around the table at the wisdom of his words.

'Don't give Kett an argument to use against you. It is only a matter of time before chaos breaks out. Sit tight and let him make a false move. When it goes wrong, I'll see his neck is stretched.'

Further disagreement was spared by a knock on the door.

It was the sentry. 'Prey forgiveness, my Lords. I have two visitors outside.'

'Who?' enquired Codd.

'One is from London. The other claims to be an emissary from the rebel camp.'

'Send in the man from London,' said the mayor.

Moments later the councilmen were greeted by a man dressed in the robes of the clergy. He was slight in build, his hair was greying, and his skin pale from a life indoors. The door closed behind him.

'I have been sent from London to disperse the rebels,' he introduced himself.

'Alone? Have you brought men?' asked a disbelieving Steward.

'I am a man of God, sir. I am alone, save for the protection of the Almighty Father.'

Steward laughed. 'Then how in God's name do you propose dislodging a thousand men from the gates of this city?'

'A thousand men?' The preacher looked confused. 'I was told to anticipate a hundred?'

The mayor and his deputy exchanged a look. For once even they were in agreement.

'I am permitted to offer them the king's pardon. God will do the rest.'

'Well, preacher, you'll need the luck of the devil,' quipped Steward.

The preacher made the sign of the cross. 'All his majesty's forces are employed in Cornwall and Scotland. It could be months before an army can be raised. For now, we must trust in the almighty.'

Having established that the preacher needed no further support, Mayor Codd dismissed him. The preacher would be escorted to Mousehold heath where he would be left to work his divine intervention. Mayor Codd sat at the end of the table surrounded by his fellow councillors, but feeling very alone.

He shouted for the chamberlain to show in the rebel emissary.

'My name is Thomas Garrod,' said the man who stood before them, his clothes ripped and stained. His boots were muddy from the morning rain, and his jittery hands looked ripe for a wash.

'I'm here to invite representatives from the city chamber to join Mr Kett and his council on the heath.'

Flowerdew shifted in his seat. His nose creased with disapproval.

'Mr Kett personally guarantees your safety and would welcome your presence so we can achieve the peaceful resolution of the people's grievances. He wants no trouble with the city and its people. As a show of good faith he has forbidden the rebels to enter the city without good cause and written consent from himself. He asks that you close the gates to all without the appropriate permit to enter.'

The councillors were dumbstruck. The mayor felt relief. As he'd imagined, Robert was taking every reasonable step to safeguard the city's people.

Flowerdew broke the silence. 'This council of Mr Kett's, of whom is it comprised and what is its aim?'

'Two men elected by their peers representing each hundred in attendance,' replied Garrod. 'They're to ensure no trouble in the camp and are responsible for carrying out Mr

Kett's orders and to assist with the dispensing of justice.'

'*Justice?*' said Flowerdew.

'We are taking prisoners,' explained Garrod, 'only the rich and powerful, men such as your good selves. They face trial and punishment, unless, of course you cooperate, and then there shouldn't be any need...'

Mayor Codd coughed. 'Thank you, that's quite enough,' he said. 'Please, wait outside.'

Steward was the first to speak. 'Mr Kett is quite the outlaw. Norfolk's very own Robin Hood,' he remarked. 'What say you, Mayor Codd?'

'I will volunteer to meet with Mr Kett and his men, and I recommend the deputy mayor also join me so we can achieve a peaceful resolution for all.'

Steward disagreed. 'Should some misfortune befall you during your visit to the heath, then I trust all will agree that I, more than any other man here, have demonstrated that I'm best placed to supervise our defence.'

To Codd's frustration, everyone consented. He'd hoped by having Steward with him so he'd be complicit in whatever happened, but the politician had wriggled free from direct association with the rebels. Heaven knows what he might attempt in my absence, worried Mayor Codd.

Augustine Steward sat back in his chair. A wry grin spread across his face. 'The king sends us a preacher, and the rebels send an emissary!'

He shook his head and made a victorious arch of his fingers.

19

14th July, Surrey House Cellar

Alfred sat on the hard floor near the cellar gate, resting his back against the flint wall. His backside was numb, but the throbbing in his swollen eye was starting to ease. So far his day had been uneventful. Master Peter had brought some scraps of food down to them this morning, and Alfred had spent the rest of the morning being quizzed by the preacher Mr Kett had locked up yesterday afternoon. To Alfred's disappointment, the preacher was concerned only with the salvation of his soul. He made no attempt to understand Alfred's circumstances before proceeding to lambast him for his sins, promising that he would face judgement in the next life. Alfred had heard it all before. The more the members of the clergy threatened him, the less he cared. He'd closed his eyes and waited for the preacher to fall silent. Around noon Master Peter had called for the gentlemen Sir Roger, whose carts Alfred had helped to raid.

Right now, Sir Roger was facing trial for crimes against the common man. Alfred hoped Mr Kett found him guilty. He had no idea whether he'd committed any crime, but his dismissive manner when Alfred had tried to engage him in conversation had been typical of his type. The gentry were only interested in themselves and wouldn't be belittled by talking to a commoner. Alfred had resigned himself to missing the rebellion and the opportunities it presented. Worse still, his public altercation with Lynn meant he would most likely lose his job. Mr Kett had made it plain he wanted good behaviour, but Lynn had provoked him.

He heard the lock turn at the top of the stairs. The hinges creaked as the gate swung open. Sir Roger, the gentlemen prisoner, came down the stairs. He passed Alfred without saying a word.

'Alfred, get your arse up here.'

His legs were stiff as he climbed the stairs to find Mr Kett waiting for him at the top, leaning against the wall, blocking his exit.

'Alfred, I don't know what the issue is between you and your wife…'

'She…'

'Nor,' interrupted Mr Kett, 'have I the time to put you on trial. I have a hundred things to attend to. People want to see their landlords face justice, not one of their own. Besides, you're forgotten about already. So, I'm offering you a deal.'

Alfred nodded. He felt wounded to be *forgotten about*, but a deal sounded promising.

'I don't want you going into the camp. From what I hear of your wife it won't be long before she provokes you again. Stay here in this house, away from her, and act as my page.'

Alfred couldn't believe his luck.

'Thank you, Mr Kett, for your kind offer.'

'Good. There is much work to do, woman's work. You can start by cleaning up the dining room. Then the kitchen. Scrub everything. Air the beds. Keep us supplied with ale and food. Keep the cellar clean and the prisoners alive. I don't want disease descending on this filthy house.'

Imprisonment replaced by servitude.

Anything to get out of the cellar, he reasoned, away from Lynn and under Mr Kett's nose, where he could finally make a good impression.

All at the heart of the rebellion.

Deal.

20

Mayor Codd's hopes that Robert's emissary wouldn't return were dashed when Thomas Garrod arrived at the guildhall in the early afternoon. *Would it have been too much for him to get lost or fall waylaid, and spare me this visit into hostile territory?* It was wishful thinking.

It had since been confirmed that the rumours of Sir Roger Wodehouse's disappearance were true, and that he now resided in Robert's charge. Mayor Codd had managed to delay his visit to the heath by a day. An extra night to compose his troubled thoughts. Today was Sunday, the Lord's day. A helpful reminder to otherwise law-abiding people that God was watching, judging. With the Lord's judgment in mind, the mayor had attended the service at St Peter Mancroft church this morning. The only talk amongst the city's subjects was of the rebellion. After the service Mayor Codd had addressed the congregation, personally reassuring them he was to meet with rebel leaders and negotiate a peace between them. So far there had been no trouble.

Mayor Codd had found strength in another beaker of wine.

Now up on his white horse, the mayor had opted to leave

his regalia in the guildhall. His gold chain and ceremonial sword would prove tempting trophies to hungry rebels. His hat and white feather were the only articles that marked him out as a man of office. The short journey through the city meant that they soon arrived at the stone gatehouse that marked the city's eastern boundary, now the last outpost of the city's rule. The gatehouse straddled the city end of the stone bridge that crossed the river Wensum, connecting the city to the coast and the cities of Low Countries across the sea.

Normally, by day, the thick oak doors of the gatehouse would be open, but the arrival of Robert Kett meant they were locked and the guard had been trebled. The council had agreed to stop short of raising the militia, but they were on standby should rebel activity threaten attack. Six watchmen stood at the top of the parapet, their longbows visible between the crenulations. The gatekeeper, on a three-legged stool, sat at the base of the tower warming his face in the sun.

'Asleep at your post?' asked the mayor.

The gatekeeper opened one eye. On recognising the mayor, he jumped up.

'Sorry, my lord.'

'Open the gate.'

'Mayor, you are not going out there surely?'

'Do as I say.'

Each day small contingents of rebels travelled into the city sourcing supplies. Some traders, ever opportunistic, had welcomed the arrival of so many new customers for their produce. Others, quite rightly, took a more cautious approach to the men from the countryside. The mayor noticed that his escort Thomas was watching everything the guards did, where the key was kept, how the door was secured, how many people were at hand. It occurred to him just how many people must have seen the state of the city's defensive readiness.

Kett was issuing permits to enter, but the city had no checks in place to see that they left.

Mayor Codd made a mental note that forthwith he would assume Kett's spies were everywhere.

The gate creaked open, and the bridge's flagstones came into view. The mayor reminded the guards to remain vigilant then passed beneath the arch of the gatehouse. The river was low, the water murky. At the bridge's far end, a man with a hand cart stopped and waited for the mayor to clear the bridge. He nodded as they passed. He was missing an eye. Mayor Codd wondered he had seen the man before. When he saw his cart loaded with flint stones, he remembered: One Eye Wulfric, the flintman, had carried out some repairs to the guildhall in the spring.

'What are you doing, Wulfric?' asked the mayor.

'Your deputy, Mr Steward, asked me to fetch some flints in case the rebels attack.'

'Why?' asked the mayor.

'Scrapshot for the cannons.'

'What?'

'To use instead of stone or lead cannonballs,' Wulfric continued, 'it's more deadly against men; the flint blast out the end and cut those in front of it to ribbons. If you ask me that ain't right to use it against your own countrymen. Against the French of course, but not your fellow Englishmen. Still, I'm just doing what I'm told, and I've got to make a living same as everyone else.'

'Wulfric, tell me, are you sympathetic to the rebels?'

The mayor smiled to reassure him.

'Well, I don't support 'em as such. In truth, I don't like them being up there either, but I ain't prepared to kill 'em.

The way I see it, they wouldn't go to all that strife if they didn't have something proper to complain about.'

'How many other's feel as you do?'

'Enough. I don't know for sure. People are scared of course, but how many turn out to fight I couldn't say, and if they did that would only be to defend their properties. They ain't gonna fight for the likes of...' Wulfric came to a halt.

'Wulfric, my thanks for your trouble. I bid you good day.'

On the other side of the road, beyond the bridge, was a steep slope that led the way to the base of the escarpment. Through the trees that clung to the side of the bank the mayor could make out Surrey House perched at the top, like a buzzard surveying its prey. It didn't seem that long ago that it was a priory filled with pious monks.

His escort led him along the dirt road that ran parallel to the river before peeling off right into the gulley that led up to the heath. The surface was hard and dusty from the summer heat, and as they neared the top it was dyed red from the blood of slaughtered sheep: an ominous welcome to Robert's camp. They caught up with some yeoman farmers carrying provisions and hand tools.

'Where are you from?' asked Garrod, the mayor's reins in his hand.

'Yarmouth,' said a sunburned man through missing teeth. 'Our Lord Paston attacked us and smashed our camp up. So, we come here instead.' He nodded seemingly excited at the prospects that Robert's camp offered them.

'How many were at your camp?' asked the mayor.

'I heard eight hundred.'

Garrod gave the mayor a knowing look.

At the top, the land levelled out, and the sight of a man on a white horse prompted whistles of alarm from the camp. Dogs barked. A rebel sentry shouted for him to stop.

'We're here to meet Mr Kett,' called out Garrod.

The sentry pointed over to Surrey House on the edge of the escarpment. Mayor Codd was shocked at the extent of the camp: there were sheep pens, a butcher's yard, hundreds of wooden shelters, and as far as the eye could see, a population of thousands.

An entire city.

Thomas picked a path towards the house, and the mayor continued to take in what he was seeing; young children running around, playing games; people moving with supplies of wood and water; men laughing and women gossiping; fires burning; women cooking pottage, making ale, the smell of food and smoke.

As his horse made its way past a wooden shelter, the mayor heard the unmistakable sound of a fornicating couple. He turned his attention in the other direction, a chicken coup filled with hens, guarded by children calling, 'Eggs a penny each!'

Ahead was more concerning: A short-haired man with a scar down his cheek was leading a party of men pushing two cannons.

Mayor Codd shuddered. Where the devil have they got cannon from?

Others were rolling powder barrels and carrying plungers and wadding.

Christ, Robert, you promised to spare the city, what the devil have you planned?

Their progress was slowed by the hustle and bustle of this sprawling settlement. Now, as the mayor neared the house, he attracted the attention of a group of men sat on the floor playing cards. They whistled and cheered.

Mayor Codd felt distinctly exposed. The sanctuary of the city was a quarter of a mile away. It might as well have been in Suffolk for all the good it afforded him here.

'I'll have somebody guard your horse for you, mayor,' said Garrod as he looped the reins around the post that held up the porch. The mayor readied himself to enter the lion's den.

Robert's a reasonable man, he reassured himself.

As the door opened, he could hear shouting from inside.

*

Robert's spirits were flagging. Today had seen men from another four districts arrive, all needing to be assimilated into the camp and made aware of Robert's rules regarding conduct. The new representatives joined their brethren in the dining room, bringing the total to thirty-two people, eager to have their say. Those that didn't get seats stood against the walls. This alone had been enough for a dispute to flare up. Members who had been with the rebellion from the outset had objected to newcomers beating them to a seat at the table. They reminded Robert of unruly children. The one consolation was that, despite having limited time, the boy Alfred had made the room presentable again.

An argument was underway about food supplies. With their numbers swelling, the pressure to keep everyone fed was mounting. Robert knew only too well that people with empty bellies were soon tempted to take matters into their own hands.

He was delighted when the door opened and in strode Thomas Garrod, who introduced Mayor Codd to the assembled company. The mayor looked crestfallen at the sight of so many people, all of them unwashed.

Robert, however, was eager to deal with the cause of this rebellion: the enclosure of land.

'Let's clear some space for you, mayor. Bossell, please

vacate your seat for our guest.' Bossell begrudgingly surrendered his place.

'Gentlemen, please don't let me intrude. I had hoped for a private audience with Mr Kett?'

A murmur of disapproval rippled across the room.

'Whatever you wish to say you are free to say in front of my men,' said Robert.

The mayor looked anxious as he took Bossell's empty seat near the door.

'Mayor, let me start by thanking you for accepting our invitation to join us so we can resolve our grievances peacefully and locally, something I know we are all keen to achieve,' said Robert.

'Thank you. I think it in our best interests if I come straight to the point,' said the mayor dispensing with any of the formalities of his usual meetings. 'I fear that won't be possible, locally at least.'

Men around the table shifted in their seats and exchanged glances.

The mayor, looking increasingly uncomfortable, continued. 'For my part I am willing to do whatever is required to prevent violence and bloodshed.'

'Stop enclosure then,' demanded one of the representatives.

Robert told the man to let the mayor speak.

'Your presence here on the heath creates fear in the city. My alderman colleagues would like your sworn assurance that you will not attack the city.'

'Pah,' said Anders Marshwell. 'Once you have that, what do we get in exchange?'

'You have my word,' said Robert 'that your safety is assured, provided you give us a ruling on enclosure, banning it once and for all in the county.'

'Robert, I don't have the legal authority to enforce your request. It would be flouted, and we would be powerless to act. The authority to do such a thing rests in London, with the king.'

'Pox on you, you coward,' Bossell banged his fist on the table, prompting jeers of derision.

'And if we attack the city?' asked William Kett.

Robert shot his brother a look.

'We are well provisioned with both armaments and men. We are confident we can withstand an assault.'

'Enough,' said Robert. 'What would you propose then, mayor?'

'Our official position remains to ask you to disband and return home. We are mindful of your grievances and will take what steps we can to encourage London to address them, once you have gone.'

'*Bollocks*,' muttered Anders Marshwell.

'You are only willing to consider such measures because we are here in the first place,' said William.

'I give you my word,' said Mayor Codd.

Mocking laughter erupted around the table.

'You have my word that we will debate and address your grievances. But I must make clear to you that if you attack, we shall repel you with all force necessary and in the name of the King Edward VI.'

A chorus of boos and hisses broke out.

Two representatives stood up and left the room, shaking their heads. There was an uneasy silence while others decided if they should follow.

Thomas Garrod spoke for the first time, his arms raised: 'How can you claim to be operating with the license of the king? We are his subjects. We obey his laws. It is you and your aldermen who abuse his laws to your own ends.'

Thomas recounted what he and his neighbours had suffered.

Robert wondered what card to play next. Their current conversation was going nowhere. To launch an attack wasn't an option, but the fear of assault might grant them some concession from the mayor. Disbanding without any commitment from the authorities was not an option. He determined that the threat of insurrection would see how far he could push the mayor and buy him some loyalty around the table.

The door opened, and Alfred slipped in quietly. He made his way round the side of the room and whispered in Robert's ear.

'Mayor,' said Robert. 'We aren't disbanding. If you are not going to help us politically, then we will attack. I've just had word that we have captured two cannon that were destined for your defences.'

Around the room the rebels exchanged glances and a ripple of smiles spread across expectant faces.

The mayor pursed his lips. 'I have one suggestion which you may see as palatable?' he said, at last.

'Go on,' said Robert.

'The authorities see you as rebels. If you could legitimise your complaint it might be possible to see you as *campaigners*.'

The room was silent, the mayor continued, 'My advice would be to petition the king with your demand to end enclosure. The Lord Protector Seymour is rumoured to be sympathetic to such complaints. Other rebels, albeit much smaller in number, have been pardoned previously.'

'How could we guarantee it would find the lord protector safely?' asked Robert.

'I could see to that. If it were completed today, now even, I could have it with him by tomorrow.'

This was real progress, thought Robert, who nodded at the mayor, sensing a mutually agreeable solution was at hand.

'But we aren't here just for enclosure.' It was Bossell who now spoke. 'What about the other abuses of the nobility? This is our chance to make a difference. We shouldn't squander it.'

'My advice to you is you will fare better if you stick to one demand,' said the mayor.

'The people of my hundred have walked forty miles to be here,' said a man who'd arrived that morning. 'They won't be happy when they hear that three-quarters of their complaints are to be neglected.'

'I agree, this is about more than just enclosure, rivers must be free too.'

'The lords must no longer be entitled to keep doves or rabbits for their pleasure. They are destroying our crops.'

'The rent for copyhold land should be put back to the level it was under Henry VII.'

'That's enough!' shouted Robert, silencing their complaints. 'I came here to end enclosure. Nothing more. Nothing less. It is not within our gift to remedy the entire realm. I agree, we make one demand of the lord protector: no more enclosure.'

The representatives turned on Robert, roaring their dismay.

'Then I'll lead!' declared Bossell.

'Over my dead body.' William leapt to his feet.

Arguments erupted across the table as others volunteered to assume command.

'Enough,' said Robert, cutting through the discord. 'I have led this cause, and we protest enclosure, that's all.'

'Then what about the church?' said a short man stood by the fireplace. 'My chaplain hasn't even preached one service since the lord of the manor moved him in. He's nothing but a money-grabbing scobberlotcher. When a shepherd doesn't even live amongst his flock, what is that a sign of, if not his desire for profits?' He raised his finger and thrust it forward. 'We want our old priest back!'

Round the room heads shook, voices raised again. This was like herding cats: impossible. Robert closed his eyes and asked God to grant him the patience to resolve the matter before it was too late.

'Silence,' shouted William.

Robert was relieved to hear his brother's voice.

'Here's what we'll do: Alfred fetch a parchment, a pen and some ink. I will scribe and commit your grievances to paper. Then we'll send it, courtesy of the mayor, to London.'

Once again heads were nodding as the representatives were appeased. The mayor signalled his consent to Robert, who nodded his approval to William. Alfred returned with writing materials. The demands of the men now poured forth, as William committed them in ink. Robert and Mayor Codd sat in silence throughout. When they'd finished the list totalled twenty-nine injustices. William passed the finished parchment to Robert for him to add his signature.

Sign this and you're signing…

As the quill hovered over the page, Robert felt the knot in his stomach twist.

…your life away?

He glanced at his brother. They had committed to the cause the moment they left Wymondham, he thought, there was no going back, and with that he signed the scroll.

'I have signed our list of demands. This is a legitimate protest and a legitimate document detailing its causes. To give it the legitimacy it requires, I now invite the mayor to sign his name next to mine.'

The parchment and quill were passed around the table until they arrived in front of the mayor, who looked queasy.

'Robert that would be treason?'

'I am sure he will not want his subjects disturbed by our protest,' said William, reminding the mayor he had no room to manoeuvre.

'Then as an act of faith you must surrender your cannon,' demanded Codd.

'Sign the document, mayor,' insisted Robert.

Thirty-two pairs of eyes bored into the mayor, who shuffled in his seat and adjusted his robes before accepting the quill and signing his name.

'I shall have it sent to London tonight.'

A round of applause broke out, and Robert bought the meeting to a close. The representatives filed out of the room in a jubilant mood.

'God have mercy on your souls for trapping me like that,' said the mayor, as the room emptied, and he prepared to take this leave.

'Tell me that what we ask for isn't just and fair?' said William.

'Fairness has nothing to do with it, William.'

'These aren't reasonable people you are making a request of. They'll take one look at this,' he held up the scroll, 'and place a ransom on your heads for interrupting their hunting, or their tennis.'

'Enough, both of you,' said Robert, slapping his brother on the back. 'We've earned a drink.'

He shouted for Alfred and moments later they were furnished with a jug of ale. Robert picked up his tankard. 'I feel a lot better having your name alongside mine.'

The mayor wasn't amused.

'I haven't asked you to do anything I haven't done myself.

Besides, we both want the same thing.'

'I fear we will both suffer the same fate,' said the mayor, his voice heavy with foreboding.

'You can say it was under duress,' said William.

'If any of you are still alive to corroborate my version of events. I fear your cause would have been better served if you concentrated your efforts on just enclosure. The other matters are minor.'

'It gives us more chance of getting something,' said William. 'To ask only for one thing means we risk coming away empty-handed.'

'I disagree,' repeated the mayor.

'I remind you, mayor, that a mutiny in our camp doesn't benefit Norwich,' said William.

'It's done now,' concluded Robert. 'You should be glad. We've saved Norwich from being sacked.'

'Pray it be so,' said the mayor, finishing his drink.

'Godspeed,' said Robert, walking him to the door. 'Don't fret over the cannon. I will keep Norwich safe.'

'You'll be a head shorter if you don't, Robert.'

Outside, Mayor Codd's horse was nowhere to be seen.

21

15th July, Palace of Whitehall, London

'Check.' John Dudley swapped his bishop for Lord Protector Seymour's pawn.

Seymour scratched his chin through his beard. Dudley was now in for an agonising wait while Seymour weighed up every option and the consequence of every move. Dudley hated placing chess with Seymour. He was forbidden to talk during the game unless it was his turn to move. He leaned back into the chair, his belly full of pork, and fiddled with his wedding ring. Since his outburst at council, Seymour wouldn't let him out of his sight, and as the kingdom fell apart, Seymour was becoming increasingly paranoid and had banned Dudley from leaving the palace.

He hated London in the summer, it stank. Fearing for the safety of the capital, Seymour insisted the council remain at Whitehall, rather than retire to the clean air of Greenwich or Windsor.

There was a faint knock at the door.

It was the chambermaid who entered. She curtsied, her eyes trained to the floor, a burning taper in her hand.

'Carry on,' instructed Seymour.

She started her way around the room, lighting the candles, leaving a trail of amber flames to illuminate the tapestries, carved furniture and silk drapes. While he waited for Seymour's next move, Dudley watched the maid. A young girl, no more than sixteen, she was a pretty young thing. Their eyes met, she smiled and looked away. Dudley held his gaze, her rosy cheeks spurring him on. After turning down Seymour's bed she stole a final glance at the earl before exiting backwards out of the room and closing the door.

Seymour's private chamber, illuminated by the array of candles, was an impressive room, its grandeur very much at odds with the man who occupied it.

Seymour moved a pawn. Keeping it between his fingers, he moved it back again.

'Has your grace reached any conclusions with regard to the rebellions in Cornwall?'

'Ssshh.' Seymour moved his knight to block Dudley's bishop.

He cleared his throat.

'Conclusions? What is there to conclude? People who are hungry, losing their lands and not guided by the correct interpretation of the bible, are prone to take matters into their own hands.'

Dudley hoped his eyes did not betray his contempt for the lord protector. He turned his attentions to the board. His feint had worked. He moved his queen out from behind his pawns.

I've got you now.

Seymour took a sip of his wine.

'Indulge me, what conclusions does the Earl of Warwick draw?'

'If the land cannot support the people then it is not the

land which is at fault, there must be too many people. It is natural that people must die so that there is enough space for others to live.'

'Dead people do not pay taxes.'

There was another knock at the door. It was the household chamberlain who now entered the room, delivering a scroll sealed with wax.

'A messenger brings word from Norwich.'

'Send him in,' said Seymour.

Seymour asked, 'Good news, I hope?'

The red-headed messenger, his accent typical of the region, was refreshingly candid.

'No, sire. Quite the opposite. Four thousand rebels camp outside the gates, poised to overwhelm the defences.'

Seymour's eyes widened.

'The city's mayor was summoned to meet the rebels, and they forced him to sign their demands.' He gestured towards the scroll. 'Mayor Codd begs that you accept their demands or if not send an army to save the city.'

'What's his nature, this Codd fellow?' asked Dudley.

'A fair man is Mr Codd,' said the messenger.

'A strong man?' Dudley probed.

'Fair is a better description, sir.'

'What is it they demand?' interrupted Seymour.

'The rebels, sire? I don't know. You will have to read the scroll,' replied the messenger.

Seymour unfurled the scroll. 'Before I read, let us pick up where we left off. What became of the preacher I sent?'

'He's being held prisoner, along with some other gentleman,' said the messenger.

'*Other gentlemen*? On what grounds?' asked Dudley.

'Lawyers and Landowners mostly.'

The creases on Seymour's forehead deepened. 'I won't

hear of it.'

'It seems the rebels accuse them of taking the law into their own hands and enforcing it to suit their own needs.'

Seymour offered Dudley a knowing look. As expected, and as elsewhere, laws were created to control such men. Unfortunately, all too often men of resources and poor nature exploited them to their own gain.

Returning to the scroll, Seymour was outraged: 'They make twenty-nine demands!'

He read each one, shaking his head. Looking up, he asked, 'Can Norwich defend itself?'

'The mayor thinks not. Others are more confident.'

'The city is protected by a curtain wall, is it not?' asked Seymour.

'Yes sir, but only on three sides. The river acts as the fourth side. The wall was conceived principally for taxation purposes.'

'Have the rebels attempted to attack?' asked Dudley.

'No. As yet they have committed no crimes against the city nor its inhabitants. Their leader, Mr Kett…'

'*Kett?*' said Dudley. Where had he heard that name before?

'A peaceful man. He's a merchant farmer from the nearby town of Wymondham. He owns the rights to the town's tannery. He has some properties and farming interests.'

'Wymondham?' said Dudley.

'Has he ever served in the army?' asked Seymour.

'Not to my knowledge.' The messenger continued, 'Kett's reputation is that of a fair and reasonable man. You may be able to appeal to his commercial instincts.'

'I see. Has he been in trouble in the past to your knowledge?'

'No. To my certainty he is a law-abiding man. Has been all his life.'

'How old is this Kett?'

'I am not sure Sire, I would fancy over fifty.'

Dudley took in a sharp burst of breath. Only last year he had sold a piece of land in Norfolk to a fellow named Kett from Wymondham. It must be the same man. His age was about right. He remembered Robert Kett with certainty because he'd tried to re-negotiate the price they had agreed at the eleventh hour. Dudley remembered thinking he was a bit sharp for a tanner. What was he doing laying siege to Norwich?

'Thank you, that will be all,' said Seymour dismissing the messenger. 'Not a word of this to anyone. Is that clear?'

The messenger nodded.

'Rest up and stay close at hand. The chamberlain will organise you some board and lodgings in the servants' quarters.'

The messenger closed the door behind him.

As soon as they were alone, Dudley leaned across the chessboard. 'Seymour, I beg of you, their numbers have already swelled. Let me take an army and wipe these rebels out so we can quell this nonsense.'

'I need time to think.' Seymour put the list of demands on the table and fell back in his chair. 'This gentleman, Kett seems like a reasonable man. But twenty-nine demands is a lot. Perhaps he wants to negotiate.'

'This is ridiculous.' Dudley inspected the scroll: '*Gentleman shall not be allowed to keep dovecotes unless it is by ancient tradition*? Look at this one, *prices should be put back to the reign of Henry VII*, that was nearly a century ago. Honestly, Edward, don't indulge this petty nonsense. You'll only encourage more of it.'

'These things matter to people, John. The devil is in the detail.'

'Edward, it is simple: Find this man Kett and stretch his neck.'

'John, you forget yourself. You also forget we have war to the north, and fighting to the west. If we send what few troops we can muster east, French spies will send word to Paris, and before we know it, we risk war to the south as well. War on all four points of the compass.' Seymour sounded weary.

'Edward, forgive me, but I cannot with clear conscience watch our realm tumble into such commotion. If you won't fight then I must warn the king that his kingdom is at peril.'

'Clear conscience?' Seymour banged his fist on the table, sending chess pieces flying. 'You talk to me of clear conscience?'

He stood up, turning his back on Dudley to begin pacing the room.

'It is the greed of you and the likes of your kind that put me in this predicament. You take what isn't yours, you deprive people of their ability to feed themselves and then accuse me of mismanagement.' He faced Dudley. 'It's your neck I should stretch, you and your conspirators on the council.'

'Conspirators? Edward, you have me wrong. You enjoy my full support,'

'Pox on you, Dudley. How dare you threaten to speak to the king? I'm the acting king. I will bring this land to order, and what's more, I will do it without your interference and treachery. I swear on my life you will play no part in what follows.'

Dudley closed his eyes and counted to five. 'It is a relief to me that my name will be spared any association with your plans.'

'Out. Get out. Out of my sight. I've heard enough.'

Dudley rose to his feet. As he left the room, the door slammed.

Seymour refilled his wine glass from the decanter and savoured the taste. It felt good to stand up to Dudley. The man was a bully with no respect for hierarchy, due process or the law. Seymour paced up and down, enjoying the soft tread of the sheepskin rugs. As he calmed, he regained his thoughts, evaluating his options. He needed a plan. Timing, he knew, would be crucial. Harvest couldn't wait any longer than a month.

What would Kett do next?

How long would his supplies last? Who else was involved? All this, and yet Exeter still held out against his troops. How much longer could they hold on? How to handle the council? What would Dudley do? How to neutralise him? Should he tell the king?

So much to consider before he could work out a plan and mitigate the risks. He would speak with the messenger again in the morning in case he had neglected to ask something which may turn out to be important.

Despite all his worries, his mind returned to Dudley. The man incensed him. Like too many of the regency councillors, Dudley liked to plough straight into things without taking the trouble to understand them fully. Unlike the thugs of his regency council, Seymour was divined by God to this office. There was a proper way to administer a country, and in time he would show the last king's cronies on the council how it was done.

He said to himself, 'Edward Seymour understands his people and the rule of law.'

Too tired to wrestle with the details, but too worried to sleep, he left for the chapel.

Tonight he needed God's guidance.

22

19th July, 3 Bishopsgate, Norwich

Jan sat down by the window next to his loom; the package he'd just collected on his lap. Piepen, the canary called out a greeting from his cage. Jan carefully untied the string and unwrapped the rough outer layer. He studied the newly fulled black fabric inside, smoothing the soft material and lifting the weave closer for examination. He sniffed it, savouring its fresh, clean aroma. It was perfect. As good as anything he'd made in Flanders. Touching it brought back memories of home and of Katherijn, his late wife. Two years had passed since her death. Home was as remote as a previous life. One he was keen to leave behind. He had no time for nostalgia.

He returned his attention to the weave.

David Fuller had done an excellent job, despite its late delivery. Jan was due to call upon Augustine Steward in an hour's time and felt the tension of the last week slip away now that the package was here, in his hands. He'd been recommended to David for his workmanship but had been warned to ensure extra time due to David's poor timekeeping. To fail to honour his first appointment with the deputy mayor would have been a bad start to their relationship.

Tiniker bounced into the workshop, her step full of spring.

'Is it good, father?' she asked in her native Dutch.

'Ja, my little spinster. It's as good as anything on the continent.'

She smiled. 'That was a close call, your appointment is on the hour, nee?'

'Ja. I must get ready, do you want to come?'

She twisted her mouth.

'Why not? It would do you good. One day I may not be here, and you'll have to take care of business and your little sister.'

'I know. But he gives me the creeps.'

Jan frowned.

'The way he looks at me like he's undressing me in his mind. It's horrible.'

Jan shook his head. 'If I only sold cloth to people I liked we'd be living under a bridge like trolls.'

Tiniker nodded, having heard her father's expression many times before.

'Tiniker, you are a pretty woman. Blonde hair and violet eyes, you will always attract attention from men. Wanted and unwanted. You cannot hide here. We came here to rebuild our lives. You must turn your good looks to your advantage.'

Tiniker grunted.

'Come with me,' continued Jan, 'Mr Steward's a wealthy mercer. If he likes this material, this will be our biggest order since we arrived in England. He has served in their parliament in London. He's well connected. We should meet him and earn his favour, Ja? Or would you rather go hungry?'

Tiniker nodded again. 'I know. What about Margreet?

Can't she go instead?'

'No. You know very well she is too young and far too foolish.' Jan clicked his tongue in his mouth. 'Go and put your best clothes on. Be quick.'

'Ok, first let me see what it is we are selling.' She knelt and stroked the fabric with her delicate hands. 'They don't have bombazine here already?'

'Not to my knowledge. That's enough, we need to leave shortly.'

Piepen whistled as she left the room.

Jan folded the package and retied the bow. All his savings were invested in this one silk sample. He held it tighter than was necessary. Tiniker coming was good. Nothing like a pretty girl to soften a man's bargaining. He knew he was going to impress today. Pull this off, and they would eat for a year, even at the current prices. Or so he kept telling himself.

Tiniker met him at the front door wearing the blue dress she reserved for church.

'You look nice, my girl. You carry the parcel,' he passed it to her, 'hold it out in front, don't crease it.'

'I know how to carry a parcel.' She glared at her father.

Tiniker's younger sister shouted goodbye from upstairs, as Jan closed the door behind him.

Outside, twenty yards to their right stood the imposing tower of the gatehouse of Bishopsgate Bridge. Jan looked up at the heath beyond. He couldn't see the rebel camp, but they were still there. On the opposite side of the river, a thin column of people were heading up into the camp.

'Looks like more people joining the rebellion.'

'Are we going to be safe, father?' asked Tiniker.

'Ja, of course,' he lied.

The presence of so many angry peasants the other side of the river worried him. But Jan had sunk his worries in his work. Weaving was laborious and tiring, but the repetition and solitude afforded him some temporary peace of mind.

They turned left in the direction of the city centre.

A short walk later they stood outside Mr Steward's narrow half-timbered house, which faced the cathedral gate, overlooking the great golden work of religious devotion.

Jan offered a quick prayer of his own.

He wasn't yet accustomed to practising his faith in plain view. Doing so at home would have cost him his life. With God on board, he reminded Tiniker, reverting to English.

'Now remember to smile. Look up. Stand tall.'

She tutted at him.

The large oak door opened and they were ushered in by the housekeeper to Mr Steward's private quarters on the first floor where the door was closed behind them.

Mr Steward was cloaked in his black gown, sitting at his bureau, facing the wall.

He turned to greet them.

Tiniker felt Steward's gaze undress her.

'Your lovely daughter is here, I see.'

'Yes…' said Jan.

'Tiniker,' she curtsied, smiling as she rose.

Mr Steward raised an eyebrow. She saw the corners of his lips twitch. His cadaverous complexion made her blood run cold.

'Well, Mr Vinck,' said Mr Steward. 'Given the current state of the city, my time is short, so let's see if this cloth is everything you have claimed it will be.'

He motioned them towards the small circular table in the centre of the room. Tiniker unwrapped the parcel and gently pulled back the cover, exposing the black cloth.

She stood back and let Mr Steward examine it.

He pulled the sample from the parcel. Rubbing between

his fingers and thumbs, he studied the weave. It was excellent. Soft and pliable like a normal woollen and yet with a fine smooth finish like a worsted weave.

Mr Steward nodded: 'It is a satisfactory cloth.'

Her father was no stranger to the tricks of mercers.

'Begging your pardon, your grace, but I am sure if you look closer you will see it is an *exquisite* a piece of material. The only one of its kind available in Norfolk, if not all of England.'

Steward held up the cloth in front of him, to see its sheen through the light.

'If it is of no interest to your grace, I can take it with me now and leave you to your duties?' He stretched out a hand.

Steward looked at him from the corner of his eyes and studied it again.

'Tell me,' dropping his pretence, 'how do you achieve this finish?'

Jan smiled. 'I cannot say, sir.'

'Well if you want me to buy it from you…' Jan hesitated. 'Unless you would rather I do business with somebody else?' Steward threatened him.

'No, your grace, not at all.' Jan pulled out a small piece of raw fleece from his jerkin. 'We take the outer layer of the fleece, like with a conventional worsted,' he showed Mr Steward the sample, 'but instead of soaking it in urine as is the normal practice, we soap it twice, which when carded, gives it a softer neater appearance, but importantly, it still keeps its shape when cut and pressed.'

'I see.' Steward nodded.

'That makes the weft. The warp is silk, which gives it the sheen and the good drape. By combining the cheaper local wool with silk, we achieve the ideal cloth for formal wear. Smart, yet affordable.'

'When it is tightly woven,' added Tiniker. She picked up the other end of the sample and folded it in her hands.

'Then we rub it in butter,' said Jan, his enthusiasm getting the better of him, 'but not the pig fat you English use for butter. Only cow's milk will do.'

'It's very nice, I grant you. This cloth is available in your home country?'

Jan nodded. 'Ja, yes, but the tax is so high on silk that it's unaffordable for all but the very rich.'

'Is that why you are here?'

Jan nodded. 'Taxes, yes, but wherever you go there are taxes! Worshipping the new religion in Flanders can mean you meet God sooner than you hoped, as my wife found out. Not so here. My country is going to hell, mark my words there will be war again, and we have nowhere to retreat. It's bad there.'

Steward grunted. 'There are more people who can weave like this in Flanders?'

Jan nodded. 'Ja.'

'We'd better talk money,' said Steward, his expression hardening.

For several minutes, the two men went back and forth as they tried to agree a price that was acceptable to both. The mechanical clock on the sideboard struck one and chimed. Tiniker had never seen a clock indoors before. She marvelled at its complexity. Moments later, the church bells outside sounded one also.

Why would anybody living in the city need such a device when there were church bells to sound the time?

With growing impatience as the two older men haggled, Tiniker couldn't resist interrupting. 'Any man rich enough to afford a clock in his room can afford to pay a fair price such as the one my father is asking for our excellent cloth.'

'Tiniker,' Jan upbraided her.

'He'll pay, father,' she said in their native tongue. 'Let us leave to prove my point.'

She picked up the cloth and headed for the door. She had not made three steps before Steward called out. 'Not so fast, young lady. Come back here.'

She stood where she was.

'There are other merchants who would be dearly grateful to be offered this cloth, Mr Steward. We've granted you the privilege of being first, but it seems we should speak to them instead? We shall take it to the Worsted Seld on Saturday…'

'Tiniker, how dare you speak to a man, an alderman, like this?' Jan hissed.

Steward smiled. 'She drives a hard bargain, Mr Vinck.'

Tiniker smiled and curtsied.

'I'll take it.' Steward stretched out his hand.

Tiniker returned to the table with the cloth. Steward shook the weaver's hand then stopped, mid-air.

'There is one further question I have, Mr Vinck.'

Jan's smile fell from his lips.

'Yes?'

'You may have noticed that a number of our fellow countrymen have assembled on the heath above the city.'

Jan nodded.

'You may have also noticed,' continued Steward, 'they have been rounding up the county's sheep to sustain themselves.'

Jan nodded again.

'Let me speak plainly, should they stay resident on the heath eating our sheep, how will you source your wool?'

Jan stuttered. He hadn't considered this. 'Rumour has it, your grace, they intend to attack the city any day?'

'Oh, I dare say rumour will have them doing a thousand

things by the end of the week, but the fact is their protest is about enclosure, and therefore wool, no?'

Jan nodded.

'Well it seems our interests are more aligned than we may have first thought, Mr Vinck. Whilst our mayor parleys with them and generally appeases them, it falls to me to protect the inhabitants of this fine city.'

Jan looked at Tiniker, unsure where the deputy mayor was headed.

'The trouble is, I cannot be certain of the rebel's intentions, nor, being frank, do I trust our current mayor to handle this crisis with any skill. The sooner I understand their intentions and capabilities, the sooner I can get them off that heath.'

Jan felt still uneasy. 'I would help in any way I can, sir, but as a weaver they would never expect me to be sympathetic to their plight. My own survival depends on a ready supply of sheep's wool.'

'You're quite right, that was not what I meant.'

Jan waited for whatever was coming next.

'Men make for clumsy spies in my experience.' Steward looked at Tiniker. 'Women, on the other hand, are most adept.' He smiled with malevolence. 'Especially unmarried ones with beauty and vigour.'

Tiniker's stomach started to fill with butterflies.

'Mr Vinck, you need those rebels off that hill. You need my money. I will pay your price, even though it is too high, but I need a spy. Your daughter will infiltrate the rebel camp and use her,' he winked, '*charm*, to learn their intentions. She will then report to me daily with her findings.'

Jan looked as frightened as Tiniker felt.

'This city has taken you in, welcomed you, let you practise your religion in safety. You are indebted to us, and in such times, Mr and Miss Vinck, we must all perform our civic duties. I don't profess to understand the customs of your homeland, but here, a man of office like myself is required to make contributions towards the upkeep and improvement of his city. I have invested too much into this fine city to see it placed in peril. My duty now is to keep this city safe, for which I request your help.'

Tiniker ran through all the hardships of the past years — the countless risks they had taken. Norwich had given them nothing without its share in return. Everything their family had achieved had been on their own merits, but there was no sense pointing this out now.

Tiniker could see her father was at a loss for words, so she spoke.

'Mr Steward, if the rebels attack the city, our house is one of the first in their path. If I agree to help you, with your power and influence, would you agree to keep us safe and offer us your protection? You have resources available to you.'

'Of course, my child.' Steward nodded.

'Should our house succumb to fire, would you rehouse us?'

'Yes, Miss Vinck. You have my word.'

'In which case, how do I fulfil your demand?' Tiniker had never spied before.

Steward cleared his throat. 'Befriend one of their number. Not Kett, he'll be suspicious. Somebody close to him who knows his intentions; somebody vulnerable to persuasion.'

'I won't doxy,' retorted Tiniker, protective of her virginity, 'not for you, or for anyone. I don't care how rich or important you are.'

'I'm sure that won't be necessary,' said Steward, shaking his head, 'but just because you make a promise doesn't mean they have to be kept. God will understand the difference.'

Tiniker look at Jan. A mix of pride and the worries of a father etched all over his face. 'I can do it, father,' she reassured him. She had to, not only to secure the cloth sale, but Deputy Mayor Steward could make life very hard for them if he chose.

'Mr Vinck, every day their numbers swell. Our arrangements are for nothing if we are not safe in our beds at night.'

Steward turned to Tiniker, a look of sombre sincerity on his face. 'I know many of the people in the city. Let me reassure you that very few possess the courage and resource of your daughter. She will do her duty. That's settled then. I look forward to receiving my first delivery of one hundred ells of bombazine by the New Year.'

Jan looked at Steward. They shook hands.

Tiniker took in a sharp breath. That was a bigger order than they could have dreamed of. It would be enough to feed their family for two years.

'I'll organise a down payment for your troubles of a tenth of the price, but on the condition that I want the exclusive rights to your fabric, and you must keep your methods secret. If you supply any other merchant at all, our arrangement is null and void.'

Jan nodded. 'Yes. Thank you, Mr Steward.'

'I will keep this sample as a yardstick for your quality. Match this, and you shall be paid in full on delivery.' There was a brief silence. 'Very well, I think our business is concluded for the day. Mr Vinck it has been a pleasure. Please show yourself out.

Jan and Tiniker retained their composure and turned to leave.

Mr Steward called out, 'One more thing. The city council

is meeting this afternoon to discuss the rebels. I intend to call upon the guilds to raise the militia. Your guild will require you to be at arms, Mr Vinck.'

Jan nodded.

'We don't know the rebel plans *yet,*' Steward fired another look at Tiniker, 'but I anticipate their approach to be directed at Bishopsgate Bridge. I will have you placed in charge of defending the bridge. Since our contract and its proximity to your home, I can think of nobody with greater incentive than yourself to keep those rebels out of our city. Good day, Mr Vinck.'

Steward smiled and returned to his bureau.

23

21st July, Surrey House

'Ouch.'

Robert slapped his neck, taking his tally of bites to thirteen. Fleas, mosquitoes and horseflies had all dined on his flesh, and he itched like a leper's armpit. They'd been camped at Mousehold for nine days now and as each day passed the wait became more agonising, the stakes higher and his mood more volatile. He climbed the stairs, his tired mind revisiting the events of the meeting he'd just finished. Every morning the elected representatives assembled in the dining room and agreed, or more recently disagreed, on the administration of the camp, which continued to grow at an alarming rate. From all over the region people were drawn to the promise of change. There were now twenty-four districts present, each with two people elected to represent their share of the nine thousand people that had joined Robert's cause. And now the representatives were split; half wanted to attack Norwich and secure much-needed supplies. Robert had refused. Attacking the city would condemn them all as traitors.

For now he had enough support around the table to overrule the suggestion, but as people grew hungry it would be harder to prevent mutiny and insurrection.

Mayor Codd and his fellow aldermen had abdicated their responsibility to those in higher authority in London, which meant that nine thousand angry commoners were left waiting on word from Lord Protector Seymour. They had received the twenty-nine demands a week ago. Since then, only a long and agonising silence had been returned to Norfolk.

That greasy fool Bossell had accused Mayor Codd of trickery.

Robert disagreed; the mayor had nothing to gain by refusing their demands, other than increasing the likelihood of Norwich being attacked. A point Bossell had been too impatient to grasp.

Robert had an hour to rest before presiding over a trial of captured gentleman. He now held eleven against their will, landlords and lawyers. The latest captives would face charges of corruption and abuse of power. Accusations levelled at them from their tenants. This quick and public dispensing of justice had done much to appease the angry commoners. Robert had worried it was proving to be a distraction that consumed his time and would one day ensure he had more enemies than anybody in the county.

William had persuaded him that it enhanced his legitimacy, helped keep the camp orderly and at least in captivity the gentry were safe.

So every day Robert's followers searched the county for people to charge. There was no shortage of lawyers or embittered commoners who'd been on the wrong side of their judgements, all eager for justice or revenge.

But one lawyer still evaded Robert's clutches: Flowerdew. He'd sent Fulke and a party of men to Hethersett to find him. According to his household servants, Flowerdew hadn't been seen since the day the march started. He was rumoured to be hiding in Norwich. Robert had more than enough to do without devoting effort to capturing his nemesis, yet it seemed remiss not to exploit his authority and settle a few personal vendettas.

Standing at his bedroom window, he observed the camp that stretched east as far as his ageing eyes could see. People scurried about in all directions like lice on a fleece. The grass that had covered the heath when they arrived was now worn away. Word had reached him of other local protests, but they were small and contained, and so easily dispersed by the gentry. Yet instead of heading home, these protestors had headed for Norwich, seeking safety in numbers and lending their weight to his cause. Above the camp, the sky was cloudy and grey, like his mood.

'God, give me a sign that I have done the right thing.'

He didn't usually ask The Almighty for help. Guidance, yes, but he felt pleading for help meant you had taken the wrong path, which was a precursor to pleading for forgiveness. He lay on his bed, breathed deeply, and offered a prayer to let the lord protector see sense. Exhausted, he fell into a deep sleep.

'Robert, you smell like you have rotten fish in your undergarments.'

Robert opened his eyes, disorientated.

Sitting on the edge of the bed was Alice. 'Am I dreaming?'

'No, my love.' She leant forward and kissed him on the lips. Her eyes sparkled, and her grey hair was tied back into a bun.

'You're a sight for sore eyes.'

'Well, husband, if you want any more kisses you're going to need to wash. It's a wonder you're not all sick.'

In thirty years of marriage Robert had never spent twelve days away from his wife. For days he'd been dealing with the worries of men, none of whom had shown any concern for him. Seeing his wife now, her plain and earthy beauty, he realised how much he'd missed her. He sat up and threw his arms around her and buried his head in her shoulder. Her scent was the finest thing he'd smelt in days.

'I've missed you, love.' Robert sat up.

'I too.' Alice stroked his back, and together they shared a moment's peace. 'It looks like you've been busy whilst you've been away.'

Robert brushed hair from his face. 'You could say that.'

'My husband is the talk of Norfolk, it seems.'

Robert eased his legs over the side of the bed and sat beside his wife. They held hands. 'My love, I fear I have been reckless. I am out of my depth. I came to petition the mayor. Now I find myself in command of an army.'

'Robert, I won't deny that I am fearful, but for all these people to join you and choose you as their leader shows you the justice of what you are doing.'

'Since I've been here, all I've wanted is to wake up in our bed with you.'

'God has chosen a different path for you, Robert,' she squeezed his hand, 'even Moses had to endure the plagues before he could lead the Hebrews to safety.'

Moses parted the sea and was issued Ten Commandments from God. Robert was camped on a heath and making twenty-nine demands of his monarch.

'You can wake up in this bed with me if you like?' offered Alice. 'But first let's get you clean. I am not sleeping with you smelling like a sheep's carcass.'

Robert began to undress. Alice shouted out the door, 'Thomas, would you please bring up my bag?'

Moments later, Thomas Elmham appeared at the door clutching a leather bag. 'Last time I saw you, Mr Kett, we were playing dice at the Green Dragon. I suspect your days since have been more interesting than my own.'

'Thomas, good man, they have indeed. I'll save you the embarrassment of embracing a man in a state of undress.'

'Thomas kindly rode with me this morning. He's helped at home too,' said Alice. She took a linen cloth from her bag and began to scrub her husband's skin. 'Robert, the state of you, look…' She offered him sight of the muck collected on her cloth.

'Well, Robert,' interrupted Thomas Elmham, 'time would appear to be on your side.'

'How so? What do your friends in the church tell you?' asked Robert.

'The rebellion in Cornwall rumbles onward. Unlike here, the rebels are in the city while the government troops lay siege.'

'How does that help?'

'Exeter's lost, for over a month the army have failed to recapture it. Norwich, thanks to your good grace, hangs by a thread. That's two of the country's three main provincial cities that are now effectively under rebel control.'

Robert winced, and Thomas continued. 'By a simple fate of geography and some fortuitous timing, the government can't protect Norwich. No general wants war on two fronts. They are at your mercy, Robert.'

Robert couldn't hide his delight. This was the best news he'd had since he left. He wondered if his policy of good conduct could be leveraged to endear the authorities to his cause.

'Arms up,' said Alice, still scrubbing his torso.

'My advice, Robert,' said Thomas, 'offer them a quick solution. If Seymour can snatch the frying pan from the fire with no loss of face, he'd be a fool not to take it. Then he can concentrate on Exeter, not to mention all the other protests.'

Robert heard Mayor Codd's words ringing in his ears. Were twenty-nine demands twenty-eight too many?

'There is one problem I can foresee,' continued Thomas, 'none of this has done Lord Protector Seymour any favours. People are questioning his ability to rule and maintain order. Pressure must be mounting on him.'

'So?'

'If he were toppled, you could expect a much tougher time from somebody wishing to assert their authority.'

Robert froze.

'Is there really talk of the protector being toppled? He's the king's uncle. Surely the king wouldn't…'

'There's always talk, Robert,' interrupted Thomas, 'who knows, but the sooner your demands are agreed or negotiated, the better.'

Robert nodded. 'You are characteristically well informed as always, Thomas. Do you believe we'll prevail?'

Thomas pursed his lips, which was his way of showing he didn't want to comment.

'Events elsewhere have been kind, for now.'

'Now the bottom half,' said Alice.

'I think I'll leave you to it,' said Thomas, sensing it was time to take his leave.

'Thomas.' Robert looked him the eye. 'Thank you, for looking after the old girl.'

'My pleasure, you'd have done the same for me.'

Alice finished scrubbing her naked husband. 'I brought you a change of clothes. I suggest we have these washed.'

'Alfred,' shouted Robert.

Alice took out a boxwood comb from her bag and combed his hair. 'You have some lice in here, my dear.'

Alfred appeared at the door. He looked embarrassed to

see his master with no clothes on.

'Alfred, please take my husband's dirty clothes and wash them in the river.'

'Alfred, some ale for us, please,' added Robert.

'Yes, Mr Kett,' said Alfred nodding dutifully.

'Oh, Alfred, please could you bring me a light?' asked Alice.

Alfred returned moments later with ale and a burning candle. Placing them on the sideboard he gathered up Robert's clothing. Alice took a looking glass from her bag. With her other hand she picked up the candle and held it underneath the glass. She waited while a layer of black soot formed on the glass then she put the candle down and wiped her finger across the soot.

'Open your mouth.'

With her finger she rubbed the soot against his teeth, cleaning each one.

Robert Kett was starting to feel like a new man.

*

The camp was subdued, the frenetic activity of previous days over. On his way to the river, Alfred sensed an uneasy heaviness in the air. People were moving slowly, their expressions dour. As he picked his way through the shelters, Alfred conceded that he had landed on his feet; he would be reluctant to swap the hard tiles of the kitchen floor for these hovels. Despite doing women's work, and not having a moment to himself, he had taken advantage of his circumstances to demonstrate to Mr Kett his diligence in performing his duties. Yesterday, Mr Kett's elder brother William had winked and nodded his acknowledgement when Alfred cleared away table after supper, unprompted.

There were no roads through the camp, more a spider web of muddy paths, and Alfred made sure to give Richard and Lynn's shelter a wide birth.

'Oi oi! Look what the cat's dragged in.' It was Fulke, hands on his hips, unshaven, filthier than the last time they'd met, giving him a beady-eyed stare.

'Fulke!' Alfred stopped where he was, feeling distinctly uncomfortable.

'I thought you were locked up for battering your Mrs? I see your black eye is healing.'

Alfred filled him in on events since then.

'Is that Kett's washing?'

Alfred hugged the load tighter. 'Yes.'

Fulke laughed. 'Alfred, you must have offended a cat to have such bad luck! While you're scraping the skid marks out of Kett's underwear, we've been stealing cannons, kidnapped the gentry and extorted them too, slept under the stars and bedded as many strumpets as we can afford.'

Fulke was laughing at Alfred's misfortune. Alfred felt stupid. Once again his old friend made him feel like a dolt.

'Kett isn't buggering you, is he, Alfred? I heard he likes boys?' said Fulke, deliberately mocking him.

'Lay off.' Alfred turned to go.

'When are we planning to attack Norwich then? You must know.'

Alfred shook his head. 'Honestly, Fulke, I have no idea. I'm not privy to Mr Kett's thoughts.'

'I said he's too yellow to attack,' said Fulke. 'Stop wasting your time and join the rebellion.'

Part of Alfred was tempted to follow Fulke, but he needed this job. The rebellion wouldn't last forever, and he had a child to raise.

'I better be getting on, Fulke.'

Fulke frowned. 'Suit yourself, pick the lice from Kett's arse if you'd rather.'

Making his excuses, Alfred mused on Fulke's evident enjoyment of outlaw life. Alfred had to be careful not to put himself in a position where he could be pressured for information. Mr Kett wouldn't take kindly to be spied on. He was a good man trying to do the right thing. He didn't deserve that.

Alfred walked down the blood-stained track into the gulley. He shook his head to brush away another fly. Coming up the hill from the river were two women walking side by side, each carried a pair of sheep's stomachs filled with water over their shoulders. Alfred nodded to them. They smiled back. This small act of civility had the effect of relieving Alfred of his earlier thoughts. There were definitely fewer women around the camp now.

Opposite the gulley, nestled in the bend of the river, was Cow Tower, a fifty-foot redbrick tower with said cows grazing in the meadow in its shadow. Beyond were large orchards of apple and pear trees, all overshadowed by the giant cathedral.

As he near the bottom of the gulley, Alfred counted six archers stationed at the top of the tower. Presumably more were garrisoned within, peering through the arrow loopholes. He felt the archers' eyes on his back as he headed towards the river, praying not to be shot for the sake of Mr Kett's washing. The edge of the road was littered with shells, broken pottery, scrap wood and loose stones. Not wanting to damage his leather boots, he took the middle of the road. The hillside had been carved out for mining chalk and flint, their entrances overgrown with bracken and nettles.

A small wherry boat approached from upstream. Aboard, a cargo of dried peat, no doubt destined for a kitchen oven or a furnace somewhere. Alfred watched the elderly pilot struggle to row against the gentle flow of the river with his boat's load. Beyond the wherry was a stone bridge, framed by another fortified tower. The gatehouse door was closed and guarded by four men. On top of the tower stood more archers.

Alfred didn't fancy doing his laundry within their range.

There was no reason to suspect he'd be shot, but what was to stop a bored sentry shooting a peasant boy for a bet.

He kept walking downriver until he came across a party of women washing clothes in a shallow gravel area ideal for their task. Bent over to scrub their garments, they presented Alfred with a row of backsides.

He tried not to stare.

Alfred didn't much like water; he couldn't swim and was wary of rivers. Doing women's work amongst a party of *women* risked further ridicule. Catching another whiff of Mr Kett's clothing, he headed down to the bank, threw down the clothes and proceeded to take off his boots and roll up his shirtsleeves. The water was cold and refreshing. The sharp gravel underfoot made him hobble as he slapped Mr Kett's breeches against the water. He was aware of one of the women exchanging glances with her companion as she held up a shirt she was scrubbing and examined it for stains. Twisting it into a snake, she wrung out the water. Alfred swished his master's breeches then half-heartedly rubbed the linen between his hands. The water looked murky. He wasn't confident the clothes would be any the fresher for their wash.

'You've never done this before?' said a young woman who couldn't have been more than twenty years old with blond hair, piercing blue eyes and a wicked smile.

Stunned by her beauty, Alfred stuttered, 'No, I'm not, I'm, I don't normally do laundry, I…'

'I can see that,' she said.

She was leant forward, furiously rubbing a soap against a pair of breeches. Alfred chanced a glance. Beneath her open-necked linen smock, her breasts shook as she scrubbed.

His cheeks reddened.

'May I ask your name?' said Alfred, curiously.

'Who's asking?'

Alfred cursed himself. 'I'm Alfred.' It was customary for men to introduce themselves first.

'Tiniker.'

'*Tiniker*? That's a strange name?'

'Thank you,' she said sarcastically.

'Sorry,' he replied recovering his manners. 'I've just never heard that name before.'

She shrugged without looking up.

Alfred berated himself, *Carter, you fool*. The first pretty girl you've spoken to in ages and you mess it up. At least Fulke wasn't here to witness his clumsiness. Alfred took his frustration out on Mr Kett's breeches.

The other women began to pack up and leave.

Alfred stood up and swung Mr Kett's breeches, slapping them against the bank, making a spray of water.

Tiniker laughed.

He must look like a clumsy farmer whipping an ox.

'Let me show you,' she said, making her way towards him. 'Where's your soap?'

'Soap?'

Tiniker picked up an undershirt from the pile.

'Here. Like this.' She methodically worked the soap over the garment. 'See?'

There was something curious about her accent. It wasn't local, and she had a confidence that impressed.

'Where are you from, Tiniker?'

'Flanders.'

'Oh, Flanders, of course,' said Alfred. He'd heard about Flanders. That was where all the wool was sold to.

'My father, sister and I moved to Norwich two summers ago.'

Alfred was about to ask what of her mother and then thought better of it. 'Your English is excellent.'

'You have little choice but to learn when you come to a foreign land.'

He'd always been told that people from overseas ate dogs and slept with their mothers. The French especially. On the evidence of Tiniker, they were more like him than he'd been led to believe. She went back to scrubbing the clothes, and Alfred watched as she carried on with her washing.

'How old are you?' he asked.

'Seventeen. You?'

'Eighteen,' Alfred lied.

'Don't expect me to do it for you,' she said. Tiniker passed him the soap and motioned for him to do the same. She rubbed the fabric against itself, working up a lather, before rinsing it in the water.

'Who normally does your washing?' asked Tiniker.

'My wife.'

'You're married?'

'No. She, urm, she died.' He coughed.

'My father won't let me marry a man of my choosing. I am waiting for him to find me someone suitable.'

'You are still a maiden?' Alfred smiled.

'Don't remind me,' said Tiniker, now inspecting the shirt she'd been scrubbing for Alfred.

'This is too small for you. Why are you washing somebody else's clothes?'

'These are Mr Kett's clothes,' said Alfred with a touch of pride.

'Really? We are washing Mr Kett's clothing?'

'Yes.'

'I work for Mr Kett,' said Alfred.

'Why does he have a man doing his laundry?'

'If you must know, I'm doing this as punishment. I was fighting another man.'

'That would explain your black eye. Why were you fighting?'

'He'd insulted a woman.'

'Somebody you fancied?'

The image of Lynn came to his mind. 'No. Not at all. She was attacked. I saved her,' said Alfred, lying with ease.

Tiniker held up the shirt once more, this time to check she had rinsed out all the soap. 'Captain Mischief's undershirt.'

'Who?'

'It's his nickname in the city. Everybody says Kett's a troublemaker.'

'Bah. He's a good man. If only there were more like him.'

On the other side of the river a donkey, dragging a small trailer of manure toward the gatehouse, hee-hawed as it was whipped by its driver.

Then it occurred to Alfred what had been troubling him, 'You live locally?'

'Ja.' Tiniker nodded, ringing the water from Mr Kett's undershirt.

'Then why are you on this side of the river?'

Tiniker's eyes flashed down, then up. 'This is the best place for laundry. Everyone knows. I live there, in the pink house.' She pointed. Between two white buildings sat a pink timber house, just three along from the gatehouse and the bridge. She was close to home. 'What's it like? The camp?' She tilted her head at him.

'It stinks. Lucky for me, I'm up there, with Mr Kett.' Alfred pointed to Surrey House.

She took a moment to finish wringing out the shirt. 'Will they attack the city?' she asked, laying out the clean shirt on the bank.

Alfred laughed. 'Mr Kett is determined to keep law and order.'

He watched Tiniker retrieve her woollen kirtle that she'd left on the riverbank and slip it over her head, lacing up the front to support her ample cleavage.

'Walk me back?'

Alfred, delighted and surprised by her forwardness, beamed.

Maybe girls were like this in Flanders. If only he could think of a way to see her again.

They walked side by side, her purposeful stride keeping pace with his gait.

'Alfred.' Tiniker turned to meet his eyes. 'Would you take me to the camp? I've never seen anything like it. I'm interested to…'

'Sure,' interrupted Alfred. 'Now?'

'Why not.'

With the sun on his face, his feet cool and clean, Alfred smiled to himself, momentarily content. For a brief moment he felt something he hadn't felt for days, fleeting happiness. On the bridge as they passed, he spotted two men on horseback, speaking to the guards. One, in a black velvet hat with a feather, looked familiar. Where had he seen him before? The other was in a brightly embroidered coat. Alfred had never seen such an impressive garment. It was quartered in red and blue. Three gold lions on the red squares and gold flowers on the blue squares.

Alfred gulped.

'Tiniker, *look*.' He pointed. 'The man in the hat, that's the mayor, we ate his last horse.'

'The other man, in the embroidery, I think it's the king's standard. He must be important. This must be word from London. Quick, we'd better run. I've got to warn Mr Kett.'

Tiniker nodded, looking awestruck. Together they ran up the hill back to camp. This was the moment they had all been waiting for.

24

Alfred barged through the door, Tiniker following him into Surrey House, both short of breath. Anders Marshwell was in the hallway, talking in hushed tones with Thomas Garrod at the foot of the staircase.

'Mr Marshwell, sir, excuse me,' said Alfred to the reeve of Hethersett. 'Begging your pardon for the intrusion,' Alfred collected his breath, 'where might I find Mr Kett?'

Anders glanced at his companion Thomas, his eyebrows raised as if to convey some private meaning.

Perhaps they had been discussing Mr Kett.

'Our leader is in his bedchamber.'

'Thank you, Mr Marshwell.'

Alfred turned his attention to his new friend. 'Tiniker, you better wait here. I'll be back down in a moment.'

Tiniker nodded. Alfred grinned, after days of nothing, this felt important.

'What's the urgency, Alfred?' interrupted Anders, laying his gnarled old hand on Alfred's forearm. Alfred hesitated. 'Out with it, lad.'

'I believe we have word from London.'

The consternation on Mr Marshwell's face made clear the

magnitude of what was at stake. Alfred suddenly felt less confident in his assessment of what he and Tiniker had witnessed at the bridge. Nevertheless, he bolted up the stairs, leaving Tiniker alone with the echo of the creaking wooden treads.

She looked around, keen to take it all in. People pushed past her, she felt invisible, and her palms were clammy. She clenched her fists to stop them shaking.

Her timing couldn't be better.

If this was word from London, she could warn Mr Steward of the rebel's intentions. She had to find a way to stay in the house, remain inconspicuous and stay close to Alfred. She removed herself from the centre of the hallway and stood in the corner, waiting in the shadows for Alfred to reappear.

*

Back from presiding over the trials at the oak tree, Robert was looking forward to a few hours of sanctuary with his wife. As they lay in each other arms on the bed, Robert thought he must ask William, who also shared the room, to leave them be this evening. One night alone would do Robert more good than all the potions of the apothecary.

'Mr Kett, sir,' said Alfred.

Robert sat up and was about to scold the intruder for disturbing his peace, but he could see from the lad's startled face something was up.

'What the devil has got you into such a flurry?'

'My apologies, Mr Kett.' Alfred was embarrassed at finding Mrs Kett lying next to her husband. 'I just saw the mayor leaving Norwich.'

'You barge in here, and that is all you have to tell me,

Alfred? Have you nothing but earwax for brains?'

'Accompanied by another man.'

Robert felt his frustration bubbling like a pot coming to the boil. All week he'd been subject to such ramblings. Now, enjoying a rare moment of peace, he was interrupted by this cloth-eared boy making a song and dance about a couple of strangers leaving the city.

'Robert, listen,' said Alice.

'I think he was wearing the king's coat of arms. It may be word from London. They're coming here now.'

There was a pause.

Robert sat up and swung his legs over the bed with the speed of a man half his age.

'Alfred, throw everybody out of the house except my brother. Alice, you wait here. Alfred, ready some drinks for our visitors.'

Alfred nodded and closed the door behind him.

Robert felt oddly calm. Their fate had been determined, somewhere far away by people he didn't know. Was it their intention that he should succeed or fail? Never before had his life rested in the hands of a stranger. Alice squeezed his arm.

He turned to look at her lying beside him, then knelt and offered a prayer. As long as he was granted concession on enclosure, he would have enough to send people home victorious and with his honour intact. The other demands could be sacrificed; anything else was a bonus. With the army nowhere near, he knew he held the whip hand.

Another knock. It was William who now entered. 'They're here: a royal herald and Mayor Codd.

William looked preoccupied. He wore the same worried expression that Robert recognised from childhood. They had played together as children, worked together as men and prayed together as subjects of God. This, they were well aware, would be a defining conversation of their lives.

'Young Alfred is asking everyone to leave,' reported William.

Robert could hear voices. as Alfred welcomed their visitors. They had made him wait all week, so he was of a mind to make them wait a while. Alice kissed him, wished him luck, he took a deep breath and left the room.

At the bottom of the stairs, Robert squeezed his brother's shoulder and they exchanged a nod of acknowledgment, before walking into the dining room together. The herald, an imposing man, was standing with his back to the wall. His gold-embroidered tunic radiated its brightness against the wood panelling.

Highwaymen would gladly relieve you of that splendid outfit, thought Robert.

Mayor Codd managed a brief and unconvincing smile. This isn't going to be easy, Robert realised.

'I'm Robert Kett.' Robert offered his hand.

The herald's grip was on the painful side of firm. His hazel-coloured eyes were blank, beneath a square cut a fringe of dark hair. He's not giving anything away, wouldn't fancy playing cards with him, thought Robert.

By contrast, the mayor looked pale.

'Please, take a seat, herald,' said Robert.

'I'll stand.'

'If it pleases you. I am too old to stand, so you'll forgive me if we are seated.'

'As you wish.'

'Mayor, won't you take a seat?'

'I'll stand also.'

'Very well.' This didn't bode well, feared Robert.

Alfred appeared at the door with four ales.

'Gentlemen, a drink at least?' offered Robert.

'No, thank you.' said the herald.

Mayor Codd declined. Robert shook his head at Alfred to dismiss the drinks.

'Well, if you won't sit and you won't drink, you'd better have something worth listening to,' said Robert.

'I bring word from His Majesty's Lord Protector, Edward Seymour, First Duke of Somerset.' The herald relayed the message in an emotionless delivery. 'The lord protector is in receipt of your demands.'

Robert thought the herald's manner of speaking almost effeminate. He relayed his master's words with no intonation, yet his accent was soft and at odds with the blank expression on his emotionless face. Robert feared this was a man who was not able to negotiate. A simple messenger. I have a feeling I am not going to like this, Robert thought.

'The lord protector will fully consider them in due course,' continued the herald.

Robert looked to Codd for reassurance. Codd averted his gaze.

Not good.

'First, however, you must disband your forces and return home. Once you have done this, you will be pardoned, and your demands will be considered.'

What? Robert waited for an explanation. In the silence that followed, the herald stared ahead, as still as a sentry guard.

'Go on,' said William.

The herald bowed. He had nothing more to say.

'That's it?' asked Robert with growing incredulity and anger.

'Indeed.'

'We have waited a week only to be told to go home?' Robert looked at the mayor. Mayor Codd shifted his feet.

'There are ten thousand of the king's subjects on the other side of that door. You expect me to tell them to go home and wait for consideration?'

'Quite so,' replied the herald.

Robert was disbelieving. 'What assurances can I give that their grievances will be upheld?'

'The lord protector is known to be sympathetic to the people's concerns of enclosure,' stated the herald.

'Well a damn lot of good that has done people. They are starving. They don't have enough for winter.'

The herald said nothing. Robert looked again for reassurance from Codd, who finally spoke.

'I have been ordered not to supply material or provisions from Norwich. The city is to be closed to you and ready its defences.'

'What?'

'I'm sorry, Robert.'

Robert sprung from his seat. 'You will be sorry. You expect me to go out there and say the king is sorry. Just go home and die quietly?'

Codd examined his feet. Robert could see the mayor disagreed but that he was powerless to interfere.

'Don't you see what you have done?'

The herald stood motionless — his expression blank.

'Then you leave me no choice.' Robert knew he ought to contain his anger, but his frustration was too much to bear. 'We are not going home without our demands met and if you close the city to us,' he paused, 'then we'll take it for ourselves.'

The herald spoke, 'Raising an army against the king is treason.'

'Seymour has left me no choice. How can I back down?' Robert demanded, 'You've given me nothing. *Nothing.*'

Robert's face was red with anger. If he bit any harder, his teeth would shatter. He pointed his finger at the herald. 'If Seymour wants a war, I'll give him a fucking war.'

The herald turned his lips downwards.

'Next time I see you here you'll be on your hands and knees begging for your city back. Get out.'

The herald turned to leave. Robert couldn't bring himself to look at Codd.

'Robert,' said William. 'Leave the door ajar for them. Give him something to take back to London.'

Robert shouted at the herald's back, 'Tell Seymour I have ten thousand men, and I'll raise merry hell until he ends enclosure. Tell him he'll be forever haunted by the name Robert Kett.'

Mayor Codd stopped when he got to the door.

'Robert, Seymour couldn't give you what you wanted. He is powerless to end enclosure.'

'What do you mean? He's practically a king. He can do what he wants?'

Codd shook his head. 'Power is rarely that simple, Robert.' The mayor closed the door.

An eerie silence followed.

Robert couldn't bring himself to look at William. Both men started to pace, furious with Seymour. Robert's mind ran through the possibilities, the eventualities. Why could he not see what would happen? *He gave me no choice, that damned fool. We're short of food.*

'He's brought this on himself,' said Robert. '*Fuck*,' he shouted, his profanity resounding around the room.

In the silence that followed, the stinking reality of their situation hung in the air like an open plague pit.

'Robert, if we do this, there's no turning back.'

'I am well aware of that, brother.'

'There must be another way.' William looked at him.

'Can you please be so kind as to share it?'

Robert waited for his brother to reply. When he didn't, Robert sat down. 'We attack.' Robert swallowed hard. 'You are free to leave, William.'

'I said I'd support you. And I will, even though I don't like what is required of me.'

'Thank you, William,' he said. 'I can't pretend to like it any more than you do, but we have started this for a lot of good and honest reasons. For those same reasons we must now see it through. If God is with us, he will see to it that we prevail.'

Robert made a fist of his hands. 'Enough of this chatter. We must call in the representatives.'

'Robert, unleashing ten thousand men on the city, well, there might not be a city left at the end of the day.'

'I know. We must plan our movements. Everybody must be clear in their duty. We must retain order and control.'

'Easier said than done.'

'Well, do it we must. Let's start.'

'If you are to plan an attack, brother, let them see you with a clear head. They will be less willing to risk their lives for a man in a rash temper.'

Robert sighed, trying to calm himself. Every time his thoughts turned to Seymour, his temper began to race. Again, why could they not see what was so plain.

'Alfred,' called William.

Moments later the lad appeared at the door. 'Yes, Mr Kett?'

'Fetch us some food. Give us half of one hour in private, then summon in the representatives. At which point, keep us watered.'

'We've run out of food, Mr Kett.'

'Find some, lad.' said William, unable to conceal his own frustration.

An hour later, the dining room was full and drinks were served. Three of the men present had military experience, and with their help, the Kett's set about planning their attack.

25

Jan stood by the open gate as the mayor and herald rode through, their horses blowing after the short canter down the hill.

'Who's in charge here?' asked the mayor.

'I am,' replied Jan.

'Close this gate. Nobody is to pass through, in either direction.'

Jan nodded. Was Tiniker in the camp? He'd watched her walk up there with a young man, an hour ago. Now she'd be trapped outside the city.

'Is that understood?' asked the herald.

'Yes, sir,' confirmed Jan.

'Good,' the herald continued, 'you will be attacked. It is your duty to defend the city and repel the rebels. King Edward orders that you show them no mercy. They are traitors one and all.'

This was it then.

Jan had hoped to escape violence and bloodshed, but it had followed him here. As Augustine Steward had warned, the militia had been called up this morning. With bitter resignation, Jan closed the gate, fastening the metal bolts and slotting the oak beams in place. They won't get in here without a fight; he cursed the rebels and their troublemaking.

He should be busy making bombazine.

The mayor beckoned him over.

'This is our weakest point,' he came straight to the point. 'You should prepare to face the brunt of their forces.'

'When?' asked Jan.

'You are on guard until further notice. Have your men fill the bridge with earth to protect the gate. See to it that they construct earth ramparts on either side of the tower should the enemy attempt to swim across the river.'

'Reinforcements, will they be coming?'

'Have your men at their quarters, no rest watch. Prepare water to douse fires.'

'Arrows?'

'I'll send you every arrow in Norwich.'

Jan swallowed the lump in his throat.

'Create a fallback point farther up the street. Build a barricade in front of the hospital.'

'With what?'

'Anything you can find.'

'What about the cannon?'

'The rebels are mostly unarmed. We can't risk the cannon falling into rebel hands.'

'If you're overrun,' the herald interrupted, 'you may retreat, but the king commands we must fight to the end. Spare no one.'

'Jesus,' said Jan to himself. 'How many of them are there?'

'All told, maybe ten thousand,' replied the mayor, looking pale.

The herald kicked his horse and trotted up Bishopsgate, closely followed by the mayor. Jan stood in stunned silence as they rode off to find safety away from the front line.

By the end of this year he would have earned a tidy sum.

But now all his plans, after everything he'd overcome, just at the very point of making good, were threatened.

I'll kill every damned rebel I can see, he promised himself.

'Men,' he shouted, summoning his garrison. 'Assemble on me.'

The nine men making up his garrison gathered around him under the gatehouse.

Ten thousand rebels?

Jan knew there must be a lot, but the thought of ten thousand made his blood run cold. He did a quick calculation: there was said to be about twelve thousand souls living in Norwich. Half were women. Of the six thousand remaining, a third must be too young or too old to fight. Another proportion too rich or too sympathetic to the rebels. At best, he reckoned the city could hope to field three thousand fighting men. Outnumbered by more than three to one, he didn't like the odds. He would have to make best use of the defences and weapons, without them they'd be swamped.

His small garrison, like him, were civilians, a collection of tradespeople: two other weavers, two farriers, two wheelwrights, a cooper, a saddler and a fletcher. Obviously, they were proficient with a longbow, but none had experience of hand to hand combat besides an occasional drunken brawl outside an alehouse.

Using a stick, he drew a map of the river and the bridge in the dust. He briefed them on the need to start work on the earthen ramparts. He reassured them and said the sooner they built the ramparts, the safer they'd feel.

'All of Norwich will come to the defence of this bridge.'

They didn't look convinced.

With his men set to work, Jan now ran to warn Margreet. Looking up at the gargoyle above the door as he arrived at his door, he entreated, 'You better earn your keep today, there's a lot of evil to keep at bay.'

His youngest daughter was beating a rug in the hall.

'Hello, father.' She smiled.

'Not inside, Margreet. You don't beat a rug indoors.'

His reprimand punctured her mood.

He put his hands on her shoulders and looked into her eyes. She looked frightened. Good. He needed her to understand this was serious.

'Margreet, the rebels are coming. There is a good chance they will attack the bridge.'

Tears welled in his daughter's eyes.

'I need you to be a big girl today. They may try to burn our house. You need to be alert. Put the cooking fire out. Don't save any embers. Drench it. Have some water ready. Fill every bucket you can. As soon as you see flames, put them out. If you run out of water, beat the flames with a wet sack.'

She started to cry. Unlike her older sister, the trials of the past years had done nothing to embolden Margreet. Where Tiniker had grown up fast in the face of adversity, Margreet had remained a child. At fourteen years of age, she still confided in imaginary friends and preferred to inhabit her make-believe worlds.

Today the real world was coming whether she liked it or not.

'Where's Tinky?' she sobbed.

'She'll be back soon.' Jan hoped he was right.

'I want Tinky,' Margreet sniffed.

'She'll be here soon.' He hugged his daughter, 'Margreet, you have to pay attention. You're a big girl today. If you listen to papa, everything will be all right. Stay out of sight. Don't look out of the windows. Hide upstairs and under no circumstances unlock the door to anybody. Nobody. Understand?'

'What about you, father?' asked Margreet.

'Yes, you can unlock the door to me, just not to strangers.'

'Where will you be? Stay with me, Papa.'

'I'll be safe. Half of Norwich will be outside that door. I'll be up in the tower at the end of the street surrounded by men and weapons.'

Margreet broke into more sobs. He hugged her tightly again.

'You remember what to do?'

'Yes, keep the door locked.'

'And?'

Margreet looked puzzled.

'Fetch as much water as you can. Soak some sacks.'

She sniffed and nodded. 'Please stay with me,' she pleaded.

'I can't. Be brave. Make sure you brace the door behind me.'

Jan wiped a tear from his eye as he left his home. For the sake of his two beautiful daughters, he vowed he would fight these blasted rebels to the death.

26

With four pewter tankards full of ale in each hand, Alfred leant, pushing the dining room door open with his shoulder, careful not to spill the drinks. The pungent waft of men assaulted his nostrils. They had been planning their attack for an hour already. Alfred pushed between the two closest representatives and placed the tankards on the table.

He was just in time to catch Mr Kett speaking.

'I disagree. The most important thing is that we minimise the loss of life to our own side, a carefully planned attack will be much safer.'

Alfred handed the last tankard to William Kett, who whispered, 'Please empty the piss pot,' motioning to the corner of the room.

Alfred nodded.

'We have to go now. You have to act fast and capitalise on the element of surprise,' argued a fellow at the back. 'If you give them time to prepare, take it from me as a man who has fought in campaigns, it will be easier for them to defend their position than for us to attack. The longer you wait, the more you hand them the advantage.'

Alfred appraised the metal chamber pot full to the brim with urine. Easily a gallon's worth. Down the wooden panels of the wall behind the pot were the streaks from the spray of men relieving themselves. Alfred picked up the metal handle resting against the side of the pot. It was wet. He lifted the pot, slopping its contents from side to side.

Very carefully he made for the door, cursing himself for not checking the pot earlier.

'If we go in a hurry, it will be chaos,' countered Robert. 'Men are full of ale by night-time and are at their most vengeful. If we go at dawn, they will be more alert and less disposed to set fire to everything. I remind you that all we need to achieve is to capture the alderman. Then we can assume power peacefully. Believe me I wanted to thrash them too when that herald left, but on reflection, sending all our forces will risk destroying the city and the risk to life is too great.'

Alfred rested the pot on the floor beyond the dining room door and heard the man by the fireplace speak.

'We must storm the bridge with overwhelming force, this evening. In war, you must take the initiative.'

Fulke will be pleased, Alfred thought.

He emptied the pot in the garden hole and returned it to the dining room. In the kitchen he found Tiniker alone, filling a row of tankards with ale from the barrel.

'Has Mrs Kett gone?' he asked.

'Yes. She went to walk around the camp.'

Pleased to be alone with Tiniker, Alfred thanked her.

'It has been a hundred times easier with you here this afternoon.'

She smiled. 'I'm not sure I was much help.'

'I'm doing my best for Mr Kett, but it's not easy on your own,' he said, hoping she may volunteer to help him again.

'You are fond of him, Mr Kett?'

'Yes. If it weren't for him I'd have no job. He offered me work at his tannery.'

'Don't you hate the smell?' said Tiniker.

Alfred's mind flashed back to being thrown into pit thirteen and the foul water's taste that made him want to gag.

'It's better than going hungry,' he said, at last.

'I'm thirsty, shall we share one of these?' she said picking up on of the tankards, a mischievous smile on her face.

Before Alfred could stop her, she took a big gulp, wiped her mouth with the back of her arm and let out a satisfied burp. She passed him the tankard, and Alfred laughed and took a swig. It tasted good. He took another mouthful. It was strong, must be the first draft. Tiniker snatched the tankard from his hand and giggled as she took another mouthful. She passed back the tankard and lifted herself on to the table. Alfred had to take another sip to stop himself from becoming lost in the beauty of her cornflower blue eyes. She patted the table next to her. He followed her invitation and sat beside her.

'They've been in there for an age,' said Tiniker nodding her head in the direction of the dining room, 'What are they planning?'

Alfred swallowed his mouthful and passed her the dregs of the ale. She finished it and put the tankard down.

'From what I overheard, we're going to attack the bridge.'

Tiniker shuddered. What would happen to her father? God let him be safe.

'When?'

Alfred tried to recall the conversation he'd overheard.

'One man wanted to attack now. But Mr Kett was talking about doing it the morning when men were sober.'

'I hope my house will be safe.'

'You can stay here.'

'Alfred, it's getting late, my father will be worried about me. I better go home.'

'Will you come back tomorrow?'

Tiniker looked directly into his eyes. 'Alfred, tomorrow, the world for us is going to change. Your kind are going to attack the city. My family and I might lose our home.'

Alfred frowned. 'But Mr Kett has done everything he can to avoid violence.'

'Alfred.' Tiniker turned back to the window as the memories came flooding back. 'I've seen what happens when mobs of men roam the streets in the name of justice. Such things happened in Flanders. Nobody is spared from their anger.'

Alfred shook his head. 'I know Mr Kett as well as anybody. All he wants is to settle matters peacefully.'

'Then he's naive.'

'Whose side are you on?'

A silence followed. Why wasn't she supportive of their aims? Alfred couldn't understand. People like him were being evicted from their homes so rich men could make room for more sheep. How could anybody ignore that?

'I'm not on anybody's side, Alfred.' She pushed herself forward and slid off the table. 'I just want my family to be safe.'

Alfred succumbed to an unexpected wave of panic. Who was Tiniker? He'd now confided everything in her, and with everything she now knew, she could alert the city. They would know Mr Kett's plans. He rubbed his head in panic. The rebellion would fail, and Alfred would be to blame.

'You can't go.'

'I must.' Her face was red.

Alfred grabbed her arm.

'You have to stay. It's too dangerous.'

She snatched it away. Anger flashed across her face. 'Don't touch me.'

'Wait,' said Alfred as she ran towards the door.

'Alfred, get off me!' She pulled her arm away for the second time.

'Tiniker, let me explain, please,' pleaded Alfred.

She stood still, her arms folded across her chest. Tiniker was headstrong, she stood up for herself, which Alfred found it impressive, attractive even.

'This afternoon, with you, has been,' he paused and looked at his feet, 'the best afternoon I have spent in as long as I can remember since my wife died,' he added, remembering his earlier lie. His heart fluttered as she smiled briefly. She was exquisite, even when riled. He had to make this right. 'It's just… I have told you too much. If you were to go home and tell of our plans, Mr Kett might be defeated, and well that would be my fault. I'd be in so much trouble, I…'

'I'm not going to tell anybody,' said Tiniker, her cheeks flushing.

'You have to promise. If you don't…'

Tiniker stood on tiptoes and planted a kiss on his lips. For a brief second Alfred felt like singing to the heavens. 'I promise.'

Alfred breathed a sigh of relief. He managed a brief smile too. He believed her. 'Thank you.'

'Can I go now?'

He nodded.

'Can I see you again?' asked Alfred.

Tiniker grinned at the clumsy but handsome man stood before her; there was something endearing about him about his innocence, yet also something slightly dangerous about him. When he'd grabbed her arm, she'd felt vulnerable. It had surprised her because there was a vulnerability to Alfred also; maybe it was because he'd lost his wife so young? His misfortune compelled her to care for him. Tiniker had lost her mother and knew the pain of bereavement. Tiniker stopped herself from dwelling on such sentiments; emotions were dangerous. She dismissed them. They were the influence of the ale.

She flashed her eyes. 'Walk me back?'

Alfred agreed willingly.

They slipped out of the kitchen door into the small orchard behind Surrey House. He went first, over the low wall that enclosed the orchard, and then held Tiniker's hand as she clambered over. Together they made their way through the camp at the rear of the house. Everyone looked anxious and expectant, as they awaited Mr Kett's instructions. She was struck by a sense of impending danger. The air crackled with nervous energy like the calm before a storm. Everywhere she looked she saw weapons: bows and arrows, axes, clubs, knives, hammers, scythes, sticks, rocks. She was filled with dread.

Steward had sent her here for this very reason. She was a spy. Providence had brought her to Alfred so she could leverage some advantage for the defenders.

*

Sensing her fear, Alfred tried to reassure Tiniker with a smile. Was this love? He didn't know, but he liked it. Picking their way through the camp, he thought of Tiniker discovering that his wife was both alive and living here. Then, too, she would learn that working for Mr Kett was punishment for beating his wife with a stick. These revelations would be sure to put an end to his burgeoning friendship.

A man approached with a roe deer draped over his shoulders. The arrow that had killed it was still poking out from the beast's heart. Tiniker pressed into Alfred as they lent back to avoid him.

It was Adam Catchpole. Alfred dropped his chin to his chest, and marched quickly, head down.

'Alfred, long time no see.'

In vain.

'Adam,' said Alfred, feigning surprise.

'Who's this pretty girl with you then?' he grinned.

'Just a friend,' said Alfred nervously.

'Hello,' said Tiniker, doing a small curtsey, mockingly.

'That stag looks heavy, Adam, you best be getting on. Eat well.'

Alfred hurried on, walking Tiniker to the bottom of the gully, before squeezing her hand and saying goodbye. He was disappointed not to get another kiss. He offered to call on her and her family tomorrow and reassured them there would be no harm come to them if he had his way. He watched her walk back towards the bridge.

She didn't look back.

*

On the far side of the bridge, Tiniker knocked on the closed gate.

'Be off with you,' a voice called out.

She knocked again, before realising that she was locked out. On either side of the gatehouse, teams of men were hastily piling up banks of earth in the hope it would keep the rebels out. She pitied them, knowing as she did what was to come at them.

She considered her options, to the left the river was shallow enough to cross — she would have to brave the waters.

'Tiniker!'

From the top of the gatehouse, between the crenulations, her father was waving. He ran down and after laboriously unlocking the gate and removing the oak beams, let her back in.

Tiniker hugged her father, relieved to see him.

'You have been in their camp?' he quizzed her, in his native tongue.

'Ja.'

'Thank God you are safe.'

She might be back within the walls of the city, yet she felt more in danger now than she did in the camp with Alfred, amongst their enemies. Had she knowingly walked back into a trap? She could see the anguish on her father's face.

He hugged her again.

'They attack tomorrow, father,' she whispered.

Jan had been convinced they could come now, at any minute. Now they had time to finish their defences.

'I must go and tell Mr Steward, father.'

Jan agreed.

'Then go home. Margreet needs you.' He kissed her goodbye, his stubble scratching her soft cheek.

As she rounded the bend by the chancel of the cathedral, a troop of soldiers approached. She counted fifty, in uniform and carrying halberds. She pressed herself against the wall to let them pass. A few whistled at her, the rest ignored her, preoccupied with their task ahead. Behind them followed archers, hundreds of them with unstrung longbows. With every archer who passed, her confidence mounted. They will look after father, she reassured herself. Then came a horse and cart laden with barrels full of arrows. She wondered how many would die here tomorrow? Why did men have to be so stubborn and resolve all their differences with violence? The land would be a better place if it were run by women.

Looking up at Mr Steward's door, she knocked. No answer. Frustrated, she turned to face the street.

'Well, well. Look who it is. My little spy.'

It was Augustine Steward, approaching from the street, closely followed by a clerk carrying armfuls of vellum parchments. Towering over her, closer than was necessary, he wore a self-satisfied expression that made her want to retch. His breath smelled of wine and garlic. Although she resented being referred to as 'his', she bowed and acknowledged his greeting. He brushed past her as he pushed to open his front door. Together they made their way upstairs to his parlour were she dutifully recounted all that she had learned.

*

As the evening sun fell behind the city, the rebel camp assembled at the Oak of Reformation. There was a crackle of expectation in the evening air. Alfred found himself at the back of the crowd and had to stand on tiptoes to see. There was a tap on his shoulder. It was Fulke. Beside him, Geoffrey Lincoln and Adam Catchpole.

'Alfred, you old fox. Twice in one day!'

'Fulke,' said Alfred, surprised. 'What are the chances of seeing you here?'

'I'm like a bad penny, Alfred,' grinned Fulke, 'you've been in Surrey House, what's the news? Between friends.'

Alfred leant over, and in a whisper, said, 'We're attacking Norwich. Of that I am certain.'

'Excellent.' Fulke rubbed his hands together. 'Alfred, you little legend. Tonight?'

Alfred felt privileged. He knew what everyone wanted to know. It was nice to have the answers, for once.

'Tomorrow.'

'Damn you, Kett. Making me wait. There's a city full of gentlemen to beat up, women to rape and plunder to steal. How does he expect me to sleep tonight?'

'Alfred won't be raping anyone, now he's got his new fancy girl,' said Adam.

Fulke turned his head to look at Adam, making sure he'd heard him right, 'What's this?' he said, 'You keeping secrets from me, Alfred?'

'No!' Alfred's cheeks reddened.

'You've been rutting some girl in that fancy house?'

'No,' Alfred shook his head.

'They were walking hand in hand when I spied them,' added Adam.

'You sneaky bastard,' said Fulke, 'where is she?'

Alfred gritted his teeth. 'She's just a girl from the city, that's all.'

'If she's with the enemy then she's fair game tomorrow then,' said Fulke.

'She's not the enemy, Fulke.' Alfred's patience for this nonsense was breaking.

Fulke moved behind Alfred and grabbed his arm, twisting it behind his back. Alfred wriggled, but he was trapped in Fulke's vice-like grip.

'Her name?'

'Stop it, Fulke,'

Fulke twisted harder.

'All right. Tiniker.'

'That wasn't so hard was it? What sort of name is that?'

Fulke's grip loosened, and Alfred snatched his arm free. 'Piss off, Fulke.'

'Oi, you young scroat, don't forget who you're talking to,' said Fulke, pointing his finger at Alfred.

He was spared further interrogation by the arrival of Robert Kett climbing up on to his dais under the oak tree. There was an almighty cheer from the crowd. Mr Kett started to speak, and they fell silent. Alfred had to strain to hear him at this distance.

'My fellow men,' Kett began, 'we have come a long way. We wanted to make our voices heard. I am sorry to say that we have not been heard. The time for talking is over. The time for action is upon us.'

Jittery excitement and shock ran through the crowd.

'We have been peaceful. However, our goodwill and offer of peace is to be punished. The lord protector has ordered the city to close its gates to us and no longer supply us with food.'

The crowd booed and jeered.

'He may well close his gates, but we shall take his city,' declared Kett.

Fulke cheered. So did a great many others. Watching the crowd around him, Alfred thought for every man who cheered, there was another in stunned silence.

'Tomorrow we capture Norwich. This will not be easy. The city will be heavily defended. You must know that some of you may lose your lives. I remind you, therefore, that every man here is here of his own free will. I won't think less of any man who wishes to retire.'

Mr Kett let his words drift across the heads of the crowd. Nobody moved.

'I am confident with God's help and our superior numbers that we will capture the city. I remind you also that we take up arms against our fellow Englishmen. They have orders to repel us. Unlike us, they don't choose the orders they are given but are required to obey them all the same. So, I beseech you defend yourselves with all your strength, but so long as this protest bears my name, there shall be no wanton slaying of Englishmen, no plundering and no torching of property. Many of us sell our wares in Norwich, and we stand nothing to gain by destroying it. We must act with mercy if we are to be successful in achieving our reforms.'

'Bollocks to that,' whispered Fulke under his breath. 'You'll never get another chance for a dust up like this again.'

Alfred's stomach lurched.

Mr Kett continued, 'Your representatives will meet with you this evening and communicate your battle orders. I bid you goodnight. Say your prayers and fill your stomachs for tomorrow. You shall need all the strength you can muster.'

Alfred heard a faint noise carried on the evening breeze from the city. Then the noise, a faint boom, came again. Screams rose up in the distance.

He tried to see what had just happened.

Two further booms.

People were running. Panic spread across the crowd. People were thrown forward, flattening those in front of them trying to flee. Hysterical screams pierced the air. Crowds ran in all directions, tripping over one another as they dashed for shelter. As Alfred turned to look at Fulke, something flew through the air and knocked over a woman behind him. Blood sprayed from her mouth as she flew forward, only to be crushed underfoot.

It was then that Alfred understood what was happening. It was the city's cannon. They were being bombarded.

27

22ⁿᵈ July, Mousehold Heath

Fulke lowered the smouldering taper to the powder hole, his ears still ringing like church bells from the night before, a broad grin stretched across his face.

'Good morning, Norwich,' he said to himself.

There was a brief fizz as the taper touched the powder hole, followed by an almighty bang that shook the ground. Flame and white smoke spat forth from the barrel. The cannon lurched backwards against its chocks, and the trees rustled as birds fled for cover. A lead ball the size of a baby's head flew from the heights of the escarpment towards Norwich. It had no particular target, but it was sure to hit something.

Jolted by the blast, Fulke regained his footing.

His heart thumped.

Norwich lay sleeping, its kitchen fires smouldering, streets still beneath a veil of mist. Fulke watched as the puff of dust indicated where the cannonball had hit the wall of a house.

'I wouldn't want to be in that bedroom,' he said.

He hadn't used cannon before last night, but they were simple enough to operate. A measure of gunpowder, a rag to act as wadding, pad them down, roll in the ball, a little extra powder in the hole and boom. The rest was for God and the devil to work out between them.

Fulke's barrage had started shortly after the city guns had opened fire last night. Apart from the casualties of the opening salvo, the bombardment had done little to injure the rebels. The city's shots either fell short of the high ground, thudding harmlessly into the face of the escarpment or passed overhead into Thorpe wood.

While everyone else had dashed for cover, Fulke had run in the opposite direction, towards the cannons to begin loading them. He hadn't waited for orders. He regarded the cannons as his property. He had stolen them after all. His short fusillade had only lasted until darkness fell, by which time Kett had appeared, but Fulke knew that his work had been done; he must have terrified the inhabitants of the city as they turned in for the night, unsure if they would wake up alive.

Fulke hadn't slept such was his excitement at using his cannon.

With half their powder supply spent, Kett had determined they should wait for the morning. Fulke had waited. He now lit the second cannon's powder fuse. A loud boom heralded a lead ball sent to tempt the devil to seal somebody's fate. Fulke dampened the barrels using the sponge, a water-soaked piece of fleece wrapped around the end of a pole. He loaded up another two shots, a measure of powder, rammed into place with some rag to act as wadding, then the cannonball. Prime the powder hole, and he was ready to fire.

His firing had woken up the whole camp and packs of children stood around, fascinated to see the machines in action.

'Mr, can we help?'

'No.' They could watch, but that was all.

Fulke loosed another salvo before William Kett appeared, accompanied by another man.

'Morning, Mr William,' said Fulke to his employer.

William Kett looked tired.

'Fulke, stop that,' said William.

The distant streets remained quiet; people preferring to take their chances indoors than meet a cannonball head on. The church bells started to peel, a continuous chorus of ringing to warn the inhabitants of an imminent attack, and to summon the off-duty militiamen to join their comrades at their posts.

'Fulke, this here is Miles, a former gunner in the king's royal army.'

Fulke mumbled a half-hearted greeting and carried on.

'Fulke, stop what you are doing right this moment. I am placing these cannon in the care of Miles.'

'They're mine,' said Fulke, furiously, and stood his ground, stick in hand.

How dare you take them away from me? If it weren't for me, you wouldn't have anything but pitchforks to fight with, he thought.

'My brother and I are grateful for your efforts in securing the cannon. We have limited powder and shot and therefore need to make the most of them. It is practical to see that they are commanded by the most skilled man available.'

Fulke clenched his jaw. He looked at Miles, who was taller than Fulke and just as broad. His forehead looked too big for his face. He returned Fulke's stare without flinching. This man would be no pushover.

'Being as you're here, you may assist Miles during the attack today, but for now, cease the barrage, it is pointless. You're no more a nuisance to the enemy than a mosquito is to a bull, and we need the shot for some proper fighting later,' said William, concluding the matter.

'As you wish,' said Fulke.

He returned the cannonball to the pile and folded his arms across his chest. He begrudged the return of this hierarchy, but the promise of proper fighting to follow was a consolation he would accept, for now.

'In the meantime, you men find some breakfast. You're going to need it today.'

*

Their target was the gatehouse over Bishopsgate Bridge. The gatehouse was well within range, but it sat in the shadow of the escarpment, and they couldn't point the barrels low enough to hit the tower. At the angle required to fire downhill, the cannonball would roll gently out of the barrel before the shot could be fired.

The iron barrel of the cannon sat in a wooden cradle, on four small wooden wheels, and wasn't easy to move. Fulke now invited John Robertson, Alfred's neighbour from Hethersett, to assist. He was strong and could handle himself in a fight. They were assigned twenty other men, under Miles's command. Fulke appointed himself second in command and was happy to wait for Miles to make a hash of things so he could take over the reins. They manoeuvred their two cannon down from the heath, followed by the powder barrels, balls and other apparatus. Their progress was slow. Carefully they inched their way down the gulley that led from the heath to the river. Two men held each cannon to prevent it rolling downhill.

As they approached the treeline, Fulke could make out Cow Tower, the tower that stood in the bend of the river. He could see the archers at the top.

They shoved the cannon left, keeping tight to the side of the gulley. It was a few more paces before they could slip into the trees at the base of the escarpment slope. Fulke heaved his weight into the second cannon, together with John and another man on each side. As they pushed one of the wooden wheels stopped, stuck against a large flint. John moved forward and knelt down to dislodge the flint.

'It's jammed, push the cannon back.'

The two lads at the front pushed, and John knocked the flint clear.

'Now, move on.'

Whoosh.

The two men in front slumped forward and fell to the ground, arrows in their backs. Fulke heard the cries of agony from other men in their party. He glanced behind and saw fallen men writhing in pain on the ground. His cannon started to roll. Unable to hold it, Fulke felt it slip between his fingers. Before it could gather any momentum, its carriage wedged itself against bodies of the two fallen men in front. Fulke leant sideways to check it would hold. He saw a man's lifeless face staring back at him, as blood trickled from the man's mouth.

Miles shouted, 'Take cover behind the trees.'

Fulke did as he was told and sought refuge behind the nearest oak tree, his back pressed against the bark. John Robertson and another man up-ended the powder barrels so they wouldn't roll downhill.

Whoosh. The next wave of arrows arrived. One struck his tree with a sickening crack. The man helping John Robertson was struck in the face, fell back and released the powder barrel. John scrambled to reach it, in vain, instead, forced to watch it roll away down the gulley.

Fulke looked on in horror as the small hogshead barrel bounced down the slope and rolled into the river with a splash.

John scrambled for the cover of the trees.

Fulke poked his head around the tree. Another volley of arrows thudded into the ground. Everybody was safe, for now, but they were also trapped, pinned down by the archers. Both cannon were stranded a few feet away on the edge of the gulley at the mercy of the archers' arrows. The last remaining powder barrel was exposed. Fulke counted six corpses lying on the gulley floor. Another man, an arrow in his leg, crawled desperately for the cover of the trees. That left sixteen men to recover the cannons. Fulke looked up the slope in front of him. He could make out men huddling behind the trees.

Fulke took another peek towards the tower. He reckoned it was three hundred yards away. He saw a glint of light and pulled his head back, as he felt the impact of another arrow hitting the tree, others landed silently and harmlessly into the ground, their long shanks burying themselves into the soft loamy soil.

Fulke composed himself.

A party of boys, no older than ten, appeared from nowhere, creeping through the undergrowth. They must have been watching the cannon descend from the top of the slope. They rushed around and gathered up the fallen arrows that were reusable. The children, too young or small to fight, must have been tasked with gathering the enemy's spent arrows, he realised.

The rebels had archers, but precious few arrows.

Fulke overheard Miles saying, 'We're pinned down. We need shelter to move the cannons. Doors would be ideal. Anything big enough to hide behind and thick enough to stop an arrow. Two inches minimum. Send archers to cover us.'

With handfuls of arrows the children scarpered up the slope with Miles' message.

Miles called out, 'Can everyone hear me?'

There was an assortment of confirmations. Fulke stayed silent.

Miles continued, 'Once we have cover, we'll push the cannon into the trees. We want the barrels pointing towards the gatehouse. From this distance, we can hit the bridge once we have clear sight of it. The only archers we need to worry about are those in the tower opposite. Stay out of their sight. If they can't see you, they can't hit you. Understood?'

When everybody had acknowledged this, Miles reassured them, 'Stay hidden. We'll be fine. They won't leave their defences.'

Fulke noticed how calm the gunner Miles remained. He wasn't short of breath. He was able to think clearly. He knew what to do.

Fulke reminded himself that he would be the same given the opportunity to fight like a professional soldier. Fulke couldn't help feeling a little relieved to know that. He didn't see himself as easily scared but facing an arrow storm for the first time had unsettled him. He looked at the two dead bodies slumped in front of the first cannon. One moment they had been alive, conscious, full of thoughts and desires, the next they were dead.

I'd rather look a man in the eye, thought Fulke. Better than being shot in the back: a fool's death.

After what seemed like an age, Fulke heard voices. Men emerged with six wooden doors evidently from Surrey House. Behind them came a posse of archers, at least fifty. Fulke recognised the man at the front. He had red hair and pox scars. It was the man who had shot the Sheriff's horse when they camped at Bowthorpe marsh, John Cooper.

Cooper was calling out orders as he ran. Once again, the fearful whoosh announced another volley of arrows from Cow Tower. They had targets again. Fulke saw an archer hit in the arm, he shrieked in pain and dropped his bow.

Miles pointed. 'In front of the cannon. We move while you shelter us.'

Once the doors were in place, he shouted, 'Right lads, as we were, move the cannon.'

As instructed, Fulke bolted and took his place behind the lead cannon. He heard the whack of arrows hitting the doors. They heaved, and the cannon started to roll, resuming their progress until at last they reached the cover of the trees. They cannons slowed as they sunk into the soil, but they had shelter and were obscured by the trees.

John Cooper's archers now poured forth using the trees as cover. As soon as the next volley of enemy arrows landed, they stepped clear and loosed fifty arrows in return.

Fulke couldn't see if they hit their target, but everybody cheered, relieved to be returning fire.

The defenders fired another volley, but fewer arrows landed this time. The rebel archers stepped clear of their trees. In one motion they drew back their bowstrings, but before they could release them there was another whoosh. Ten rebels archers fell to the ground, tricked into thinking they were safe.

Cooper shouted, 'Watch it lads, no more volleys.'

They took cover.

The cannons crept closer to the bridge. The archers' exchanges were now limited to the occasional arrow aimed at a careless rebel in plain sight.

Miles set the cannons in position behind the cover of the

doors. Illuminated by the morning sun stood the gatehouse, two hundred yards away. From their position on the treeline it was now directly in their line of fire.

Miles adjusted the pitch of the cannons.

'Load,' he ordered.

Fulke and Miles lowered their burning tapers to the powder holes. Bang. Bang. Two lead balls were fired. They overshot, clearing the top of the gatehouse and smashing into the roof of the house beyond.

'Too high,' confirmed Miles before the thud of arrows hit the doors sheltering their position.

Miles raised the tail end of the cannon by two inches and propped it in place with a stone.

Fulke followed his lead.

'Load.'

Miles gave the order to fire. A short fizz, an almighty bang, white smoke. This time, they hit. One ball glanced off the front facia, and the other caught the corner of the crenulations. The rebels cheered.

'Load,' ordered Miles, sounding composed.

Between them, they discharged another six cannonballs, four of which hit the top of the gatehouse. They had half a keg of powder and nine cannonballs left. They had to make their shots count. John Robertson carried the next cannonball and lifted it into place at the end of the Fulke's barrel. There was a brief whistling noise, then a boom and John disappeared. All around them, the trees shattered. The wooden doors smashed with splinters flying in all directions. Fulke flinched as he tried to extract a shard of wood buried in his arm.

The two men holding up the door that served to protect his cannon screamed, their faces and torsos were shredded, blood pouring from their wounds.

John lay limp on the ground, his face a pulp of bloodied flesh.

Fulke looked through the smoke and the trees. On the meadow behind Cow Tower he saw white smoke clearing.

He counted six cannons being reloaded.

'Oh, Christ.'

'Lads, quick, turn the cannon to our right,' commanded Miles.

The young boys scarpered back uphill to safety, closely followed by the archers retreating from the firing line.

'Wait!' barked Fulke. 'Cooper, you coward, come back.'

They didn't look back. The gun crews were on their own.

'They're reloading,' said Fulke, watching the city cannon on the meadow.

'Move your cannon, Fulke,' barked Miles.

Fulke rushed to the front, ready to lift the barrel and swing it around.

'Fulke, don't touch the barrel, you'll burn yourself.'

Miles looked calm. He spoke directly to Fulke as if nothing had happened.

'You have to move it from the rear.'

Miles, with the aid of another man, inched his cannon backwards and forwards. Fulke copied, helped by a man who stepped in to take John Robertson's place. Together they pointed their gun in the direction of the meadow, their barrel positioned against the side of a nearby tree trunk. Fulke sheltered behind the thin trunk, and his partner went to recover the cannonball John had dropped. Another volley of arrows struck, and Fulke's partner screamed as he was hit in the shoulder. There was another hiss.

Six more cannonballs bounced past them. There was a cry from Miles' partner as he fell. A ball had bounced in front of him, travelled up and hit his shin. He lay toppled on the ground, the white tips of his shin bones poking through his breeches.

Fulke's partner struggled to his feet, his right arm hung limp, the arrow stuck in his shoulder. With his left hand he dropped the cannonball into the muzzle. Fulke heard it roll into place.

'You're good to go,' said the loader. He collapsed to the floor and crawled to the safety of the nearest tree.

'Right, Fulke, let 'em have it.'

It was time to light the powder hole.

Where was his taper? He must have dropped it. There was now an almighty bang, and the shock of it nearly knocked him off his feet. Miles had fired. On the meadow, Fulke could see people running.

The ball fell short.

Miles moved over. He checked Fulke's cannon and touched his taper to the hole. Nothing happened. Fulke had forgotten to charge the powder hole. Miles took his powder bag, looked again into the distance, poured a measure of powder into the hole, moved his hand clear and blew on his taper, which glowed orange. He touched it to the powder hole. Boom. Through the smoke, the two men watched the ball smash into the wooden footings of middle cannon, shattering its carriage. The cannon slumped to the side, the barrel pointing harmlessly down toward the ground.

Fulke cried out with joy, 'Got ya!'

'One down. Load up, Fulke.'

More arrows struck the trees and ground around them, one lodged into the wheel of Fulke's cannon.

The men returning to the enemy cannon were exposed in the meadow. Last night the city cannon had been positioned around the higher ground of the castle keep. They must have moved them in the night, thought Fulke. Fulke cursed all the time they'd wasted waiting for shelters. If the Ketts knew what they were bloody doing, they would have thought this through and made preparations.

Now they were trapped, outgunned five to two.

Miles fired both cannon.

Again, their enemy scattered unharmed. Fulke waited impatiently while someone emptied powder into the cannon's muzzle, another man stood ready with a cannonball.

'Fulke, look for your taper,' ordered Miles.

As he looked about he heard shouts in the distance, 'Cease fire, cease fire.'

Two men with white flags ran down the gulley towards the river.

'What the devil are you doing?' Fulke shouted toward the heath above.

He spat in their direction. People would call him a coward. He may have been terrified, but that was no reason to surrender. They had better positions, more cover, a better rate of fire.

'Kett, you coward,' he shouted in vain.

'Fulke, let's move these cannon back now,' said Miles.

'Why the hell are we surrendering?'

'We aren't. If we stay here, we'll lose these cannon. They're buying us time. Let's get them to safety.'

Miles seemed very certain of himself. How did he know that without being told? Perhaps it was tactical, but Fulke didn't like the thought of going back up to the heath with his tail between his legs. Miles shouted for help. The remainder of the gun party assembled. Together they pushed and heaved the cannons back up to the safety of the heath.

*

Jan pumped his fist at the sight of the two white flags coming towards him. He'd stationed himself in the most strategically vital position at the top of the gatehouse, grimly aware this would draw the bulk of the enemy's fire. Fearing a charge, he'd posted twenty archers on the top of the gatehouse, as many as he could fit. Those that had survived the initial bombardment were cowering on the floor. Jan's eyes strained to see through the distant trees. The rebel cannon appeared to be retreating up the gulley to the heath.

'Their cannon are withdrawing,' he announced.

There was a small and unconvincing cheer from his dazed militia as they got to their feet. Now he had a moment's respite, his first priority was their casualties and to survey the damage. For most of his men stationed at the top of the gatehouse, the worst they had suffered was minor cuts and grazes. They were serviceable. Jan ordered them to tidy the rubble on the floor. He didn't want them tripping over if the rebels returned.

Some of his men had not been so lucky; sustaining serious injuries. One man cupped his eyes with his hands, blinded by flying masonry. Another lay flat, knocked unconscious when the ramparts in front of him suffered a direct hit and exploded in his face. Worst of all was Jan's deputy, James, the wheelwright. He had caught a cannonball full in the chest. It had knocked him back into four others behind him, flattening them all. James had ended up laying on top of his stunned friends, shaking and juddering as he fought to hold onto life. Jan had never heard noises like that coming from the human body, not even at hangings. Once James' tremors had stopped, and he'd slipped into the afterlife, Jan had thrown his body over the side into the river below. He'd needed to clear some space and preferred his men not to have to stare at their dead friend.

No sooner had James' corpse splashed into the water than Jan realised his mistake. Men not used to battle didn't fancy their sacrifice being rewarded by a watery burial without prayer, and James' fate had sent the archers into a panic. Three men had rushed for the spiral staircase that led to the guard room underneath. The third man lost his footing at the top and fell. He tumbled on top of the first two men as they descended the narrow stone stairs. Together they ended up in a pile on the floor of the guardroom. Jan threatened the rest with flogging and hanging to get them to stay. He apologised and promised none of them would suffer the same treatment as James. The men stayed put but made no attempt to conceal their contempt.

Jan descended the narrow staircase and assessed the fallen men's injuries. Between them a sprained ankle, three broken bowstring fingers and the other unharmed beyond some bruising.

'That's what you get for running away. Get back up to your posts,' barked Jan.

'But my fingers are broken?' protested one of them.

Jan's temper surged. He drew his knife. 'I'll cut your fingers off unless you're back up those stairs.'

The archer avoided Jan's glare, got to his feet and followed his brethren cowards back upstairs to the battlements.

Their attempted escape would have been in vain. From the guardroom, the staircase continued down to the street level, where Jan had had the good foresight to lock the door at the bottom. There was no flight from the gatehouse.

The men garrisoning the guardroom above the gate were unharmed. They were covered in a layer of dust, but their defences were intact. They were the lucky few, able to hide behind the walls and fire their arrows through the loopholes.

A man was stationed at each of the four narrow slits in the wall, with another in reserve to pass more arrows. They could alternate and rest their arms and backs from the strain of repeatedly firing their longbows.

Jan told them to quench their thirst from the barrel of rainwater in the corner then return to their posts and ready for a counter attack.

Downstairs, he stepped outside, locking the wooden door behind him. The church bells sounded noon. The street was bright but eerily quiet. Norwich was closed for business. Everybody was hiding in their homes. Those that hadn't were lined up ready to fight. The only things out of place were some cracked wooden roof tiles laying in the street.

More archers and men at arms were stationed behind the earth ramparts on either side of the gatehouse. Last night they had dug a series of defensive trenches in the cow meadows and orchards that formed Norwich's eastern boundary. At best, all the ditches would do was slow a rebel advance. The defensive bank that flanked the gatehouse for a hundred yards along the riverbank in both directions was shoulder height, so hardly formidable, but it provided a hasty shield behind which a thin line of archers and swordsman were stationed.

From his vantage point, Jan reckoned he had barely five hundred men defending each side. Far fewer than the mayor had promised. What was wrong with the townspeople? Did they not want to defend their homes?

He didn't understand the English sometimes.

Having inspected his defences there was little else Jan could do. The cannon on the meadow had done their job, halting the rebel approach. From the other side of the gatehouse, Jan heard someone calling, 'Open up.'

Jan ran to the locked gates and peeped through the open

Judas hole. The bridge was covered in large a spoil heap to impede the rebels. He could see a white flag poking over the top of the earth.

'It's open, you're safe,' he called out.

A rebel scrambled over the top of the earth barricade and met Jan at the gate. He was in his twenties, reckoned Jan, with blond hair. Behind him came another younger man. Both appeared unarmed.

'State your business,' asked Jan.

'My name is Peter, an employee of Mr Kett. I come as an emissary to seek peace.'

'Well you'll need to speak to somebody more important than me for that.'

'Where is the mayor?' asked Peter.

Jan pointed up the street and sent the rebels towards the guildhall. An hour passed before the two rebels returned, their flags waving high for all to see.

'What's the verdict?' asked Jan.

The blonde man replied. 'Well you're not backing down, and so I expect you'll be seeing us again shortly.'

Jan grunted. He'd feared as much.

'Good luck,' said Peter as he passed through the gate back into no man's land, followed by his younger companion.

Jan closed the gate.

As the younger of the two reached the top of the mound blocking the bridge, he turned and faced the defenders. 'For every man you have here we have ten more. You will be overrun in no time. Save yourselves, return to your homes.'

An arrow loosed from the top of the gatehouse struck him in the chest. The young rebel collapsed, falling down the other side of the soil heap.

Dead.

'What's wrong with you? Can't you see the white flag?' shouted the rebel named Peter.

'Cease firing,' shouted Jan, 'Let him leave.'

At least it was one less to fight.

*

The rebels now descended from the heath. Remaining behind the treeline, they ran fast between the trees. There were thousands of them.

It had started.

Let's get this over with.

'Take aim,' said Jan.

A fleeting moment passed before he issued the order to fire.

A thousand arrows made a spine curdling whirr as they flew across the river, before coming to land amongst the trees at the foot of the embankment.

Rebels dropped to the floor. They were soon overtaken by hundreds more.

'Let them have it,' shouted Jan.

Another volley of arrows thumped into the rebel line. More men fell. Jan could hear the screams of men dying in agony. In no time the rebels were opposite his position and taking cover behind the trees and in the craters left by the chalk mines that pockmarked the face of the embankment.

The city cannon fired. Six cannonballs smashed into the rebel front line, producing chaos and terror.

Jan shouted to the men.

'Fire to the front. Keep them away from the bridge.'

There was another hiss. The man next to Jan fell backwards, an arrow lodged in his forehead. An arrowed sailed straight past Jan's head. He ducked. The rebels weren't firing in ranks. They're firing randomly, trying to keep us pinned down, he realised.

He stole a glance over the top of the tower. The earthwork bank had absorbed many arrows. A few of the archers behind it had been hit, and he counted five bodies, then another dropped as he watched.

'Keep firing,' he yelled.

Jan heard a cry.

Thousands of men were now pouring out of the woods, screaming bloody murder as they ran.

Jesus, thought Jan, taking the saviour's name in vain. I hope we have enough arrows to flatten this lot.

'Keep firing. Let them have it,' he shouted.

The defenders were crouching behind their bank.

Jan cursed their cowardice. 'On your feet, you dogs, fire your bows,' he shouted.

They couldn't hear him, the rebels war cries drowned out Jan's orders. He stretched out over the edge of his fortification. 'Fight back, you cowards!'

Below, nobody moved. Jan felt a searing pain across the top of his shoulder. Dazed, he collapsed on the floor. He tried to move, pain seared through his body. His tunic was turning red.

He was hit.

*

Alfred peered out from behind the tree before the next wave of arrows peppered the air around him. Behind him a small boy wailed in pain as he stared in horror at the shaft of ash buried in his forearm. Alfred tried to take his mind off the boy's screams. Not wanting to accompany his father-in-law with the Hethersett men, he'd elected to join those from

Wymondham for the attack. They were happy to have every extra man they could. William Kett and Luke Miller had briefed them on the plan of attack. Even to Alfred's unseasoned ears, it had seemed simple in the extreme. The plan relied on the rebels' superior numbers to overwhelm the defences at the closest point, the bridge.

Alfred, Fulke, Master Peter, Luke Miller, David Fisher, Adam Catchpole, Geoffrey Lincoln and the other Wymondham men had run the gauntlet through the trees at the base of the escarpment, past the bridge, to their rendezvous point opposite the end of the earth ramparts shielding the city's defenders on the far side of the gatehouse. Here they would cross the river precisely where Alfred had done Mr Kett's laundry with Tiniker's help. Alfred crouched down, panting heavily.

All that remained was to cross the open ground, navigate the river and overwhelm the defenders. A battle cry went up, as the men from Attleborough and Hingham charged directly at the bridge. The abundance of moving targets approaching the gatehouse had the effect of drawing the arrow fire away from the trees.

Alfred poked his head round. The view offered no respite from the screaming boy behind. To his right, rebels ran down the slope like water in a rainstorm. The enemy couldn't fire quickly enough. In no time the rebels were at the bridge and scaling the spoil heap. Their bodies littered the approach to the bridge; arrows stuck out from the ground like spines on a hedgehog. The screams of the wounded turned Alfred's blood cold. He'd never seen so many men die at once. It was chilling. He wanted to count the bodies, but there were too many. To his left, David Fisher panted, staring wide-eyed at the scene before them. David wasn't a violent man, and Alfred doubted he'd ever had a fight in his life.

Alfred hadn't slept well last night, worried about what today would bring.

Some will live, some will die, according to Mr Kett.

Alfred had wondered what fate had in store for him as he lay on the kitchen flagstones, staring into the darkness, waiting for sleep, yet not wanting to miss what may be his final hours alive. In the early hours, he wondered again and again if today would be the day he met his parents in the afterlife or if would he be seeking out Tiniker after the battle. Nothing he could think of made it any clearer, and yet that was all he could think about: his life would hang on the turn of a card or the roll of a dice. Win or bust. He resolved that he would fight as hard as he was able, overcome his fear and do his duty as best he could. That small honour was a much as he knew he could affect. With that small crumb of comfort he slid into a fitful sleep shortly before dawn.

'Fulke!'

Although he had been an irritant of late, Alfred took comfort in seeing his friend pop out behind David Fisher, a meat cleaver in his hand and a look of bloody murder on his face. 'Where the hell are they? What's taking them so long?'

Then came Geoffrey Lincoln, Adam Catchpole, Master Peter and Luke Miller. The Kett brothers weren't amongst the first wave of attackers, and Luke Miller was in charge of the Wymondham men. Between them they had sickles, knives and hatchets. None had bows. Alfred was handy with a bow but as yet hadn't got his hands on one. He hoped to pick one up from a dead man. Otherwise, his weapon was a blunt knife he'd taken from the kitchen and an axe handle he'd found in the house.

The rebel archers took positions behind the trees. Their first volley pinned the defenders behind their earth wall. The city cannon boomed.

'Right boys,' shouted Luke. 'I want as much blood spilt today as you can.'

Alfred frowned. Luke's instruction seemed at odds with Mr Kett's wishes.

Luke continued: 'We charge on the count of three.'

This was it. Alfred made the sign of the cross.

'*Three*,' shouted Luke.

Alfred waited, shaking like a man with a fever.

'Two.'

Time slowed down. He thought of his dead parents, his wicked step-family and then Tiniker. I'll see you tonight, he thought with a flare of affection.

'One!'

Together they roared so loudly that the hairs on Alfred's neck stood on end. The moment he moved clear of his tree and stepped into the open, he felt as alert, calm and alive as he'd ever experienced. His nerves vanished, and he ran with all his strength straight toward their enemy, roaring from the bottom of his lungs.

Men he'd spent his ordinary life with, were today doing something extraordinary, as they ran together like an army. Fulke's stumpy frame pounded forward, his cleaver raised, ready to chop. Even David Fisher looked like a lion in for a kill as he charged down the slope to the river. Heads appeared above the ramparts on the other side.

The tips of their longbows emerged and raised as the defenders pulled back their bowstrings, one by one they rose above the mound ready to fire.

This is it.

Alfred powered his way towards the threat. He saw a defender on the far side looking at him, taking aim, and he saw a sliver of wood speed towards him. He felt a small gust of air past his right cheek. It had missed. He lived, for now.

To his right, he heard a retching noise. He glanced over and saw David Fisher fall, blood spurting from the arrow buried in his throat. To his left, more screams. He didn't look. Over Alfred's head a volley of rebel arrows returned fire, destined for the defenders. The man who'd shot at him was hit, the arrow landing square in his forehead. His head snapped back and disappeared from view. All the defenders behind the bank disappeared from sight, hiding behind the earth.

Alfred reached the water's edge and made for the shallows. He heard the splashes of men barrelling their way into the river. He waded as quickly as he could, the water rising above his legs, and his waist as he lost his footing. He fell forward, put out his left leg and stopped himself from toppling. At the halfway point the water was no deeper than his armpits. On the far bank, the earth ramparts loomed. In front an archer was felled by a rebel arrow. His body bent forward, toppled down the rampart and landed on the riverbank. The bow fell into the river, but now the string was wet, it would be no good for this fight.

Alfred reached the far side and crouched down beneath the rampart.

Fulke stooped beside him.

'David Fisher?'

'Dead.'

Adam and Geoffrey arrived safely across. Adam grinned like a man who'd won a prize at the fayre. On the bank they had come from, children left the cover of the trees and scurried forward to recover the spent arrows amongst the fallen rebels.

Luke, sickle in hand, shouted, 'Men, let's finish this.'

Rather than scaling the rampart, he now ran to its extremity and shouted a blood-curdling cry as he rounded the end of the earth bank to face the defenders. Alfred squeezed the grip of his knife in his left hand. This was about to get grim. He'd never killed a man before. Fulke roared, and Alfred followed him and Luke, his axe handle held high behind his head.

Alfred saw Luke knock the bow from a man's hand and barge into the next man. Beyond them, stretching to the bridge was a long line of folk facing forwards.

Fulke charged and brought his cleaver down to meet a defender's neck. His victim fell to the ground. Fulke pulled his weapon free and moved on to the next in line.

Alfred ran up the inside slope of the rampart, the soil shifting beneath his feet, he passed Luke and Fulke ready to attack.

Before him stood an older man in a faded woollen hood that covered his head and shoulders. The face it framed had a look of terror and determination. His bow was drawn, the arrow tip pointed at Alfred. The defender pulled his bowstring back the final two inches, and Alfred lifted his axe handle ready to swing. As the man's two fingers released the string, Alfred lunged, and his weight shifted, the spoil of the earth defences giving way under his foot. He tumbled forward as the fletching of the arrow glanced against his cheek. The slip had saved his life. The determination on the old man's face vanished, leaving only terror, as he dropped his bow to surrender his hands and beg for mercy.

Alfred snarled and swung his axe handle into his head, knocking the man down.

Fulke trampled over Alfred's fallen opponent, and sliced his cleaver down the side of the next defender's bow stave, slicing the man's fingers from his hand as his blade fell.

The man screamed in pain as the bow fell to the ground.

Luke yelled with rage as he flanked round and swung his sickle at the next man in line. He missed, and the defender raised his sword ready to bring down on Luke's head. He's had it, thought Alfred, as he leapt forward and drove his kitchen knife into the man's guts. After a moment's resistance, the blade slid forward deep into his stomach, his head and shoulders buckled forward, the air driven from his mouth, followed by blood. Alfred stood still, holding his weight on his knife close enough to smell the man's final breath. Alfred pushed him over, drawing his blade from his stomach. Alfred's first kill. A feeling of power surged through his body to his fingers and toes. Alfred roared, as alive as the other man was dead. Luke nodded at Alfred, the simplicity of the gesture somehow more than enough to acknowledge the enormity of Alfred's quick thinking.

Behind them, more men poured around the flank of the ramparts, yelling their battle cries. In front, the first of the rebels appeared at the top of the earth bank, only to be felled by arrows. They were immediately overtaken as more men climbed the ramparts and poured into the defenders' line. The rebels' superior numbers began to pay as streams of men descended over the top. Alfred surveyed their advance, for the first time, confident they could win. He picked up the sword of man he'd just killed, charged forward and hacked at the next man in the line. The defender ducked, and Alfred's sword glanced off his back. He swung his sword in reply. Alfred stepped back, and its point sliced harmlessly in front of him before its tip lodged in the earth bank. Alfred kicked the blade, forcing the hilt to fly up out of the boy's hands. Seeing his weapon lost, the boy began to raise his hands in surrender. Alfred lunged forward, driving his sword point into the boy's ribs. His face filled with terror as he realised he was meeting death. Alfred roared into the dying boy's face.

Next to him, Fulke swung his cleaver into another man's head. Together they moved forward. The faces of the defenders betrayed what was now plain to see: they were about to be slaughtered. Sensing their fate they turned and ran, a line of people running for their lives, back to the safety of their homes. Alfred swung his sword. He missed and gave up the chase. The rebels cheered at the sight of their foe fleeing across the meadows towards the cathedral. Alfred ran back and scrambled to the top of the rampart. He held his arms up and yelled with the full force of his lungs. The relief of surviving, the thrill of battle tore through his body.

He turned and surveyed the scene around him.

*

Jan watched through the embrasure. He shouted down, ordering his men to turn and fight, his voice too weak to be heard. The shaft of the arrow protruded out from his shoulder, stuck against his collar bone, poking clear through his back. He'd left it in place, not wanting to lose more blood. The right side of his tunic was soaked, but the wound had sealed around the arrow. He moved, wincing in pain.

'We're being overrun!' warned one of his men.

'Shoot them,' he mumbled with as much force as he could muster. His body weighed a ton, though his head was light. He gritted his teeth. He had to fight on.

'We need more arrows,' shouted another one of his defenders. 'I only have five left.'

Jan picked a path through the bodies that littered the roof of his gatehouse. They'd lost six men to rebel arrows. At the top of the stairs, he yelled down for more arrows to be brought up. He took the place of fallen man, filling the gap in the line at the front of the gatehouse. To either side his men fired arrows at the rebels pinned down behind the earth dumped on the bridge. Those that had made it over banged on the gate beneath. Their thuds shuddered through the gatehouse. They wouldn't be able to beat the door down, but they were close.

Jan could see in the faces of his remaining men that the rebel presence below, their banging, shouting and threats, was undermining the defenders' confidence.

They began to reposition themselves, to concentrate their arrows between the gatehouse and Cow Tower.

The children had cleared the field of spent arrows, re-supplying their own archers, a group of thirty, gathered near the treeline opposite the bridge.

Suddenly they turned and dropped their breeches. They bent forward and bared their arses. They swung from side to side and bounced up and down, their pale buttocks, a mocking insult of their impending victory.

Bile rose in Jan's mouth. He'd show those filthy creatures. The fight was not lost. The gate would hold. He had to win the left flank.

'Men,' he shouted, 'everybody fire to the left, give it everything you have.'

'We need more arrows,' shouted one of his men.

Jan looked around. The only arrows he could see were those stuck in his fallen militiamen.

'Lads, we're beat, time to save ourselves,' said the defender closest to the stairs, as he disappeared down into the gatehouse guardroom. The others exchanged glances, dropped their bows and followed their mates down.

'*Sorry*,' said the last one to go.

'Get back here. Fight, you cowards.'

Jan was alone at the top of the gatehouse.

He picked up a bow and arrow from the floor and took position on the left side. Streams of rebels crossed the river and scaled his makeshift fortifications. Jan watched as his left flank crumbled, in small groups they dashed back across the meadow, chased by the rebels. The cannon crews abandoned their guns to flee back to the cover of the city.

'Fight. Damn you, English.'

Livid at their betrayal, Jan held out the bow in his left arm. He wanted somebody important, Mr Kett, Captain Mischief himself, perhaps.

Unable to recognise anybody of authority, he put the arrow to his bow, the string to the notch behind its goose feathers. He would make this shot count. He yelled in agony as he struggled to pull the string with his right hand.

The English made it look so easy. He tried once more.

His arms shook with pain.

Searching for a target, he settled on a young man with dark hair standing on top of the rampart, his arms raised, his sword in the air.

Jan closed his left eye and took aim.

From the corner of his eye, he saw an archer on the far bank looking at him. The archer drew back his bowstring. Jan changed his aim, pulled as hard as he could and looked down the arrow shaft at his target. Their eyes met. Jan could make out the man's features, red hair, smallpox scars, freckled skin, Jan watched the man release his string.

Jan did the same, the string scuffed against his fingertips, and his shoulder stung with the jolt of the bow's tensions being released.

Jan saw a streak of movement headed in his direction. He felt a warm sting in his neck. The arrow entered above his outstretched arm and lodged itself at the base of his throat. He fell back, his head thumped against the stone floor, his view turned blue, his hands and feet relaxed, his body went limp, his pain faded.

He thought of Tiniker and Margreet.

He wanted to tell them he loved them.

So close, he thought, to a new life, riches, now slipping through his fingers. Jan gave up his fight and succumbed to death's soft embrace.

28

Robert, Alice and William stood hand in hand on the edge of the heath outside Surrey House.

Their hopes rose as at last their men came into view down below as they entered the river, turning it white with splashing. They watched as the distant figures swarmed the far bank. A moment later the city's defenders were fleeing under the weight of the attack. Robert shook both his fists in the air before he embraced his brother. Alice squeezed his hand and kissed him on the cheek.

'We've done it.' Robert felt overjoyed.

With the bridge taken, the city was again open to them. They would be able to eat once more.

'Robert, we better get down there before these lot run riot. Our cause won't be well served if the city is razed.'

Robert looked at Alice. 'Don't feel you have to come, Alice, if you'd rather stay…'

'I was thinking,' she interrupted, 'there are plenty of women left in the camp, they'll all be worried about their husbands, perhaps I should accompany them down so they can be reunited.'

'Good idea.'

'Some may also need some comfort for their losses,' she added.

Robert nodded and squeezed her hand. They hugged, and she went into the camp to round up the women. The two brothers headed for the gulley.

The camp looked almost deserted. As Robert walked he felt his shoulders drop. If their attack had been repulsed, his adopted cause would have faltered and collapsed. If the consequences of failure for him personally weren't so dire, he might have been relieved to leave the heath for good. Now they had all but captured Norwich, the government would be forced to negotiate.

Once he got around a table with them, he could thrash out a deal and talk his way out of trouble.

'Robert, what are you going to say?' asked William as the rounded the corner at the top of the gulley.

Robert wasn't sure. It occurred to him they had spent so much time planning the attack, they'd neglected to plan for the aftermath.

'It's no good winning the war only to lose the peace.'

'Fine words, brother,' said Robert. 'It's a fair walk from here. We've got time to plan it now.'

As they reached the treeline, they passed a body — an arrow buried in his heart.

'Poor bugger,' said Robert as he stopped to look at the body, a boy, probably no older than thirteen. Robert shook his head. 'I don't want to leave him here, but…'

'Robert, I think you better take a look at this,' said William, his gaze fixed ahead across the slope that led to the river.

Robert rushed up. His mouth fell open. The ground was littered with his followers, slaughtered, the grass red with their blood. Already a muster of carrion crows hopped about the ground, deciding which bodies to strip of their flesh.

'Help me,' cried an injured man.

'William.' Robert stood frozen.

Neither had seen so much death in one place. Across the battlefield came a chorus of coughing, spluttering, whimpers and cries as their fallen clung to life. Robert covered his nose. At the top of the slope, a group of young boys and a girl turned over a corpse, looting the body.

'Stop that, you brigands!' he shouted, incensed. They looked up, then ignoring him, carried on their search.

'The sun will cook them,' he realised, shaking his head.

'Help me!' came the repeated plea.

Robert found the man crying out as he tried in vain to crawl away, an arrow lodged in his hip. Robert knelt and placed his arm on his shoulder, toying with the idea of pulling out the arrow, but it was too deep.

'They shot me,' he mumbled.

Robert shushed him. 'Lay still, rest.'

'You're Kett aren't you,' the man realised, 'look what you've done, dead. Everybody. Dead.'

'You lay still. I'll get somebody to help you.' The man had lost a lot of blood, and Robert wasn't certain he'd live. He stood up while he considered what to do.

'Don't leave me,' begged the injured man.

Robert moved away. It was too much to bear.

'William, what should we do?'

'We have to keep moving. All hell could be breaking loose in Norwich.'

'Those bastards. I offered them a truce. All we wanted was food. This could have been prevented. So many dead.'

'Robert.' William took his brother by the arm. 'We need to go.'

'We can't let the women see this,' Robert said, 'my God,

we've got to stop them.'

William steered Robert away, cupping his elbow. They picked a path through the carnage. Robert now buckled over and vomited. As he spat on the ground, his eyes watered.

'What have I done?' he whispered.

'We will organise burials, and a proper service for the fallen,' his brother assured him.

Robert nodded. His brother was right. The dead could wait. First they must attend to the living.

They reached the bridge, blocked by the spoil heap, ten feet tall and a dozen corpses piled up, having fallen down the slope. The tangle of bodies made Robert's stomach lurch. They used their hands to scale the mound, then slid down the other side to find the gate open. Under the arch lay a uniformed soldier, his throat slit, a puddle of drying blood coated the stone floor. They stepped out from underneath the gatehouse.

'Stay where you are,' sounded an angry voice.

In the shadow of the doorway leading up to the guardroom was a soldier, brandishing his sword. He staggered forward, his movement uneasy, his face caked with dried blood. He looked hard into Robert's eyes, then William's, as he smirked and spat on the floor.

'Brothers, are you?'

Robert took a step backwards.

'The Kett brothers I'd say,' slurred the soldier, pointing his sword tip at Robert. 'Which one of you is Robert?'

'I am.'

'Get on your knees, Kett.'

29

As the bells of St Peter Mancroft tolled one, Mayor Codd was ripping up floorboards. The counting room of the guildhall was a box room where the city's tax receipts and cash reserves were held. When all of this was over, and he was questioned over the loss of the city, he could adequately claim that he had done his best to broker peace, but when faced with a superior and motivated force he was powerless to stop their capitulation. What he wouldn't be able to defend was the city's treasury falling into rebel hands. One small consolation of the low tax receipts of recent years and London's hunger for funds was that the city's reserves were at their lowest level in years, which just now meant fewer coins to hide.

He upended the large wooden chest and sent the coins spilling into the void between the ceiling below and the floorboards of the counting room. The fewer people who knew the location of the city's reserves the better. Mayor Codd intended to keep it a secret. He swept up the last of the coins that lay on the floorboards pushing them into the recess. He looked up to reach for the floorboard he had removed and nearly jumped out of his skin.

Watching him from the door of the counting room was Augustine Steward.

'Steward, you frightened the life out of me.' The mayor's nerves were already frayed.

'Sorry, mayor.'

'As you can see,' said Mayor Codd laying the floorboard back in place and reaching for the hammer, 'I've hidden our reserves, just in case.'

Steward cleared his throat, 'Very prudent. I assume the mayor knows how much he's buried? Wouldn't want any of it to go missing, would we?'

'Of course,' lied Mayor Codd, he hadn't had time for such precautions. I must hide the ledger books too, he realised. If one of the rebels can read, we'd have some questions to answer, he thought as he hammered the nails back into place. 'The less people that know, Steward, the better.'

'I quite agree. You never know who you can trust nowadays,' said Steward.

Mayor Codd grunted.

'I'm glad I've caught you, mayor. I have a proposal for you.'

Mayor Codd stood and began looking for the most recent ledger from the bookshelf. 'Go on. I'm listening.'

'Should the worst happen, I wish to remain free of your friend, Mr Kett's, clutches.'

'Quite why you think he's my friend I am not sure, but why would Kett agree to that?'

'Because if Kett captures Norwich, he will need somebody to administer the city for him. You have been at pains to stress his desire for peace, and I will help him, purely for the benefit of our inhabitants, you understand.'

'I'm not in any position to make you promises, Steward,' said the mayor as he selected the relevant ledger from the shelf and tucked it under his arm.

At the door, Steward blocked his exit with a cold stare and stale breath.

'If you don't keep me out of his captivity, you'll face charges of conspiracy and treachery.'

'Tosh,' dismissed the mayor, 'on what grounds?'

'You rode out in the dead of night to meet with Kett in secret. You must have been privy to his intentions and can be shown to have done little to hinder his progress since.'

Mayor Codd's eyes widened.

How did Steward know?

'Bowthorpe Marsh on the ninth of July. I had you followed,' said Steward.

'You bastard.' barked Mayor Codd.

'It pays to keep one's friends close.'

'Huh.' And one's enemies closer still, thought the mayor.

'I am sure Kett is a persuasive man, it would be understandable, although not forgivable, if you had come round to his way of thinking.'

'Steward, you defy words. At this time of crisis, how can posture for your own self-advancement…'

Steward interrupted him. 'Do we have an understanding, mayor?'

Mayor Codd eyed his opponent with contempt. 'We do,' he finally acquiesced.

'Excellent. Why don't we join the others in the chamber?'

Mayor Codd locked the door behind him and followed Steward back into the council chamber.

Flowerdew leant against the corner windowsill, checking for activity outside. The king's herald sat at the council table, stroking his chin as Steward took up his usual seat. Mayor Codd paced the room. The rest of the city's aldermen had stayed away, preferring the anonymity of their own homes.

The chamberlain entered the chamber and broke the silence. 'The cellars are locked. These are the only keys,' he said, before tucking them into the side vent of his gown.

They couldn't risk the guildhall's underground storerooms falling into rebels hands. That was where they kept the last of their munitions.

Mayor Codd nodded.

Flowerdew sprung to attention. 'There are people, in the marketplace, five of them.'

'Ours or theirs?' asked the mayor.

'Not sure.'

'It's hard to tell whose side people are on, mayor,' said Steward, looking at the herald.

'Wait, there's more,' reported Flowerdew.

Mayor Codd joined him at the window. Outside, streams of men poured into the marketplace. Yelling and waving their weapons in the air as they gathered around the market cross. More joined them from the side streets.

Watching their numbers swell, the mayor tried not to sound perturbed. 'It's the rebels. They're in.'

He now watched one of the rebels outside, point towards the guildhall, and his companion looked in their direction.

'Hang on to your heads, gentlemen, the mob are coming,' said Flowerdew.

The mayor's heart thumped in his chest. He turned to the chamberlain and double-checked, 'Is the entranceway locked?'

'Yes, your grace. And barred.'

'Herald, our city has fallen. What would your king propose we do now?' said Mayor Codd, unable to conceal his anger.

'*My* king, is he not your king also?' replied the herald.

'Take a look out of this window, you see for yourself what you've done.'

Banging came from downstairs.

'Gentlemen, they are at the door,' said the chamberlain.

Mayor Codd walked around the table and stood opposite the herald, his hand outstretched, inviting the herald to take charge.

The herald remained where he was.

'It's *your* city, mayor. I have no precedence here.'

The banging on the door below grew louder.

'I doubt very much that I do now, thanks to you.'

Flowerdew reported from the window, 'Hundreds of them. We're overrun.'

There was a loud smash. Shards of broken glass flew across the room. They all jumped. A sickle hung in the broken window, its blade caught in the lead of the diamond panes. Mayor Codd made the sign of the cross.

Below, the door started to creak.

30

The soldier swayed on his feet. Robert looked down the length of his sword, its point waving back and forth like a cat's tail and refused the soldier's invitation to fall to his knees. The soldier swung his sword, but he missed, lost his balance and fell to the floor. Robert trod on the sword blade, pinning it under his foot. The injured soldier, his red and yellow tunic coated in brick dust, appeared to give up.

He had nothing left.

'You killed my friends. You ought to die,' he slurred.

Robert stood over the soldier and held out his arms like a preacher. 'If I'd died, would it appease these people's concerns?'

The soldier groaned. 'They're dead. Because of you. You're a coward.'

Robert nodded. 'It sickens me that we live in a time when slaughter is necessary just so the ordinary man can be heard. A time when the fortunate few treat the common folk with such contempt. If you'd have killed me, there would be ten thousand angry people ready to take my place.'

The soldier closed his eyes. 'Then make sure you win, Kett. So this slaughter wasn't in vain.'

'Come on, Robert, we haven't got time for this,' said

William as he picked up his fallen sword.

The brothers walked up Bishopsgate side by side.

William spoke, 'From now on, neither of us travel in this city on our own. We're targets.'

Robert agreed. It dawned on him now, that in his quest to preserve the freedom of others, he had sacrificed his own.

They walked through the city, Robert working through in his head what he would say when he addressed his followers. The hard earth streets were quiet and deserted. An occasional broken window, a few arrows protruding from various walls, a dropped bow on the ground, were the only evidence of the fighting that had taken place. Down side streets they could hear small isolated scuffles as their forces took out their revenge on the defenders. The city streets narrowed as they approached the centre. In the area known as Tombland they passed a small party of rebels relieving a baker's shop of its bread. Such infractions were now inevitable. They had to concentrate on legitimising their control. As they neared the marketplace, they could hear the din of a mass of people. The victors were singing and chanting. The air buzzed with a mixture of elation and anger.

Pray, Mayor Codd is still alive, thought Robert.

Making their way into the crowds, pushing past people, the brothers found themselves in the impressive marketplace full of country folk, enclosed by three-storey timber buildings. Their pointed rooftops encircled the marketplace like the teeth of a dragon. The market stalls had been cleared of their produce. Some tipped over and scattered. Beyond the stalls loomed the church of St Peter Mancroft.

'Kett is here,' a voice rang out.

A moment later, he was met by a sea of smiling faces. His back was slapped, he was thanked, his arms held up for him. As the hysteria mounted, he felt himself lifted from the floor, his legs perched on the shoulders of two men he'd never met. He fought to keep his balance, briefly managing a wave, surrounded by a sea of faces. Amongst the thousands he glimpsed Alfred, Fulke, Anders Marshwell, others from dining room meetings and home in Wymondham. He felt like a conquering general as they carried him towards the porch of the guildhall. The grand knapped-flint building stood proud in the northwest corner of the marketplace. It was narrow like the nave of a church with windows to match. Its roof finished with crenulations giving it the pomp of a castle, to show off the city's strength and authority despite having its windows smashed, besieged by his mob.

In front, the crowds cleared a path.

'Make way for the great Mr Kett,' somebody shouted. 'Long live Kett. Kett for King. Kett, Kett, Kett.'

Robert gestured for silence, nearly losing his balance in the process. He had to grab the heads of those who carried him and a ripple of laughter spread through the nearby ranks.

'I think I better get down, my friend.'

They lowered him to the ground. 'Mr Kett, an honour to carry you, sir. You're a man as great as you are heavy!'

Robert laughed. 'Thank you, both.'

He arranged his clothing and turned to see William pushing his way through the crowd to join him. The people fell silent and stepped aside from the guildhall door.

Robert knocked on the door. Nothing. He knocked again.

'Is anybody home?'

Another wave of anxious laughter spread through the massed rebel.

The lock clanked.

The door creaked.

An ashen-faced Mayor Codd stood in the doorway. A chorus of boos and hisses erupted from Robert's followers.

When they subsided, Robert spoke. 'Hello, Thomas. I believe this belongs to me now.'

The rebel cheers reverberated through the marketplace.

'Then you'd better come in,' said the mayor, his trembling hand betraying his fear.

As he entered a few onlookers outside hissed with disapproval. Robert hesitated, unsettled by their reaction. He didn't want to conduct these negotiations in public. He continued and closed the door behind him, leaving William to keep order outside. The chorus of boos, jeers and demands for justice faded to the background.

'Thomas, we haven't long. Keep that lot waiting, and they'll pull this building down.'

'Very well, Robert. What do you propose?'

'Who's here?'

'Most of the council have fled. The bishop has left. Steward's here. The king's herald is still here. You could make some use of him?'

'Good idea. I'm afraid you will have to show your face, mayor. It was you we came to see in the first place.'

'Robert, why? What do you hope to gain?' The mayor's fears were clear to see.

'I'll go easy on you, Thomas, but I can't promise my followers will do the same. They aren't the most obedient lot. Nevertheless, fetch the herald and everyone else here. I want all of you outside.'

'Robert, please, we'll be lynched.'

'Don't argue with me, Thomas, or I'll lynch you myself. Outside now. Everyone,' barked Robert.

'Ok, ok. I will. Just remember, Robert, you are now responsible for what happens here,' the mayor reminded him.

'Then what would you suggest?'

'With the Sheriff ill, we'll need the cooperation of the

justice of the peace and his watchmen. Especially after dark.'

'I agree. Get it done.'

A startled expression passed across the mayor's face before he did as he was told and made his way up the staircase to fetch the others.

The crowd cheered as Robert opened the door. 'Clear some space, plenty of room, move back,' he ordered.

Moments later the crowd roared at the sight of the mayor sheepishly making his way out of the guildhall, followed by a defiant-looking deputy mayor, Steward, who Robert knew of, but had never had occasion to meet. Next to file out was the herald. The sight of his royal quartered robes prompted a renewed welcome of boos from the onlookers. Then an official man in robes, who Robert didn't recognise. Just when he thought that was everybody, another man appeared at the door. Robert couldn't believe his eyes. Ginger hair and a fox-like face. It was him. Flowerdew.

I've got you, you rat, thought Robert rubbing his hands together.

'William, look what the cat's dragged in.'

William rested his weight against the hilt of the sword.

'Now's not the time to deal with him, Robert. Remember our aims.'

The men of the guildhall stood shoulder-to-shoulder facing the victorious mob who taunted and spat at them.

Robert approached them, then turned to address his followers. He caught a glimpse of Fulke, next to him, Alfred. Pushing his way to the front was John Bossell.

Trust Bossell to have made it through unharmed.

A few rows back he recognised the face of Miles, the gunner. A bonus. He couldn't see Master Peter. Then he saw Luke Miller, his face spattered in blood. Many of this lot will have lost friends and family today, thought Robert. If I leave them here, reprisals will run through the night.

He clapped his hand and raised his voice.

'A fortnight ago I came here in peace to see the mayor. They,' signalling his captives behind him, 'closed the city. They refused to talk.' Boos and hisses. 'Well, they'll talk to me now!' A cheer ran through the crowd. 'Men, I thank you for the sacrifice you have made today. We came here in peace, and it is to peace that we must now return.' The crowd fell silent. 'This man here was sent by the king,' said Robert pointing to the herald. 'Today he will return to the king, and tell him we have rescued his city from the corruption and greed of his officials.' More cheers. 'He may have it back,' continued Robert, 'when his government accept our demands.' A roar sounded across the marketplace. Applause broke out, and people started singing Robert's name.

Robert grinned as the chant of *Kett, Kett, Kett* spread like fire in a barley field.

'To rescue the king's city,' said the herald in his effeminate voice, 'and attach conditions to its safe return, is to hold it to ransom in the eyes of the law.'

The people at the front spat and cursed him. William had to raise his sword to stop two burly men from pressing forward.

What is it with this fool? Robert thought.

'You,' said Robert, turning to point at him 'Are the cause of all this trouble.' More cheers. 'Herald, you will ride to London without delay. Our message is simple: the city in return for our demands.'

Cheers once more. The herald blew air from tired lips. Robert raised his eyebrows and opened his arms, gesturing at the crowd behind him.

The herald nodded his acquiescence. Cheers and clapping now merged with taunts and jeers.

'If you disband, you may still be pardoned,' called out the herald.

His suggestion was met by a chorus of boos.

'Enough,' snapped Robert. He beckoned for Fulke to come over. 'Take this fool indoors before he gets himself killed.'

Fulke nodded. He grabbed the herald by the arm. When the herald resisted, he was met with a punch to his ribs, which was enough to persuade him to return to the safety of the guildhall. Once the crowd's laughter subsided, a man shouted, 'How can we trust him?'

Robert didn't have an answer for that.

'He'll lie!' shouted another.

'Kill him, that will show the bastards we mean business.'

This thirst for revenge was what Robert feared. He grasped the sword from William's hand and held it aloft towards the heavens.

'Silence!' he ordered. 'The kings of this land have claimed their thrones with trials by battle, victories ordained by God. Well let me tell you that today our victory was a trial by battle. We won, and our cause is ordained by the almighty.'

Roars of approval filled the air.

'We must offer God our thanks, let us pray. Kneel.'

To a man, the crowd dropped to their knees and bowed their heads. Robert breathed a sigh of relief before leading them in prayer.

Amen, he lifted his head.

'Men,' he resumed his address, 'today you have fought for the justice of our cause, and now I must ask one more service of you. Many of our fellow men lay dead and injured on the slopes beneath our camp. Whilst there is still daylight, we must honour their sacrifice and intern their bodies to the ground.'

He swallowed. 'I ask that each of you return to the scene of our hard-fought victory and lend your hand in preparing the ground for our fallen brothers.' As the words left his lips, the simple humanity of his request, seemed to him, hard to refuse. Here and there men whispered to each other, but for the most part, he had their attention.

Behind him somebody cleared his throat. 'Mr Kett.'

Robert turned to find a man in a black gown, his hand raised.

'If I may,' he said, 'I could offer you the services of the city's barber-surgeons for your injured, and our clergymen, for your fallen?'

'Thank you, that would be appreciated.'

The man bowed his head. 'Augustine Steward, Deputy Mayor, at your service, Mr Kett.'

Robert nodded again while observing Mayor Codd's forehead crease.

Robert faced his followers. 'I summon the representatives of the hundreds to join me in the guildhall now. Let me make it clear, you will each be responsible for the conduct of the men of your parish.' The representatives pushed forward. 'For the rest of you,' continued Robert, 'I will have all the ale in this city sent to the heath, and you may toast the departed and celebrate your bravery. Now, please return to the heath and bury our brothers.'

'What about them?' called a man, pointing at the captors.

'They will accompany us to camp, as our prisoners.'

'And you? What about you? What will you be doing while we bury those who fell because of your plan?' asked the man again.

William, to Robert's relief, now stepped in: 'We must see to it that this time our demands are accepted so that today's losses are not in vain.'

'You heard the herald,' said Robert, pointing his sword in the direction of the guildhall, 'you're pardoned. You're free to leave if you'd prefer?'

'You want me to leave? After what happened today?'

Robert shook his head. 'No, but I haven't risked my neck so you can create merry hell in my name. You go back and start digging a hole, or I'll have you arrested for disturbing the peace.'

'How can we trust the herald not to make mischief with the king?'

It was Bossell. It was a fair question.

'Mr Kett, if I may?' said Steward, doffing his hat.

Robert nodded, inviting him to continue.

'I was a member of parliament for some years, and despite what you may think of politicians, some of us are bound by a belief in service. This herald, the one you are now sending to London, has he not made matters worse at every turn?'

Mr Kett thought for a moment, then nodded.

'I know the council of the king. Send me with him, and I will see that your demands are considered fully.'

'Why should I trust you?'

'Because I can make them aware of what is at stake.'

Robert shook his head. 'If I wanted to do that there is nobody I'd rather send than my own brother.'

Mr Steward appraised William Kett. 'Indeed. Although he has no knowledge of the men with which he must parley. Indeed, they may take him hostage. An eye for an eye, so to speak.'

The Kett brothers exchanged glances.

The deputy mayor pressed on. 'Besides, you have a city to run now. You will be responsible for all that happens here under your command, legal or otherwise.'

Mayor Codd came forward. 'Robert, let me ride to

London. I know better than anyone what you seek to gain.'

Robert denied him his request. 'Mayor Codd, I think I would prefer your assistance here.' He turned his attention to Steward. 'Why,' pointing at him with the sword, 'should I trust you?'

'I love this city, and there is nothing I wouldn't do to save it from being destroyed. Because, together, we must do what is necessary to achieve a peaceful outcome.'

'Mayor Codd, can I trust this man to represent us in London?' asked Robert.

The mayor hesitated. Steward gave him a small slow nod. The mayor looked uncomfortable. 'I think, like me, he has only the best interests of the city at heart.'

'All I seek is peace, Mr Kett. It seems to me that satisfying your demands is the easiest way for us to achieve that.'

'Very well, you shall accompany the herald to London.'

'I see you wear a cross around your neck. Take it off and give it to me,' said Mr Kett, pointing at the deputy mayor.

Steward pulled a gold chain and crucifix over his head and passed it to Robert.

'Kneel. Swear your loyalty to the people of Norfolk and to ensuring our demands are met.'

Steward dropped to the floor and with raised arms, cupped his crucifix and repeated Robert's words. He seemed sincere, thought Robert. The crowd seemed more sceptical.

'This man has, in the presence of God, sworn his allegiance to us,' declared Robert. Then he turned to Steward. 'When you return from London, you will meet with me in person.'

Steward nodded. 'Of course.'

'Very well, be gone.'

William touched Robert's arm. 'Robert, we're responsible for what happens here tonight. If we have learned one thing today, it is that we need to think further ahead.'

Robert nodded. Part of him regretted that his moment on stage had passed. Planning meant arguing, meant details, but William was right. Robert thanked the last of the crowd and promised to free them from the yoke of the gentry. Slowly they dispersed, melting away into the side streets. For the most part they went in the direction from where they had come.

There was much to be done. With his chest puffed up, Robert followed his captives and his representatives into the guildhall. Tonight, Norwich was his responsibility. If it were to go up in flames, so would his chances of success. He caught sight of Fulke and Alfred standing by the door. 'Fulke, join us, tonight I have need of a man with your skills.'

31

The justice of the peace and his two heavies left the council chamber, followed by a worried-looking Mayor Codd. Robert dropped his head into his hands. The justice of the peace had finally agreed to attend to his duties, but it had taken all of Robert's persuasion to reassure him he wasn't committing treason by cooperating with Robert. Robert, supported by the mayor, had explained that the justice's duty of keeping Norwich safe remained the same, whomever assumed charge of the city, and that he risked a charge of neglecting his duties if he abandoned his post. Eventually, the justice, a man whose physicality exceeded his intellect, had agreed that all parties wanted the same thing. With the aid of the night watchmen that hadn't been killed in the fighting earlier, he'd agreed to ensure the city gates were locked and a curfew enforced within the walls from sundown to sunrise.

Earlier, Robert's representatives had been dispatched to order all the city's taverns and alehouses to close for the night. By now their drink should have been confiscated and be safely on its way to the heath. Robert and the mayor had come to cross-purposes when Mayor Codd protested that the landlords should be afforded his protection or at the very least compensated for their loss. Mayor Codd had quickly recanted to Robert's demands when he'd offered the mayor a cell for the night if he disagreed.

Thereafter, the representatives were instructed to account for their living and see that they remained on the heath.

The city's clergymen had not shared the concerns of their civic counterparts. Theirs was a moral duty to carry out the Lord's work. They had agreed not to follow the example of their bishop, who'd fled, taking with him as many of his valuables as he could fit into his carriage. Instead, they were attending to the dead and the injured.

Robert racked his brains for anything he might have overlooked.

The door opened, and William entered, looking haggard.

'Six hundred dead. Five hundred ours.'

Slumped in the chair at the head of the table, Robert remembered the moment when Alfred had arrived to warn him of his enclosures being vandalised.

How different things would have been if I'd stayed at home, he thought, wanting nothing more than to be home, sitting by his fire, stroking his dog and chatting with Alice.

Instead, he was in charge of Norwich, and in open dispute with the lord protector of the realm.

Too late now to run away.

'How long before we hear from London, do you think?' asked Robert.

William did the calculations. 'Steward left with the herald around two. If they ride fast without stopping, they should arrive in the early hours. What happens then, only God knows.'

'Can we trust him?' asked Robert.

'Who? Steward?' William shrugged. 'We have to. But, where we now find ourselves, brother, I doubt we can trust anyone.'

Robert nodded.

'Still, at least you've caught up with Flowerdew at last.'

Even that felt like a hollow victory. After the events of today, the Flowerdew affair felt petty and irrelevant.

Maybe in the morning, if he were able to get some sleep tonight, he would find some shred of satisfaction from imprisoning him.

'Do you want me to stay?'

'No, no,' lied Robert. 'I've posted a party of guards downstairs under Luke Miller's command. We've enough weapons to keep out the most determined of assaults. You keep our folks on the heath and out of the city.'

'Don't go out alone, brother.'

'Give Alice a kiss from me.' Then from nowhere, his tired thought, 'Oh, and keep an eye out for Master Peter. I haven't seen him this afternoon. It's unlike him.'

As William went to leave, Alfred appeared.

'The bridge is clear. The earth mound has been moved. They're using it to cover the dead.'

'Very well, Alfred. See to it everything makes it back safely. Lock the prisoners in Surrey House. The mayor can be spared the indignity of the cellar. Give him a room.'

Mayor Codd had agreed to act as a symbolic prisoner to show the city's surrender.

Alfred left the chamber.

*

Earlier, Alfred had joined Fulke in the guildhall. Together, they'd found a stash of weapons in the cellar. Mr Kett had ordered them to load up their new weaponry and take it back to the Surrey House. Between him and Fulke, they piled up three stolen carts with pikes, powder, cannonballs and arrows. In the absence of horses or donkeys, the plan was for the prisoners: Mayor Codd, Flowerdew and seven other aldermen rounded up from the comfort of their homes throughout the afternoon, to push the haul up to the heath.

Mr Kett had explained he wanted people to see the good and the great doing peasant labour.

Alfred joined Fulke and Miles outside the guildhall. Together with two other rebels, they stood guard over their gentlemen prisoners and the haul of weapons.

Miles was congratulating Fulke for fighting bravely. Fulke nodded in a way that suggested he didn't need to be told.

'All clear,' said Alfred through a yawn.

The prospect of supervising this convoy of carts back to the heath was tiresome, but he promised himself an ale when he got back to the heath. In fact, having survived today, he thought he should get royally drunk.

'Let's go,' said Fulke, clapping his hands.

The indignant-looking prisoners took their places, three to a cart. Miles guarded the lead cart, Fulke the second. With the aid of the sword he'd captured during battle, Alfred took watch over the rear cart, which was being pushed by his former landlord, Flowerdew and two other gentleman prisoners.

They trundled through the streets, past the cathedral and onto Bishopsgate, which led to the heath. Alfred found little satisfaction in seeing Flowerdew push the cart. After everything he'd caused, it seemed like a trivial punishment. The ginger-haired lord hadn't given Alfred a second glance all afternoon. Flowerdew didn't appear to remember him, despite having evicted him only sixteen days earlier.

'You don't remember me, do you?' accused Alfred.

Flowerdew stopped pushing and turned to study Alfred.

He shook his head. 'Should I?'

Flowerdew would take more notice of shit on his shoe than he would me, thought Alfred.

'Perhaps I should give you cause to remember me.' Alfred drew his sword from his belt, its blade still red from the bloodshed earlier.

Flowerdew took another step and looked into Alfred's face. He was a fraction smaller than Alfred. 'Going to kill me, boy?'

'I should. You evicted my family from our cottage.'

Flowerdew's face lifted as he remembered. 'Ah. You're the boy who got that ugly Smith girl pregnant.' He grinned.

'How dare you,' said Alfred, raising the tip of his sword to Flowerdew's throat.

Flowerdew's natural authority wobbled as he felt the blade press against his skin.

'Now now, don't be silly. If you kill a powerful man you'll be condemned to an eternity in hell. Once they've hanged you.'

Alfred shook his head. 'Not now Mr Kett's in charge.'

Flowerdew laughed. 'Do you honestly think Mr Kett is going to make it out of this alive?' He shook his head. 'You fools don't realise what you've done. The government won't let you get away with capturing a city. They'll come and slaughter every last one of you. Then they'll string Kett up by his neck, mark my words.'

'Shut up,' said Alfred, shifting uneasily on his feet.

Flowerdew pressed his finger against Alfred's sword and slowly lowered it. Resentment coursed through Alfred at Flowerdew's nerve. All afternoon the dying faces of the two young men he'd killed had haunted Alfred, and his hand began to shake. He'd learned to kill today, why not add Flowerdew to his tally? Now was the moment.

The carts had carried on without them. There would be no witnesses. One strike and the lord would be dead. Last chance, thought Alfred. His hand twitched. Could he stomach that same helpless look in Flowerdew's eyes? That would be killing in cold blood, not the heat of battle. In Flowerdew's eyes he saw power, control. His arm longed to lunge forward yet his instinct wouldn't let him.

Flowerdew pushed the blade to the side. The moment had passed.

'You should be careful about making powerful enemies, boy. I won't forget you again.'

Alfred's muscles were coiled. He read the relief on Flowerdew's face. The lord *had* been scared, and for a brief moment they'd been equals.

'What say you and I make a deal, boy?'

'My name's Alfred Carter,' he told Flowerdew.

'You want your cottage back?'

Alfred failed to hide the surprise on his face.

'In return, you let me go, unharmed.'

Alfred knew it was wrong to be tempted by such an offer. It was a small damp cottage, but it had also been home: a roof over his head.

'How can I trust you?'

Flowerdew smiled. 'I give you my word as a gentleman.'

Alfred shook his head. As if the word of a gentleman counted for anything.

'You don't rise to the top in life by breaking your promises, Carter. You can have your cottage back. I swear it on my life.'

Alfred squinted. It was a good offer. He searched for a reason to believe Flowerdew but couldn't find one. Without witnesses, Flowerdew could easily deny it later.

Flowerdew appeared to sense Alfred's hesitation.

'After today, even if this rebellion ended right now, there are enough dead littering that slope that I'd wager I've already gained more land than I could by evicting you. I don't need your family land now. I already have the land of your dead comrades.'

The nerve of the man.

'If I stick this sword in your belly, then I can have my cottage back regardless,' countered Alfred.

'But then my estate will be passed down. And a new landlord won't take kindly when he learns his tenant murdered his lord. You let me go, and I'll gift you the rights to your cottage.'

'To *me?*'

Flowerdew nodded. 'You have my word.'

In one handshake, his life transformed for the better. Alfred couldn't believe his luck. He was as householder. He'd been vaulted from impending destitution to having property of his own. His family had never owned anything.

He looked up. Flowerdew was gone.

Alfred ran back down the road to catch up with the carts.

He couldn't wait to tell Richard.

'Where's Flowerdew?' asked one of the two remaining prisoners left pushing the rear cart.

'He's dead! Keep pushing, or I'll gut you too,' barked Alfred pointing his blood-stained blade towards them.

They looked terrified and renewed their pushing. Alfred smiled to himself and slid his sword back between his belt and his tunic.

The front cart drew to a halt by the gatehouse. While they waited for the gate to be unlocked, Alfred noticed the dead had been cleared. Patches of blood in the dirt were the only trace of their last stand, and the place took on a ghostly atmosphere in the twilight. Alfred shivered and turned his head away, eager to bury the memories of earlier.

On his right he'd drawn level with a pink house in between two white buildings. He jolted as he remembered his conversation with Tiniker at the river. This was her house. He was relieved to see it wasn't damaged, although the shutters were closed. His heart skipped. He couldn't resist seeing her. He crossed the road and knocked on the door. What better way to celebrate his survival than her smile and big blue eyes? He listened. No noise.

He knocked again.

'Tiniker!' No answer.

'Tiniker?'

Alfred jumped. 'Fulke! Where did sneak up from? You made me jump.'

'So this fancy woman of yours lives here.'

Alfred frowned, unsure what to say.

'Let's have a look at her then. Get her out here. I fancy a play.' Fulke banged on the door. 'Does she know you're married?'

Alfred flushed. 'She's not here. He put his hand on Fulke's arm and pulled him away.

'Shame. We'll come back later.'

'Mr Kett wants us to stay at the heath tonight.'

'I don't give two turds what Kett wants. Victor's privileges: rape and pillage.'

The gate was open. From behind the front cart, Miles gave the order to push.

The carts began to roll.

Alfred cursed himself. How could he have been so careless to disclose Tiniker's house to Fulke's attention?

He followed the last cart across the bridge and breathed a sigh of relief when the gates closed behind him.

A trench had been dug. A pastor moved along the shallow grave offering prayers for the fallen. Somewhere in that long line of unfortunates would be David Fisher. Alfred, deciding they could manage without him, took the opportunity to pay his last respects to David. He edged his way along the trench, only now beginning to appreciate the true cost of today's victory. He wasn't old enough to remember the last plague outbreak, but he could recall his father telling him how it had devastated communities. Every dead man had left a town or village short of a blacksmith, a carpenter, a stonemason, a butcher, a baker.

Or, as Flowerdew had already remarked, land without a farmer, animals without an owner, homes without a tenant, women without a husband.

Occasionally he recognised a face: somebody he'd seen in camp, in Surrey House, a face from Wymondham. He'd walked nearly the length of the trench, which stretched out beyond the bridge opposite. Alfred found himself standing where, earlier today, he'd made his charge to the river. Seeing it again now, clear of bodies, free from flying arrows, silent from the shouts of battle, it was at odds with the flashbacks of his memories, sights and sound he knew would never forget. The faces of the men he'd killed popped into his mind: their agony and their acceptance. This was the price of survival.

He came across David Fisher, lying prone with a peaceful look of resignation on his pale face. His expression at contrast with the violence of his end, thought Alfred. He glanced at the next man in the trench. He blinked hard to ensure his eyes were not deceiving him. His mouth fell open. He stood frozen as his thoughts came to terms with the sight of his father-in-law. Dead.

He hadn't liked Richard. He was a petty, small-minded man, but he hadn't deserved to die. He'd finally taken a stand, and it had cost him his life. It was Alfred who had encouraged Richard to join the march after Flowerdew had evicted them.

Alfred felt a pang of guilt for that, and for allowing Flowerdew to escape.

He remembered Flowerdew's visit to their cottage.

How he'd tossed the sovereign coin into the dirt and left.

The coin, where was it?

Richard would never have spent it. He'd never let it out of his sight. An uncomfortable thought occurred to Alfred. Was Richard about to be buried with it? A sovereign could feed Alfred for months. There was no point allowing it to go to waste. Glancing up, he saw that the burial gang were a way off yet. He stepped into the trench and knelt, resting one knee on Richard's stiffened thigh. The aroma of death seeped its fleshy scent into his nose. He patted Richard's corpse searching for a purse or the coin. His flesh felt dry, not yet cold, and Alfred gagged. Alfred checked him all over again. Nothing. His stomach turned with each moment he spent in the trench. He may have hidden it in his shoes, but they were missing, already looted.

Would Richard have left it in his shelter on the heath? Alfred thought not, that coin never left his sight. A far ghastlier notion dawned on Alfred: would Richard have hidden the coin up his bottom? There was nowhere safer, coins and purses were often dropped, but nowhere would Richard's grip be tighter than his own backside. Alfred shuddered at the prospect. He saw in an instant that the decision he faced condemned him to a life or continuous torment, as he would forever speculate on the bounty buried safely in his father-in-law's arse, or the indignity of having looked. The idea seemed typical of Richard, able to exert one final humiliation to forever sustain the disapproval he had formed of Alfred. Only finding the coin would vindicate Alfred. Then and only then would he have the last laugh.

He took another deep breath, grabbed Richard's legs and heaved the rigid body onto its side. He was heavy, and Alfred lost his balance, falling on David's corpse. He stifled a gag and righted himself. He pulled Richard over. His hose were soiled. His bowels had discharged their contents after death. Alfred felt bile rising in his throat. He patted the cold, damp buttocks in the vain hope that the coin may have been evacuated. He tugged at the top of the hose, fumbling to loosen them before his breath ran out. He yanked them down, exposing Richard's pale backside matted in his own manure. He leant in to look closely for the glint of gold and grimaced as he parted the buttocks with his palms. He rehearsed in his mind what he would do. A quick and precise insertion of one finger as far as he could reach. Alfred stretched out his first finger and stiffened it.

'What the fuck are you doing?' cried a voice from behind him.

Alfred froze.

'You thieving nave!'

The voice was familiar. Alfred twisted his head and looked over his shoulder. At the foot of the trench stood Lynn. His heart sank. He was too ashamed to go red.

'Alfred. You shit!' she slurred, swaying on her on feet.

She stumbled, trying to correct her balance, but she fell.

She was drunk. Alfred got out from the trench and took a breath of fresh air. Lynn lay on the floor, her cheeks damp with tears.

'Lynn, it's not how it looks,' said Alfred. He sounded

pathetic, yet he felt somehow relieved; her appearance had spared him the ignominy to which his greed had blinded him.

'Yes it is,' she slurred. 'I know what you want, you thieving...' her words trailed off as she tried to push herself up.

'How much have you had to drink?'

'Piss off,' she tried to spit at him. Her spittle landed on her chin, where it stayed. Her eyes fell shut.

'I've spent it,' she declared.

'Spent what?'

'What you were looking for. My money.'

'Spent it? How? Not on drink?' The shame in his own indiscretions faded as he realised what she'd done. 'Your father died and you...'

'Yes.' She sounded defiant. She rolled over onto her front and wriggled onto all fours, rocking back and forth as she searched for the strength to push herself up.

'All of it?'

Lynn purred and closed her eyes again. 'I have some change. But you won't be getting any.'

She heaved herself upright and rested on her knees. 'I beat you to it, Alfred.'

Alfred winced as he thought of his wife searching her dead father for loot. He was staggered she could be so callous. His heart sank for the prospect of his unborn baby in her belly. What kind of child would they have with a mother like this?

'He was a shit,' she garbled in the direction of her dead father.

'I pity you, Lynn.' Alfred shook his head.

Lynn rolled her eyes.

'You're a fool, woman. Drinking the money we need to feed our child?'

'Shut up, Carter,' she hiccupped, 'there's no baby.' She started to giggle.

'What do you mean?'

'I'm not pregnant. You're such a,' she hiccupped again, 'such a fool. You didn't realise.'

Alfred lurched forward and grabbed her shirt, twisting it in his fist.

'I made it up.'

Alfred raised his fist. She lolled drunkenly in his grip, refusing to meet his stare.

He let go, and she dropped to the ground.

She laughed as she tried to push herself up. 'You fell for it. You're nothing but a silly boy. And you married me.' Lynn laughed.

Alfred felt tears of disbelief welling in his eyes. How could she? What sort of person made something like that up?

'Why?'

'Nobody would ever marry me,' she hiccupped.

'You'll go to hell, you lying cow.'

'I've been in hell my whole life.'

Alfred frowned as the revelation sunk in: he wasn't going to be a father. He'd been tricked. He felt stupid, and yet this was the best news he could have been given. The past few months made no sense. His life had been bent on a lie. Looking at Lynn in the dirt he longed to put a noose around her neck and hang her from the nearest tree and yet, for all her ills, she had just set him free from a purgatory — an existence that he'd wanted nothing more than to escape from.

Alfred looked back at Richard, lying face down in the trench. Did he know? Alfred wondered. It didn't matter now.

Lynn hiccupped.

'You may not have been dealt the best cards in life, Lynn, but that doesn't give you the right to deny others of their own destiny. I was tricked into marrying you. As far as I'm concerned our marriage is null and void.'

'Not in the eyes of God,' she mumbled.

'I'll let you explain that to the devil when you meet him. I got the cottage back. It's mine now.'

Lynn snorted, her head lolled from side to side.

He took a final look at her. 'Goodbye, Lynn.'

Alfred turned his back on her drunken laughter and left her alone to wake up next to her father's grave. He staggered, light-headed, towards the gulley. He looked back towards Norwich, at the battered gatehouse beyond the bridge: Tiniker's house and the cathedral spire. There was smoke. In the northern part of the city, a building burned, illuminating the grey evening air, and he saw another house on fire in the background.

Alfred shook his head. He'd had enough trouble for one day. He needed a drink.

Today he'd taken lives, and been given back his own. What's more, he'd come out of it owning his own house.

He managed twenty yards before he fell to his knees and vomited up the contents of his stomach.

32

23rd July – The Palace of Whitehall

Dudley stood in the corner of the council chamber parleying with Archbishop Cranmer in hushed tones. Seymour was the last member to enter the chamber, his complexion even paler than was customary, his stride uneasy, like a man trying to walk on ice. To Dudley's eye, the lord protector looked like he'd been awake all night. In his wake came the royal herald and another man who looked familiar. Something must have happened. He glanced at Archbishop Cranmer. Dudley racked his brain to remember where he'd seen the tall, sallow man before.

'Be seated,' said Seymour, doing his best to sound authoritative.

The assembled men shuffled to their places, Catholics on one side of the table, Protestants on the other.

Seymour remained on his feet at the head of the table. His two companions beside him. 'Kett's rebels have taken Norwich.'

There was a collective hush.

Dudley inwardly smiled. Don't say I didn't warn you, Edward. That's two cities we've lost now, he thought.

Only York, Bristol and Newcastle of any consequence were left. How long before the next two were inspired to rise up and the latter fell to the emboldened Scots?

Seymour introduced the royal herald and Augustine Steward, the deputy mayor of Norwich. 'Mr Steward, please tell the council what you told me.'

The council sat whilst Steward recalled how the rebels had overwhelmed the city's defences. He made great play of the fact that many of the city's inhabitants had refused to take up arms against their fellow countrymen.

To Dudley, the deputy mayor's message was clear: They had not the means with which to defend themselves, and nor did they have the appetite locally to resolve what was clearly now a national issue. The deputy mayor was washing his hands of the entire debacle.

'Did you offer them the lord protector's pardon?' Dudley was the first to speak up.

'To Kett, yes, in private, then again to the masses once they occupied Norwich. I think it is fair to report that they had little confidence that anything would change once parliament was recalled from its summer recess,' replied the herald in his effeminate tone.

'You see, gentlemen,' said Seymour, 'because of your behaviour, the word of the lord protector now counts for little. It is because of the way you, and those you command, abuse your powers that people have not the confidence to know that they will be treated fairly.'

Councillors exchanged looks.

'That's a touch simple, Seymour,' said Sir William Paget.

'Is it, Sir William? Am I not the one they call The Good Duke? These people are loyal to their king and their lord protector. If we are to control the angst that grips our kingdom, you all have a duty to reform. Otherwise, these disturbances will go on.'

Dudley clenched his jaw.

How could Seymour not see that his actions had encouraged the very thing he was accusing them of?

'How many times must I resort to force against those that are afflicted by your actions? I won't do a thing until I receive a solemn promise from each of you that you will take down your own enclosures. Everyone. You must lead by example. All your enclosures must go. Immediately. The good people of this land must see that I am in command and that you are loyal to the reforms that I have promised.

'Your grace, if I may,' interrupted Dudley, 'your reforms are well intended, but we risk losing our kingdom to our own people, if not the French or Scots. Believe me, our perils will not be assuaged by removing enclosures. Now is a time for action.'

'You may not,' declared Seymour. 'I've heard quite enough from the Earl of Warwick recently.' His voice trembled as he gripped the back of his chair. 'My duty is to my people, and they are starving.'

'And yet your grace has managed to appropriate sufficient funds to build yourself a new palace on The Strand?'

Around the chamber you could hear a pin drop. Dudley had said in public what everyone was only prepared to condemn in private. The protector's hypocrisy exposed, as plain to see as the building site intended for Somerset House.

'Your council, Mr Dudley, is surplus to my requirements. I request that you leave us.'

Dudley's head rocked back, his cheeks red with rage.

'You heard me. Your presence at this table is no longer required.'

Dudley stood up, took one last look at the faces of the councillors and then, against his better judgement, stalked out of the council chamber.

He needed a walk.

Seymour seemed to have made up his mind, but surely the loss of Norwich would create some debate. Dudley inhaled the smell of horses, their manure and bedding straw. Better to wait here in the courtyard, he concluded. Seymour couldn't let a city fall and do nothing, even he wasn't that stupid. Dudley cursed himself for speaking out too quickly. He would have been better to bide his time, but it was difficult when the solution was so blindingly obvious.

He took refuge against a wall opposite the stables and studied the assorted buildings that made up the palace. They were as irregular as those who occupied them, part timber frame, others red brick, then the white stone that gave the palace its name. It had all the hallmarks of a place built up gradually over time, without any cohesive, or strategic vision.

Not unlike the regency council, thought Dudley, who preferred buildings to be uniform and symmetrical.

A wolfhound ambled across the yard. It stopped to root through the pile of mucky straw beside the stables, discovered a tasty lump of horse muck and made off.

Here I am, thought Dudley, the most capable general that Seymour has, thrown out on the muckheap. After a career spent advancing his reputation, winning the favour of those above him, John Dudley knew he would never be content with a life without power, rooting out manure at the bottom of the pile. His rightful place was top of the heap.

*

It was three hours before council broke. William Parr, The Marquess of Northampton and brother to old King Henry's last wife Catherine Parr, was the first to emerge to fetch his horse. Parr wouldn't have been Dudley's first choice to confide in but, swallowing his pride, he forced himself to approach the young man. Parr wore his ginger hair short and his beard long. It made his bold features seem bigger.

He put on his leather gloves while the ostler went to fetch his horse from the stables.

'I'm not sure I should be speaking to you, John,' said Parr, evidently enjoying Dudley's fall from favour.

'At the very least put my mind at ease that there is a plan to recover this latest debacle.'

'There is. I'm to leave for Norwich with a force of fifteen hundred soldiers and recapture the city.'

'You?'

'Yes,' grinned Parr.

'But you've no experience commanding men in the field?'

The ostler arrived with a fine black stallion and gave Parr a leg up. 'I have generals. Besides they're nothing but a rabble of farmers, poorly armed. No match for a modern fighting force.'

'You're outnumbered nearly four to one?'

'Jealous are you, John?' said Parr, looking down from his horse as it wriggled between his legs.

The sun shining behind his shoulders blinded Dudley's view.

'You better get used to being in my shadow once I take back Norwich.'

Dudley fumed. 'Why won't he give you more troops?'

'He wants to keep London, and the king, safe. Besides, fifteen hundred skilled soldiers will be more than enough.'

'Don't rush straight into the city, William, fight them on open ground.'

'That's your problem, Dudley, always think you know

best, telling everyone what they should and shouldn't do. Look where it has got you. Skulking around stable yards searching for titbits of information. You overplayed your hand, John. What you fail to see is you're too powerful for the duke. Seymour's intimidated by you. You're a threat to him.'

'I was trying to save him from blundering into an even bigger disaster.' He shook his head, despondently.

'Well, there's a new order now, John, things are going to be different in the future, Seymour wants to create a commonwealth where all Englishmen prosper. You're the old guard. Your time was up when King Henry died.'

'Then you better take back Norwich, Parr, otherwise this commonwealth of Seymour's will only ever be a dream. Take me at my word. You can't govern with idealism. Fail, and this government falls. Forget politics. You have to get that city back.'

'That's exactly what I plan to do. Now if you'll excuse me, John, I have a name to make for myself.' Parr kicked his stallion.

As Dudley watched him trot out of the courtyard, he had to concede that perhaps he was jealous. Politics was a poor substitute for the cut and thrust of battle. He was most at home on a horse at the front of an army or at the helm of a ship bristling with cannon. At those things, there was no one better in the land. Poncing around the council table was for the likes of Parr.

He shouted at the ostler to fetch his horse.

'May I ride with you?' It was Augustine Steward, the Deputy Mayor of Norwich.

'Don't think me rude, sire, but I'd rather not. It's been a trying day, as I'm sure you'll understand.' Dudley didn't like the look of this fellow. There's nothing as tiring as a provincial man with ideas above his station.

'Of course. Just one question if I may though?'

'Very well,' said Dudley, distractedly.

'Rumours abound about the health of King Edward, is there any substance to them?'

Without looking up Dudley answered. 'He's a sickly child. It wouldn't surprise me if God had other intentions for him.'

Steward nodded. 'Well, based on the calibre of those I've observed here today, it might be better for him if he was to die.' He kicked his horse and ambled out of the courtyard.

You cheeky bastard, thought Dudley, that's nigh on treason. Ride up here and pronounce your judgements.

As he rode the short distance back to his house at Holborn, he wondered if that was it for him, at forty-six years of age, would he ever get the chance to lead men again?

The gentle rhythm of his horse rocked his body, dislodging the thoughts that crowded his mind. His wife often said the best thing for the inside of man was the outside of a horse. Dudley turned right onto The Strand and caught sight of Somerset House, Seymour's folly.

What would happen if Kind Edward died? In all likelihood, his older half-sister Mary would succeed him. Mary was a devout Catholic, her accession to the throne would throw the Pope's cat amongst the Protestant pigeons. Seymour would no longer have blood ties to the royals and given the strength of his reformist views, he wouldn't last an hour.

Unfortunately for Dudley, he'd thrown in his lot with the Protestants, believing it was their doctrine that would prevail.

Then it dawned on him: a plan formed in his mind. He kicked his horse and broke into a canter. If he were to topple Seymour, there was not a moment to lose.

33

24th July, Framlingham Castle

The wooden bridge creaked under the thundering hooves of Dudley's horse. Behind him the sun cast a warm pink glow over the Suffolk market town. The castle, a large flint structure interrupted by a series of rectangular towers, was functional and old fashioned. The tall, red brick chimneys that protruded inelegantly from each tower were the only sign of modernisation. On first glance he thought the castle a deliberate slight to its resident, an out-of-favour member of the royal family. Dudley's horse, the third he'd ridden that day, came to a halt at the gate. It snorted, exhausted from the thirty-mile canter from Colchester. Foaming spittle dripped from its bit onto the dusty ground as Dudley patted its neck, equally relieved to be here.

'What's your business, sir?' enquired the burly man who emerged from the side entrance.

'The Earl of Warwick, to see Princess Mary.'

The man offered a quizzical look. 'Normally your sort has a retinue?'

'This isn't a normal visit,' retorted Dudley.

'Is she expecting you?'

'Now be a good fellow tell her John Dudley is here seeking an audience with her on important matters of state.'

The guard weighed up his options. 'Very well, wait here, please.'

A runner was dispatched and soon disappeared into the bailey.

'I've ridden ninety miles today, I need to get off this horse, let me through,' insisted Dudley.

'Of course,' said the guard recovering his manners, 'forgive me, sire, we can't be too careful with all the troubles in these parts.'

He took the horse's reins, and Dudley swung his right leg over the horse's rump and landed on the ground with a thump. His legs were shaky, his old war injury on his right leg ached. Even he had to concede he was getting too old to make such long journeys in one day. As he regained his balance, he let go of the saddle.

'Have you had problems here?'

'Briefly. Usual thing. Commoners protesting. We nipped it in the bud,' he said proudly. 'Broke up their party and hung a few of them in the marketplace.'

That was precisely how you handled a rabble.

'The rest left, headed north to join up with Kett in Norwich.'

The guard showed Dudley to the hall where he left him with a maid to organise refreshment. It wasn't long before he was greeted by Mary's lady-in-waiting.

'Lady Mary is engaged at present, but she will be glad for you to join her for supper shortly.'

Dudley was invited to freshen up first and was shown to a guest room.

He woke with a start to find somebody knocking at the door.

It was dark. Having washed his face and body in the clay basin, he'd afforded himself a moment's rest in a chair and drifted off. He rubbed his eyes and cleared his throat.

'Coming,' he said, cross with himself. His head was thick from resting, and the last thing he needed was muddled thoughts when he was about to commit treason. He pushed himself up from the chair, his legs protesting the effort. A chambermaid led him through a modestly decorated corridor illuminated by rush lights. In the small dining room, beyond the empty table was a roaring fireplace in front of which sat the king's older half-sister Lady Mary, accompanied by a man.

They rose to greet Dudley's arrival.

'Lady Mary.' Dudley kissed her outstretched hand and curtsied. She eyed him with a mixture of charm and suspicion. Her once fair beauty was now strained by her years, many of them spent in partial exile from court. She was too close to the throne, and too attached to the old religion to be allowed in the circles of influence.

Dudley turned his attention to her companion. 'Ah, Lord Sheffield, how are you, Edmund?'

They shook hands. The young man's grip was firm, his greeting warm. Mary summoned some wine for Dudley, and they returned to their seats around the fire. Dudley took an empty chair between the two, opposite the flames.

'John, to what do I owe this unexpected pleasure of your company?' Mary Tudor was always direct.

Dudley cleared his throat. He hesitated. 'My Lady, I,' he rubbed his hands down his thighs and adjusted his cuffs. 'I hoped I might be able to discuss a matter with you in private?'

'By all means,' she said, her voice steely.

Dudley looked at Lord Sheffield.

'Edmund and I are cousins.' Mary didn't smile. 'We have

no secrets from each other.'

Sheffield smoothed the thin moustache that sat beneath his hawkish nose, quite evidently a man of confidence, at ease with himself.

Was there more to the relationship than met the eye?

'How long have you been here, my lady?' Dudley continued.

'Only a week. Given the trouble in Norfolk, I thought it best to leave Kenninghall and come here until things settle down.'

Dudley swallowed, his mouth dry. He told himself his plot was for the good of the country as well as his own prospects, but there was no taking back these words once they left his lips. He clenched his fist.

'My lady, your brother, the king…'

'How is he, my brother Edward VI? Are the rumours true?'

'They are. He is a sickly child. Rumours persist about his fate. I understand yesterday evening, Seymour was forced to ride through London with the young king to prove he was still alive and quash a rumour that he'd died.'

Mary nodded. 'Will he live?'

Dudley shrugged. 'Some say not.'

'What would Seymour do then?' asked Mary.

'With the way things are, I'm not sure Seymour will outlive his nephew. But regardless of who were to die first, it would leave you next in line to the throne, my lady.'

'My brother is staunchly Protestant. He would never sanction the realm reverting to Catholicism.'

'He is. But without an heir of his own what choice does he have?'

'Lizzy?'

Dudley shrugged. 'The king is young and impressionable.

If Seymour were out of the way, then Edward might be encouraged to see things, differently.'

Mary's gaze appeared to indicate she was not disinterested.

'Go on,' she said.

'As you know, rebellions are breaking out like a pox. At present, all our efforts have been aimed at the western rebellions. Seymour is making a hash of matters. His actions are responsible for the current strife. Each day he's delayed, Kett's rebellion in Norwich has grown.'

Dudley glanced at Sheffield, who was listening intently.

'Seymour has finally decided to send troops to Norwich. Their numbers are small, but believe me, any experienced and well-armed force is capable of defeating a motley bunch of farmers. He should now be able to quash this uprising and restore order to the realm. If he were successful in putting down these rebellions, his position as lord protector would be consolidated. Unless…' Dudley paused.

'*Unless?*' asked Mary.

'Unless, the rebels were to be victorious. Well then Seymour would be finished. No council member would support his rule.'

'That would still leave my brother as king?'

'It would, yes. And about that we can do little. But with Seymour gone, I could become lord protector and…'

'Ah, this isn't about me is it, John? This is your naked ambition.' Mary tossed her hands in the air.

'No,' protested Dudley, 'Please let me finish. I would be the king's representative. I would have unfettered access to him. In time, I could persuade him of your virtues, then should the worst happen, well…'

'Well?'

'You'd inherit the throne.'

'And what of you then?'

'I'd be at your service.'

Mary turned her face to the flames.

'It's all very far-fetched,' she said, at last.

'Well, yes, potentially, but if I had told you two years ago that Jane Seymour's brother would be king in all but name and the country would be tearing itself apart, you might have reached the same conclusion then.'

Mary raised her eyebrows. 'How can you ensure you're in charge of the council after Seymour?'

For the first time, Sheffield spoke. 'I may not be on the council, my lady, but I know the earl commands great loyalty from the members because of his military abilities. He could be confident of their support.'

'What about the Catholics on the council. John is,' she looked down her nose at him, 'of reformed beliefs.'

'Well,' said Dudley. 'If they knew I was going to support your accession to the throne, I am sure they would come round to the idea,' said Dudley, thinking fast.

'More wine,' beckoned Mary, 'you would have to convert to Catholicism. Do you swear it?'

'Now?'

Dudley felt cornered. Convert, and she was sure to go with his suggestion. Prevaricate, and he risked a traitor's death. This was why politicians were better suited to such negotiations. He cleared his throat. 'My lady, I am a pragmatic man, better suited to fighting. I am not best placed to understand the doctrines. If your brother were to die then it would seem very sensible to convert,' adding, 'if you were to be Queen.'

Mary nodded. It was an ugly compromise. 'So, the only small snag is that Mr Kett's rebels need to be successful in defeating Seymour troops. Will you fight for them?'

'No.' Dudley shook his head. 'I can't be seen to side with them and maintain my authority at council. Subtler means are necessary. They are led by William Parr.' He saw Mary's mouth turn down with distaste at the mention of the name of one her father's many queens that succeeded her own mother. 'He's inexperienced in command of troops. He could be *misadvised* to make mistakes.'

Mary nodded. 'Yes. We need a man on the inside. Edmund,' she looked over at her friend, 'would you do me this service?'

Dudley sat back in his chair, relieved to no longer be doing the talking.

The young Lord Sheffield flashed his charismatic smile. 'For you, my lady… anything.'

Dudley was relieved. 'Good, then it's agreed, join Parr's forces and see that they are defeated. I have a spy amongst Kett's ranks by the name of Luke Miller, a good Catholic you can trust.'

Lady Mary held her glass aloft. 'Gentlemen, a toast, to the success of Robert Kett and his rebels, and the downfall of Edward Seymour.'

'And, to Queen Mary,' said Dudley, clinking glasses.

PART 3

Isaiah 40:31
³¹ *but those who hope in the Lord will renew their strength. They will soar on wings like eagles; they will run and not grow weary, they will walk and not be faint.*

34

31st July, Surrey House

The barber surgeon clicked his tongue against the roof of his mouth as he examined Master Peter's swollen hand. The tips of his fingers were turning black, and the rest of his arm was a vivid red. The injury he'd sustained to his right forearm when they'd attacked the bridge nine days ago wasn't healing, and pus seeped from the arrow wound. Alfred put his hand over his nose to guard against the smell that filled the small bedroom that had been cleared for Mr Kett's foreman. Mrs Kett wiped the fever from Master Peter's brow as he lay on the bed. The linen of the straw mattress was soaked in his sweat. He'd been in bed for days and wasn't getting better. The surgeon brushed a fly away.

'We'll have to amputate above the elbow. If we go any lower the malady will return.'

Alfred shuddered. He edged closer to the open window. Mr Kett stood at the foot of the bed, looking drawn and tired. 'What are his chances?'

The surgeon shrugged his shoulders. 'If you keep the windows open to prevent the build-up of miasmas, bleed his good arm with leeches, apply a fresh poultice of cow manure to his stump each day, then he may live. I'd recommend praying for him at least four times a day.'

'Very well,' said Robert, 'do what you have to do.'

Master Peter groaned.

The surgeon turned to Alfred. 'I'll need you to hold him down. First, fetch a bowl for his blood.'

'God be with you, Peter,' said Robert, wiping a tear from his eye. Master Peter had worked for him since he was a boy.

Alice kissed Master Peter's forehead. 'I'll pray for you,' she whispered. She took her husband's hand and led him away. Alfred returned and placed the bowl by the side of the bed. The surgeon untied his canvass bag, unravelling it to expose the tools of his trade, none of which would have looked out of place in a carpenters' workshop. Alfred shivered.

'Tell him to bite on this,' said the surgeon, passing Alfred a small round shaft of oak wood, the teeth marks of previous patients visible.

Master Peter waved his hand to stop Alfred. 'Alfred,' he strained to find the words. 'You have a good soul,' he struggled to swallow. 'Be warned of Fulke.'

'Come, bite on this,' replied Alfred.

'His father was a bad man,' mumbled Master Peter, his face pale and damp. 'He beat them. His mother too. Fulke killed them both. Burned their house while they slept.'

'Sshh,' said Alfred, unable to think about these revelations just as he was about to assist in removing Master Peter's arm.

Master Peter gripped Alfred with what little strength he could muster. 'The apple didn't fall far from the tree, Alfred.'

Alfred placed the wooden bit between Master Peter's teeth.

Why are you telling me this now? Alfred thought.

'Kneel on his arm, and put your weight on his chest,' instructed the surgeon. 'He's weak, but you'll be amazed how much strength they can find when I hit the bone.' The surgeon took his saw from the bag, its blade greased, its wooden handle stained red from the blood of his previous patients.

The colour drained from Alfred's cheeks, and his palms turned cold with sweat.

Master Peter began to scream as the teeth of the surgeon's saw bit into his flesh. Alfred pushed his weight down to stop the patient from wriggling free. A trickle of blood spattered into the bowl below. Master Peter's screams grew louder as the saw blade tore its way through the muscle. Alfred's mouth began to water. He closed his eyes. Beneath him Master Peter fell limp, and his agonising cries fell silent. Alfred heard the rasp of the saw against the bone. The room fell dark.

Alfred passed out too.

*

Next door, Robert heard the thud of what sounded like a body hitting the floor. At least Master Peter's screams had stopped. Robert was grateful for the peace, no matter how temporary it would turn out to be this time. From habit he put his thumb to his mouth before remembering he had no spare nail left to bite.

'Have a seat, Robert, your pacing is making me nervous,' said Mayor Codd. He sat on a small wooden chair, shrouded from sight by the bright sunlight pouring through the window.

Robert ignored the mayor's comments. Mayor Codd had been with him every waking moment since his capture, and his relentless company was beginning to grate. The thought crossed Robert's mind again, to have the mayor transferred to the castle or the guildhall to join the other prisoners of the rebellion. Robert had moved his captives out of Surrey House to the city's cells, and their removal had created some much-needed breathing space around his headquarters. The mayor though, notwithstanding his relationship, was too valuable a piece to surrender his custody. Instead, he lived cheek by jowl with Robert, if not helping the movement, then at least providing it with the image of the legitimacy it required.

The door opened, and Alice entered carrying two jugs and a stick of burning incense. 'I thought you men might appreciate some ale.'

Thank God for Alice, thought Robert. How right she was. She placed the incense into a small clay pot on the mantelpiece and closed the door behind her.

Mayor Codd raised his jug and said cheers to a peaceful outcome. Without replying, Robert up-ended his jug and sank half its contents, the pewter rim pressing painfully against the sore that had broken on his lip at the corner of his mouth. Against his better judgment he was drinking more heavily than usual this past week. It offered temporary comfort from the problems that faced him on all fronts. Following the herald's departure there had been nothing but silence from London.

Despite Mayor Codd's reservations, Robert had met with Deputy Mayor Steward on his return from London. Steward had proved insightful. His prediction of a military response was prophetic. Yesterday, a royal army had been sited quartering at Cambridge. It would only be a matter of time before they showed up at Robert's door.

He took another mouthful and put his empty jug down on the small table opposite the empty fireplace. His legs were tired and begged to be seated. Robert resisted, whenever he was stationary, he was tortured by his fears. Since he'd captured Norwich any hopes of feeding his followers being eased were compromised by the further swelling of his camp. In the following five days an additional five thousand people had arrived. Some came from as far afield as Essex and Cambridgeshire, keen to experience life free from the clutches of their landlords. What had started as a protest against enclosure had turned into a campaign for justice — an end to feudalism. Not all the new arrivals bore such noble intentions. Young men especially, in the absence of their elders and betters were bent on revelling in the downfall of the traditional powers of state.

Robert stopped his pacing and took in the view from the window. The camp now sprawled out to the other heath beyond the gulley. Totalling fifteen thousand, Robert's followers now outnumbered the populace of Norwich living in their shadow. Despite Robert's efforts to keep his people out of the city, the lines between the camp and the city had blurred. Many of his followers had opted to move into more comfortable quarters under a roof, and all the city's churches acted as dormitories for Robert's followers. Vacant homes, abandoned by their gentlemen owners, had been commandeered as people fell prey to the temptation of sampling the splendour and comfort of those they fought. An irony that was as lost on them as it was apparent to Robert.

The nature of the city had changed. Some of the inhabitants had fled, fearing for their safety. Others with more commercial instincts were attracted by the opportunities that could be realised by meeting the needs of so many extra people in one place, all with loot to spend, bellies and bladders to fill and seed to spill. Some were making a tidy fortune, provided they could stay safe enough to keep hold of their takings.

'I still think you should keep a closer eye on Augustine

Steward,' said the mayor for the tenth time this week.

'Thomas, if it weren't for Steward, I doubt very much that Norwich would exist.'

Having returned from the safety of London the deputy mayor had met with Robert, testified to what he'd witnessed in London and then volunteered to take responsibility for the safety of Norwich. An offer Robert was only too keen to accept as it was one less burden for him to shoulder. On Robert's first night in charge of Norwich after the attack, sporadic fights had broken out, undefended homes had been looted, some of them set ablaze. Thank the heavens there had not been a wind on which to carry the flames, thereby sparing the city from destruction.

'You can't trust him, Robert.'

'Enough,' snapped Robert. 'Steward has one job to do, and he's proved himself more than capable of keeping order. The last thing I want on my conscience when I arrive at the pearly gates of heaven is having to account for why I allowed a city of God to be sacked and torched.'

'Well…'

'Well nothing. I won't debate it with you further, Thomas.'

The mayor's constant provocations over Steward seemed to Robert to reflect the mayor's own failings in his role.

How well would you be coping if you were charged with his responsibilities? Not as well, I'd wager.

With Robert's permission, Steward had drafted in notable clergymen to preach the virtues of peace and order in the city and in the camp. Only Mathew Parker, supposedly one of the most captivating preachers in the land, had stepped beyond his remit by suggesting the 'rebels' disband and return home, lest they be punished by God. He'd scurried back to Cambridge, with his tail firmly between his legs, lucky to still be in the clothes he was wearing.

'I know him, Robert.'

'God give me peace, man,' barked Robert, as William appeared in the room; his expression serious. 'Brother, the king's army is here. A mile from the city gates.'

35

William Parr's horse flicked its head to the side, brushing away the fly that circled its eye. Parr twitched his reins.

'Have you been there before?' he asked Lord Sheffield, mounted to his right.

From the highest point of the road, a mile outside of Norwich, they could see the cathedral spire, the battlements of the castle keep and the shadowy flint church towers. The city lay still, like a dog basking in the afternoon sun.

'I make it my habit to avoid cities as a rule,' replied Sheffield.

What sort of bite would this dog have? Parr wondered as he nodded. His horse swung its head again, narrowly missing Sheffield's horse. Parr tugged on the reins and clicked his tongue twice. On the road immediately behind them waited his generals: Southwell, Warner, Paston, Cornwallis, Bedingfield, Clere and Walgrave. The column of the army stretched out beyond them like a restless snake. Five hundred mounted cavalry, followed by a thousand men at arms. Amongst them, four hundred Italian mercenaries and a further two hundred Swiss mercenaries. At the rear, teams of horses attached to carts laden with cannon, powder, shot and other supplies.

Earlier, the herald had been sent ahead demand the surrender of the rebels. While they waited for him to return, Parr's mind turned to where they could camp for the night. They had been late leaving Thetford that morning as Lord Sheffield's horse had unhelpfully fallen lame just before they were due to leave. Precious time was wasted while he sought a replacement. Having since marched hard all day, it was now early afternoon.

To the north the clouds threatened rain.

The flat terrain of Norfolk rolled into a series of small hills and valleys south of Norwich. Parr preferred to camp on flat ground. It gave better visibility of any approaching forces should Kett attempt to pick at the edges of his camp under cover of darkness.

It's what he would do in Kett's position.

He considered his options. Parr had been on campaigns before and was no stranger to battle, but this was his long-awaited first command. He was thirty-six years old and now realised how easy the commanders he'd fought under had made it look.

Now it was his turn in the saddle. The full weight of the decisions facing him and the consequences of each weighed on his mind. His orders were clear: capture Norwich, arrest Kett and his deputies and disperse the rebellion.

'Here he comes,' said Sheffield, as the galloping horse of the returning herald came into dusty view.

Parr threw back his shoulders. He wanted to look authoritative in front of his generals, some of whom he knew were sceptical of his unproven abilities.

Get to the facts, he reminded himself.

'Well, herald, what news have you?'

In his effeminate voice, the herald simpered, 'The gates were open.'

Parr frowned.

'I was greeted by the deputy mayor, Augustine Steward.'

Parr remembered that name. He was the hawkish fellow who had attended the council meeting in Whitehall. 'And?'

'I demanded the city's immediate surrender.'

'Well?' asked Parr wishing this fellow would get to the point.

'Steward said he wasn't in a position to grant the surrender, as that must be done by the mayor, who was still in office. However, he was at pains to point out that the city is not hostile to you, your grace.'

'Are you saying that the city is offering no resistance to royal authority?'

The herald looked uncertain.

'What about Kett?'

'He and his forces are situated on an area of heathland outside the city's eastern boundary.'

'He doesn't hold Norwich captive?'

'No, sir, not directly. He does hold the mayor captive and a great many of the aldermen.'

In all the time Parr had spent thinking about the probabilities he faced, this wasn't one he'd considered. He'd expected a siege, similar to that in Exeter.

'So, Norwich is undefended?'

The herald nodded. 'The gates were open and the walls unmanned, barring a few interested folk straining for a view of your grace's army.'

Parr stroked his chin. This must be a trap. It was too easy. He glanced up at the sky, checking the sun's progress shrouded behind the clouds.

'Go back and fetch this Steward fellow.'

The herald sighed but, as instructed, once again made his way back to Norwich.

In the period that followed, Parr reflected on these unexpected events. The cavalry had dispersed to graze their horses. The soldiers formed groups, playing cards, dozing, chatting and joking. Parr ignored the comments he overheard from one of the generals, bemoaning the lack of discipline. To Parrs's mind, after their late start, the more rested they were, the better. He'd placed scouts and trumpeters half a mile to each flank. However unlikely a surprise attack might be, they would have time to ready themselves.

The herald and deputy mayor drew to a halt.

'The city of Norwich remains loyal to King Edward and extends the hand of friendship to you all,' announced Steward.

Was that a note of sarcasm, he detected. The figure in a dark robe continued, 'I bring with me the city's sword of state, as a symbol of our welcome and in hope that you shall deliver us from evil.'

Parr dismissed his earlier concerns and beckoned over the deputy mayor. From their saddles they shook hands.

'Where's Mr Kett, and where are the rebels?'

He went on with his list of questions; why were they staying out of the city, how many of them were there, were they armed, what was the heath like, what surrounded it, and so on.

For the most part, he found Steward cooperative, occasionally evasive, but above all, Parr was satisfied he was honourable, although his answers provided the young commander with little comfort. Any approach to the rebel camp from the south was rendered impossible, the river protected their southern flank, and there wasn't a suitable crossing between this road and where the river met the sea at Great Yarmouth over twenty miles to their east. Any attempt to outflank them to the north was risky as they would be forced to cross the river on a narrow bridge at the village of Hellesdon. The village was known to be sympathetic to the rebels, and once word spread of the army's movement in that direction, they would be sitting ducks if the rebels could mobilise their archers to take advantage of the bottleneck. It was the sheer size of the enemy that gave the young commander his biggest headache. Even if the deputy mayor's reports of fifteen thousand rebels were exaggerated, he was outnumbered ten-to-one. Combined with the rebels terrain advantage, this rendered an attack impossible, even with professional soldiers.

He would have to defend.

'Let me ask you, Mr Steward, if this heath on which our rebels are camped is impregnable, what is the key to drawing them off their perch?'

'You, sir, are the military man. You will know better than I. The only comment I can make is that after nineteen days, their living conditions are nothing short of squalid. It won't be long before the rats outnumber the rebels. They have scavenged every living beast within twenty miles. They are now entirely dependent on the city to feed them. It is my understanding that what little funds they had have been exhausted, so they cannot buy fish from the coast or produce from further afield. Indeed, I haven't heard of a boat entering the city for over a week, for fear of piracy. They are surviving on the city's grain reserves. Without our bakeries and breweries, they will starve, so I would suggest you target them,' he concluded, in a tone that suggested he was happy to wash his hands of any further responsibility.

Parr nodded. 'Have all the grain loaded up and sent to me here.'

Steward frowned in disbelief. 'I'm not at liberty to take the grain. It is guarded by men loyal to Kett. My throat will be slit if I so much as set foot…'

Parr grunted.

'This is a trap, Steward…'

'No,' said Steward, sounding indignant. 'I make no suggestion; just relay the facts as you seek them, and as I find them to be.'

Parr could sense his generals' impatience. He had to make a decision. He didn't like any of his choices, but he knew he only really had one.

'If I may offer a suggestion, your grace?' asked Sheffield, who'd kept his counsel quiet until now.

'By all means,' said Parr.

'The heavens threaten to open. We can't stay here. A wet and hungry army will not fight well. Let us take Norwich, and show these beasts we mean business.'

'Sheffield, can you not see it's a trap?'

'Then lets us walk in, and take their bait. Our forces can easily overpower their guard. We'll burn their granaries to the ground; then we've got them.'

Steward interrupted. 'If you burn the granaries, the subjects of Norwich will lynch you themselves, and I must say I'd be tempted to help them. You were ordered to save the city, not to condemn it,' his voice growing louder as he went.

'Enough,' snapped Parr.

'I apologise,' said Sheffield. 'Then we merely capture the grain. Once they know it's gone then…'

'Will he negotiate?' asked Parr.

'Kett?' Steward said. 'If you ask me, he's in over his head. He'll be keen to avoid violence at all costs. The sacrifice of his rebels when they stormed the city was said to take a great toll on him.'

That was good. Parr knew from the experience of

previous campaigns that a cowardly opponent was easy to manipulate. Going into the city was dangerous, but it confirmed what Parr already knew. It was his only choice. If he could secure the food, Kett would be forced to accept his invitation to negotiate. He would snatch this jumped-up tanner as he walked back into his own trap. It wasn't without risk, but if all went according to plan they could be on their way back to London by tomorrow. Parr tapped his clenched fist against his mouth as he considered his only doubt: Kett must be expecting him to take this course of action. What response would Kett have planned?

'Deputy mayor, we are vulnerable in the city. You will be obliged to feed us, and your subjects must quarter our men in their houses. All being well, we'll be gone by tomorrow evening.'

Steward agreed, adding, 'On condition that the troops conduct themselves by God's laws. The foreign ones especially.'

Parr signalled his agreement by reaching for the ceremonial sword, which Steward carried. 'Then you better lead the way, deputy mayor.' He turned and spoke to the trumpeter, 'Sound your horn. We are leaving.'

*

A drumbeat pounded from the top of the city's main gate. St George's flags flapped in the wind. Rose petals blew past Parr's head as subjects threw them from the top of the curtain wall. Their heads peered over between the crenulations, some eager to welcome their saviours, others to assess the strength of their enemy. Whatever their allegiances, Norwich's inhabitants were excited to witness the rare spectacle of a royal army entering their city.

Parr had an uneasy feeling of being watched as he and his column followed Steward through the vaulted flint archway of the gatehouse.

Women reached up to give him flowers, and dirty-faced children moved about his horse like cats brushing against their masters' legs. They jumped up to touch his armour and saddlecloth, their gap-tooth grins and excited questions swirled around him. Behind Parr, his trumpeters sounded the royal tune. The street ahead was wide, plenty big enough for two carts to pass in opposite directions on its pitted and dry surface, lined with three-storey timber frame houses belonging to the merchant class. Amongst fine well-kept houses, were others that bore the hallmarks of decline. Their thatch had turned dark with green mould at the edges, missing wooden roof tiles, windows crudely boarded up, weeds taking root on any flat surface, the colour of the walls faded, the edges of the oak beams creeping inwards as they rotted. The mixed fortunes of the residents were evident in the look of the place, which was once wealthy and had since fallen on harder times. The crowds followed them closely as they made their way to the end of the street, into the marketplace.

Parr was surprised by its size, equal to any of London's. Only a few stallholders waited behind their wooden carts hoping to cash in on the arrival of the army. A gathering of strumpets in their striped hoods were gathered around the market cross.

Steward barked at them to be gone and threatened to have the constable arrest their husbands.

Parr turned to his general. 'Pass on the order, form the army into ranks across the marketplace, let us parade our strength for all to see. We will meet at the top there,' pointing to the large flint building in the corner of the sloping marketplace, 'to receive your orders.' Sheffield and Cornwallis nodded and relayed the instructions back to the others. 'Steward, you stay with me,' said Parr.

Half an hour later the church bells rang four of the clock. Parr's generals formed around him and Steward in a half circle outside the guildhall. The rain that threated had not darkened the earth of the streets.

Behind the generals amassed the fifteen hundred troops standing in straight lines that neatly filled the marketplace. From the wooden buildings, local faces could be seen looking on in awe from every window. In the streets that led to the marketplace, people stood nervously peering out at the army, waiting to see what they would do.

Parr cleared his throat. 'Men,' he turned his attention to the battle-hardened men of all shapes and sizes that comprised his generals, 'listen carefully, we have only five hours to prepare ourselves before darkness. We must be ready for an attack. Our plan is to draw Kett in to negotiate.' They listened intently, motionless. 'To do this, 'he continued, 'we must capture the granaries. Paston, that's your job.'

The old man nodded, without issue.

Turning his attentions to the deputy mayor, he continued, 'Mr Steward. You will impose a curfew. I don't want anybody on these streets other than my men after seven o'clock. No beggars, no vagrants, none of your constables. Anyone other than my men found on the streets will be treated as a rebel and dealt with accordingly.'

'The authority to do that rests with Mayor Codd.'

Parr brought his hand to rest on the hilt of his sword. His scowl made it clear he would not tolerate the protocol of petty politics.

'Very well,' acquiesced Steward. 'I'll have the criers posted, and the bells sounded.'

Parr continued, beginning to feel at ease. 'We don't have enough men to adequately hold the entire city, so we will concentrate our strength on defending the heart of the city here. Steward, please point out the main approaches to the generals.'

Steward nodded and cleared his throat as he thought for a moment. 'I would expect the rebels to approach the city in the most direct fashion, as they did last time. If you look beyond the castle keep over there, you will see for yourselves the heathland that forms their stronghold.' Steward waited for the generals to return their attention to him. 'To prevent them entering the heart of the city there are five streets which you will need to control. One is north of the river leading from the Pockthorpe Gate to the bridge at Whitefriars. However, they are most likely to approach on Bishopsgate, so I would counsel you to form the bulk of your defences in that area beyond the cathedral. The cathedral is walled, which will force their movement around it. If they move south, around it, you can pin them down in the streets between the cathedral and the castle. One further blockade beyond the castle should be enough.'

'Good, thank you, Steward,' Parr turned to his generals. 'That's five streets. You will each be responsible for establishing and defending a blockade across one of those streets. We'll split the cannon, one for each street. With buildings on each side and narrow streets you'll knock the rebels over like skittles, and they won't be able to capitalise on the supremacy of their manpower.'

His men nodded.

'What if the rebels attack us from above, from the windows and rooftops?' asked Clere, who was always quick to question rather than think for himself.

'Place gunners in the windows first,' snapped Parr, making

it clear he wanted no further interruptions. 'You will each be responsible for holding the rebels at bay from your blockade. If you fail, the king shall hear of your incompetence.'

Parr looked around the faces of his generals, making sure to meet eyes with each of them. 'When, we hold off any rebel attacks, Kett will have no choice but to negotiate from a position of weakness.' A prospect, which Parr could feel himself already looking forward to.

'It is a full moon tonight, which is to our advantage. I will appoint you each a trumpeter. Sound the alarm if you fall under attack. I will hold reinforcements here and send them to those of you under attack.'

Parr looked to the most elderly of his generals, Sir William. 'Walgrave, it shall be your job to build a bonfire in each corner of the marketplace. I want it to be as bright as day.'

Walgrave nodded.

Steward cleared his throat. 'Given the thatch,' he said indicating some of the surrounding rooftops, 'would it be safer to construct one larger fire in the middle of the marketplace?'

Parr ignored the deputy mayor. 'What he's saying, Walgrave, is don't set fire to the city.' A murmur of amusement trickled through the circle of men.

'But, sir,' protest Steward.

'But nothing,' interrupted Parr pointing at Steward. 'For your own safety, the law requires you to build with wooden roof tiles in a city. If your city has ignored the law, don't later expect its protection.'

'How will it be to your advantage if the marketplace catches fire, Mr Parr?'

Parr glared at the deputy mayor.

'I appreciate your comments regarding the law,' said

Steward in a more conciliatory tone, 'but you have seen for yourself the depleted nature of our tree stock.'

'Very well, Walgrave, one fire in the middle. Now, Steward, take us to each of the streets leading inwards from the rebels' position, then,' he looked at his generals, 'we'll divvy up who goes where. Lord Sheffield, you watch over the army in the meantime.' Parr felt relief that his first briefing had passed without incident. His plan was robust.

*

For Sheffield, it had been a day of mixed fortunes. He'd successfully delayed their departure, which had now reduced their preparation time. Parr had been lured into the city where his cavalry would be ineffective. They were outnumbered. The threat of harrying attacks in the tight maze of narrow and unfamiliar streets had, unfortunately, been defused by Parr who had begun to prove himself a proficient commander.

He had, however, made his first mistake: in his haste he'd neglected to appoint a bodyguard for himself. If Sheffield could send word to Princess Mary's spy in Kett's camp, Luke Miller, then perhaps the rebels could happen across the undefended Parr inspecting his defences on foot.

How he might get word to the rebels without arousing suspicion, was uppermost in his mind.

36

There was a knock at the door. Tiniker wiped the flour from her hands on her apron and left the dough resting in the bowl. It was Alfred. She tried not to betray her gladness as she invited him in. Since the death of her father she had come to look forward to his visits more than she was comfortable admitting. He brought sunshine to her otherwise cloudy days. She was frightened that she was starting to rely on him.

Tiniker didn't want to come to depend on anyone but herself.

Alfred paused as he passed her, but Tiniker looked away. They hadn't kissed again since the day they met, and he'd led her home through the rebel camp.

Tiniker was adamant she wouldn't fall for him while she was in mourning. Her late mother had warned her not to take risks with her heart when vulnerable.

The room darkened when she closed the door behind him. The only light came from a window that overlooked the orchards and meadows to the rear of the house. There was no glass, only wooden shutters that opened inwards against the wall.

'Where's Margreet?' asked Alfred.

He stopped by the modest wooden table in the centre of the room, its uneven surface pitted with the small holes of woodworm.

'Sleeping,' said Tiniker, her eyes motioned upwards. 'She's been bad today.'

Alfred nodded knowingly. Without saying much he had a way of understanding what she and her sister were suffering. She'd discovered he'd already lost his parents, as well as his wife. His unspoken empathy had been the only comfort Tiniker had found in the previous week. She noticed he looked paler than usual.

'You all right?'

'Hmm, yeah fine, just a sore head,' he said, dismissing her concern.

'I'm afraid I don't have any herbs left.'

Alfred poked his finger through the bars of the wire cage on the table. Piepen squawked and fluttered his little yellow wings. Tiniker had brought him downstairs from the weaving room to keep her company. Alfred was fascinated by the canary, having never seen one before; every day he'd gently tormented it, fed it and studied it.

Tiniker smiled, the house was a better place with life in it. Even the burgeoning friendship between a little yellow bird and an Englishman was enough to briefly take her mind off her father's death and the circumstances she now faced.

'Now you're here, would you help with fetching the sack of flour the next room. I've just finished this one.'

Each day, Tiniker made lists in her mind of jobs she could get Alfred to do when he visited. He had lots to do for Mr Kett, but the longer she could keep him here was a moment less lonely. Her nights had become hours of sleepless despair. She couldn't bring herself to use her father's mattress, so she still shared her bed with Margreet, who slept soundly every hour of the night and many during the daylight. Tiniker tossed and turned, fretting: how would she find enough money to survive?

Would Mr Steward be good to his word and let them keep the house? She had only heard from the deputy mayor once since the city's capture.

What would become of Margreet? Should they return to Flanders? Where was home? Her tired mind tried to make sense of matters, always arriving at the same conclusions: without money they would starve, without shelter they would perish. Defeated, she'd finally drift off, sleeping through into the morning. Not that it mattered, it was better she stayed indoors and saw that the house was safe. She'd seen rebels walking past back to the camp with arms full of loot relieved from people's homes.

Alfred propped the heavy sack of milled flour against the wall away from the fireplace. 'Have you heard?'

'What?' asked Tiniker.

'There's a royal army on its way to fight us. They may even be here by now.'

'Alfred, will you stay here with us, keep us safe?'

'You'll be safe. Their fight isn't with you.'

Tiniker instinctively checked the bolt on the front door.

'It's us they're after,' said Alfred, proudly.

He was so naïve.

Soldiers routinely took women as a prize. Her house, by the bridge, had been at the heart of the last battle. She wiped tears from her eyes.

'Please? Alfred.'

He took her in his arms. She felt small wrapped in his embrace —her cheek pressed into his chest. For a moment, she allowed herself to feel safe, loved even as Alfred's hand smoothed her back.

'Dank je,' she whispered.

They heard a noise near the door. Swish. There followed two knocks.

'What's this?' asked Alfred, breaking their embrace. 'Somebody's just pushed something under your door.'

Tiniker turned to see a piece of paper, bright against the hard earth floor. Puzzled, she walked over to pick it up. It was folded in half, on the inside a message.

Find out Kett's intentions. AS.

Tiniker closed it and folded in half again, pressing it between her hands.

'What is it?' asked Alfred.

AS... Why did the devil have to pick such poor timing?

'Tiniker?'

She turned to face him, putting her arms behind her back, clenching the note in her hands. Standing opposite each other with him looking down at her, she felt bare. His frown turned from quizzical to wary.

'You look guilty? It's a note from another man, isn't it?'

Tiniker looked away. 'No,' she muttered.

'What is it then?'

'It's a warning,' she said before adding more confidently, 'about the army arriving.'

Alfred shook his head. He didn't believe her. She looked away, desperate to think of something to say.

'Show me.'

Tiniker shook her head; tears welled in the corner of her eyes.

'You're hiding something.' He frowned. 'Every afternoon I come here and do everything you ask. It's another man, isn't it?'

His accusation stung. 'No.' She shook her head. 'I love

you, Alfred,' she said, tears streaming down her cheeks.

'I thought you were too good to be true,' said Alfred as if resigning himself to his fears. 'You're beautiful, and you could have any man. Good things never happened to me.'

'No,' said Tiniker, tears rolling down her cheeks.

'People who love each don't have secrets,' he said. 'Nor do they tell lies.' He barged past her as she sobbed. 'Goodbye, Tiniker.'

*

The finality of those words hit Alfred just as hard as he emerged from the gloom of her house to the glare of the grey evening sky. The street was deserted. Whoever her mystery messenger was, he'd gone. Alfred wiped a tear from his eye. He shouldn't have come — her arrival in his life coincided too readily with Lynn's departure. She had been sent to taunt him; it would have been better never to have worked his hopes up. He cursed himself for allowing himself to believe that she could be real.

This wouldn't do, he said to himself, wiping his eyes with the sleeve of his shirt. There was much to be done at camp, and then he had soldiers to fight.

37

'Where the hell are they?' demanded Robert as he paced the floor tiles of the hallway. 'They should be back by now.'

His thoughts battled for attention against the hum of the lively discussions taking place in the dining room next door. William looked doubtful. Their scouts had left for the city shortly after the army had arrived, and they were supposed to be back at Surrey House by seven o'clock. It was now a little after eight.

'Steward will betray you,' repeated Mayor Codd.

'Mayor, if you don't leave this room immediately, I will have you thrown in a cell.' Robert pointed to the door that led down the steps to the cellar. 'Indefinitely.'

The mayor shuffled out of the hallway in the direction of the kitchen. Robert felt a surge of relief to have finally rid himself of the presence that had slowly chipped away at his patience.

'Robert, we may yet need the mayor,' said William.

'He won't be hard to find. He's spent the past week closer to me than my own shadow.'

The door from the dining room opened, filling the hall with the emboldened rhetoric of the representatives within.

Anders Marshwell rested his hand on the knob, and his weight against the doorframe.

'Are they back?'

William shook his head.

'I think you two should come back in.' Anders' tone suggested things were getting worse.

Robert sighed and followed his brother through to the dining room, determined not to succumb to the blood lust of ignorant men.

*

Parr had expected to face the strongest rebel advance, closest to the heath, at the barricades in the shadow of the cathedral. General Cornwallis had done a thorough job. His soldiers had relieved the neighbouring houses of their tables, barrels, floorboards and together with a fruit cart, dragged them across the street shielding the men at arms that knelt behind them. At the centre of the barricade, amongst the assemble of wooden materials, was a small porthole from which it was just possible to make out the muzzle of a cannon.

'They won't see it until it's too late.'

Parr nodded. 'Your arquebusiers?'

'In position. Out of sight.'

'Well, if I can't see them, the rebels won't either. Good work. The foundries are making you extra shot as we speak.'

'I doubt we'll need it, sir.'

'Well, I am leaving nothing to chance. Small details can make all the difference.'

Cornwallis nodded.

Parr looked beyond the barricade down the street. The flint wall of the cathedral precinct on one side and a row of houses on the other made the perfect corridor into which the rebels would be funnelled as they rounded the corner from Bishopsgate.

The curfew had ensured the streets were deserted. Windows were shuttered. Doors bolted. This desertion had made apprehending Kett's returning scouts easy.

They would, under torture, be revealing their secrets at this very moment.

The light was fading. A breeze stroked Parr's face, taking with it the stench of the city. The threat of rain had passed, much to the gunners' relief; they would not need to worry about their powder getting damp.

'Anybody passing to the north of the cathedral has to pass through your barricade. Nobody passes you,' ordered Parr, pointing at Cornwallis.

Parr's plan was robust, and his forces well prepared. But an ambush was only effective if it was a surprise.

'Give them hell, general. You have my permission to kill anybody on these streets tonight. The rebels must be kept in the dark. You've got Lord Sheffield in reserve if you need him.'

*

'No,' said Robert, barely holding his temper as he stood. 'This is not a violent movement. We *must* negotiate.'

Around the table sat as many of the camp's representatives as could be seated, the rest leaning against the wood-panelled wall of Surrey House dining room. Two-thirds of them jeered. The rest exchanged whispers between themselves or stared at Robert. None came to his aid.

'How,' exclaimed Bossell, pointing his stubby finger at Kett from across the table, 'can you say, now, that this isn't a violent movement when a good number of our men lay buried in the very slope you commanded them to run down into a storm of arrows?'

'Don't simplify,' pleaded Robert.

More jeers. Robert was losing their good faith. He needed a new approach. Behind Bossell, he caught a glimpse of Alfred stood by the door.

'Fetch us some ale.'

Alfred shook his head. 'I regret we have run out, sir.'

'See,' shouted Bossell. 'We have no provisions. We will be starving by noon tomorrow.'

Bossell was right. Fifteen thousand people would not wait patiently with their bellies empty. Robert knew he had to get across the table from the army commander before the evening was out.

'Very well,' said Robert. 'We will attack,'

People on both sides sprung from their seats amidst a contradictory chorus of cheers and boos.

'After,' shouted Robert making himself heard over their tumult. 'I have visited their commander in person.'

The room fell silent.

'I will negotiate our demands. If I am unsuccessful, we will attack.'

The room was still, only the movement of a few heads gently nodding.

Thank the Lord, thought Robert, common sense has prevailed.

'No!' came a voice.

Robert looked at him, askance.

'*No*,' repeated William shaking his head. 'Brother, your intentions are honourable, but as the day is long, I swear you shall not return from the negotiations. Not at least with your head attached to your neck.'

What?

Did William not realise his words were committing hundreds to die and sealing their fate as outlaws?

'Robert, if they had really wanted to negotiate they would have sent that lousy herald of theirs. Instead,' he tapped the table with the blade of his hand, 'they have come and taken positions and readied themselves for battle.' He raised a finger, 'If you, our leader, walk into their jaws, even with a thousand men for protection, they'll take their opportunity.'

An uneasy silence hung in the stale air.

'If they kill you, the rebellion dies.'

'You,' snapped Robert, 'will take my place.'

'And we'll fight anyway,' said William.

A murmur of agreement rippled through the room. 'Robert, your death will achieve nothing and prevent nothing.'

'Precisely,' added Bossell. 'Let us negotiate from a position of strength. With our numbers we cannot fail.'

Amongst the cheers and declarations of agreements, Robert was conscious of his failure. He'd lost the room. There was little sense in putting it to a vote. He was outnumbered and had been outmanoeuvred by Bossell, with his own brother to thank for nailing his coffin shut.

'Very well,' he said, meeting as many sets of eyes as he could. 'I am only here because of what I believed was right and with all my heart I cannot find it within me to lead men once more in a course I cannot condone. If I no longer have your support, then I am no longer fit to lead.' The room listened in stunned silence. 'I wish you the very best for your attack tonight, but I will have no part in it.'

'Robert,' breathed William.

'No, brother,' interrupted Robert. 'You've said quite enough already.'

Robert felt the pang in his stomach ease as he walked past

the shocked faces of his representatives and left the room.

*

'What will you do, Fulke?'

'What the hell do you think I'll do? I'm going, of course. I wouldn't miss this for all the fools in government!'

Alfred smirked and wondered why he'd asked.

Adam Catchpole slapped Fulke on the back.

'What about you, Geoffrey?'

Geoffrey Lincoln shook his head. 'No.'

'What do you mean, no?' snapped Fulke 'You staying loyal to that old windbag, Kett?'

Adam laughed and pointed to Geoffrey's guts.

Geoffrey nodded. 'Poor Geoff's got the trots!' grinned Adam.

'Worried about shitting your breeches are you, Geoffrey?' asked Fulke.

'Yeah, you'll never let me live it down.'

'Ah well, your loss.'

The atmosphere in the camp was noisy, one of confusion and uncertainty, as people debated between themselves what to do. News of John Bossell's challenge to Mr Kett had been met with mixed reactions. Those that had wanted violence were glad of their chance to act. Those that believed in Mr Kett, which seemed to Alfred to be the vast majority of the camp, were left bewildered. A rumour circulated that a few people were packing up their things and going home. Alfred was past caring what happened. If men far cleverer than he couldn't make their minds up, how could he know what was right?

He rested his hand on the hilt of his sword, tucked into his belt.

It calmed his busy nerves, although they were not as bad as the time before.

He knew he had what it took to fight.

Last time, he'd set off with nothing than a blunt kitchen knife. Now he had the sword he'd scavenged from the battle. He'd cleaned and greased the blade and sharpened it so much he dare not touch it.

He watched Fulke retie his bootlaces and search for his cleaver. Master Peter's words came back to him, and he wondered if it could be true, would Fulke have murdered his own parents? Alfred imagined his parents trapped in their burning house and shuddered at the thought.

'You staying here to scrub Kett's backside, then?'

'No, I am not,' replied Alfred, indignant. 'I'm coming too. It's what we came here for.'

He wasn't sure it was, especially since Mr Kett hadn't sanctioned the attack, but the sight of Master Peter having his arm cut off and the discovery that Tiniker had another man had left Alfred feeling that somebody should be made to suffer for the things he'd witnessed today.

'Good lad,' replied Fulke, cuffing Alfred's arm.

'Right then, I'm ready,' said Fulke, 'Let's leave these cowards and join with the rest at the oak tree.'

*

The livestock pen had been commandeered to corral the cavalry horses. Most of the horses slept with their saddles on. A few cast their noses about the ground in search of the last of the hay that been spread about their hooves earlier. Parr had retired to Steward's house for dinner, so Sheffield had volunteered to keep watch in the marketplace. He stroked a horse's nose as it chewed. As his fingers touched the soft pad of the drowsy beast's snout, he pondered how it was that a horse could be so docile one moment, then so strong and alert the next. The glow of the bonfire reflected in the animal's eye. Sheffield watched as hot embers drifted skywards.

An hour earlier he'd followed Parr's messenger sent to the heath with a note inviting Kett to negotiate. Sheffield had intercepted him and volunteered to take the message himself. When the messenger had refused, Sheffield had stuck the point of his knife into the man's guts. He'd kept the note to show Lady Mary. It was scrunched up in his purse. Now returning to the door of the guildhall, he saw a string of small, bright flashes coming from the direction of the heath. Moments later he heard the unmistakable faint bangs of distant cannons firing. In the near distance behind the houses surrounding the marketplace, he heard breaking glass and cracking timber as the cannonballs thumped into their unsuspecting targets.

Sheffield stretched out his arms.

Good for you, he thought and went to fetch his horse.

*

The rebels charged, down the bank, over their buried brethren and splashed into the river. Alfred's heart pounded as he struggled through the water and climbed the far bank, the blade of his sword glistening in the moon's light. The defences were empty, deserted. They made their way past Tiniker's house and up Bishopsgate, towards the cathedral.

*

The soldiers, positioned just past the sharp bend at the end of

Bishopsgate, sat crouched behind their barricades. The rebel cannon fire had ceased. Now came rebel voices. Through the gaps in the barricade, the soldiers peeked out at the road in front. In the moonlight the rebel's faces appeared at the end of the street, closely followed by more, carrying burning torches. They poured around the corner, swept along by the momentum of those behind them as they pushed farther into the narrow street. Spotting the barricade, the rebels realised their path was blocked and alarm rippled through their ranks.

The soldiers remained as still as statues.

There was no turning back for the rebels, and their walk quickened to a jog, weapons raised aloft. The night air filled with the roar of their battle cries. Behind the barricade came a short fizz of tinder burning as a flint was struck, a hiss of gunpowder then a bang loud enough to make ears bleed. A bulk of broken flints flew forth. Screams erupted from the rebels as the men at the centre of their approach were cut to ribbons.

Parr's trap was sprung.

*

In Surrey House, Robert finished his wine and put his empty tankard down on the table. He felt numb. Too tired to think, too ill at ease to sleep. As Wednesday passed silently into Thursday he watched the distant flashes of cannon muzzles briefly illuminate the streets of Norwich, and the cathedral briefly lit by small flashes followed by the crack of gunfire. Wherever Bossell had taken his followers, they would come across an opposition unlike anything to which they were accustomed.

How has it come to this? Robert wondered.

He felt lousy. Beaten. Sick. He felt a hand on his shoulder.

It was Alice. He hadn't even heard her come into the room.

'How is he?' asked Robert, referring to Master Peter in the next room.

'Feverish, sleeping,' said Alice softly. 'He's dreaming. Making some funny noises.'

She put her arms around Robert's waist and leaned to the side to see out of the window. 'What do you hope for them?'

'I don't know. Victory, I suppose. A safe return. Or a quick death.'

Alice said nothing. He knew she would want to know what he planned to do next, but he loved her all the more for not asking him tonight. That was a decision for a different day. He closed his eyes, as another boom punctuated the night air. He heard the shriek of a horse whinnying, the clash of steel, the screams of men.

'Come to bed, love. There's no good to come from listening to this.'

She was right. There was nothing more he could do.

It was some time later when their bedroom door flew open, a worried-looking William entering the room. Robert lay awake on his bed. Still dressed.

'Brother?'

'Robert, get up.'

Robert heaved himself up from the bed and followed William downstairs. The house was quiet. Mayor Codd stood in the hallway next to a panic-stricken man holding his cap in his hands. His skin was splashed with blood.

'They ambushed us,' he trembled.

'Now, lad, take a deep breath and steady yourself. Tell me what happened.'

'We crossed the river, no problem. As we got close to the cathedral they'd blocked off the roads, when we got close,' the man shook, 'they opened fire, cannon cut right through our lads. They had gunners on the rooftops. We tried to retreat, but their horses charged us from behind. They come out of nowhere.' Tears welled in his eyes. 'We was trapped.'

'Did anyone survive?'

The man's lip trembled. 'They were cutting us down as we ran away.'

'Bossell?'

The man shook his head.

'Robert, there could be our men still trapped in the city. It will be daylight shortly. They will be killed if they're caught,' said William.

Robert nodded and let out a deep sigh.

He would have to lead after all.

38

1st August, Norwich

Fulke woke with a start. His mouth was bone dry. It took a moment to remember where he was. He'd slept tucked up against a wall, under a window. Above him was a thatched roof. He pulled himself up onto his elbows, his body stiff from fighting. Alfred lay fast asleep on the floorboards. Stealing a look through the window, Fulke quickly drew back. They were directly over the enemy barricade. He watched a soldier take a piss against the wall. Behind the barricade rested the cannon, a small barrel of powder and a pile of flints and stone shot. Soldiers crouched against the barricade. Those farther back looked tired but wary. In front of the barricade the street was covered with the bloodstains of rebels.

Fulke thought back over the events of last night.

With the luck of the devil, he and Alfred had been at the rear of the rebel attack. They'd been following the others when the cannon fired into their front ranks, and gunners, posted on the rooftops, began firing from above. Fortunately, he and Alfred had been in the shadow of the buildings. Their problems had started when the cavalry took up the rear, and they had almost been crushed against the wall. In the stampede that followed, Fulke had been winded and had dropped his meat cleaver, but they had managed to push their way clear as the troops on horseback hacked into the nearest rebels. Fulke grinned, remembering picking up a discarded hatchet and throwing it at a horseman, knocking the man forward with a single blow. He'd been unseated by some rebels and killed.

Together, a handful of rebels had retreated down to Bishopsgate, but their hopes of going that way were cut short by the arrival of more cavalry who gave chase.

Fulke and Alfred had run as fast as they could, leaving the slowest to be trampled beneath the charging horses. Fulke vowed to kill at least two of the enemy to make up for the shame of running.

Alfred coughed and shifted position.

'Fulke?'

Startled, he got to his feet.

'Where are we?'

'Take a look for yourself,' said Fulke in a hushed voice.

Alfred walked over to the window, swore and ducked out of sight.

Fulke grinned.

'What happened?' he whispered, looking confused.

'We were chased by cavalry,' said Fulke in a hushed tone, 'past the hospital and through the orchards until we got cut off by the river.'

Across the silvery surface of the river, the street on far side had also been barricaded. Cavalry patrolled the road back to camp. They were trapped. They'd crept through some gardens and broken into this house, relieved to find it empty.

Alfred nodded as the images came back to him. 'What about Adam?'

Fulke shook his head. 'Didn't see him.'

'What's the plan?' asked Alfred.

Above them, the thatch rustled, and they heard men talking. Alfred froze. Fulke squinted and put his finger to his lips. The gunners were on the roofs above them.

'Where's your sword?'

Alfred shook his head and whispered, 'I lost it.'

They were unarmed.

Downstairs, the front door creaked open.

*

Lord Sheffield stepped out of the Maid's Head tavern to be greeted by birdsong. He'd been up all night. Now, after a hearty breakfast of ham, eggs and cheese washed down with local ale, he was tired and uncertain what to do next. The rebels had blindly wandered into Parr's ambush, and those that hadn't been slaughtered had been repelled.

No word as yet on the fate of Kett.

If he were dead, then Sheffield's plot would be a failure. Not a prospect he relished relaying to Princess Mary. His orders had been to remain in the marketplace and reinforce any defences that threatened collapse under rebel attack. The trumpeters had sounded, so he'd sent the smallest number of reinforcement he could, but the rebels had been trapped like fish in a barrel.

After the fighting, he'd counted their corpses. Three hundred had forfeited their lives in the attack.

The new day brought an end to the curfew, but only those with a pressing need would brave the city's streets. In front of him a few people moved busily through the open area between the cathedral and Steward's house, anxiously looking over their shoulders as they walked.

Sheffield fetched his horse, tethered to the railings outside the tavern. His limbs were tired from yesterday's ride, and his sore backside protested as he positioned himself back in the saddle. Sheffield turned his animal and caught sight of the herald running towards him from the east. He looked excited. He must have news, thought Sheffield. He positioned his horse in the middle of the street to block the herald's path.

'A party of thirty rebels has arrived at the gate on the other side of the river.' The herald pointed north. 'They are surrendering!'

Sheffield concealed his alarm.

'Is Kett amongst them?'

The herald shook his head. 'They claim to represent Kett and all the rebels.'

'Very well, notify Parr. We better go and greet their demise.'

While Sheffield reconciled himself to the opportunity lost, the herald roused Parr and Deputy Mayor Steward from the latter's home. A short while later, accompanied by twenty knights and as many men at arms, they travelled the short distance over the bridge, past another barricade, which had yet to see any fighting, and at the end of the street, they mounted the tight spiral staircase of the flint gatehouse.

From the top they looked over a posse of rebels gathered on the far side of the ditch.

'I am William Parr, commander of His Majesty's Forces. Present yourselves.'

A broad man with a large forehead raised his arm. 'My name is Miles. I represent Mr Kett and his followers. It is our wish that we might discuss peace with your good selves, such that more men may be spared the loss of their lives.'

Parr's head gently nodded. 'You seek a pardon?'

'A pardon, sir? We maintain we have no need for a pardon

as we have done nothing wrong.'

Parr smirked. 'Are you prepared to surrender your weapons and return to your homes?'

Miles nodded.

'Yes.'

*

In the sanctuary of their bedroom at Surrey House, Robert hugged Alice as if his life depended on her. Neither spoke. It would only be a matter of hours before he would know whether his gamble had paid off. With so many lives at stake, these promised to be some of the longest moments of his life. He cupped her wiry hair against her head with the palm of his hand, inhaling her scent. With nothing to do but hope and pray, he broke their embrace, and together they knelt at the foot of the small bed. With their eyes closed and their palms pressed together, Robert spoke his prayer out loud. He offered thanks to the Lord and asked for him to grant them and their people safe passage through the day.

When he ran out of words, Alice continued, asking that their children, and that their children, would be granted peace, prosperity and love. She wiped a tear from her eye as she spoke. She reminded the Almighty of two lives lived full of good deeds and asked that he grant their endeavours with his grace.

*

Alfred stood facing the wooden planks of the door that concealed their whereabouts. Slow and purposeful footsteps echoed from the room downstairs.

He heard a man's voice. 'Show yourselves if you want the Lord's mercy.'

The accent was strange.

Fulke pressed his back against the wall and shook his head. He moved toward the door, careful not to make any noise.

The footsteps came up the stairs and stopped outside the door. From the centre of the room Alfred watched the black metal latch rise with a clunk. The door slowly swung open, its hinges creaking as it opened. Alfred trembled at the sight of the soldier. He was short with tanned skin and the beginnings of a beard. He wore a metal helmet and breastplate that covered a scarlet tunic. He had a small knife in a sheath on his belt, and in his hand, a raised sword pointed toward Alfred. He smirked. 'On your knees, rebel.'

Alfred shook his head. 'I am not a rebel.'

The soldier spat on the floor. 'Then I am a lady of the court. On your knees,' he barked.

Alfred took a step back.

'Knees, boy.'

Alfred fell to his knees and bowed his head. 'I beg of you, believe me, this is my house. I am not a rebel.'

As the soldier stepped through the doorway into the room, he rested the tip of his sword against Alfred's heart.

'If this is your house, what colour is the tapestry that hangs downstairs?'

Alfred had no idea.

'Red and green.' he guessed.

He heard the soldier laugh, and felt the tip of the blade spike his chest.

From behind the open door, Fulke stepped up behind the intruder and whipped the soldier's knife from his belt, slashing its edge across the man's throat. There was a gurgling noise, and Alfred found himself covered in a spray of warm blood. The soldier collapsed with a thud. He gasped for air as blood flooded from his neck across the floor into the gaps between the floorboards, surprise etched onto his face. He put a hand over his throat in a vain attempt to stem the blood.

Fulke grinned. 'One down, one to go,' he said.

Alfred shuddered. There was noise from the thatch above. The soldiers on the roof shouted. They must have heard their comrade hit the floor.

'Here, take this,' said Fulke passing Alfred the knife.

Fulke picked up the dead soldier's sword and ran downstairs. He bolted the front door closed. Outside, the soldiers on the street shouted as they realised there was a problem. They tried the latch. They banged on the door.

Amid more shouting outside, Fulke ran back upstairs.

Alfred was still on his knees, staring at the dead man.

Fulke patted the body up and down. 'Come on, help me search him.'

'What for?' asked Alfred.

Fulke lifted the body over and dropped it face down, and the corpse twitched as the last of life's magic vanished. Fulke found a small leather pouch fastened to the soldier's belt above his backside. Inside, he found what he'd been looking for: a flint, a steel and a small pouch of tinder — essentials carried by soldiers on campaign to keep themselves warm and fed.

Fulke now placed a wad of tinder on the surface of the flint and struck it with the steel. Sparks flew, but the tinder didn't take.

The banging on the front door grew louder.

Fulke struck again. There were more shouts above their heads from the rooftop. He struck again, and again. This time a spark landed in the fluff of the tinder, which started to glow.

Fulke blew on the small flame. 'Alfred, you're taller than me. Put this to the thatch.'

'But we'll be burned?'

Fulke snarled, 'Just do it.'

At the corner of the room nearest the street, Alfred held the flame to the underside of the thatch. The dry stalks of reed smouldered and took the flame, and Alfred blew to fan the flames. He'd blown too hard.

It went out.

'You stupid leper,' barked Fulke.

Alfred blew on the tinder and held the flame to the thatch again. This time it caught quickly. He watched as the bright orange light spread across its surface, turning into a soft flicker. He waited, listening to the shouts above and the banging below. He blew, and this time the flame billowed. Fulke unstrapped the dead soldier's metal breastplate and used it fan the fire, and the room started to fill with smoke. Fulke smashed the window to let the air in, causing the flames to surge. There was panicked shouting from above as the smoke leached through the top of the thatch. In the street, they could hear the soldiers arguing. In no time, the roof was ablaze. The room grew hot as it filled with smoke.

Alfred followed Fulke downstairs.

The front door shook in its frame as soldiers frantically tried to kick it open.

'What now?' asked Alfred.

'We wait.'

They heard a soldier jump from the roof and shout in pain as he landed on the street. The intensity of the fire drew air upwards, creating a draft downstairs, and the roar of the flames grew as the timbers of the roof took.

'We'll burn.'

Fulke laughed. 'I know what I'm doing.'

Fulke's words reminded Alfred of Master Peter's warning, moments before his arm was cut off.

'Fulke,' said Alfred loud enough to be heard over the fire, 'is it true you burned your parents?'

An evil grin spread across Fulke's square face. Above them, a roof timber collapsed, causing the building to shake. The banging on the front door stopped. The window next to the door was shuttered, so Fulke pressed his face against the wooden boards and peered through the gap. He watched as a soldier climbed the barricade in a hurry and lost his footing. He fell and landed on his chin. He lay on the street, doubled up in pain. A lump of burning thatch landed on him. There was a loud bang, and a bright flash as the soldier's powder purse exploded, showering his smoking entrails all around him. His dying screams sent panic through the fleeing troops as they sought safety behind their defences.

With the soldier's sword in hand, Fulke unbolted the front door. The last of the soldiers was mounting the barricade. Alfred felt bile rise in his throat as he watched Fulke plunge his sword into the man's kidney, who screamed in pain and fell in a heap at the foot of the barricade. 'That's two,' said Fulke.

*

Fulke felt the immense heat warm his head and back. He glanced along the street, to see that the fire had spread to the neighbouring houses. A trumpet sounded as the royal soldiers cowered away from the flames farther down the street to the rear of their barricade. He heard a whoosh above him as the blazing thatch fell through, sending a large puff of smoke out from the open roof. He leapt over the barricade and rolled the powder keg against the cannon. Fulke removed the barrel's lid, leaving the explosive black dust facing the elements. He looked up at the sky filled with floating embers of reeds. Two soldiers dashed towards him and then thought better of it when they realised it was a giant tinderbox they were entering. Fulke leapt back over the barricade and ran back into the smoke-filled house.

'Let's go,' shouted Fulke to Alfred, who was crouched on the floor with his sleeve over his mouth.

Fulke unbolted the rear door to on the back garden. There was a bright flash, as an explosion tore through the house and threw them to the floor. The ground shook, followed by silence. His ears ringing, Fulke regained his footing. He poked his head clear of the front door. The air was thick with the smell of rotten eggs. The barricade had been smashed to pieces, scattering debris across the street. A small crater of scorched black earth was all that was left of the gunpowder barrel. The cannon had been thrown against the flint wall opposite. Thrilled, Fulke felt his senses recovering. Figures at the end of the street were approaching from Bishopsgate. He ducked back in and closed the door behind him, then joined Alfred in the garden at the rear of the house.

They climbed the fence and dropped down into the orchard beyond.

Handfuls of men were running between the fruit trees.

'Are they ours?' asked Alfred.

'They're carrying sickles and axes. They must be.'

The first party of rebels ran in their direction.

'What's happening?' asked Alfred.

A rebel crouched down beside them, short of breath. 'Kett's launched a counter-attack. We're swarming the whole eastern side. Every man who is fit and able is headed in this direction.

Fulke grinned. Kett had grown a backbone after all.

*

From the top of Pockthorpe gate, William Parr heard the blast of a trumpet. He turned just in time to see a plume of orange flame erupt over the distant rooftops. Then came the bang.

'That's your barricade at Bishopsgate,' said Steward, trepidation carved into his face.

'Look to the right, they're moving through the orchards on the far side of the river,' said Parr. 'This charade is a decoy!' He faced the posse of rebels gathered in front of the gate. 'You'll hang, everyone one of you,' he shouted.

Steward placed his hand on Parr's forearm. 'Your grace, if we don't cross the bridge soon, they will cut us off from the body of your forces.'

Parr cursed Kett. If the treacherous tanner were here, he'd gut him himself. He forced himself to suppress his anger.

'Sheffield, take these knights and men at arms, cross the bridge and drive the rebels back.'

'Very well, sir.'

'Now, man, move!' screamed Parr.

*

Sheffield ran down the spiral staircase, his mind racing as fast as his feet, wondering how he could legitimately fail his orders whilst appearing to comply.

He mounted his horse and shouted to the assembled cavalry, 'Right men, head for the fire, make haste.'

It was the order the cavalry had been waiting for, and with their lances held aloft they broke into a canter automatically forming ranks of three with Sheffield following to their rear. As they crossed the bridge, rebels appeared to be impaled on their lances. More streamed forward and were trampled by the horses. A sickle flew through the air, piercing a knight in his face, who was pulled from his stead, kicked and beaten. Sheffield passed the rebels, swinging his sword and decapitating one of them. The men at arms followed on foot, over the bridge, and drove their pikes into the huddle of rebels, easily overpowering them.

Sheffield followed the cavalry past a church into the street where their barricade had stood. The street was littered with the blast debris. The houses on the left were burning. The rebels were skirting the walls, moving forward carefully to avoid the heat of the burning houses. The cavalry gave chased as the rebels as retreated. The horses mowed down the men Sheffield was supposed to be helping.

He stopped by the remnants of the barricade and wondered what to do.

*

Fulke moved stealthily through the churchyard, Alfred behind him, as the cavalry charged past. Rebels clashed with soldiers in the open area in front of the church. Beyond the fighting, reinforcements approached from the direction of the marketplace. If he ran into the melee, he and Alfred would soon be outnumbered. He stepped out from the shadow of the church tower and looked down the street where the barricade had been.

The cavalry had cleared the rebels. Only one man on horseback remained. He didn't wear a helmet or armour, but his clothes were fine.

'*Silly man*,' muttered Fulke, 'Follow me, Alfred.'

Fulke ran crouched over as he approached the solitary rider from behind. He kept as close to the burning houses as he could manage. He drove his sword point into the horse's flank, between the rib cage and the rear leg. The hilt hit the animal's flesh before it had a chance to react. It lurched forward with a howl of pain, unseating the unsuspecting rider who landed on his back with a thud that knocked the air clear from his lungs. The horse landed on its back legs and crumpled in a convulsing mass as it thrashed its front legs, desperately trying to escape the pain of the sword lodged in its belly.

Fulke stood over the fallen rider with a broad smile on his face. He watched the man fight for breath, unable to speak.

'Alfred, pass me your knife.'

Alfred hesitated. 'Fulke what are you going to do?'

'Teach this fellow a lesson he won't forget.'

Fulke smiled as the man on the floor waved his arms, shaking his hands and his head. 'Alfred, pass the knife.'

Alfred refused. He picked up the fallen man's sword instead.

Fulke smiled. 'Very well, we'll do this the old fashioned way.' He dropped to his knees, pinning his victim's arms to the ground. Fulke brushed the man's cheeks and thin moustache with the backs of his fingers and stroked his hair with a tenderness of a parent caring for a child.

'What is it you're trying to tell me?' asked Fulke.

The man gasped for air in short burst. 'Lord Sheffield,' he sputtered, 'don't kill me,'

'Oh, you're important, are you?' asked Fulke as he placed his hands on the man's throat.

Lord Sheffield nodded. 'I am a nobleman.'

'I know,' said Fulke, his hands started to squeeze.

The man's eyes bulged, terror written on his face.

'Ransom me,' he pleaded in his strained voice. 'A fortune for you.'

Fulke smiled. 'All the money in the land couldn't buy this.'

'Fulke, stop,' said Alfred, horrified.

Fulke tightened his grip as hard as his strong hands could squeeze. He laughed as Sheffield's face turned purple.

'Fulke. Stop,' repeated Alfred.

Sheffield's eyeballs turned upward like a man falling asleep. He kicked his legs helplessly against the ground as Fulke threatened to squeeze the last of his life out of him. Fulke released his grip allowing in a moment's air. Sheffield coughed and inhaled, with Fulke's hands resting limply on his neck. Fulke lowered himself so their noses were nearly touching.

He squeezed again, crushing Sheffield's throat between his fingers. 'Goodbye, Lordy,' he whispered before kissing the lord on the lips as he gripped with one final squeeze and pressed the life from the nobleman's body. When Sheffield's body stopped moving, Fulke inhaled, gulping from himself the last of the man's strength.

Alfred retched.

Fulke stood up and felt power surge through his body. His muscles rippled, and he sneered at Alfred cowering against the wall. 'Keep your sword then.' Fulke looked back towards the church. A group of three soldiers on foot headed directly towards them. Fulke faced them, spread his arms wide and roared to invite them to do their best.

He was unarmed and smiling like a madmen. 'Alfred, how about that sword now?'

Alfred grabbed the knife they had taken from the soldier in the house and threw it at Fulke's feet.

Fulke waited until the last moment. As the soldiers arrived, Fulke ducked the sword that swung at him, grabbing the knife from the floor. He shoulder-barged the first attacker into the next one as he rose. The soldier nearest the wall swung at Alfred.

Alfred swerved, and the soldier's sword sparked against the flint wall.

Alfred kicked his attacker in the groin. He buckled over in pain.

Alfred plunged his sword down into the soldier's back, crunching against his ribs.

Fulke struck his man in the face and bayed the other to take him on. His savageness caused the soldier to hesitate. Fulke leapt forward, his shoulder hitting the closest soldier in the stomach, knocking him off his feet. Alfred sliced his sword across the arm of the other. Fulke grabbed his man and twisted him round into his grip and held his blade to the man's throat. The remaining soldier took a step back, his arm turning red. He held his sword up in one hand and showed the palm of the other as he retreated slowly.

Beyond, Alfred saw six more soldiers coming. 'Fulke.'

Fulke, his blade still poised over the soldier's throat, nodded. 'Back off, you lot, and I'll let your mate go.'

The injured soldier continued pacing backwards in Fulke's grip.

At ten yards distance, Fulke lowered his knife and turned the man he held to the right. With both arms, he shoved the man clear, straight into the burning buildings. The oncoming soldiers gave chase. Fulke was confident they could outrun the armoured soldiers.

Around the bend at the end of Bishopsgate, they came face to face with the returning cavalry. They were pinned, soldiers to their rear, cavalry to their front.

To their left were the hospital and its gardens.

To their right, another wall, waist high.

'They killed Lord Sheffield, those two,' shouted a soldier.

Without saying a word, Fulke and Alfred scrambled over the wall and ran for their lives. Glancing over his shoulder, he watched as two horses leapt the wall and galloped after them in pursuit. They ran through vegetables, herbs, over grass patches, night soil heaps between fruit trees, and behind them, the thunder of horses' hooves grew louder and louder.

Fulke could hear the blowing of the horses' breath. He twisted round to take another look and heard Alfred shriek as a lance punctured his left arm.

The force knocked Alfred off his feet and slammed him into the ground. He screamed in agony as he tried to stand but collapsed.

Fulke dashed back and wrapped his arm around him.

'Alfred, quick, get up, they're coming back.'

Fulke pulled Alfred to his feet as the two cavalrymen circled to resume their charge.

Fulke looked about for a place of safety. The gardens were open, nowhere to hide. Alfred pointed with his good arm. 'There.'

Fulke looked along the row of houses and saw the shuttered window Alfred was pointing to. It was the house of Alfred's fancy girl. 'Come on then,' said Fulke, taking Alfred's weight. Alfred stumbled and fell to his knees, screaming as the pain seared through his arm. His sleeve was soaked in blood. Alfred's head flopped forward. He was passing out. His legs wouldn't move.

The horses thundered towards them — the riders lowered their lances ready for the kill.

39

On Whitefriars Bridge, Parr watched the fighting from the vantage of his saddle. He cursed the rebels as they poured forward like rats fleeing a fire, blocking his route back to the marketplace.

'Steward,' he called over his shoulder. 'We can't cross here. Take me back to the marketplace another way.'

Steward kicked his mare and led Parr in a trot up Fishergate and across the river over the next bridge upstream. The royal herald trailed behind, running as fast as he could. As they passed the Maid's Head and Steward's house, rebels appeared through the cathedral gates. Parr kicked his horse into a canter. The rebels shouted at the sight of their quarry passing. Parr felt a gush of air just behind his head, and a spade clattered on the ground, just missing him. His horse shrieked in pain and lost its footing. Parr glanced back and saw an arrow buried in the animal's rump. He kicked it as hard as he could, drawing level with Steward on his inside. The next arrow pierced the horse's ribs, flattening it and throwing Parr forward. He leapt clear of the saddle and landed on his feet. He grabbed Steward's leg, leapt up and wrenched the deputy mayor clear from his seat.

Steward was left stunned in the dust as Parr mounted his

horse and galloped back towards the marketplace.

*

Alfred heaved himself through the open window, as Fulke pushed him from underneath. He slid through and thumped to the floor, screaming in agony as his landing reverberated through his injured arm. Behind him, the smashed shutters hung limp on one hinge as Fulke's block-shaped head and hands appeared at the window. He grunted as he flung himself in, using Alfred to break his fall. Outside, the sound of the horses' hooves passed the window.

Fulke laughed with relief, but Alfred was still groaning from cushioning Fulke's landing.

He turned very pale.

'Who goes there?'

A startled young woman stood in the doorway, brandishing a cooking knife in her hand. Her face relaxed when she recognised Alfred, but her mouth fell open when she saw his blood-soaked sleeve.

'You're hurt.' She ran over.

Alfred let out a groan that rose from somewhere deep inside of him. Fulke admired her figure as she felt Alfred's forehead. 'You're cold.'

Alfred leant over and vomited a thick, stodgy mouthful of bile and food onto the rush matting. She wiped his mouth and held back his hair. His body went limp in her arms, and she stroked his hair. 'Ssshhh.' She looked at Fulke, who found himself admiring her blue eyes and her blonde hair.

'What happened?' she asked.

'He was lanced,' said Fulke as he peeked out of the window for any sign of the final rider. 'Lucky for him he was with me, otherwise he'd be dead.'

'I'm Tiniker.'

'I can see why he likes you,' said Fulke.

She ignored his compliment, and Alfred groaned in pain as he lay slumped across her thighs.

'Help me,' said Tiniker. 'Let's lay him flat so I can take a look at his arm.'

She took his legs while Fulke lifted his torso, causing another agonising groan from Alfred. They laid him down, and Fulke caught a whiff of the girl's scent. Once Alfred was flat, Tiniker used her knife to slice his sleeve. Then she cut his shirt down the side and peeled the material clear of his wounds. The ball of his arm was torn open, leaving a clean slice of flesh hanging from it. She couldn't tell if his arm was broken. There would be plenty of bruising. 'I've seen worse injuries. He should survive, provided it doesn't become infected. I need you to pee on his arm.'

Fulke grunted.

'It will clean his wound.'

Fulke stared at Tiniker, who obligingly turned away as he untied his codpiece and fished for his manhood. His exertions had robbed it of its size, so he turned his back at Tiniker and started to piss.

Alfred groaned as it stung his wound.

'Wat is er gaande?' came a feeble voice from the corner of the room.

'Margreet, Nu bovenaan!' barked Tiniker.

The young girl at the foot of the stairs was pretty, but awkward-looking. Her sister, Fulke assumed. Alfred's found himself a right little foreign pleasure nest here, he said to himself.

Alfred groaned again as the young girl scurried away.

'Please, give me some space,' said Tiniker as she knelt to examine his wound.

Fulke watched Tiniker as she cared for Alfred. She looked like she knew what she was doing.

From outside, came the shouts of people fighting and screaming. Fulke decided that was preferrable to the sound of Alfred's whimpering and the smell of his sick. There was still fighting to be had, and he'd been forced to run away again. 'I'll leave you to it.'

'Very well,' said Tiniker, 'show yourself out.' she said, nodding the in the direction of the door.

Fulke slid the bolt clear and closed the door behind him.

*

Parr had made it back unscathed to the relative calm of the marketplace. At the barricades, Parr's soldiers fidgeted as they waited for their enemy. Steward's horse twitched its legs as he decided where to position himself, whilst Parr wrestled with what to do. Finally, he summoned four men to act as runners. They were to inspect each of the remaining barricades and report back. No sooner had they left, than soldiers poured back into the marketplace, bursting through their own defensive lines as they pushed their fellow soldiers out of the way. Parr trotted down the slope, screaming at his men to close the gap. His front line reformed and blocked off the street that led to the cathedral. Parr reached down and grabbed a soldier by the sleeve — his face was splatted with blood and was short of breath. 'What is happening?'

'There are thousands of them. Too many to hold.'

Parr released the man's arm. Around him, exhausted men were bent double from fighting. Now, at the far end of the street were gathered a mass of rebels, filling the street and taunting his troops: beckoning them forward with their hands, mocking, bearing their tails and waving their farm tools.

Parr watched as one man pushed through the crowd of rebels. He had ginger hair and carried a longbow. He walked forward five paces and put an arrow to his bowstring. The rebels cheered. He drew back his bowstring with a sinister smile spread across his face. Parr felt himself twitch. The arrow flew, and a soldier screamed as it buried itself in his guts. Cheers and laughter rippled up the street from the rebels. The archer put another arrow to his bow, and the front line of soldiers shifted from side to side in a vain attempt to find safety. The archer waved his bow from left to right, imitating a drunk. The rebels put their thumbs in their armpits and flapped their arms like capons.

'Somebody shoot that damned archer,' yelled Parr.

The next arrow flew. Another man fell. The line faltered.

Parr leapt down from his horse. 'Give me that gun,' he said as he snatched an arquebus from a soldier who had just finished loading it.

'Make way,' he barked as he pushed his way to the front. He put the weapon to his shoulder, catching a whiff of the burning taper as it smouldered next to his right eye.

'Five pennies for the man in the blue,' he heard one of the rebels call.

The archer took another arrow, but Parr pointed the gun, and the rebels fell silent. He pulled the trigger, and there was a flash as the gun recoiled, slamming into his shoulder, a bang and a puff of white smoke that clouded the street. A young man standing behind the archer fell.

Parr grimaced at his miss.

The rebels charged.

Parr retreated and threw the gun to the ground.

'Hold them,' he ordered, leaving the soldiers to perform their duty.

'Your grace,' said William Walgrave, Parr's elderly general. 'The men return with tragic news. Lord Sheffield is dead. Murdered in cold blood.'

Parr's eyes swelled. All around him came the noise of the side streets filling with rebels. They were being overrun.

*

Robert and William stood in silence outside Surrey House in the late morning sun listening to the faint din of fighting in the city below. Their view was obscured by the smoke of burning houses that drifted up from the far end of Bishopsgate.

'Robert!' The brothers turned to see Luke Miller running towards them. 'You've done it!'

'Done what?'

'Beaten them. They're routed! You've done it,' his speech was frantic as he drew breath.

Robert felt his eyes well with tears. 'Truly?'

Luke nodded. 'Oh yes, truly. They have fled like a scolded dog.'

Robert grinned from ear to ear, raised his arms and shouted with all his might. He leapt up and down like a man thirty years his junior. His brother hugged him, and still he jumped.

'We've done it,' he yelled, his words drifting out over the city.

'Robert Kett, the saviour of Norfolk,' Luke cheered.

*

Fulke looked at the bodies on the street. Amongst them, Adam Catchpole, his shirt stained red around the chest wound that had claimed his life. Fulke carried on, puffing his chest out as he passed the barricade he'd destroyed. The street was still ablaze, but nobody made any attempt to put it out. He thought it was a shame the wind wasn't stronger; the fire could have really spread. The open area in front of the church was deserted apart from a few people looting the fallen corpses on both sides. As he picked a path through the bodies, the ground was slippery with blood that clung to his soles.

In Tombland, an angry mob of rebels crowded outside a doorway.

Fulke approached and asked, 'What's going on here?'

'It's the deputy mayor's house.'

'And?'

'He's one of them, isn't he?' said the man, puzzled.

Fulke snorted and barged his way through the people to try the door handle.

'We had thought of that,' said a man sarcastically, disgruntled at being barged out of the way.

Fulke bent his elbow and pulled his right arm tight in against his torso. He sprung forward and barged into the door. There was a crack as the wood holding the bolt to the doorframe splintered. The door swung in and slammed against the wall. 'Well, you didn't try that, did you,' he said, looking back at the man.

Fulke walked in and gazed around the opulent hall as the rest of the mob piled into the house. An ornately-carved wooden staircase and balustrade dominated the hall. Tapestries and a painted portrait of the deputy mayor adorned the walls. The sideboards displayed clay ornaments, candlesticks and even a bowl of fresh apricots. Fulke headed for the kitchen, where he found a housekeeper trembling in the corner of the room. Fulke beat the man repeatedly round the torso. Satisfied that he'd established his command, he closed the door and ordered the battered housekeeper to prepare him a meal. Moments later, a plate of bread, butter, fried bacon and cheese appeared, which Fulke washed down with some wine.

He didn't especially care for wine, but when in Rome, as the saying goes.

Fulke, having been briefly interrupted by some inquisitive rebels who he deterred from searching the kitchen, finished his meal and belched. His belly was full, and his pains numbed from the wine.

'Clear up this mess,' he ordered the housekeeper. 'And I'll be back this evening for roast meat. If it isn't ready,' he stared at the terrified servant who refused to meet his eye, 'I'll eat you.'

He chuckled to himself as he left the kitchen. The other rebels had done a fine job of looting the house. The hallway had been cleared — only the portrait remained, but the deputy mayor's face had been slashed with a knife.

Fulke could hear an argument upstairs. Invigorated by his meal, he bounded up the steps two at time. In a large room, adjacent to the top of the stairs, a man in a black gown, who Fulke took to be the deputy mayor, protested that they leave his mechanical clock alone. Ignoring his pleas, a rebel smashed it with his hatchet, scattering brass cogs and springs all over the floor. The deputy mayor closed his eyes and fought for composure. Meanwhile, another rebel rummaged through papers on his desk. Finding nothing of value, he urinated on them.

'All right, boys, that's enough. Leave the man alone,' said Fulke leaning against the doorframe.

There was a moment's hesitation between the rebels as they decided if they should follow his orders. 'Come out, there's nothing here for you.'

The men ran out of the deputy mayor's private chamber with bundles of clothes in their arms. Fulke and the deputy mayor were alone.

'Thank you,' said the deputy mayor.

'Steward, isn't it?'

Fulke approached the important man, and Steward squirmed. Fulke stepped even closer. Close enough to smell the garlic on the man's breath. Fulke raised his hand and stroked Steward's cheek. His skin was cold and dry.

'What is it you want?' asked Steward.

Fulke touched Steward's hair, fascinated by the colour and texture. Grey. Coated in oil.

Steward shuddered.

Fulke looked at him. 'I don't know yet. But for now, just you remember that I saved you.'

Steward summoned the resolved to meet Fulke gaze.

'I'll be back,' said Fulke, wiping the hair oil on Steward's gown. He turned and walked out. 'Bye for now.'

*

Steward dashed over and closed the study door. He surveyed the destruction and tried to compose himself. On the floor lay the remnants of his clock. A piece of mechanical genius worth a fortune, smashed to pieces. What had they proved by its destruction? Steward sighed at the futility of it all. Outside his door he could hear the yelps of excitement from the rebels as they left his house, their arms full of his possessions. He hobbled to the window, grimacing in pain from his hip and his ribs. The former from being yanked clean from his horse, the latter from being assaulted whilst he lay on the ground.

In the street below, a stream of people leaving his front door ran in different directions, clutching their loot. Smoke poured from behind the cathedral close. It had taken him years to accumulate his wealth; a life's work had been pillaged. He stared at the cathedral spire as he'd done a thousand times before. The sky was filled with smoke and screams, and a heaviness grew in his chest. He'd invested heavily into this city, and the duty of his office demanded he make civic contributions — how many of those assets would be in ruins by nightfall? How much of a city would remain for him to officiate and trade in? He shuddered. The city was going down on his watch. Order must be restored at any cost. Those blasted fools from London cared not two hoots, and their incompetence had only made matters worse. Steward rubbed his face with palm of his hands and wondered what was to be done.

Where, he asked himself, was the divinity in all this madness?

*

Fulke was irritated that the royals had fled so soon. His annoyance was partially eased by his act of mercy and his breakfast; it paid to have friends in high places. Nonetheless, his thirst for suffering had yet to be sufficiently slaked. Fulke entertained himself by taking a burning timber and using it to spread the fire. He torched nearby houses that had so far escaped the burning. He took some satisfaction from torching the hospital. It was a grand building, which roasted nicely once the mattresses and linen took light. Hotter than hell, he thought, as he watched the glass windows shatter.

Above, the sky blackened with smoke.

He'd set Norwich ablaze, but still he felt restless. Unfulfilled. He began to wonder why: the houses he'd burned were empty, his work was unopposed and unappreciated, he'd lacked the satisfaction of seeing peoples' fear. He gave up and walked back down Bishopsgate toward the camp. He thought of Alfred and wondered if the foreign girl had saved him, and that reminded him of another need that had so far gone unfulfilled.

He tried the door handle. It was still unlocked, so he pushed it open, taking care to avoid the watchful snarl of the gargoyle, its carved teeth bared to keep evil at bay. He walked in. Before him appeared the young foreign beauty, anxious at the sight of him entering uninvited, her cooking knife in her hand.

'How is Alfred?' asked Fulke.

'Unconscious.'

'Good.'

Tiniker looked confused. Before she had time to react, Fulke stepped forward and grabbed her shoulders. He swung his leg behind hers and threw her to the ground. She hit her head and lay dazed on the floor. Then he kicked the knife from her hand and knelt down, pinning her arms with his knees. He gripped her throat with one hand and covered her mouth with the palm of his other. He saw the terror in her eyes, as her nostrils flared over the edge of his hand.

His loins stirred as his manhood start to swell and press against his breeches.

He grinned at her. 'You and I are going to have some fun.'

40

Tiniker glanced to her right. The knife she'd dropped was out of reach, and Alfred lay unconscious on the floor under the window. The canary hopped up and down in his cage, tweeting. Her nostrils flared, and Fulke could smell her fear. He had her arms pinned beneath his knees. She kicked her legs underneath him but couldn't dislodge him.

She's a fighter this one, thought Fulke.

Her eyes betrayed the helplessness of her predicament. He wondered if he should let her plead for mercy.

'Now, you need to do exactly as I say. If you don't, I'll snap your neck like a chicken. Blink if you understand me?' Fulke was enjoying himself.

She blinked.

'Good girl.'

Fulke let go of her throat, keeping her mouth covered with his other hand. He twisted his shoulders, leaned back and moved her white apron to one side to reveal the lower half of her madder red kirtle. He gripped the fabric between his fingers and inched it back, one fold at a time, exposing her smock. His hand muffled her scream as she kicked her legs frantically from side to side, forcing her pelvis up in an attempt to unseat him.

'I see you're getting excited too,' said Fulke, grinning. 'Has Alfred had his way with you yet? Blink once for yes.'

Her eyes stayed open.

Fulke rubbed his hand up the inside of her thigh. He felt the brush of her pubic hair. She squealed. The ceiling above them creaked.

Fulke looked up. 'Is that your sister? Is she upstairs?'

She wriggled with all her might; her eyes scrunched closed. Fulke grinned. He brought his fist crashing down on her chest, driving the wind from her lungs. He released her mouth, and she strained to find her breath. As she writhed on the floor, fighting for air, Fulke stood up and collected the knife from under the kitchen table.

'We don't want to leave things like this lying around, do we? Somebody might hurt themselves.'

He took a cursory look at Alfred.

Still unconscious.

Tiniker rolled over onto her hands and knees, gasping for air. Fulke walked back and held the knife blade under her throat. She froze.

'Try and escape, and I'll cut you,' said Fulke. He twisted her arm behind her back and lifted her to her feet. With the blade against her throat, he whispered in her ear, 'Upstairs, do anything silly, and you die.'

She led the way up the narrow staircase, its wooden boards creaking under their weight. The stairs opened into a large room, before carrying on to the weaving room above, its whitewashed walls stained with patches of mould. An open window overlooked the meadows and provided plenty of light. A plain wooden bed frame had on it a straw mattress covered by a blanket and resting on the floor in front of them was another smaller straw mattress.

'This should do nicely,' said Fulke as he looked about. 'Now, where is she?'

Fulke pressed the blade harder into her throat. 'What's her name?'

'Margreet.' She sobbed.

'Good girl. Margreet, come out wherever you are. Otherwise, your sister will suffer.'

The room was still. Fulke pinched the skin on Tiniker's neck between his thumb and forefinger and twisted as hard as he could. She yelped.

The wardrobe door creaked open, and a delicate, pale leg stepped out.

Fulke smiled. That was easy, he thought. 'Good girl, come here.'

The young girl stepped out of the wardrobe, trembling with fear at the sight of her elder sister held at knifepoint. Tears welled in her eyes.

'Tiniker wat gebeurt er?'

'English. Speak English,' demanded Fulke as he watched the younger one stop in front of him.

'Take off your clothes.'

'No,' cried Tiniker.

'Shut up. Do it, or I slice your sister's throat.'

'Please, no,' begged Tiniker.

'Take them off.'

Margreet looked to Tiniker for reassurance and found none. Her eyes started to stream tears. Fulke reissued his instructions, and slowly Margreet unlaced her dress and let it slide to the ground, sobbing as it landed at her feet.

'Keep going,' said Fulke.

Margreet's hands shook as she tried to unbutton the cream blouse that formed the top half of her undergarment. A wet mark appeared on the front of the fabric and spread outwards. Fulke groaned as he watched her piss trickle down her legs and pond on the floor. The undergarment slid down to her feet. She was too young for fully formed breasts, but she raised her arm to cover them both. Her other hand covered her small patch of hair. Her skin was pale, her body lithe. She looked at the floor, snivelling.

Tiniker wriggled, the blade slicing at her neck. 'Please no. Stop this. Take me. She's a child.'

'Not from where I am standing,' replied Fulke.

'Please. Please,' begged Tiniker. 'I'm a maiden. I'll do anything you want me to. Just leave her.'

Fulke had waited long enough.

'You, stand over there in the corner.' He pointed the knife at Margreet and nodded his head in the direction of the corner. 'You can watch your sister learn to be a woman.'

Margeet ran to the corner of the room and sunk to the floor with her back to the wall, as she pulled her legs up to her chin and sobbed onto her knees.

Fulke moved Tiniker forward and bent her over the end of the bed frame. 'Try and escape, and I'll stab you.'

She buried her face in the blanket and clenched a mouthful of fabric between her teeth as he lifted her kirtle and smock.

Margreet wailed. Her windpipe bulged in her throat as she howled in misery.

Fulke grinned. Their sobbing and screaming excited him. He took off his shirt and threw it on the floor. He unlaced his hose, ready. He rubbed his hand between Tiniker's buttocks. She shuddered and clenched the blanket between her hands.

Fulke groaned in anticipation when her body clenched in terror. It was time.

Fulke heard a creak behind him, and as he opened his eyes and turned around, a blow thumped him on the nose.

Everything went dark.

Another blow came down on the back of his head.

Alfred swayed on his feet and dropped the kitchen pan onto the floor. Tiniker shrieked at the sight of him and pulled her dress down. She picked up the fallen pan and brought it crashing down on Fulke's head for good measure. His body didn't move. Alfred turned and planted his backside on the bed, his torso wavering from the effort of getting up the stairs.

He tried to speak but found no words.

'Get him out of here. Get this monster out of my house,' screamed Tiniker.

Alfred slumped backwards onto the bed and passed out.

*

Robert watched the columns of smoke drift upwards peacefully to the heavens. Buildings that had taken months, years, to build were gone. From what he could make out from Surrey House, it was the nearest part of the city that had taken the brunt of the fighting. He watched as two men scurried across the meadows with buckets filled with river water, rushing to douse the flames.

'It's no good, Alice. I have to see it for myself.'

Alice had spent the afternoon by the empty fireplace in the sanctuary of an oversized upholstered chair.

'If you must, then at least take William with you. You shouldn't walk alone.'

'I doubt I have many enemies left.'

'You may have some new ones when people see what's become of their homes.'

Robert enlisted his brother as Alice suggested, then found the mayor and together they made their way down the gulley to the city. The smell of charred wood carried on the breeze. They crossed the unmanned bridge and walked up Bishopsgate where they chanced upon a man supine in the middle of the road. His bare chest was moving — he was breathing.

'Is that Fulke?' asked Robert. He crouched down. 'His breeches are undone?'

Robert held Fulke's thick jaw in his fingers.

'He must be unconscious.'

'Or drunk,' suggested William.

Robert leaned in. No scent of ale. He blew in his face and tapped his cheek. 'Fulke, wake up.'

Fulke grunted. Robert tried again, and Fulke's eyes popped open, startled by his surroundings, he glanced around to get his bearings.

'You all right?'

Fulke blinked as he gazed up to the sky. He rubbed his head. Robert watched his puzzled expression as he searched for his last memory. Fulke frowned and twisted, stretching his back.

'What happened?' asked Robert.

Fulke coughed. 'I don't remember.'

'Why are your breeches undone and your shirt missing?' asked William.

Fulke frowned and retied his codpiece to his breeches.

Robert said, 'Come on, you well enough to stand?' Fulke grunted and with Robert's help, pulled himself onto his feet, steadying his balance as he rose. 'Come with us. We'll find you a drink.'

They walked up the street with Fulke hobbling alongside.

'It was a proper fight,' explained Fulke. 'They blocked the street ahead and ambushed us as we approached. We gave them hell, but they had horses, cannons and better weapons.

I blew up their barricade. That allowed us to push them back.'

They passed the smouldering hospital. The thatch and timber of the roof was missing. Two boys dressed in rags were making their way around the side of the building, and they stopped to peer through a window. One pointed to the other something he had seen inside.

'They're going to loot the hospital!' exclaimed an appalled Mayor Codd. 'You two, come here,' he shouted.

The two boys looked over their shoulders and fled.

'This is scandalous,' said the mayor. 'Who in their right mind would burn our hospital? Thank God, we evacuated the patients the day of the herald's visit. They'd have been roasted alive.'

Robert's pained expression signalled his displeasure. This was not what he'd intended. The hospital was one of the city's most important civic buildings. It was the embodiment of society's most noble values, to care for the weakest and sickest.

'We must stop this,' he declared.

Fulke nodded.

'People have been looting all day. I caught several in the deputy mayor's house earlier.'

'I haven't always seen eye to eye with you, Fulke,' said Robert, 'but these are extraordinary times, and they call for men of certain, skills. Can I trust you?'

Fulke returned his stare.

'I need somebody to help keep law and order here. Somebody with your strength and presence.'

'Me?' Fulke looked surprised. He thought about it. 'I'd need paying.'

'This isn't about money, Fulke.'

'I appreciate that, but I need to eat, and I can't be stealing food to survive and then in the next breath catch people for doing the same.'

Robert nodded. 'I'm not worried about food theft. I need to guarantee the safety of people and their property.'

'Agreed.'

'I'm not in a position to pay you now, but I'll allow you half a silver coin a day to keep order, reporting to me only.'

'Deal,' said Fulke, a grin across his face.

Robert assessed his lieutenant. Fulke was brave and tenacious. He hoped this responsibility would bring out the best in him.

'In which case, you can start now. Go and see Steward. He'll give you a key to the castle cells and the guildhall. Anyone you catch burning things or terrorising people, stick them straight in.'

'No trial?'

'Not yet, no. There is no time to prosecute. Justice must be swift.'

Delighted, Fulke sauntered off to find Steward.

'Fulke, you fought well today,' Robert called out after him. 'Find yourself a shirt,' he added.

Fulke didn't look back. Once he was out of earshot, the mayor confided his doubts. 'There's something menacing about that man, are you sure you can trust him to keep order?'

'No,' said Robert, 'but as the saying goes, hire a thief to catch a thief and frankly, mayor, I'd rather have him acting for me than against me.'

William nodded. 'He's capable. Damn good butcher too.'

41

3rd August, Bishopsgate

All that remained of the houses between St Martin at Palace Plain and the hospital were charred stumps and burning embers. Thankfully, the Lord had seen fit to send the rains and limit the fire's reach, although the air was damp and thick with the smell of charred wood. Steward had spent the day locked in his home, wondering why God favoured the rebels. His house had been spared the flames but had been plundered three times, and there was nothing left of any consequence to take. Fortunately, that brutish fellow Fulke had offered to stand guard in exchange for hot meals.

Word reached Steward that the justices of the peace had been attacked and were refusing to carry out their duties. This news enraged him. It was time to act.

On his way to the rebel camp, he banged on the door of the weaver's daughter's house. As the door creaked open, a young girl peered through the gap. She looked frightened.

'Hello, my child. What's your name?'

'Margreet.'

'Hello, Margreet. I'm here to see Tiniker. Is she home?'

The girl shook her head.

'Is she your sister?'
Margreet nodded.
'When will she be home?'
'She has gone to fetch water.'
'I'll try later, on my way back.'
The bolt slid back into place.

*

'Who was that?' asked Alfred.

Margreet shrugged her shoulders. 'He's visited Tiniker a few times. She won't say who he is.'

Alfred bounded up the stairs, ignoring the pain in his shoulder as his sling jolted with every step. He peered out of the window and watched the stranger passing under the gate. He was evidently a man of some standing. He was tall and dressed in a black gown that gave him a sinister appearance. Was this the man who'd passed Tiniker a note a few days earlier?

Until now there had been little to gain by mentioning the incident again. He was happy to stay here with them and had little desire to return to the filth of the camp where he risked seeing Fulke. After knocking him unconscious, the girls, between them, had dragged Fulke's weight down the stairs and dumped him in the street. When Alfred had finally recovered from his exertions, he'd woken in Tiniker's bed as she cleaned him with a warm cloth. Although his shoulder protested in agony, the sensation of being soaped with a scented clothe was divine and when united with the Tiniker's aroma on the bed, Alfred, in his drowsy state, was left wondering if there really was a heaven, and if he'd woken up in it.

Tiniker had later demanded to know why he'd brought

such a monster into her home, to which Alfred had protested that he hadn't known the man well, they'd just happened to be fighting alongside one another.

Master Peter's warning now rang in his ears.

Lying back on the bed, Alfred groaned as his shoulder sank into the straw mattress. The pain made him tire quickly. He stared at the ceiling. This room, simple as it was, was preferable to his cottage in Hethersett. He still hadn't got used to the idea of having a freehold. He hadn't enjoyed such security since his parents had died. He wondered when would he go back. Then it occurred to him, Tiniker's father had died and yet she seemed to have no concerns regarding her own security. More questions fell into his thoughts: How would she afford to live here without her father's income? Was that what the mystery visitor was — her landlord demanding rent? Perhaps the shame of not being able to pay was what had upset her? Alfred cursed himself for his jealousy.

She could live with me, he thought. An image of Lynn came to mind. Even if he could get rid of Lynn and her mother, the rest of the village would know he was married. Tiniker would be an outcast. But if Lynn were to die, as a widower he could do as he pleased. How could Lynn die? His eyelids hovered. This was all getting too complicated for his weak mind. He closed his eyes and drifted off to sleep.

*

'God rest his soul,' said Robert.

Alice sobbed at the foot of the bed. Master Peter's soul had moved into the afterlife.

Standing next to his brother, William made the sign of the cross over his chest and whispered a prayer.

'Robert, he was of the old faith,' said Alice, 'should we not have found somebody to administer the last rites?'

Robert shook his head. Master Peter had chosen his faith, and that was his business, but this rebellion, that was the second time today Robert had caught himself using the 'r' word, wasn't going to be risked further tainting by associating it with heretics. A reformed death was all Robert was able to offer his loyal servant. His death came as a blessing. The poor fellow had suffered for days, and the miasmas in the room threatened to make the whole house sick. Robert had resigned himself days ago to losing poor, wretched Peter. He'd seen people die of lesser wounds and all the prayers in the world weren't going to save the poor man. With one arm, he'd have been no use to man nor beast, better he made his fortune in the next world.

'William, could you have someone move the body for me? See that he gets a proper burial in one of the churchyards.'

Robert and Alice followed William out of the room and closed the door behind them. At the bottom of the stairs, Robert thought he should raise a tankard to lift his own spirits and say farewell to Master Peter, and Alice headed for the kitchen to find him a drink.

Alfred had failed to return from the last raid, so was presumed dead, and Robert hadn't replaced him now Alice was here. She worried less when she had tasks to keep her occupied.

Mayor Codd joined him in the empty dining room, and together they drank ale. What to the outside world looked like a victory felt anything but to Robert. More lives lost. His forces were scattered and no longer at his command, the representatives arguing between themselves. They were out of food, and to top it all, Master Peter his trusted servant of fifteen years, was dead.

Robert took a long swig, and between them they debated

the next step in the rebellion. Mayor Codd recommended taking their protest south, marching to London and submitting their protests directly to the council or the king. Robert wasn't convinced that walking into the lion's den was the right step, particularly when Mayor Codd admitted he wouldn't be joining them on the journey south. The mayor's advice was tinged with self-preservation. Understandably, he wanted the rebels off his patch and to escape further complicity.

Robert dismissed the suggestion. He'd never been to the capital, and by all accounts London was a labyrinth of alleyways and dark corners where a man would kill you for your pocket change or the shirt on your back. Raiding a poorly defended Norwich was one thing, a heavily fortified London quite another. Better for their foe to make the long journey instead, he reckoned.

Alice appeared. 'There's a man claiming to be the deputy mayor here to see you, Robert, Augustine Steward?'

He swapped a glance with Mayor Codd, who looked characteristically suspicious. 'Send him in.'

Steward's gaunt frame at the door bore the hallmarks of a man deprived of sleep. Robert knew how he felt. Steward bowed his head and then acknowledged the mayor.

'Mr Steward, welcome to my castle,' said Robert. 'We're not accustomed to seeing you up here on the heath. To what do we owe the pleasure of your company?'

'May I?' asked Steward, pulling out a chair from under the table.

'Of course,' Robert nodded and offered his palm. An uneasy silence hung in the room. Robert glanced at Mayor Codd, who was frowning.

Steward cleared his throat. 'Very well. I'll come to the point.'

'Please,' replied Robert. He caught himself indulging in his status, nice to have county officials pay *him* their respects for once.

'They are calling you the King of Norfolk.'

Kett grunted his acknowledgement of this fact. The nickname amused him.

'Well, I don't claim to be a king,' continued Steward, his voice sounding strained, 'only an alderman of Norwich. I have served this city all my adult life.'

Codd snorted. 'And yourself.'

'It's true,' admitted Steward. 'I have prospered too, but I have a love of this city and its people. It has been good to me, and I have been good to it. It has taken more of my time than any women or child.'

Alice came back in with more ale. Robert took a swig and returned his tankard to the table with some force.

'Mr Steward, let me clear one thing up before we start. Whose side are you on?'

Steward cleared his throat and met Robert's gaze. 'Mr Kett, for you this past week I have been to London to issue your demands, I have kept order in the city and until recently, prevented your rebels from causing untold damage. I have brought in a succession of the clergy to preach a message of peace and reconciliation, all of which serves to keep the name of Kett from being tarnished, and you ask me whose side I'm on?'

'And yet William Parr ate dinner at your residence and spent the night as your guest?'

Steward smiled. 'With whom do you think he would have preferred to stay, the candlestick maker? The baker? Or the nightsoil boy perhaps?'

Robert snorted. 'I see your predicament, Deputy. But my question remains.'

'It's a question I have asked myself, Mr Kett. In the last two days, I have seen my home ransacked, my possessions looted and my servant abused. I witnessed parts of the city burn at the hands of your followers. Your rebels have done untold damage,' Steward's voice started to shake with anger.

'Compose yourself, Deputy,' ordered Robert, 'this is regrettable, and should have been avoided. But the city had refused to cooperate, and by locking their gates they brought this misfortune on themselves. I've since taken steps to restore order.'

'Perhaps you will succeed where I appear to have failed, Mr Kett. I don't profess to understand it, but it seems that at every turn, God has favoured you and your rebels.'

Robert smiled. 'It would seem so.'

'What are your aims, Mr Kett?'

'I want my demands met. When I left Wymondham, all I sought was to put a stop to enclosure, but in the time I've led these people and listened to their stories of evictions, of bribery, of their landowners manipulation of their demense, I have realised that this movement is fundamental to returning us to a time when we were governed fairly. The more I've learned in these past weeks, the more I will accept nothing less than a return to all our ancient traditions where a Lord bore as many responsibilities to the men he ruled as they did unto him. No longer can men of power exploit the common man, and so ruthlessly apply the rules to their own gain.'

'And are you going to get what you want, do you think?'

Robert hesitated.

Steward cleared his throat. 'You know that one of your followers murdered Lord Sheffield, don't you?'

Robert froze.

'You didn't know, did you?' Steward pushed him.

Mayor Codd stayed silent, seeking comfort in his tankard.

'The king's cousin?' Robert sank back in his chair. The knot in his gut tightened.

'You're supposed to capture the aristocrats, not murder them.'

'I'll have to…'

'To make matters worse,' said Steward, interrupting him, 'you've buried him in a pit alongside your hoi polloi. I can't see the king taking kindly to that. Or his sister, Lady Mary; they were reported to be close.'

Steward smirked. 'It doesn't make a compelling case for being seen on your side.' His gazed fixed on Mayor Codd. 'I hear your rebels also captured a soldier and dragged him up here, tortured him, and then hanged him?'

'Enough,' said Robert banging his fist on the table. 'Who killed Sheffield?'

'Search me,' said Steward, 'but it will be you they blame for it.'

'Have you come here to antagonise me?' Robert stood up, his chair legs scraping across the floor. 'Because I remind you, Mr Steward, I am in charge, and you are only free to sit here at my pleasure. I have cells full of men like yourself, and unless you wish to join them in their squalor, you'd better start by helping.'

'I will do anything to keep Norwich, and it's people safe from tyranny.'

'You accuse me of tyranny?' barked Robert.

'No more than I do those fools from London.'

'Mayor Codd, what do you propose I do with your deputy?' asked Robert, his fists pressed into the table taking his weight.

Mayor Codd shrugged, turning his gaze towards the window. 'See what he offers.'

Steward cleared his throat and looked more at ease. 'Mr

Kett, if you'll pardon me for speaking plainly, I believe circumstances demand it. We must look forward. Have you ever prodded a wasps' nest with a stick?'

'I thought you were speaking plain?' retorted Robert.

'When you disturb a wasps' nest, the wasps don't negotiate, they don't seek to understand your intentions, even if they are honourable. No, the wasps sting you. All of them. I have served in parliament. I know London, and I've seen the people on the other side of your actions. You need to understand that they can't give you what you seek because they don't know how. Now you have killed Lord Sheffield, you have crossed a line. There won't be any more negotiating or posturing, just the wrath of angry wasps.'

Robert clenched his jaw. 'And?'

'My city bears the scars of this dispute. By the time you are both done, I doubt there will be anything left.'

'Your city?' piped up Mayor Codd.

'I treat it as if it were my own,' replied Steward.

'Taking its fruits as you please.'

'Enough.' Robert clapped his hands.

'Mr Kett,' said Steward, 'if you are serious about your demands, you can't wait for them to be handed to you, like alms to the poor. If I have learnt one thing during my career, it is if you want something you have to either take it or build it.'

Robert gripped the table with his hands. 'What do you propose?'

'You have two choices. You up sticks and take your army to London while his majesty's forces are predisposed in Cornwall. Batter down the door and refuse to leave until your demands are met.'

'What happens if the king, or Seymour, refuse?'

'You must be prepared to kill them.' Steward's cold eyes

bored into Robert's skull, watching for his expression, testing his resolve.

'You'd be a marked man for the rest of your life, Robert,' added the mayor.

Robert nodded.

'Or, you stay here and ready yourself for whatever is coming this way.'

Steward rubbed his chin while he waited for him to respond. Mayor Codd took another swig, larger than his previous one.

'Is that the extent of your advice, Mr Steward?'

'Only, you can't wait,' Steward cleared his throat. 'You have no food.'

'You seem to be enjoying this too much for my liking, Steward.'

Steward sat forward. 'You need supplies. You need to make them think you can last longer than they can. You need a port. You need money. You need weapons. You need order and discipline.'

'Nobody is more aware of my current needs than I.'

'At present you are a target, sitting here in the dark like a flaming beacon. A direct attack will test you and most likely defeat you.'

Robert frowned.

'If, however,' continued Steward, 'you were *three* targets? What then? You are blessed with the sea on three sides. You can't be encircled, and with a seaport or two, you can be resupplied. Mr Kett, you must secure King's Lynn to the west and Yarmouth to the east. You must commandeer their treasuries.'

'And find them as empty as yours?'

Mayor Codd shuffled in his seat.

'If you want to defeat a king,' continued Steward, 'you

must start thinking like one, and what is more, acting like one.'

'And what about you, Steward?' asked Mayor Codd. 'What will your part be?'

'I am here, making a contribution, am I not, Mayor?'

'Hedging your bets perhaps,' replied the mayor.

Robert leaned back in his chair. Steward's suggestions raised more questions than answers in Robert's mind. He decided to keep his counsel quiet for the time being.

'Thereafter,' said Steward, 'wherever they choose to attack, must be where you, Robert Kett, are not. You must attack them under the cloak of darkness or when they move, whittling away their numbers and their supply lines avoiding a direct confrontation. You must fight dirty.'

'There is no honour in it, Robert,' declared the mayor.

'True, but there is no victory to be had in the alternatives.'

The door opened. 'William, you're just in time, come and hear the deputy mayor's plan for defeating the king.'

'You are on our side, are you?' said William, standing at the head of the table.

'I doubt it,' said the mayor.

William mouthed to Robert, 'Peter is in the ground.'

'Then you negotiate. Whatever demands you want to make. Whatever spoils you want for yourself,' Steward went on.

Robert shook his head. 'This is not about my personal gain. I am not a politician.'

'It will be. It always comes to that once you realise the extent of the sacrifice you have made for others. But that's for another day. Once you have won, you can do as you please. Form a new kingdom, break away from England if it pleases you?'

Robert laughed. 'One thing at a time, Steward.'

'Robert,' Mayor Codd leaned forward, 'remind me, what is the deputy is offering you?'

'Do you know. I'm still not sure.'

'What say you we have him placed in the cells, out of harm's way, with the rest of his kind?' suggested William.

'Good idea, brother. Better to be safe than sorry.' Staring directly at Steward, he added, 'We can't be too careful nowadays.'

William strode over to Steward and gripped his cloak, 'Come on, you, up you get.'

'Wait,' said Steward.

William winked at Robert.

'Go on.'

'I have no desire to be imprisoned. I believe I can be of more profit to you out than in.'

'So you keep saying. How exactly?'

William twisted his grip on Steward's gown. 'I have a property at Welborne, not far from your own land holdings. You may hide there, keep it for as long as it pleases you. I have no need of it.'

'Deputy mayor, it pities me that you should judge me by your own standards. I have no desire to hide and even less to profit from this situation. William, take him away.'

William marched him towards the door.

Steward turned to face Robert. 'What if I could get you money?'

Mayor Codd jerked round in his chair.

'Yours?' asked Robert.

'No, I have little wealth left, thanks to you. The king's money.'

'Go on.'

William released him.

'There are plenty in London who'd take delight in seeing

Seymour fail, and,' Steward spoke in a hushed voice, as if the treason was somehow a lesser offence when spoken in a whisper, 'the child king. One friend in particular at the exchequer could extend you a line of credit from the treasury.'

Robert laughed. 'Now we are talking, Mr Steward.'

Mayor Codd let out a sigh.

'No less than a thousand gold coins,' said Robert.

'That is an enormous sum!' gasped Steward.

'It is, you're right, but that is the price of your freedom, and with it I shall restore order in the city you claim to love so much.'

Steward cleared his throat. 'Well, if you'll excuse me, I better be going. I have work to do.'

'Remember, Steward, we have nothing, and therefore at this stage, nothing to lose. A thousand gold coins, no less. The king can pay for his own rebellion,' grinned Robert, unable to conceal his delight. There was nothing like a minor victory to restore one's belief in one's own actions.

Steward straightened his cloak and exited the room.

Once the door had closed, Mayor Codd leant across the table. 'What if he double-crosses you?'

Robert shrugged. 'Then he knows what we have in store for him.'

William picked up Steward's full tankard. 'Well, I propose a toast,' he lifted his drink, 'to Augustine Steward.'

Robert laughed and followed suit. Even Mayor Codd raised his drink.

42

6th August, Norwich Cathedral

The overgrown lawn had been trodden flat by the crowd now gathered in front of the cathedral doors. Here, leading to the nave, sat Robert. Before him stood John Cooper; his pox-scarred face defiant, his hands tied with twine behind his back. He waited for Robert to give his verdict. Robert wondered if his scars accounted for his behaviour. He'd seen it before with survivors of the pox, either grateful for a second chance at life or resentful about the disfiguring effects of the disease.

Behind Cooper's shoulder, Fulke kept a watchful eye on the man he'd brought to trial.

Whispers and murmurs rippled quietly through the crowd while they waited to see the measure of Kett's justice. Robert took his time, oblivious to the skein of geese that flew overhead. Behind him the cathedral doors were propped open to let the bad airs out.

After pleading with his representatives to withdraw their communities to the heath, Robert had finally resigned himself to the inevitable reality that his followers were determined to benefit from the comfort of the city. The cathedral had been commandeered as a dormitory. He rather hoped the Godliness of the surroundings might rub off on some of the more unruly members, but so far, his wishes had gone unrewarded. With so many men at large, unburdened by their normal tasks, the threat of lawlessness was never far away. He estimated a thousand or so men still braved the heath. The rest had made their own arrangements, sheltering from the morning dew in the empty homes of the city they found at their disposal.

Robert had introduced a curfew to keep his rebels indoors each night. It wasn't enforced with much discipline, but those Fulke suspected of wrongdoing were followed to ensure they weren't looting or vandalising the properties of the city's inhabitants, many of whom had fled to find sanctuary elsewhere.

Steward had reminded Robert of his earlier principles; swift justice was not enough to remedy people's wanton behaviour. Official justice needed to be seen to be done to set an example for others to follow. Robert was now presiding over the first of his reinstated open trials. The previous defendants had been landowners and corrupt nobility. They were either already in custody or had fled the reach of Robert's justice, leaving his own rebels as the only offenders guilty of crimes. The mood was proving to be sourer than that of former trials he'd conducted on the heath.

'Cooper, you have been in front of me before today, having disturbed the peace once already,' said Robert. 'Indeed, I sent you away, and yet, like a bad penny, here you are before me again. Have you anything to say for yourself?'

Cooper shrugged.

He had the loyal support of twenty archers for whom Norwich was their home. Men that would be useful in defending the city against a royal army, should one come.

However, in the meantime, Cooper had sought fit to enter a merchant's house, relive the merchant of his silver and impose himself on the merchant's wife. The merchant had appealed to Steward, who'd presented him to Robert to make his charges. He now waited at Robert's side with an expectant expression on his face.

Robert cleared his throat. 'Cooper, I order you to repay the silver you stole.'

'Can't,' interrupted Cooper, 'your man relieved me of it.' He nodded his head in the direction of Fulke.

'Fulke, do you have the merchant's money?'

'Yes, have it here ready.' His hand rummaged in his clothing before he passed the merchant a small handful of coins.

The merchant examined his money. 'This is mine, but only a fraction of what the man took.'

Fulke shrugged. 'It was all he had.'

Cooper returned Robert's stare. 'Fulke, in the shadow of his building, with God as your witness, do you swear those coins to be all that you found?'

Fulke nodded.

'Cooper, I sentence you to one week in captivity.'

Cooper spat on the floor at Robert's feet. Some of the onlookers booed and hissed. The merchant protested that one week was a pitiful sentence. 'What about the violation of my wife, surely I am due compensation?'

Robert dismissed the protests with a wave of his hand. He would negotiate an earlier release in private so that Cooper and his men would be available in the event of another attack.

'This trial is over. Fulke, take him to the castle.' Robert stood up and addressed the crowd. 'Let that serve as a warning to you all. I seek to build a just and fair society, not a lawless free-for-all. Any of you guilty of the same can expect a similar outcome. Now I beseech you, take your places in the cathedral and listen to the pastor I have organised for you.'

'What about food?' called out an anonymous face from the crowd.

Food, food, food, they began to chant.

'Bread will be served,' shouted Robert, 'after the service! Say your prayers daily. Earn your daily bread.'

As the grumbling crowd began to move toward the cathedral, Steward grabbed Robert's arm and pulled him away from the melee.

'Robert,' said Steward, 'troubling news.'

Mayor Codd approached, eager to be included.

'I see you are in dressed in new clothes. Where did this doublet appear from?' asked the mayor, pointing to Steward's purple jacket. 'I thought you'd been relieved of your wealth.'

'My attire is no concern of yours, mayor,' said Steward. Then, cupping his mouth with his hand as protection from eavesdroppers, he confided, 'Word from London this morning. Yesterday, royal forces confronted villages loyal to the rebels in Cornwall. The rebels were caught off guard. Many were captured before they could escape.'

'I see.'

Steward cleared his throat. 'Then they were executed.'

'Good God. How many?'

'Reports suggest eight hundred men had their throats cuts.'

Robert's eyes widened. He felt the knot in his twist tighter.

'Surely, such reports are exaggerated?' suggested Mayor Codd. 'Fearmongering.'

Steward ignored the mayor. 'We are dealing with a wounded animal.'

'Are the rebels in Cornwall defeated?' asked Robert as his

thoughts started to settle on the implications for them.

'No. Many escaped. We can assume they will keep the army tied down there for a time yet.'

'I cannot bring myself to believe such rumours,' said Mayor Codd, determined to call Steward's information into question.

'What news have *you*, mayor?' retaliated Steward.

Robert shook his head. The two men had been bickering like siblings ever since Steward had made good on his promise to secure money from the government. Having exploited his associate at the treasury, he had extracted three hundred pounds of silver coins from the government coffers. The money had been a godsend. The night watchmen yesterday, upon reinstatement of their pay, had agreed to resume their patrols. Carpenters and blacksmiths had been commissioned to repair the city gates; the bakeries were provided with flour, and the brewers were supplying ale again. Even the prisoners could look forward to some overdue nourishment.

Robert had bought a wherry full of salted fish. He had cringed at the price, but the merchants were canny enough to know how desperate he was and that he didn't have the time to go elsewhere. When the boat had arrived this morning, he'd remarked that it was the most expensive piece of fish he'd ever eaten.

The deal had confirmed what Steward had suggested; they needed to secure a port. Rather than take one by force, Robert had compromised. Yesterday he sent William, with a force of one hundred men upriver to the coastal town of Yarmouth. They took with them a letter and a chest of silver. The letter stated they had come to administer the town in the name of the king. The silver, to grease the palms of any alderman suffering misgivings.

Robert now planned to head back to Surrey House, eager to see Alice. He expected word from William at any moment. If he'd been successful, it was Robert's intention to leave William in charge of Yarmouth.

'Mr Kett.'

It was Thomas Garrod, one of the representatives who'd been with Robert since the first days of camp.

'Walk with me,' said Robert.

'Sir, the men of my hundred grow restless.'

Robert frowned. 'Do you want me to have a play organised for them?'

'They want to return to their homes.'

Robert sighed.

'They fear for their harvest. The weather has been dry. They have much work to do.'

'I understand, Thomas, but what of our cause if we all return home? Would you have me fight the government on my own?'

'My words fall on deaf ears. Some of them claim to have seen a magpie possessed of evil spirits in the tree over their shelters. They say it is an omen and that we'll perish like the men in Cornwall.'

'Nonsense, Thomas,' Robert reassured him. 'It's a magpie in a tree, nothing more. It's not the devil.'

'Their minds are set.'

Robert stopped walking. 'Well, bloody unset them, Thomas.'

Thomas shook his head. 'There is one other solution which I can volunteer.'

Robert looked at him.

'They return to their fields, but instead of returning to their homes, they camp on their common as a show of solidarity to Robert Kett?'

'I have a much better idea, Thomas,' said Robert as he started to walk away. 'They stay here and ready themselves for the fight of their lives.'

Robert was fuming: how could you reason with such bollocks? As he made his way down the passage between the houses, he felt a hand brush his arm.

'Please, sir, alms for an old monk. I am without board, lodgings or my sight.'

The old beggar dressed in rags, soiled in filth, stank to high heaven.

'Fuck off,' barked Robert, pushing the beggar too hard. He hit the wall and slid to the floor.

Robert marched fast, too frustrated to feel guilt. Everybody in hard times claimed to be a monk, another innocent victim of the old king.

Past the burned houses, he turned on to Bishopsgate. A gentle breeze travelled across the meadows and cooled the anger from his cheeks. He took a series of deep breaths and gathered his thoughts. He'd been victorious at every step, and yet every victory presented new problems that required yet another victory. Yarmouth would do nicely.

The fate of the Cornish rebels didn't bode well for London's mood. What was Seymour thinking right now? Robert wondered. As he walked, Robert thought about how he could get on the front foot. If he was to negotiate peace, he needed the momentum of events on his side. Could he use Steward to send a message to Seymour? Give me enclosure, and you can have Norwich back? Sheffield's death stood in the way of such a simple deal. Could Robert offer Seymour a perpetrator? Some unlucky swine who could swing for the crime. It would be a small sacrifice that could deliver thousands from the teeth of battle. Whose face would fit?

A front door opened, and an attractive young girl stepped

out onto the street. Robert took a moment to admire her and remembered his first sighting of Alice, her pale skin and lustrous blond hair. He smiled before catching a glimpse of a dark-haired man leaving with her. It was a farther three steps before Robert stopped in his tracks.

'Alfred?'

'Mr Kett,' he stammered. His arm bound in a sling.

'I thought you were dead?' exclaimed Robert. The boy's face turned crimson, and his gaze turned to the dirt of the street. 'Where have you been?'

'Sorry, Mr Kett. I was hurt in the attack. I nearly died, and I couldn't make it up the hill. I had to rest. I'm lucky to be alive. If it wasn't for Tiniker here, I might not have lived.'

Robert glanced again at the girl. He didn't recognise her. Alfred was still talking nineteen to the dozen. 'Enough,' interrupted Robert. 'Can you work?'

'I am healing. I can't move my left arm, and my shoulder is stiff, but the rest of me works.'

'Does it?' Robert looked at the pair of them; they looked like lovers. Yet, Alfred was married. What became of his wife? Robert wondered, remembering she was pregnant. 'Lynn?' asked Robert.

Alfred recoiled, his face frozen like a man who'd just discovered a plague spore in his groin.

Robert grunted and stared at the boy. He'd offered Alfred every charity, and he'd proved himself undeserving. He'd fled work and was eloping with another women while his wife grew his child in her belly. Moreover, if it weren't for Alfred alerting him to his fences being vandalised, none of this would have ever happened. Robert smirked. It would be Alfred that would swing for Sheffield's murder.

'You must come back. I have something in mind. Master Peter died, poor fellow.'

They stood motionless.

'You too, Tiniker. Gather what you need. I'll see you both at Surrey House.

'Delighted to be in your service, Mr Kett,' said Tiniker.

Robert felt pleased as he headed back. A young girl would brighten the mood in the place, and Alice would be glad of the help. Robert passed under the arch of the gateway and crossed the bridge. Downstream, was a boat in full sail, loaded with men. As the boat drew closer, Robert saw William at the bow. Why hadn't William stayed in Yarmouth? Robert leant over the brick wall. 'William, what news have you?' shouted Robert.

William shook his head and called up to his brother.

'They wouldn't open the gates. A navy ship is anchored off the coast. Cannon were fired, a warning to stay loyal to the crown.'

Robert rubbed his face and gritted his teeth.

'If you want Yarmouth, Robert, you'll have to fight for it.'

43

8th August, Whitehall

Seymour sneezed. After a few days rest at Hampton Court, today was the first day he'd felt well enough to return to Whitehall and start preparations to raise an army. He'd spent the morning at his desk surrounded by papers and burning incense. He enjoyed the solitude of his study. Here, behind closed doors, he could work methodically through his papers, all of which demanded his uninterrupted attention so he could assess critical decisions. It was only when other people misinterpreted his instructions, or worse still ignored them altogether, that the problems would again resurface like a persistent rash untreated by his salve. If only the noble classes desisted from bending matters to their own will. With these thoughts uppermost in his mind, he'd disbanded his council, preferring to take matters into his own hands.

He took a sip of spiced wine and dipped his quill in the inkwell, before adding his signature to his order for Lord Russell in Cornwall.

Dudley was safely out of the way at home in Warwick castle.

Russell had finally, after weeks of dithering, recovered

Exeter. The last of the rebels remained at large, but without a base it was only a matter of days before they were rounded up. The execution of the prisoners was regrettable. Indeed, Seymour had shed a tear in private after hearing the news. They may have been heretics to a man, but they were *English* heretics, deserving of a more honourable sentence.

He would take this up with Russell on his return, but for now, he was content to relieve Russell of his reinforcements and ready them for his Norfolk campaign.

He folded the paper, held a lump of red wax against his desk candle and sealed the order to return half of the eight thousand troops to London.

Seymour had sent word to his nobility that he'd appointed himself head of the army and would be personally leading them to Norfolk to end the rebellion. The next paper in the pile was a petition from the people of Great Yarmouth, pledging their allegiance to the crown and asking for royal support to protect them from Kett's rebels. This was the sort of correspondence he enjoyed — one that didn't require a response but assured him of the loyalty of the people.

He would show his council, including Dudley and Russell, how to quell a rebellion. He would ride at the head of his forces. He would meet with Kett in person, offer him and his followers a pardon and an end to enclosure, bound in law. In exchange, all he would ask was that they stand down and return to their labours.

He scratched his chin and wondered if he should challenge himself to finish the insurrection without the loss of a single soul. A bloodless solution. He'd spent many an hour before dawn, lying in bed, pondering the fate of the rebels and their demands. People would always have petty grievances. If he entertained the grumbles of every man, he would be forced to conclude England to be the worst country in the world, and that he knew was far from the truth. The way to an Englishmen's loyalty was through his belly and his store.

See that they are both kept full and he will stand in line for you and fight with more ferocity than any continental.

He'd seen it for himself on repeated campaigns. Man for man, no one was fiercer than an Englishman. But ending enclosure was all it would take to win their hearts and return them to their fields.

Then a thought occurred to him, the nobility would complain about Lord Sheffield's death not being avenged. However, killing a thousand peasants wouldn't bring him back to this life. On reflection, he might have to be seen to string up someone for the crime, but that was all that was required to see justice delivered.

One life, in exchange for peace and an end to the crime of enclosure.

Seymour smiled. He was looking forward to resolving it neatly.

It would be nice to get out of London for a week and enjoy some fresh air.

He felt his stomach rumble. Time for some food, he thought. As he stretched his limbs, there was a knock at the door.

'The French ambassador for you, My Lord.'

Seymour sighed and slumped back in his seat.

'Show him through.'

Moments later, he could hear the prancing steps of the Frenchman.

'Seymour,' announced the ambassador as he appeared around the door, wearing a smug grin across his oily face.

'Ambassador, please come in,' said Seymour, rising to his feet. 'What an unexpected pleasure. Regretfully, we shall need to be quick as I have other commitments to attend to.'

'*Mais oui*,' said the ambassador, gliding across the floor in his sky blue and gold embroidered tunic. 'You have many problems, *n'est-ce pas?*' The ambassador took a seat across the desk.

'Indeed, but I can always find a little time for my good friend. Tell me, what has got you in such a fine mood on this summer's day?'

'I bring word from my king, Henri.'

Seymour frowned. There was something menacing in the man's manner. He appeared conceited. Not that that was unusual for a frog.

'Yes?'

The ambassador clapped his hands before rubbing them together. 'He has declared war on England.'

44

18th August, Surrey House

Robert cradled his head in his hands. The afternoon sun shone through the window, warming the back of his neck. He'd been enjoying a rare moment's peace alone in the solar when he'd heard the commotion outside. A glance out of the window across the heath was enough to sink his spirit: his men were returning. He slumped into the chair and waited for the knock on the door.

It was thirty-five days since Robert had left Wymondham. In one month, he'd aged ten years. He felt a fraction of the man who'd set off to deliver a simple petition to Mayor Codd. The relentless succession of daily challenges, many he could no longer recall, others he'd never forget, had taken their toll. He'd met every one of them, rising to the occasion, but instead of growing in strength, he was crumbling. Robert knew privately what he was sure others could see for themselves. He was spent. Numb. Willing to make his peace with God.

The knock on the door came. Robert opened his eyes to find William, Luke Miller and Mayor Codd filing in.

'I'm sorry, Robert,' said Luke. 'We tried everything, but—' he paused while he searched for the right words.

Robert groaned. His second raid on Great Yarmouth had failed.

'We'd captured the cannon from Lowestoft without any trouble,' began Luke, 'but when we fired on the gatehouses at Yarmouth, they were ready for us. They returned fire, and we were losing men,' now his voice trembled, 'we had to retreat. They set light to a haystack, downwind of our position. We were engulfed in smoke.'

The manner of their defeat was irrelevant; it was still defeat. No matter how valiant, it amounted to the same thing.

'They advanced through the smoke and ambushed us.'

'How many dead?' asked William.

'Twenty-seven — another thirty taken prisoner. All the guns were lost.'

The room was still, the faint hubbub outside as the story spread through the camp was the only noise.

Luke puffed out his chest. 'I'm sorry. Robert. I failed.' Tears welled in his eyes.

Robert nodded. 'You did your best, lad. I can't ask more of you than that.'

Luke fought for composure. 'I hate the swine Seymour for making us do this to ourselves.'

Robert grunted. He agreed. It was beyond his comprehension that any of this should be necessary.

'Another thousand men wouldn't have made a difference to our fortunes,' said Luke, in an attempt to offer Robert some comfort.

It had the opposite effect.

'Thank you, Luke. Gentlemen,' said Robert. 'I'd like some peace now.'

'But Robert, this changes things, our strategy has failed.

We must make new plans,' said Mayor Codd.

William ushered the mayor to the door. 'Not now,' he said softly.

*

Tiniker ran the cow horn comb through Alice's silver hair, tugging through a knot that had snagged its journey. Alice twitched.

'Sorry,' said Tiniker.

Alice said nothing. All evening she'd appeared distracted by her worries about her husband.

Outside the bedroom window, the rain darkened the dusk. Tiniker was grateful for the pitter-patter of droplets against the window. It provided some respite from the agonising silence that echoed through the house ever since the Yarmouth raiders had returned. The mood indoors was crushed between the pestle and mortar of the Kett's predicament. The rain did nothing to dampen the tension that hung in the air.

'Lice free,' said Tiniker inspecting the comb in the glow of the candlelight.

Alice sighed. 'Thank you, Tiniker. Let me comb yours.'

They swapped places, Tiniker taking the spot on the bed left warm by Alice. Alice wiped the comb on her sleeve and began to part Tiniker's hair at the centre.

Over the past ten days, the only two women of the house had struck up an unlikely friendship. In ordinary times, a young immigrant from the lower orders and an elderly yeoman's wife, more accustomed to having a maidservant than doing women's work herself, may have found little in common. Each day since Alfred's return, Tiniker had spent the daylight hours at the house. She had shared the cooking, cleaning, shopping and errands that their circumstances demanded of them. The two women had quickly seen past their differences, and as the days had passed, an intimacy had developed between them.

'Let us change the mood,' said Alice forcing a reluctant smile as she summoned the energy to cheer herself up. 'You and Alfred?'

'What's to tell?'

'Even a blind man could see he likes you.' Alice lowered her head for a closer look as she stroked the comb through Tiniker's hair. 'He stares at you as you work. He doesn't even notice that I'm watching him. He has that glaze in his eyes that young men get.'

Tiniker's cheeks glowed.

'Don't tell me you haven't noticed!'

Tiniker smiled, picturing Alfred's endearing face. 'He's nice,' she said, not wanting to admit too much.

'Tiniker, come on. You're not much subtler yourself.'

Tiniker purred as the comb ran through her hair, tugging at her scalp, relaxing her. 'He's been good to me. After father was killed, he helped with man's work at my house.' She paused. The mention of her father brought her attention back to the heaviness in her heart.

'Tiniker, do you blame my husband for your father's death?' Before Tiniker could answer, Alice continued, 'The question has been on my mind ever since you admitted your father had been killed defending the gates. I was too surprised to ask at the time and the moment hadn't been right since.'

Alice's voice was soft and compassionate. Her question aroused no emotion in Tiniker. She shook her head a little.

'No. Robert didn't kill him. His guild required him to defend the city. He didn't support the rebels, but that was only because he didn't want his home damaged or our lives put in danger.'

Tiniker smoothed the creases of her woollen dress against her thighs, her mind casting back.

'We had similar things in our homeland,' she sighed. 'Everybody does what he or she thinks is the best for themselves.'

'Come here.' Alice turned the young girl's shoulders toward her. They hugged. 'You're wise for one so young.'

Tiniker closed her eyes, enjoying the embrace. She felt welcomed by Alice, and after the past weeks, she craved the warm touch and love of another. She hadn't planned to confess that the rebels had killed her father but late one afternoon, talking in the kitchen with a tankard of ale, it had just popped out. She panicked that she might have inadvertently undermined her ruse to infiltrate the Kett's headquarters. In fact, it had had the opposite effect, serving only to increase the trust between the two women. Alice had expressed her sorrow for her loss.

'Why it should be necessary for men to kill one another I will never understand,' she'd said. 'I think we'd make a better lot of running the country if the men would let us.'

Tiniker had thought about it afterwards. From what she had seen of them, Robert, Alice and William seemed like lovely people. It was hard to deceive them, and she couldn't bring herself to tell one more lie than was necessary. It stung to know she was liable to betray them, but she needed to keep a roof over her head. Duplicity was hard. The closer she could keep to the truth, the less chance she had of tripping herself up. She never disclosed Jan's responsibility for the defences or her arrangements with Steward. Every time Tiniker had misgivings, she thought of Margreet. She couldn't see that her limited information to Steward had done the

Kett's any harm anyway.

Alice rose back to her feet and resumed her combing.

'Has he kissed you?' asked Alice turning the conversation back to Alfred.

Tiniker hesitated.

'No.'

'You're not a very good liar, Tiniker.' Alice grinned.

Tiniker froze. She was a spy, living a lie. Her nerves were frayed.

She took a breath and reassured herself that Alice was only referring to her kissing Alfred.

'I think he has a good heart,' continued Alice, interrupting Tiniker's thoughts. 'I dare say he has his shortcomings, but I see goodness in him.'

Tiniker smiled to herself. It was nice to hear her innermost feelings confirmed out loud.

'It's been the highlight of the last week watching you two flirt and laugh.' Alice sniffed, 'It's been nice to have a little dose of love and happiness in this house.'

'We're not in love!' pushed back Tiniker as her cheeks turned red.

'Come, Tiniker, I can see it clear as day, even if you choose not to.'

Tiniker squirmed in her seat. She knew she loved Alfred but refused to admit it to herself. Fearful she would fall for him, or betray him, or lose him. She had to stay strong for Margreet.

'Pretty thing like you, it's a wonder he manages to walk around the house without his horn showing. By the time you leave at night, I fancy his hose look more like a tent.'

Tiniker giggled.

She'd never heard a woman of Alice's age talk openly about matters of the flesh. Surely older people didn't…?

Tiniker had always imagined that after a certain age people must stop naughty thoughts and deeds.

'He still has one good arm.'

Alice let out a laugh. 'Oh dear, that's the first time I've laughed in days.' The comb snagged, pulling with it Tiniker's hair. She yelped. 'You'll be making more noises like that if Alfred has his way with you!' Alice laughed.

'Stop!' Tiniker's cheeks went a deeper shade of red.

She started to giggle.

She let out a small fart by accident, and their laughter grew. Alice tried to reply with a joke but ran out of air before she could get her words out. Tiniker covered her face with her hands, as Alice bent double, finding only more laughter when she fought for words. The two of them descended into fits of giggles. For a brief moment, all the pent-up worry of recent weeks was released. Neither was sure what exactly it was they were laughing at, or why it was so funny, but they enjoyed it all the same. Alice leant on the bed, laughter shaking her body. Tiniker laid back resting on top of Alice. It was several moments before they composed themselves.

'I'd like to kiss him,' confessed Tiniker, 'but I don't trust myself.'

'You'll know when the moment's right,' said Alice. She cleared her throat. 'Don't let him have his way with you though. Once boys his age have had what they want they'll vanish quicker than a Catholic's morals, and you'll be left with a baby.'

Tiniker nodded.

'You don't want to end up outcast, Tiniker,' warned Alice, her tone becoming serious. 'Do it properly. Wait till he proposes.'

Tiniker went quiet, staring at her knees.

A moment passed with only the raindrops as accompaniment.

'A penny for your thoughts?' asked Alice.

Tiniker startled, returned from her daydream.

'I'm worried Alfred won't survive the fighting to come.'

'He won't be doing any fighting with that injured arm of his.'

'Something tells me harm's going to come to him.'

Alice went quiet. Only the sound of the raindrops.

'Why don't I plait your hair?'

Tiniker nodded. 'Sure.'

A silence passed. Tiniker closed her eyes as Alice pulled her hair back. She sensed Alice needed to talk and unburden herself of her own fears. Now was the time to ask the question that had been at the back of her mind all afternoon. She threw caution to the wind. 'What will Robert do?'

Alice sighed. 'After today's news, he's as flat as a pancake.'

The door opened. William stepped into the candlelight of the room, and Tiniker cursed his arrival.

'That's a gay sound I haven't heard much of recently.' He closed the door behind him.

'Just us being silly,' said Alice. 'How's Robert?'

'Not good.' William moved past them and sat himself at the head of the bed. 'He's talking about conceding defeat.'

Alice gasped.

'He's talking about riding to London tomorrow and handing himself in.'

'He'll be hung.'

'I know. He thinks it's the only thing he can do to stop the loss of more lives. What he doesn't realise is that once word spreads, he'll be lynched by our own side for betraying them. He wouldn't make it off the heath.'

Tiniker stayed quiet.

'What word is there from London?'

'Only God knows for sure. Word is there are troops gathered, but they have no orders. The fighting has finished in Cornwall, so maybe they have simply returned. Now we're at war with France, maybe the soldiers are required to guard against invasion. This morning, I even heard a rumour that Dudley had deposed Protector Seymour! Frankly, I don't know what to believe.'

'What should Robert do?' asked Alice.

'Search me. Our best hope might be to negotiate a pardon for everybody, but he's in no condition to even manage that at the moment. We've got to find a way to pick him up, otherwise, well,' he paused, 'no, we have to get him back on his feet and leading.' His knee clicked as he strained to get back on his feet.

'I'll leave you ladies to your business.'

William closed the door behind him. Tiniker heard Alice sniff.

'Alice? Are you okay?'

The plaiting stopped. Alice sat down behind her, and the bed trembled beneath her. Tiniker turned and hugged Alice whose body shook in Tiniker's arms. Emotions, which had been simmering below the surface for days, began to overspill.

'You're the only person who's asked.' Alice's voice was shaking, 'Not even Robert has given a thought to me.'

Tiniker rubbed Alice's back.

'I have to be strong for him. He's got enough to worry about with having to reassure me,' said Alice straightening her back and wiping her nose with her sleeve. 'Pray with me?'

They knelt either side of the bed, their hands joined in the middle, heads bowed as they closed their eyes. Tiniker's mind and heart fought like cat and dog as her loyalties collided. She didn't hear a word of Alice's prayer, too busy wrestling with her conscience.

*

As night fell, the silhouette of the cathedral spire faded against the darkness of the sky. Fulke pulled his new jacket tight around his body to keep out the chill. He winced as it sent pain through his ribs. He ducked out of the rain and took shelter under Steward's porch. A long yawn seeped from his tired and aching body. It was too early to be found asleep at his post, but he was determined to get some rest tonight. This evening there was not so much as a cat to be seen on the streets, as the rain had done his work for him. Fulke had always imagined every night in a city would be noisy, but tonight was still. He rested his back against Steward's door.

Fulke had agreed to guard Steward's property at night so the deputy mayor could sleep soundly. The arrangement suited Fulke. He wanted to remain on Kett's payroll, but events in the city now exceeded his ability to dispense any semblance of order on his own. Not that he'd admit it to Kett.

Fulke didn't like the deputy mayor, but he understood how the man's mind worked. He was the sort that would see himself right. Fulke respected Steward's brand of self-interest. Steward was influential, so Fulke had decided to stay close to him. His sort paid well to keep their dirty work at arm's length.

As he relaxed, Fulke's mind drifted back to Wymondham. Beating up the constable seemed like a lifetime ago. Not in his wildest fantasies could he have expected things to go as well as they had. But there would come a time when this rebellion would finish, and life would return to normal. He felt a satisfaction in knowing that he had started and lived through something that would be talked about for years to come. He'd beaten up gentleman, extorted their cash and imprisoned them. He'd gotten and spent more money in the past month than he had in the previous year. He eaten and drunken like a prince, bedded his share of strumpets and still had money to spare. He'd set fire to fair portion of the city, killed a good many soldiers and murdered a member of the aristocracy.

He grinned at the memory of that.

Once word had spread of Sheffield's death, there had been a right hoo-ha. He'd overheard rebels saying it was good to have the boot on the other foot for once and put the frighteners up the aristocracy. Others however, feared that Sheffield's death would bring with it reprisals and that Kett's demands would not be granted. There had been a lot of talk of a bounty for the man who killed Sheffield. Fortunately for Fulke, only Alfred had seen, and he knew better than to open his mouth.

The furore had caused Fulke to think for the first time that he would do well do keep in favour of powerful men. The events of the past month had given him a taste for life and more means than he'd ever had before. When he'd started, he had nothing to lose. Now he found himself feeling a little different. He had enough money to bribe constable Morris for roughing him up in Wymondham, he had ingratiated himself with Kett and Steward, but neither would be enough to keep him from coming into harm's way for what he'd done to Sheffield. It wasn't that he was scared of dying, but dying in a fight, or better still a battle was infinitely preferable to a noose of a mere common criminal's death. That wasn't good enough for Fulke: the man who killed aristocrats.

The rain stopped. A break in the clouds let a silvery glow of moonlight shimmer against the wet. The rain ceasing threatened to bring people out and disturb his rest.

Kett's curfew was routinely ignored. The gangs that nightly roamed the streets were a greater deterrent than Kett's laws.

One such gang had forced Fulke to see the limitations of his own force. The night after Cooper's trial, when Kett sent the local archer to prison, Fulke had been approached by a young boy who claimed to have discovered a wealthy man beaten and left for dead in a back alley. Sensing opportunity, Fulke had followed the boy and true to his word, a man lay folded like a baby in the dirt. As Fulke bent down to get a better look in the darkness, the victim jumped up and accosted him. As the boy made good his escape, the narrow alleyway filled from both ends with men. Fulke gave his best account of himself but was soon overpowered and left for dead like the man he'd come to rescue. Kick after kick had rained down on him until he lay still. After they had finished beating him, they pissed on him, telling him this was the price he paid for messing with John Cooper.

In his current bruised condition, guarding Steward's door served as the ideal way to stay out of danger whilst remaining on the payroll.

He rubbed his eyes, alert to movement in the shadows across the street. His senses fired, as he strained to see a small figure in a hood and cloak run across the street towards him. As the figure bounded up the steps, Fulke raised his arms to protect himself from collision.

A shrill scream rang out.

It was a woman.

'Watch where you're going,' he said as he held her frozen body at arms' length. 'Calm,' he said, sensing the woman's agitation at being surprised in the dark.

He pulled back her hood, and she let out another scream. 'It's you!' She kicked his shin.

Fulke shouted and buckled as she aggravated a wound from earlier. She wriggled out of his hands and stepped back on to the street. When he saw her blonde hair in the moonlight, he realised it was Alfred's girl.

'What are you doing here?' she barked. 'You frightened the life out of me, you dirty rapist.'

'What are *you* doing here?' replied Fulke.

'If you touch me, I'll scream so loud your ears will bleed,' threatened the foreign girl.

'Pretty little thing when you're angry, aren't you?' taunted Fulke. 'Wonder you haven't broken my leg.'

'Touch me again, and I'll kill you.' She flashed a small blade from beneath her cloak. There was a steely menace in her voice that convinced Fulke she meant it. 'I should have killed you last time when…'

The front door jerked open.

'What in God's name is all this noise?' demanded Steward peering out from behind a candlestick.

'You have a visitor,' said Fulke.

'And you have a rapist at your door,' said Tiniker stepping forward.

Steward recognised Tiniker.

'You'd better come in.'

Tiniker pointed her knife at as she went up the steps backwards and into Steward's house, making sure to close the door behind her. Her hands were trembling as she stuffed her knife in her belt then turned to face Steward behind her.

'What the hell is that man doing at your door?' she barked.

Steward was taken aback by her reaction. He squinted. 'Hello, Tiniker, welcome,' he said. 'Come through. Let me pour you some wine.'

Tiniker followed him into the house and took the tankard he offered her. Her hand was still shaking. The wine was soothing.

'That man at your door tried to rape me.'

'Well, better he's occupied at my door than free to roam the streets, don't you think?'

'Well, if you judge a man by his companions then I can't say much for you.'

Steward's eyes narrowed.

'If you want my information, you'll have to guarantee my safety,' she said, shaking off her hood.

'I'll walk you back myself.' Steward gave his word.

Tiniker pulled out the bench and sat down. Steward did the same. The kitchen was large enough to prepare a banquet in. The embers of a fire smouldered in the hearth under an empty spit for roasting meat. She could make out sacks of food against the wall, and barrels in the corner.

'I see why you need a guard,' she remarked.

'Enough about my companions. What about yours? Mr Kett?' said Steward.

'He's done for.'

'What is he planning?'

'No, that's just it, he's done for.'

'He's surrendering?'

'He wants to. He's lost his nerve. He wants to back down.'

Steward smiled. 'Good. The sooner his fetid head's parted from his body, the sooner we can get back to our lives.'

'And you'll be happy, will you?' she challenged him. 'When a good man has been killed for standing up for his beliefs to improve other men's lots?'

Steward snorted, 'Come on!'

'You are a cynical bastard,' said Tiniker releasing her grip on her tankard.

'Young girl, don't come into my house, accept my hospitality and have the front to sit in judgement on me.'

She couldn't afford to lose his support, but it rankled that he should take such pleasure in Robert's downfall. If he had seen Alice in tears less than an hour ago, he might think differently.

'Maybe you have spent too much time with the Ketts?' Steward traced the watermark on the table left by his tankard with his finger. 'Perhaps you can't be relied on anymore.'

'Mr Steward, sir. I don't wish to upset you, as you I know I am reliant on you for my protection and survival, but having spent time with the Ketts, I have found them to be good people whose only intention is to overturn the injustices that they see.'

'When you walked here tonight, you walked over the graves of Englishmen, through a city partially destroyed by fire, and on a night when gangs of men roam free to exert their will on any who should be unfortunate enough to cross their paths. You sit in a house stripped bare of its contents, and indeed, have lost your own father.' Their eyes met. 'There is one man responsible for all of this: Robert Kett. You'd do well to remember that.'

Tiniker ground her teeth and searched for a response.

'Whatever has happened, I can tell you that his intentions were honourable.'

'I judge a man by his actions, and a more dangerous man than Robert Kett, I have yet to encounter. The sooner he's strung up, the better,' Steward wasn't budging.

Mr Kett deserved better than the treatment Steward wished on him. Tiniker took another sip. The wine warmed her, ridding her body of the night's chill.

'Well, I have told you what I know. He will back down.

No more violence is necessary. What will you do?'

'I'll let London know. What they do is up to them.'

'Have you no feelings?'

'For Kett and his troublesome followers? Kill the lot of them for all I care.'

'Will you make no attempt to…'

'Kett threatened to have me imprisoned. I couldn't care less what fate befalls him, and if he's worried for his own neck then he'd be well advised to consider that before he raises hell next time.'

'His wife told me he never intended for this to happen.'

Steward topped up her wine. It warmed her body as she drank. Steward loosened his collar and licked his lips. 'Just how much are you prepared to do to help save Kett?'

Tiniker met his gaze and placed her hand on her hip. 'Mr Steward, I have a knife in my belt, and if you so much as lay one finger on me, I'll have no hesitation in using it.'

Steward grinned as she stood up.

'Thank you for the wine. My business here is done. Now if you'll be good enough to walk me home.'

*

Robert woke up after the best night's sleep he could remember having in a long time. Alice lay in slumber next to him, her breathing slow. Robert's mind was normally busiest in the morning, but today it felt blank, devoid of inspiration, sunk in the mire of his misfortunes. But, oddly, his mood was not as black as the day before. He ignored this small sign of progress, preferring to hold onto the dismay of recent days. If he admitted to himself he felt better, he would embroil himself in the challenges he faced, and if the events of the past month had taught him anything, it was that his actions only led to bigger problems.

For now, his body knew, even if his mind did not, it was safest to stay beaten. He needed to pee but didn't want to wake Alice. Instead, he turned his thoughts to their children. He still referred to them as children even though they had long since become men and women. His daughter Jane was now the concern of another man. It had been years since he last saw her, a source of some vexation, but he had convinced himself he didn't want to interfere in her life and be a nuisance father. She would be busy raising her own children, and he'd left her husband with enough money to survive several winters.

He'd pushed his boys out to find their own paths. A tannery was no place for bright young men, and he didn't wish the hardships of his own life on them. His eldest, William had ventured to London. The youngest, George, had always dreamed of a life on the high seas. Perhaps he would succumb to the lure of the new world. Whatever they all did, wherever God placed them, Robert was grateful they were not with him. He wondered if they'd heard their father's name mentioned in the taverns and inns. Would he be a hero or a villain; would the name Kett be a hindrance to them now or would they dine out on their father's deeds? Robert had always hoped his eldest, William, might return to Norfolk and inherit the family land, but today he closed his eyes and offered the Lord his thanks for keeping them out of Norfolk.

An hour must have passed while Robert stared at the ceiling, ignoring his call of nature. His sanctuary was disturbed by a faint knock. The door crept open, squeaking on its hinge. From the corner of his eye, he could see Alfred carrying two tankards.

Robert ignored him, oblivious to the smile on the young lad's face.

'I've brought you last night's rainwater from the butts,' he whispered. He placed a tankard at each side of the bed. 'Would you like me to empty the chamber pot?'

Robert shook his head, so Alfred left.

He heard the clatter of people moving about downstairs. Coughs, yawns, creaking floorboards and chatter, the dawn chorus of Surrey House coming to life. Outside the bedroom door he listened to the footsteps of people walking along the corridor, relieved when they didn't stop at his door. It would not be long before people wanted to talk to him about the king's army, the boy who stole the milk, and everything in between. Robert wanted nothing more than to spend the day in bed.

It was early afternoon when Alice and William finally dragged Robert out of the house, with Mayor Codd close behind. Despite his protests, they refused to tell him for what purpose he was needed in Norwich. Not even the fine weather could assuage Robert's temper from fraying as they crossed Bishopsgate Bridge on the now very familiar journey.

'If I am required to lead, I should damn well know what's going on,' said Robert making no attempt to hide his frustration.

He didn't like surprises. Alice squeezed his hand and asked that he trust her.

Their walk continued in silence. They cut through the cathedral grounds, past the cloisters and over the lawn to the front doors.

'What the blazes is going on?' asked Robert when he saw they meant to enter.

'You'll see,' replied William pushing open the small door cut into a much larger one.

Robert followed his brother through. The nave was full of

people, numbering thousands. Those lucky enough to have seats rose to their feet. Every pair of eyes was trained on Robert. He wondered what in God's name was going on as a mild panic returned to his body. I better not have to address this lot unprepared, he thought. Alice took his hand in hers, and William stepped to the side. The choir began to sing, and their voices reverberated up and against the stone columns and walls, filling the air with their angelic melody. The hairs on Robert's neck prickled. He recognised the composition. It was Thomas Tallis: *Ave Dei patris filia*. His favourite.

Alice led him down the aisle, between the smiling faces, and Robert felt like the bride at a wedding. The front bench had been reserved for them. They took their seats. The rest of the congregation sat.

Mayor Codd was no longer with them. Robert looked around and saw the mayor had stayed at the back.

'Was this your idea?' he whispered to Alice. She smiled. Robert closed his eyes and let the music fill his ears.

As the moments passed, his body relaxed. The tune was magnificent. Such a composition was as impressive an accomplishment as the cathedral. He reflected on what man was capable of. How could a being capable of creating such beauty, be capable of the violence that he'd witnessed? Violence that he'd had a hand in.

How will I account to God for this?

The choir fell quiet. A pastor mounted the pulpit and offered a brief prayer, his ample voice sufficient to reach the extremities of the building.

'We are gathered here under God to celebrate the labours of Robert Kett.'

Robert tried to swallow the lump in his throat. This service was for him. He looked at Alice, whose lips betrayed a proud smile.

Robert shook his head. Sneaky mare, he thought to himself.

The pastor continued, elucidating at length the qualities required to lead men in a cause that one believed in. Qualities Jesus had shown the world.

'Virtues like those of Luther,' he continued.

Don't mention Luther, thought Robert, his name was enough to get the catholic half of the congregation up in arms. Robin Hood might have been a less controversial choice.

'Qualities that one man here has shown, time and time again. Sacrifices he has made in the service of those he leads. One man, above all others, here today in this house of God, has followed the example laid down by the son of God. That man is Robert Kett.'

Robert grew teary.

The comparison to Jesus was far-fetched, but he was now overcome by an awareness of what he'd achieved and the impact he'd had on people's lives, the community. Whatever may lie ahead, after just one brief summer, his would be a name that lived through history, a name that would pass down the generations.

He was exhausted, bruised and battered and still, somehow, he was here, at the head of his people.

He fought to compose himself.

The pastor invited a layperson to address the crowd. She was a woman in her twenties accompanied by a small boy, who stood at her hip. She told her story: how her family had been evicted, and how the courts wouldn't let them bring a charge against the lord of the manor. She'd been to see him in person. He'd beaten her and raped her. She fought back her own tears as she talked. She said she'd wished to die, and had it not been for her son, she would have gladly taken her own life. She didn't want to go on living in a land where rich men could do as they pleased with no regard for those they trod on. She said her family had joined the rebellion because Robert Kett was a good man who was prepared to stand up to those in power. She said she was prepared to lay down her life so that her children may grow up in a better world than the one in which she had.

The pastor asked her son what he wished for.

The boy mumbled: 'For my mummy to be happy and for my family to be safe.'

The pastor repeated the answer loud enough for the congregation to hear. Robert had heard the boy's own words for himself and gritted his teeth. This was why he had come this far, and that was why he must continue. These people couldn't go back and face their masters after this. They had no choice but to prevail.

The pastor invited the congregation to pray. They bowed their heads and said their prayers in English.

'Amen.'

They stood to sing.

Robert found his voice. The hairs on his neck prickled as the cathedral resounded with their voices. The knot in his gut began to loosen.

'I doubt this house of God has ever witnessed such impassioned singing,' said the pastor.

The congregation remained standing, and the pastor repeated, 'Let us give thanks to the Lord for Robert Kett.'

The service ended. Robert and Alice led the congregation out, and Robert was halfway down the aisle when everyone present burst into applause. The clapping was deafening. Robert took a deep breath, glanced at Alice, her arm wrapped around his.

Outside, he was mobbed by well-wishers, wanting to

thank him for his courage. Some asked for help with their grievances, but one man accused him of hypocrisy: jabbing his finger.

'Are you going to rebuild it for me, Robert Kett?' he hollered.

Another man came to Robert's defence, shoving the complainant away.

Robert pulled Alice away as the first blows were exchanged.

They quickly made their way back to Surrey House.

'Whose idea was that, then?' asked Robert as they waked down Bishopsgate.

Alice squeezed his hand. 'We thought you'd earned it.'

'Thank you.'

The gatehouse at the foot of the bridge was unmanned. Its brickwork bore the scars of the rebel cannonballs. Small drifts of earth banked up against the walls that enclosed either side as if the bridge were the only reminder of the mound that had briefly blocked their access to the city. It had taken a mere afternoon to unblock the road before they could send the captured weapons, powder and prisoners back to the camp. It seemed like a long time ago. Robert shivered as he thought back to that day. The day he'd failed and resorted to violence. It had only brought more violence, death, arson and burglary.

Since that day, Norwich had descended into Sodom. He sighed. He brought them to a halt at the apex of the bridge and looked over the side. The river was murky from the rain last night. Alice said nothing as he stared blankly into its depths, watching the dust and debris drift slowly towards the coast. Robert felt like a piece of flotsam himself, drifting east farther and farther from his home. How nice it would be to go home, he thought, even for one night. He could catch a boat home from here. He pictured the route in his mind, east at first, turn right onto the Yare, double back south of Norwich, then turn left where the Tiffey met the Yare at Barford. He'd tried to buy some old monastic land around there and had been outbid by Flowerdew. He'd just been appointed escheator to the king and was flush with cash from his first confiscations.

Robert jolted as inspiration hit him.

The answer to his problems had been beneath his feet the whole time. Robert had been so preoccupied that he hadn't given a second thought to his old nemesis. Amongst the trials and tribulations of the rebellion, he'd failed to see what was suddenly so obvious: Flowerdew was a direct line to the king.

Dragging Alice behind him, he said, 'Come on love, I've got a prisoner to bargain with.'

45

'What do you mean he's missing?' shouted Robert. 'You brought him back here, didn't you?'

Alfred stood in the doorway, squirming like a child that needed to pee. His injured arm sat across his chest in a sling.

'Look at me when I'm talking to you,' snarled Robert. 'Where did you put Flowerdew?'

Alfred looked away.

'Stop dithering, lad.'

'Go easy, Robert. Alfred. The facts,' said William, his voice calm.

'Here's a fact for you, William,' said Robert turning his temper on his brother. 'There's a good chance an army is going to come here and try and kill us. It would be very helpful to speak to the king and Flowerdew is one person who knows the king, and until moments ago, a man we had under lock and key. Now he's vanished like the fucking princes in the tower!'

William looked away towards the window.

'Tell me, Alfred, no better still, show me.' Robert marched round the table and grabbed Alfred by his good arm. 'Show me where you put him.'

He dragged Alfred across the hallway to the cellar door.

Alfred fumbled for the keys. 'He's not down there, Mr Kett.'

'It seems you're not even capable of wiping your own arse, so why should I trust that you have checked the cell properly?' He waited for Alfred to unlock the door. Alfred pulled the door open, and the human stench wafted upstairs.

'Good God,' said Robert. 'Come on, lead the way.'

He followed Alfred down the stone steps into the darkness of the cellar.

'Mind out,' said Alfred to the prisoner slumped at the bottom of the stairs.

'*Flowerdew?*' called out Robert. 'Where are you? I'm going to release you.' In the faint light, prisoners began to stir. 'Flowerdew, this is Robert Kett. Come out.'

'He's not here.'

'Who's that?'

'Sir Roger Wodehouse,' he croaked and stepped forward out of the gloom.

Jesus.

They'd captured Wodehouse at Hellesdon the day before they set up camp on the heath. The poor soul had been here ever since — time enough to grow a beard. He looked thin and frail, squinting against the small trickle of daylight from the top of the stairs. Robert grunted. Sir Roger would know. He lived at Kimberley, making him and Flowerdew neighbours.

'He might have been moved to the castle,' suggested Alfred. 'We moved the majority of prisoners when it became too crowded here.'

'No,' said Sir Roger, recovering from his coughing fit, 'he was never here.'

'So tell me, Alfred, where did you put him after you marched him back from the guildhall?'

'I stopped at the bottom of the heath. My father in law had been killed in the fighting. I had to pay my last respects,' said Alfred, falling over his words.

'Did he offer you a bribe?'

'*No*!'

'Alfred. What happened to Flowerdew?'

'I'm not sure, Mr Kett. He and the other prisoners were all with the carts when I left them. Everybody started pushing the carts uphill, and I wasn't needed and…'

Alfred was babbling.

'Enough,' snapped Robert. 'You're not leaving my sight, Alfred. You're going to scrub this cellar clean — so clean it smells like a spring meadow. I wouldn't keep swine in these conditions.'

Robert was ashamed at the treatment that had been allowed to occur under his feet.

'Robert, release me, please. I could help you?'

'Sir Roger, after spending weeks down here I think any man would have sufficient justification to raise an army of men hell-bent on slaughtering me. For certain, I would.'

'Please let me go. I beg you.'

'I'm sorry. I can't take that chance.'

'Save us,' came a voice from the murky depths of the cellar.

Robert turned to climb the stairs as voices start to murmur around the cellar. He stopped halfway up the stair.

'Alfred, who else guarded the prisoners with you that day?'

'Fulke, Gunner, Miles and two others I didn't recognise.'

Robert ran the rest of the steps and took a lung full of fresh air in the hallway.

That evening, Surrey House was dark and quiet when Robert

made his way up the stairs to bed. A trace of candlelight escaped under his door. Alice was lying, awake, in bed. Robert sat on the bed and untied his shoes. He dropped his clothes in a pile on the floor and got under the cover, too tired to scratch the flea bites on his neck.

'He's slipped through my fingers. I sent William to the castle. They'd never seen him there either. I'll send some people to look for him in Hethersett tomorrow. May not have worked anyway,' conceded Robert. Flowerdew was slippery and would most likely not have been good to his word. 'Would have been nice to try though. I'll try anything at the moment. At this rate, I'll have to send for a sorcerer to make us all disappear.' Robert closed his eyes.

'You poor thing.' Alice kissed him goodnight. She leant over to blow out the candle but stopped when she heard a thud downstairs. 'What was that, Robert?'

'Sounded like the cellar door to me.' A lock clunked as it turned, disturbing the night's silence. 'It's that fool, Alfred. He's been washing out the cellar all afternoon. He deserves a good thrashing that boy.'

'Go easy on him, Robert. Tiniker has fallen for him.'

'Stupid cow.'

'It's nice to see two young people in love. It brightens the place.'

'Don't you be getting all soppy. That boy's married.'

'No!' said Alice, raising her hand to her mouth.

'He had a fight with his wife the first day we were here. Whacked her with a stick, and then her dad gave him a shiner of a black eye.'

'Robert, stop it,' said Alice in disbelief.

'It's true,' he protested. 'That's why he's here doing all our chores. I had to keep them apart so they didn't kill each other.'

Alice let out a hushed gasp, 'I thought it was just because he was your apprentice at the tannery. That little swine,' said Alice. 'I'll have his guts for garters in the morning when I see him. Poor Tiniker must have no idea?'

Robert closed his eyes and smirked. 'She's pregnant too.'

'Who?'

'Alfred's wife.'

*

Alfred staggered into the kitchen to clean up the dirty pot and brush he'd left in the kitchen overnight. He'd been too tired to wash them last night, and now, just his luck, the smell of the cellar had permeated the kitchen. He wasn't too worried about Mr Kett inspecting the cellar. He'd done a half-reasonable job, and Kett had more important things to contend with.

Cross-legged on the floor, Alfred yawned and set about washing the brush with his one functioning arm using the last of the river water. He thought about what he'd say to Tiniker. She'd dashed off early last night, and he'd been too ashamed to come up and see her off, smelling as foul as he had. The thought of her laugh, her smile, and those blue eyes had been the only thing to keep him going yesterday. Maybe he could pick her some flowers?

He returned the clean pot and brush to the cupboard. He turned around and nearly leapt out of his skin.

'Mrs Kett I didn't hear you come in.'

'Alfred, I am very unimpressed.' She looked angry.

'I'll open the doors and clear out the smell. It will be gone in no time.'

'Enough of that,' she snapped. 'Why is a married man leading young Tiniker astray?'

Alfred was shocked. 'Who? She hasn't said anything to me?'

'I'm talking about *you*, you village idiot. You're married, and she has no idea.'

Alfred's shoulders sunk. 'Let me explain,' he pleaded.

She folded her arms. He could tell he would only get one chance to explain his circumstances.

'I was tricked. She told me she was pregnant, and I was forced to marry her. She lied.'

'But you'd had sex with her anyway?' Mrs Kett made no attempt to hide her contempt.

Alfred squirmed, grinding the ball of his foot into the ground. 'I was drunk, and I didn't intend to, I wish I'd never laid eyes on her,' he babbled.

'But lay on her you did, and she thought she was pregnant.'

'She knew she wasn't. She confessed to me.'

'A women cannot know for sure for at least a month. Where is she now?'

'I don't know,' said Alfred. 'After her father was killed, she left the camp. Most likely she has returned home.'

'Her father is dead and you, her husband, have left her?'

Alfred's temper flared. 'She was the most poisonous creature I ever met. I am not her husband. I was tricked — our marriage is annulled.'

'Who by?'

Alfred hesitated. 'By me.'

'Poppycock. Alfred, you took vows before God. If you have a case to plead, then make it.'

'I will.'

'Good. Then the church can decide your fate, not you.'

'Fine.'

Alfred waited to be dismissed. Instead, Mrs Kett stared at

him, reminding Alfred of how his mother used to evaluate him when he'd been naughty.

He walked past Mrs Kett and opened the kitchen door to allow some fresh air in.

Mrs Kett passed sentence. 'Alfred, you have one week to get your marriage annulled. If not, you must return to your wife.'

Who does she think she is? A magistrate? I work for her husband, not her, Alfred thought, how dare she threaten me? He opened his mouth, ready to give her the full weight of his opinion.

'If not, I will tell Tiniker the full truth of your indiscretions.' She left the kitchen.

'*Bitch*,' muttered Alfred to himself.

He spent the rest of the morning emptying chamber pots, sweeping the house, fetching water and skinning rabbits for the pot. People moved through the house conducting their business, visiting Mr Kett, but Alfred was too preoccupied to notice. All morning, his brain had been working on how to escape the curse of Lynn and save his relationship with Tiniker. He doubted he even had a relationship with Tiniker. If she found out he'd been lying, then whatever chance there was of winning her heart would vanish; she wasn't the sort of girl to tolerate lies. Not even lies with good intention.

The more he went over the matters in his mind, the more the simplest solution seemed the best. He'd worked hard for the Kett's, and hadn't always been treated well, thrown in sewage, thrown in a cell and later made to clean it. He'd depended on his job at the tannery for his survival. He'd dreamed of making a success of it, especially since Master Peter's death. Now, so many had died that work would be easier to find. Faced with the choice of losing his job or his true love, the answer was simple. Tiniker won every time. He made up his mind: He would desert the Ketts.

Just after midday, Alfred was lighting the bread oven when Mr Kett appeared in the kitchen, looking preoccupied. He announced he was hungry after a busy morning.

'There are some dried herrings left,' said Alfred pointing to the crate on the shelf.

Robert helped himself and sat at the table, chewing on the fish. An uncomfortable silence hung in the room.

Luke Miller arrived, looking worried. 'Robert, I bring news.'

Robert wiped his hands on a piece of linen. 'Good or bad?'

'Bad. An army has left London. They will be in Cambridge by nightfall.'

Alfred's ears pricked up. He glanced over his shoulder as Luke sat down opposite Robert. Alfred carried on arranging the kindling in the door of the oven.

Robert said nothing.

'They've recruited fighting men from Essex, all the lords that remain loyal to the king.'

'How many?' asked Robert.

Alfred could hear the fear in his master's voice.

'Thousands: reports vary between ten and twenty.'

The door opened. It was William.

'The army is headed for us, much larger than before,' said Luke bringing William up to speed. 'We have, at most, two days.'

Alfred placed three tankards on the table, and the three men sat in silence. Robert's eyes were closed.

'They are led by John Dudley, the Earl of Warwick,' continued Luke. 'They have cannon, cavalry, powder, guns and men at arms. He is the finest soldier in the realm.'

The Kett brothers exchanged a knowing look. Robert rubbed his eyes, resting the weight of his head in his hand.

'Robert, I think you should give serious thought to surrendering.'

Robert's head snapped up. 'You're a contrary bastard, Luke. You were one of those goading me on from the start.'

'What I meant was, seek terms with Dudley…'

'Luke,' interrupted William, 'thank you, truly. Now please be kind enough to leave my brother and me in peace.'

Luke hesitated. 'But…'

'We'll send for you shortly. Just a moment's peace, if you'd be so kind.'

Luke looked disappointed but left the table.

Tears appeared on Robert's cheeks.

'Come, brother,' said William gripping his shoulder, 'remember the words of the preacher. This is but another problem which we must overcome. God must test his subjects. There will be an answer, but we must remain calm with clear-headed thoughts.'

'Alfred if you'd be kind enough to leave us, find some work elsewhere. We need some time alone,' said William.

'Of course. Goodbye.'

Alfred left the room. I doubt if you'll ever see me again, he thought to himself.

46

24th August, Norwich Castle

From the castle rooftop, Robert observed the royal army amassing less than a mile beyond the city wall. He'd given up trying to count the lines of neatly pitched white tents.

'What do you intend to do?' asked Steward.

Robert glanced at William. 'We wait.'

He wiped the sweat of his brow. Today looked to be the hottest day of the summer, with not a cloud in the sky.

'Robert, you might be wise to make the first move. Show some goodwill, and get Dudley on your side,' suggested Mayor Codd.

'We'll look desperate,' replied William.

They *were* desperate.

Robert was unsure how many men he could field. His system of elected representatives had broken down or splintered into factions. Some had been killed, others deserted, anxious about their harvests, some exasperated by Robert's desire for a peaceful solution. Fortunately for Robert, many people still felt aggrieved at their treatment by their lords, and many feared seeing them again once this was over. Those that had been captured would threaten reprisals and those that had evaded capture would be no less forgiving. Whatever the true state of rebel minds, so far as the army outside were concerned, they needed to appear calm, in control, and able to carry on indefinitely.

The army had arrived shortly before sunset last night. It had camped on the London road, thereby blocking any supplies from the southern approach to reach the city. Rumours about their strength varied, but Robert's spies had counted fifteen hundred cavalry and anything up to another eight thousand infantry. This time the sides were far better matched than when he'd faced down Parr's army of fifteen hundred. Parr's defeated soldiers had been seen in Cambridge and had no doubt been absorbed into Dudley's army.

Robert had seen enough. The only consolation at seeing his quarry was that after five days of planning and talking about nothing else, there would be no more dreading their arrival.

Robert tried to reassure himself it was a game of cat and cat but wasn't convinced. He'd felt like an actor waiting in the wings. He'd learned his lines, and thankfully it was finally time to perform. His nerves would calm once he stepped on stage. Only William knew his plan. They had come this far and only ever been victorious. They were on home ground, and they had right on their side, and therefore God.

'Mayor Codd, I have a task for your supervision,' said Robert.

The mayor looked apprehensive.

'Our prisoners are mostly housed in this castle. Any gentlemen are to be taken in their chains and kept at Surrey House out of harm's way. Any men prepared to take up arms against the soldiers are to be released.'

'But they have been declared a danger to the community?' said a disbelieving Mayor Codd.

'Mayor, I need every pair of hands I can get. Now please be kind enough to make haste.'

Robert knew he would never be afforded a pardon himself. The prisoners were his final bargaining chip. He turned his attentions to the deputy mayor.

'Steward, when they approach, you will go on my behalf. You are to tell them Norwich is defended by men with no regard for anybody's welfare, including their own, and any attempt to enter the city will be repulsed by overwhelming force.' Robert continued, 'If his lordship will promise to end enclosure, then I will send my rebels home, and in exchange, I will offer them the man who killed Lord Sheffield so he may face justice.'

Steward looked surprised at that revelation. The deputy mayor liked to think of himself as somebody who knew all there was to know.

'Those are my terms, and I will entertain nothing else.'

'Understood,' replied Steward.

Negotiating with Dudley would prove the most important task: Mayor Codd was no good under pressure. He was scared of his own shadow and would be keen to exonerate himself. In Robert's mind, this made him liable to muddle the negotiations. Steward was more capable and had, to date, made good on all his promises. Robert reckoned the deputy mayor could be relied on to favour Norwich's, and thereby his own, survival.

What the city needed most was peaceful negotiation.

Steward would take or advise whatever action was necessary to stop violence. On that point, Robert could be certain they were of same mind.

'Stay within sight of the gates. I want them to see our forces posted to the city walls and the gatehouses.'

Steward went to take his leave.

'Oh, and Steward,' added Robert as he was leaving, 'get it wrong, and you'll never step foot in this city again.'

*

John Dudley kicked his stallion into a trot, leaving the comfort of Intwood Hall and his host for the night, Sir Thomas Gresham, behind. Never one for camping on campaign, he'd opted to stay a mile behind his forces. He'd slept soundly in the four-poster bed and hadn't been interrupted.

'What a fine day for putting down a rebellion.'

William Parr rode beside him, looking less enthusiastic. After his previous experience, he didn't appear to be relishing another fight with Kett.

Dudley thought otherwise.

The cocky Marquis of Northampton was still berating himself for his defeat. Dudley had suffered defeats of his own in the past. If you were lucky enough to survive, you had to endure them and learn the lessons for next time. Some commanders never recovered from a botched first attempt in charge, but Dudley assured Parr that Seymour had set him up to fail. With so few men, he could never have succeeded. He'd offered Parr a chance to redeem himself as his second in command, and Parr was ambitious, so had agreed. Dudley's only condition had been that Parr swear to support him in the council.

It was war with France that had tipped the balance.

When Seymour had informed the council that he intended to take an army to Norfolk, they pulled rank. How could Seymour ride around the country singlehandedly quelling every rebellion of public disturbance when France threatened to invade at any moment? The whole commotion had played into Dudley's hands. Exiled in his castle at Warwick, the council had demanded Seymour recall him. The realm's most experienced commander couldn't be left to rot while the country slipped into ever-deeper peril. Dudley knew this was his moment, and he planned on seizing it with both hands. Seymour had lost the confidence of the council. Without the support of the gentry, he was there for the toppling. The stage was set. Only Robert Kett stood in his way.

When Dudley reached the camp, he ordered the herald brought to his tent. The herald stood in front of Dudley and listened to his instructions. He repeated them back and left for Norwich for the third time this summer. The earl was at pains to remind him to ignore Kett. 'The man can't lead if we won't acknowledge his authority.'

*

The herald's horse wore his usual coat of the king's quarters.

'We meet again, herald,' said Steward.

The two men met outside the main city gate. Steward had walked far enough out of the city gate to be clear of earshot of the ranks of rebels posted to the gate and walls. This time none of Norwich's inhabitants clambered for a sight of the waiting army. They knew trouble lay ahead.

The herald returned Steward's greeting. He held his chin high, suggesting he accepted no responsibly for events. 'I demand your surrender.'

Steward sighed. 'As you know, personally, I am not in opposition to you. I am merely a mouthpiece for others.'

'As am I.'

'Then you'll understand I am not in a position to grant the surrender of others.' Steward could hear the frustration in his own voice. The herald was one of those people who got under your skin without trying. His effeminate voice and his manner were condescending. Steward reminded himself to be calm. 'Let's get this over with, shall we? What are your terms?'

'Total surrender. Kett's capture. Yours?'

'Promise to end enclosure, and the rebels will stand down.'

'Not possible.'

'Then God forbid man, you'll be raising the curtain on a scene of devastation and bloodshed. In future, the taxes raised from this city won't amount to anything. We won't be able to fund our part in your wars,' Steward went on. 'What's more, you'll create a generation of enemies opposed to Seymour, the king too. Is that what your master wants?'

'My master wants Kett's head on a plate.'

'And do you think he's just going to walk out into the welcoming arms of an army? Let me speak to your master.'

'I'm afraid that's not possible.'

'Why not? Is he worried we might actually be able to sort this out peacefully?'

'His worries are his own private matter.'

'Go back and tell your master this: Kett says end enclosure or fight. But pay attention to what I say. I know Kett, and I have agency within his camp. Tell your master he's a coward and will do anything to avoid a fight. Which is what we all want, isn't it? Offer a pardon and end enclosure, and your work here is done.'

The herald smiled. 'Mr Steward, The Earl of Warwick will look favourably on you for your information, thank you.' He pulled his reins and kicked his horse.

The church bells would toll ten before the herald returned

from the army's camp.

This time he brought two other men on horseback. One was a soldier, carrying a brace of handguns. A bodyguard, Steward presumed. The other was a trumpeter.

'Mr Steward, sir, the people shall have their pardon and God willing, your city be spared the wrath of John Dudley, this country's finest soldier.'

Steward couldn't hide his delight.

'Take me to the rebels,' the herald demanded.

Steward led the three horses through the gates under the watchful eyes of rebels above. They made their way through the city and gathered in their wake a following of rebels curious to hear the herald's proclamation. Steward left the herald and his horsemen outside Tiniker's house by the bridge leading to the rebel camp. That was as far as Steward was willing to go. Having been to the camp on numerous occasions, he had no desire to be amongst the men that had vandalised his home. Besides, this was the herald's message, and Steward didn't need to be seen to endorse it. He hadn't enquired further to the nature of the royal concessions, but all they had to do was issue a pardon and promise to end enclosure. As he walked back to his house, against the tide of people following the herald, Steward felt a sense of hope that this would all be over soon.

*

Alfred had been trying his arm out of its sling when he heard the procession outside Tiniker's house. The herald rode past the window. For Alfred, the return of the herald was good news. He'd wanted to leave the Ketts, but Tiniker had pleaded with him to stay. He couldn't understand why she was so keen for him to be involved with them, but she seemed to prefer being at Surrey House to being in her own home. Reluctantly, he'd stayed on. She'd rewarded his loyalty, kissing him with a passion he'd never experienced. It was if her life depended on it. Alfred wasn't going to argue. He could have kissed her all night, but she'd been worried that Margreet might discover them, so they'd stopped.

And since, she'd looked even more beautiful.

Tomorrow was the day he was supposed to have his marriage annulled. Otherwise, Alice would tell Tiniker about Lynn. Alfred had lain awake at night, his mind torturing him. Their relationship would be in tatters. He cursed himself for lying, but he could never have told the truth either. Alfred was trapped in the web of his own mistruths.

Getting his marriage annulled wasn't as simple as it sounded. It meant walking to Wymondham, convincing Lynn to accept his terms, convincing the pastor the annulment was legitimate and the marriage never consummated, despite Lynn claiming to be pregnant. The pastor would turn to Flowerdew for guidance, who Alfred suspected would, in turn, likely demand the return of his cottage, which meant he wouldn't be able to use it to bribe Lynn. Even if he managed to successfully annul the marriage. How would he account his vanishing for three days to Tiniker? Whichever way he looked at it, it wasn't going to work. His hopes of saving his love for Tiniker rested on the rebellion coming to an end so he could escape Kett's influence.

'Let's go outside and see what's going on.'

Tiniker shouted to Margreet upstairs to stay indoors. She had a habit of keeping out of the way when Alfred visited. They stepped into the morning sun, joined the throng of people, and Alfred held Tiniker's hand as they were swept along. Alfred caught a glimpse of John Cooper's red hair amongst the crowd. He was using the stave of his longbow as a staff. As Alfred looked around, he noticed more weapons amongst the bodies: a glint of a steel blade, a flash of a sickle, a glance of an axe head. He kept an eye out for Fulke. He was likely to be amongst the crowd. He hadn't seen his friend since clattering him over the head. Tiniker wouldn't take kindly to seeing her assailant up close again either.

The mood amongst the people was expectant. There was not much chatter as they moved along the road. A young boy with blonde hair pushed past Alfred, brushing against his leg. Alfred instinctively checked his belt to make sure he hadn't been pickpocketed. Another two boys pushed their way through following their friend. Seemingly oblivious to the consequences of the herald's visit, they sang a song about how the herald liked to lie with men. Alfred grinned to himself and checked on Tiniker, half a foot behind.

They queued to cross over the bridge, heading into rebel territory. Over the tops of people's heads, Alfred could see the herald and his two bodyguards on horseback. Once across, they were just in time to hear the herald's trumpeter sound a call on his instrument to announce the men's arrival. Eager to get a view, the crowd behind the herald dispersed across the slope, forming an arc around his party. Moments later, the remains of the rebel camp made their way down from the heath. Several thousand people now circled the herald and his two companions.

'Where's Robert?' said Tiniker.

Alfred looked around. He couldn't see the Ketts. That surprised him. Why wouldn't they come down?

The herald nodded to his trumpeter who blew one sharp note to bring the crowd to silence. The herald straightened his back and spoke, 'Subjects of King Edward the VI of England. I carry with me here your pardon,' the herald raised his arm and held a scroll aloft.

A small cheer rippled through the crowd.

'If you leave for your homes now, no more blood will be spilt,' continued the herald.

Alfred looked around the sea of faces. Amongst the nodding heads and smiles were some frowns and expressions of confusion.

'We haven't done anything wrong?' shouted a woman to Alfred's left.

'The king and his protector, the Duke of Somerset, have been most generous in this offer. I urge you, plead with you, go home and return to your lives in peace.'

'What about our demands?' shouted someone. 'Have our brothers died for nothing?'

'I remind you that you are not entitled to make demands of the king.' replied the herald, looking down his nose at the heckler. 'Nonetheless, the lord protector's enclosure commission will continue its work to understand the nature of the problem, which you have brought so violently to his grace's attention.'

Jeers of derision rang around the crowd. People shouted their complaints but couldn't be heard. The bodyguard and the trumpeter shifted in their saddles. Alfred shook his head in disbelief. The herald's going to lose the crowd again, he thought. Tiniker had a worried look on her face. Alfred cursed. Where were the Ketts? What could he do to pacify matters?

In a break in the chorus of taunts, Alfred shouted, 'What about Mr Kett, will he receive the pardon too?'

The herald looked ill at ease. 'Mr Kett is a criminal. He will face the king's justice.'

Boos rang out from the rebels.

'What justice?' shouted a voice from the crowd.

'Once he is found guilty in a court of law,' added the

herald. The herald nodded to his trumpeter, who blew a note to silence the crowd. Once they had settled, the herald stood in his stirrups.

'You have put a city under siege, you have attacked your own countrymen, you have burned and pillaged your neighbours.' He raised his voice to be heard over the catcalls and retaliations. 'I offer you a pardon and promise that, in time, your complaints against enclosure shall be addressed. Can you not see how lucky you are?'

Why does this man keep threatening people? Alfred thought.

To one side of the crowd, people began to pull back. A gap appeared as they parted. It was Robert Kett walking through; his arms raised high. When people saw their leader, they began calling out their grievances again.

Alfred noticed the herald ignored Robert.

'Go home now, and you shall be free. Stay, and you will be slaughtered.'

While Robert appealed for calm, the herald continued to ignore him and spoke directly to the crowds. 'I command you, leave and live. Stay, and you shall die.'

'Enough,' bellowed Robert.

As the crowd fell silent, the herald stood in his stirrups again and raised the scroll of pardon above his head in both hands.

'Do not listen to this man. He'll will lead you to the gates of hell.'

'That's quite enough from you, herald. Once again, your knack of irritating the good people of Norfolk knows no limits.'

'I bring these people a pardon,' said the herald.

A small blond boy stepped forward. He tapped the herald on the leg.

'Mr herald?'

The herald looked down at the young boy, his irritation clear to see. The boy stepped back a few paces. 'This is what my neighbours and I think of your pardon.'

The boy turned around and dropped his breeches, exposing his bare buttocks, before proceeding to empty his bowels onto the grass.

The crowd roared with laughter and clapped.

The herald, lost for words, turned his head away. The laughter of the crowd was silenced by a sharp bang. The herald's bodyguard held his pistol aloft, and smoke drifted from the barrel.

The boy's body slumped forward onto the ground, and blood trickled from his mouth. He'd been shot in the back.

The shout rang out: 'He's dead.'

Fury filled the air.

Alfred pulled Tiniker into towards him and shielded her with his arm. People pressed against them.

'Alfred, we're going to be crushed,' said Tiniker.

The horses of the herald and his companions, spooked by the crowd, reared up, forcing people back. The bodyguard had reloaded his pistol and fired another shot towards the heavens. Alfred gripped Tiniker and fought to hold his footing.

Where was Mr Kett?

A stone struck the herald, and a volley of cheers erupted.

'Kill the herald!'

Men moved forward, bent on avenging the herald for their fallen.

As Alfred held Tiniker's head against his chest, he caught sight of Mr Kett spreading his arms and pleading with people not to retaliate.

Robert grabbed the reins of the herald's horse. 'If you

want to live, you'll come with me.'

With the herald's horse in one hand, Robert swung his other arm to clear a path towards the Bishopsgate Bridge. Screaming at people to get back, they edged out of their way. Those close enough spat at the herald and his companions.

'Mr Kett, you will hang for your good deeds,' warned a woman from the crowd.

'Let me worry about my fate,' replied Robert as he made his way through the ranks of his followers.

Alfred kissed Tiniker's head, the golden thread of her hair soft and fragrant against his dry lips. Slowly, they followed in Robert's footsteps. Rebels poured ahead of Robert and his escorts. Some ran to make it across the bridge before him. Alfred saw a group of men standing shoulder-to-shoulder, blockading the bridge. In their middle, was the ginger-haired John Cooper. Robert drew to a halt in front of them, trapped on the bridge.

'Mr Kett, sir, pray, tell us, what do you plan?'

'Let me pass, Cooper.'

The gang behind Cooper locked arms, forming a human chain across the bridge.

'I am taking this herald back to his master, where he can do no more harm to our cause.'

'Let us take him, Mr Kett,' asked Cooper.

'If you go with your longbow, you will be killed.' Robert said. 'I will take him, and I will negotiate a settlement so our cause will not have been in vain.'

Cooper relented. 'Mr Kett, it is you they want. You are the only man who is not to be pardoned. If I will not be safe, what chance have you?'

'Let me pass, Cooper.'

'Only if we, your forces, join you and die with you in your cause.'

'I'm not planning on dying. Come on.'

'People,' shouted Cooper, 'we cannot let our leader risk his life, for then what of our struggle when he is dead?'

People shouted their agreement. Alfred looked around. People didn't want Mr Kett to leave the city. He overheard a man saying, 'The moment he steps out of the walls he's dead, and so are we.' Another man shouted, 'We'll suffer the same fate as the Cornish rebels. Promised a pardon only to have their throats cut.' A ripple of fear ran through the ranks.

Cooper broke the silence. 'The herald and his men may leave. But you must stay, Robert Kett. Otherwise, we are all dead.'

Robert looked ashen-faced as he released the reins. Cooper stepped to the side, and his gang parted to let the herald pass over the bridge.

Alfred whispered to Tiniker. 'There goes Kett's last chance of bargaining his way out of this. There's going to be an almighty fight now.'

47

Fulke washed down the last of his scrambled eggs with a swig of ale and belched. He picked up the jug of wine he'd bought and stepped out of the Maid's Head into the midday sun, feeling ambivalent about what the day had in store. The royal army were camped outside, which invited the prospect of fighting, but Fulke doubted it would happen. He'd seen Mr Kett up close enough times to know the old man hadn't the stomach for a fight. He'd try and find terms but would settle for anything that saved his own neck. Then they'd all go home, and nothing would change.

It didn't matter to Fulke.

Enough had changed to make a difference. He had some money and more importantly, in Steward, he had connections.

He wasn't leaving Norwich.

After the mayhem of the last few weeks, there was opportunity to be had in this city. Empty homes, damaged buildings, frightened merchants and unclaimed goods, the hard part would be deciding which opportunity advanced his interests fastest. The fighting had taken its toll on the city's stock of manpower. Widows needed men and the city needed to repair its defences and replenish its guards. Fulke fancied himself as a captain of the watch, or a sheriff even. For the first time in his life, he could envisage a future for himself that didn't involve chopping up carcasses for William Kett.

He crossed Tombland to Steward's house. The wine he carried was a gift for the deputy mayor. They would, in all likelihood, be celebrating the end of the siege this evening. Fulke had proved useful to Steward during the unrest, but once life returned to normal, Fulke couldn't rely on his service being requested. So tonight, after a few drinks, Fulke planned to share his thoughts on how he could be useful to the deputy mayor: his designs on how they could ensure Codd's tenure as mayor finished, following his association with the rebels.

Knowing Steward, his eye was no doubt already on his rival's station, but if Fulke could become complicit in his plan, he was another step closer to the source of authority.

Fulke heard the rhythm of cantering horses behind him. Interested to see why somebody should be riding fast, he turned to see the herald and his two bodyguards on their mounts. Fulke studied their panicked expressions as they rode either side of him. They didn't have the look of men who had just successfully granted a pardon.

Before Fulke could reach Steward's door, a stream of rebels had spilt into the open area in front of the cathedral, carrying weapons and shouting for people to ready themselves. Fulke stopped one of them, 'What's happening?'

'The herald shot a boy. He was lucky to escape with his life. We're off to man the gates ready for the fight.'

He let himself into Steward's home without knocking and found the deputy mayor coming down the stairs.

'The herald's made a pig's ear of his pardon,' said Fulke putting the jug of wine down on a side table. 'A gift.'

Steward groaned. 'That fool could drown on dry land.'

'Looks like the rebels are making their way to the gates to head off the army.'

Steward closed his eyes and clenched his fists. He took a deep breath while he composed his thoughts.

Fulke interrupted them. 'What do you want to happen now?'

'For this madness to go away,' snarled Steward. 'Let's go to St Stephen's gates and see if we can't yet talk some sense into these bloody jesters.'

*

The first cannon shots rang out in the early afternoon. Both scored a direct hit on the wooden doors of St Stephen's gate. The doors cracked. A few more hits and they'll be in, figured Steward, as he looked on from down the street. The rebels gathered behind the doors, crept back nervously and left a space clear. Men posted on the city walls were crouched down, occasionally peeking their heads above to see what the army was doing. Steward tapped his fist against his chin.

'Do you think they can hold them out, Fulke?'

Before Fulke could answer, the ground shook, and a tremendous bang erupted into the air. The gates shattered as the full force of Dudley's twelve cannons was unleashed. Splinters of wood flew into the waiting rebels — they fell and screamed. One door was blown clean off its hinges, and the broken remains of the other hung defiantly to the archway. Through the open gateway, Steward could see the smoke clearing and the soldiers readying themselves. A trumpet sounded, and they charged.

The air filled with the battle cries of both sides.

Kett was nowhere to be seen.

Nobody was in charge of the rebels. Only Steward

appeared to have any official authority. Now the first soldiers arrived at the gates. Rebel archers loosed their arrows from the walls. Stones were dropped onto the soldiers from the top of the two round towers that straddled the archway. The clash of steel colliding could be heard amongst the cries of men. Steward found the scene in front of him repellent: the smell of burning gunpowder, blood and spilt bowels.

This was what happened when ignorant men were left to their devices, he thought.

He watched with increasing dismay as the gateway began to pile up with corpses. He estimated twenty minutes had passed since the first wave of soldiers, but the rebels kept them out. The fighting was slowed by the gates forming a bottleneck which only a few could pass through at once.

Fulke spoke. 'You're fidgeting, Mr Steward.'

'I'll take kindly for you to be quiet, Fulke.'

'We need to be on the winning side,' said Fulke.

Steward looked at Fulke. He noticed Fulke's fists were clenched.

At heart, he remains a thug, knew Steward. Fulke was right though. Steward had to take a side, and it needed to be the winning one.

It was time to hedge his bets.

'Fulke, I have a task for you.'

Fulke nodded.

'Slip outside. Find Dudley. Say I sent you. You're to tell him to send some men to the St Benedict's gatehouse, two gates farther round from this one. The lock was reported broken, and I never sanctioned the repair. He may find that easier. If he gets in, invite him to lodge at my house. Go.'

*

So far it had been a day of mixed emotions for John Dudley. It was always the same with warfare, the ebb and flow of events put even the most seasoned of soldiers to the test. Afterwards, he would only remember the highs, but they would taste sweeter for having had to overcome the lows. The first skirmishes had not gone his way, and he'd begun to fear the loss of the initiative.

Then fate played her part.

The arrival of the deputy mayor's information about the open gatehouse was a godsend. Victory often depended on the smallest of details. He'd left a detachment of his forces battling rebels at St Stephen's gate while he quick-marched the rest of his infantry two gates farther along. No sooner had they found the doors unlocked and undefended, then he recovered the advantage. He'd trotted alongside his forces as they stormed into the city, taking possession of the marketplace and the guildhall. Next, they had cut off the retreat of the rebels still defending the main gates. He ordered Parr to take a force of three hundred men and capture or kill the rebels that were now trapped at the main gate between their forces.

Dudley was in.

He would soon face a counter-attack, and the more decisive his early victory could be, the better his chances faired. But Dudley knew, despite all his experience and preparation, in the chaos of war, lady luck had a role to play. So far she'd been on his side.

An hour later, Parr returned to the marketplace and cantered up the slope to join Dudley on horseback outside the guildhall. Dudley noticed the flush of excitement on the young man's face.

'Your grace, I report we have control of the gate. We captured forty-nine rebels. The rest are slain or fled.'

'Very good, William,' replied Dudley. 'Have your men sweep the streets between here and there to make sure there are no pockets of resistance.'

'Already in progress.'

Dudley gave his second in command an appraising look. He liked it when a commander showed initiative. 'Good. Well done. Bring the rebels to the market square and have them make their own gallows. If any of them protest, kill them without enquiry.'

Parr kicked his horse and left to set about his duties.

Dudley looked around the marketplace, getting a feel for his surroundings, deserted, with buildings boarded up. He was here to stay. Without supplies, Kett would soon wither. That meant they would risk all to unseat Dudley's hold on it. He had to be ready. Like Parr before him, he summoned his commanders and instructed them to place a body of guards at each of the streets leading into the marketplace.

Once they were satisfied the area was secure, they were to send for his cannon and his own supply train. The short, stocky man brandishing a facial scar reappeared.

'Remind me of your name?'

'Fulke.'

Dudley thought him a thuggish-looking sort. Despite his embroidered jacket, he was unshaven and not what Dudley would expect as the typical company of an alderman. 'You must thank your master for his assistance today.'

The man nodded. 'Thank him yourself. He invites you to join us at his house and offers you our assistance, which you'll need.'

Dudley frowned. Now was not the time to take offence at the man's manner, but he found the fellow's self-importance as unconvincing as it was rude.

*

'What should we do?' asked Tiniker.

Alfred scratched his head. Moments earlier they'd seen rebels pass the window and cross the bridge back to the camp.

'I don't want to stay here in the house if there's going to be fighting at the bridge again.'

'Well, there's bound to be. It's the only direct route to the camp.'

'I'm not leaving,' declared Margreet.

'We could go up to Surrey House?' said Tiniker.

Alfred shook his head. Being close to the Ketts risked his secret escaping and was almost certainly going to put them in harm's way if they were caught. 'It might not be a good idea to be found in the Kett's service.' He thought about this logically. 'We can't make up our minds when we don't know what's going on. You stay here, and I'll go and see for myself what's happening.'

She nodded, but he could see she was reluctant.

'Be careful, Alfred. You promise you'll come back?'

'I promise. I'm unarmed, so they won't suspect me.' He kissed her goodbye, closed the door behind him and listened for the bolt to close.

The atmosphere was eerie. The street was quiet as he rounded the corner. The farther he got from the safety of Tiniker's house, the more Alfred queried his decision to come out alone. He could hear a low rumbling noise like carts rattling and creaking under the weight of their cargo, so he paused to listen. Two soldiers appeared in metal plate chest armour, dragging a cannon behind them. They were followed by more men and more cannons. Alfred froze.

The soldiers had captured the city.

If he ran, he looked guilty.

If he waited, he risked confrontation.

The first soldier saw him as he looked up and wiped the sweat from his brow. The afternoon sun was beating down, punishing them in their labour. They approached as Alfred tried to make up his mind what to do. They must be trying to get to the gatehouse over the bridge, he thought, but why were they not being escorted by men-at-arms?

'Can you help me, young man?' said the first soldier as he drew level with Alfred. He was short of breath from tugging the cannon. He had an unusual accent, and it took Alfred a moment to work out what he'd been asked for. Before he could reply, the second soldier stood up and loosened the rope over his shoulder. The cannon stopped rolling.

Another soldier at the rear of the gun shouted, 'Stop!' drawing the convoy to a halt.

'I thought it was supposed to be flat around here? Hilliest bloody city I've been to outside Wales,' protested the second soldier.

'We're looking for the marketplace, young man?'

Alfred was bemused by their accent, but once he'd made sense of the words he wondered why he was standing face-to-face with the royal artillery. They were a long way past the marketplace. Where were the rest of the army and why were the cannon, the slowest and most vulnerable part, alone?

Alfred's mind raced. He didn't want to endanger the girls, but the soldiers were sitting ducks and most of the way to Mr Kett's camp.

'Keep going,' he said, 'around that corner then it's left past the hospital.'

'Thanks, lad.'

With his back to the cathedral wall, Alfred counted fifteen cannon, followed by a trailer of shot and powder. Donkey's dragged carts full of chests, presumably soldiers' luggage.

Beyond the church at St Martin's, Alfred could see soldiers at the end of the street, by the Maid's Head. He turned right and went over Whitefriars Bridge. He discovered a group of poorly-dressed men in conference.

'You rebels?'

'Who's asking?' said a moon-faced man.

'I work for Mr Kett. I'm his page.' Alfred was nervous. 'I've just seen all the army's cannon and luggage. They're looking for the marketplace, but I sent them towards the bridge.'

'Are you certain?'

Alfred nodded.

The man grinned. He held out his hand. 'I'm Miles.' They shook hands. 'You little beauty. Come on, boys, let's go.' He tapped Alfred on the back of the head like a proud father. 'You run up to the camp, and get as many down as you can find. We'll trap the bastards.'

*

The day's light was fading. It soon would not be safe to be out on the streets. Fulke had waited patiently in the background all afternoon, observing Dudley as he battled to control the city. He was a short-tempered man and didn't suffer bad news well. When his captain had told him they'd lost most of their canon and luggage to the rebels, Dudley struck him in the face, knocking him to the ground. Once he'd finished shouting at him, he'd repeatedly kicked his officer where he lay. The captain obviously deserved his beating. Only a fool would lose his army's cannons. The captain had protested that he had not been in command of the unit and was only relaying the news. Nevertheless, Dudley sent the man off to recover them, and he'd returned with only three cannon at a cost of thirty soldiers' lives. All the powder and shot had been lost to the rebels. Dudley had been so enraged he'd made his way to the scaffold where the rebel prisoners patiently awaited their fate with nooses around their necks. The gallows had been hastily built from scavenged wood, and each rebel stood on a chair. Dudley made his way between the gallows, kicking out the chairs from underneath his captives. One by one, they swung by their necks, with their hands tied behind their backs — their feet dancing in the air as they wriggled. Dudley's frustrations appeared to have been vented after the first twelve men, so he ordered his soldiers to finish the rest.

The bells sounded eight o'clock.

The forty-nine rebel corpses hung limply in the dusk light, their eyes bulging. Fulke walked between them to see if there was anyone he knew. He was fascinated by the expressions cast on their cold faces. He felt privileged to stare at the dead, seeing what they themselves would never see. 'You shouldn't have surrendered,' he whispered to himself.

He turned to leave the gallows.

Dudley was issuing orders to a party of soldiers. Once he'd finished, he gestured to Fulke. 'Take me to Steward's house.'

Dudley clapped his hands above his head and summoned Parr to follow them. Fulke led them the short walk to Steward's house in Tombland. The area was teeming with soldiers, and Dudley shouted to his men that he didn't want a single rebel to pass beyond the Maid's Head, and if they did, he would hang the section commander at fault.

That was leadership, thought Fulke. Strike fear into men's hearts if you want them to fight with all their strength.

He and Dudley had a lot in common, he mused.

Fulke banged on Steward's door. Moments later, the deputy mayor appeared in a linen shirt and velvet waistcoat. Steward looked over Fulke's shoulder. 'May I welcome the Earl of Warwick to my house. Do come in and join me for dinner.'

Steward held out his arm against Fulke's chest, blocking his passage. 'Fulke, please let the earl pass.'

Seething, Fulke allowed the earl to push past him to shake Steward's hand.

'Fetch my banner and have it strung up above the doorway,' said Dudley, addressing Fulke. 'I want the rebels to know I am here, and I am unafraid.'

Steward welcome Parr back as he followed Dudley inside.

'That will be all for today, Fulke,' said Steward.

The door closed, leaving Fulke standing motionless on the doorstep. He heard the bolt slide across, and his cheeks glowed red as his frustration soared. The new life he'd envisaged for himself, one of power and influence, felt like it had slipped through his fingers in as much time as it took to close a door.

He stalked off, where to, he didn't know.

I'll show them what I'm capable of, he thought. Those stuck up pricks will rue the day they turned their noses up at Fulke.

*

The door burst open. Tiniker screamed, and Margreet, mute, ran to her sister's embrace. The soldiers filed into their kitchen. The captain's metal breastplate and helmet made him look even larger than he was as he surveyed the room's entrances and exits.

'Fifteen men to a floor,' he shouted, looking out of the

rear window to the meadows and gardens beyond.

Piepen the canary tweeted in his cage.

'Oi,' shouted Alfred in vain. 'What right have you…?'

The soldiers' heavy footsteps pounded up the stairs and across the wooden floor above, and Tiniker found the courage to get to her feet, 'Excuse me,' she said as the captain approached, 'this is my house. I am guaranteed safety in this house by the deputy mayor!'

'Does he report to the king?' The soldier turned to acknowledge her for the first time. She could see the hardness in his eyes.

'I'm…' she stammered.

'I have orders to take this house and everyone along this street.'

This was what Tiniker had feared, as their house was on the front line between the rebel camp and the city defences.

'You can stay if you want, but you must keep out of our way, and you should expect fighting.'

'You can get in my way if you want,' said another soldier. He grinned, rolling the handle of his battle-axe in his palm.

Tiniker shuddered. She looked at Alfred, who glanced towards the front door. She nodded. This was no place for Margreet.

'Margreet, fetch your coat and some warm clothes. We're leaving.'

'Come on, Margreet. I'll help you. Come with me,' said Alfred.

Alfred held Margreet's hand, and they took leave of their own house to the sound of their furniture being rearranged and soldiers' voices.

On the street, Tiniker turned to Alfred, 'Where should we go? Surrey House?'

'No. We need to blend in, and look like Norwich locals.'

They would have to find shelter. There would be a curfew and anyone found on the streets after dark would be assumed to be a rebel and killed without enquiry.

As they walked, soldiers busied themselves as they prepared to defend the street from rebel attacks. They listed and dismissed places they could hide.

'I know where we can go,' said Tiniker. 'There is a wool warehouse on King Street. It was where my father used to buy his wool. Nobody will need wool tonight. It's by the wharfs on the river, out of harm's way. If we could break in there, we should be safe.'

*

'Robert, you can't surrender once you've started fighting,' said William.

'He's right,' said Alice.

'I didn't start the fighting. I was trying to agree the peace!' shouted Robert.

'Be that as it may,' said William making every effort to stay calm, 'the fighting has started, and they will hold you to account for it.'

'*Me?*'

'Us, then, if you prefer. I am not trying to argue with you, brother, I am simply pointing out that events have overtaken us, and we cannot pretend otherwise.'

'We were so close.' Robert pressed his fists onto the dining room table, taking his weight off his feet. His eyes were closed. 'We could have overcome the herald's manner, but what were the odds of some vagrant child taking a shit in front of him? What's more, that bloody fool shooting him?'

'The Lord works in mysterious ways,' said Alice, with a conviction that didn't fool her husband.

William massaged his temples.

'It's simple: we have no choice. We have to win.'

'Thanks to Miles, we have their cannon, but they're no use when we're attacking in the streets,' said Luke Miller, entering the conversation. 'We'd be better to use them on open ground in a traditional battle.'

Robert ignored Luke's suggestion. In time, they agreed their aim must be to capture Dudley. The army would be leaderless, and they would be able to negotiate surrender in exchange for his safe return. They'd heard he was staying at Steward's. Mayor Codd again pointed out that he had warned Robert that Steward was a snake.

'The bridge, the road to the cathedral and Tombland are all bristling with troops,' reported Miles, who'd seen things first hand on the streets. A direct approach was impossible. They would have to create a diversionary attack to draw Dudley's forces away from him.

'What about here? Will they not come for us?' asked Alice.

'Unlikely,' said Miles. 'We can retreat and hide in the darkness. It would be chaos. They'll take comfort from the defences of the city.

When the planning was finished, and a course of action agreed, Miles and Luke left to organise their followers who waited outside on the heath for a plan of attack. Robert walked to the far end of the dining room and stared out of the window at the evening sky. He must have watched the sunset a thousand times before, but never had the colours seemed so miraculous. As the light disappeared, the orange gave way to pink, which faded to blue into grey.

Am I getting closer to you, Lord? Robert asked in his mind. What will we talk about, I wonder?

Robert crossed his fingers.

*

Alfred took one final look down the street. All clear. Then, with a kick, he smashed down the side door to the warehouse. The door creaked. Another kick was enough to force it open. It was even darker inside. He ushered in the girls and refastened the lock from the inside. It wouldn't hold if pushed, but it would pass a casual inspection from a passing eye. Tiniker drew a sigh of relief and hugged Margreet to reassure her. They were unlikely to be found, anybody unlucky enough to be in Norwich tonight was more concerned with their personal safety than that of their woolstock. Against the walls, the wool packs were piled floor-to-ceiling. It would have been washed once already, but the stale air was thick with the dusty smell of livestock. Margreet stayed below, while Alfred and Tiniker climbed up to fashion out a hiding space by moving the bags.

It reminded Alfred of playing in the straw after harvest when he was younger. He built two spaces to conceal themselves in. They were soft and warm, and Tiniker helped Margreet into one of the spaces. She lay beside Margreet and held her hand until she drifted to sleep. Ever since the death of their father, her younger sister had been able to sleep at the drop of a coin and for as long as she was undisturbed. Tiniker envied her, as she'd spent more time awake at nights than she had asleep. Now that her father was gone, all the problems were hers to resolve. She was the parent now; bearing the weight of responsibilities she had never before appreciated. Fortunately, she had found Alfred to help her. She owed him a lot.

She checked Margreet was sleeping before creeping out of the hiding space, slipping down off the woolpacks and finding Alfred, farther along, buried between the stacks. He looked surprised as she squeezed into the small hole he'd fashioned and rested her head on his chest.

'Thank you for keeping us safe,' she whispered.

Alfred stroked her hair and said nothing. Tiniker tilted her head so she could see him in the gloom.

'What will you do when this is over?' She had found herself worrying about this lately. She feared he would return to his village and resume his old life.

'I'd like to stay with you.'

'People would talk. We'd be living in sin.'

'Suits me,' quipped Alfred.

Tiniker smiled. She put her head back down on his chest and felt herself relax.

'Will you fight with Mr Kett?'

'I don't know. If I don't, people will ask where I was, and why I didn't fight. I would be a coward.'

Tiniker gripped his shirt with her fingers. She didn't want him to fight.

Alfred paused. 'I think what he wanted was right and worth fighting for.'

Tiniker lay in silence. She felt a tear well in her eye. She had lost everything. First her mother, then her country and now her father. She had only just been spared her maidenhead as Fulke had tried to rape her.

Now her house was jeopardy. She'd betrayed the Ketts in the hoping of keeping it, and now it was occupied by soldiers and would again be in the front line of the fighting. She doubted it would escape the flames a second time.

Without Alfred, all she had was Margreet. She couldn't imagine how she would survive. Even if Steward intended to be good to his word, he wouldn't rebuild the house for the sake of a weaver's daughter. The guild wouldn't help an unmarried woman. Laying in the warm and musty darkness of the warehouse, Tiniker no longer trusted that things would turn out all right.

Looking at Alfred as he lay peacefully, she now leant forward and kissed his lips. She lingered before parting her mouth. Their tongues touched and slowly began to dance. She felt herself melt. She tingled as his hands travelled over her clothes. She knew it was wrong, but after everything she'd been through, why shouldn't she blot her pain for once?

She rolled on top of him and ran her fingers through his hair as they kissed. Her body yearned for more. Her whole life, her father had forbidden her from boys, but he was gone. Alfred's hands found their way into her linen smock and squeezed her breasts in her undergarment. He wanted her — she could feel his erection swell beneath her. She would have expected to feel nervous, having never gone so far with a boy before, but being with him, she no longer felt like a girl. She wasn't. She had the responsibilities of a parent, the body of a woman, with the desires to match. She sat up and pulled her smock over her head, exposing her body to the night air. Alfred's warm hands ran over her flesh. It was dark, but he would be able to see the silhouette of her breasts, and the thought thrilled her as he touched them. She pulled up his shirt, and he wriggled free from its sleeves. He pulled her down beside him. They tried to kiss as they removed his hose. Naked, he rolled on top of her, his weight pressing her down into the wool. She gasped as he entered her.

*

Fulke watched the flames of small torches descend from the heath like burning ships on a black sea. He followed their progress from the meadows behind the Flemish girl's house. In his mind, he could hear her sobs as he pictured her bent over her bed. She would keep for another day. Only Alfred, who he hadn't seen since, knew it was him who'd killed Lord Sheffield. Fulke was confident that Alfred wouldn't talk, but a nagging doubt at the back of his mind told him that it was a loose end he would be well advised to tidy up.

Fulke was in the mood to vent his anger at being snubbed by Steward and Dudley. He didn't care who suffered. For him, this rebellion had become a way of escaping his past. To have that dream dashed so publically, rekindled all his bitterness to those in power. He had authority of his own now, and he intended to keep it, and to use it. To what end, he was not yet sure.

The flames didn't stop opposite the bridge but continued south. Fulke waited behind the last hedge before the wharfs at the waterfront. In the distance, he could see the boom towers. He couldn't see whether the towers were garrisoned. The rebels stopped short of the tower on the far bank of the river, perhaps trying to work out if it was safe to cross. The towers were linked by a heavy chain that rested above the water line to stop boats from entering the city wharfs until they had paid duty on their goods.

Tonight the rebels used the chain as an easy method of crossing the water. The first few slid into the water and, holding onto the chain, began dragging themselves across the river.

The first arrows flew when they were halfway across.

Fulke heard the twang of bowstrings and the shrieks of men. The rebels withdrew, and he watched them cross farther upstream. Fulke cursed their foolishness. They would have been better to cross the river downstream because now they had to negotiate the gates at the end of King Street, which must also be manned since they were only a few yards inland from the boom towers. The rebels must have feared crossing the river inside the city limits in case they were met by soldiers on the far bank.

They could not know that Fulke had passed through the meadows unchallenged. Although Dudley's forces were far superior to those of Parr's original army, he was still a long way short of being able to guard every inch of the perimeter. Fulke lost sight of the rebels behind the city wall as they crossed the river in the distance. Perhaps it was a good time to get involved? He ran along the hedge line and pushed through, scratching himself against a blackthorn. He emerged on King Street. The piers and warehouses that lined the street appeared deserted. Fulke jogged down the road towards the gates. He was ordered to halt by a sentry. Fulke stopped in the road.

'I am sent by the deputy mayor. I have come to warn you of the rebel plans.' He spread his arms out. 'I am unarmed.'

Satisfied, the sentry invited him to approach, and Fulke ran the final yards. Only two soldiers on the ground guarded the gate. Fulke couldn't see how many people were in the gatehouse above.

'Here they come,' shouted a voice from the top of the gatehouse. 'Ready, lads.'

'What do you know?' asked the sentry. He had a front tooth missing. There was nothing to identify him as a professional soldier. No armour, no helmet. He carried a hand axe with a dagger tucked in his belt. These were militiamen, Fulke assumed.

'You are about to be attacked by a force of rebels. Prepare yourselves to fight to the death.'

'How many are you?'

Fulke put his hand on the guard's arm.

'Be calm, reinforcements are on their way. I will help you until then.'

A roar erupted from behind the gate. The rebels were charging.

'Hold firm, lads,' said the sentry turning his attention to the gate. Arrows loosed from the top of the gatehouse.

Shrieks rang out of shot men. Moments later, the wooden gates shook as the rebels barged into them. Fulke noticed the sentry's hand shaking. The other guard took a step back from the gates.

'I am unarmed, friend,' said Fulke. 'I could be more use to you with your dagger?'

'Here, take it,' said the sentry, fumbling for the hilt as he drew it from its scabbard.

Fulke took the dagger and examined its blade. It was tarnished, but sharp. 'Thank you.'

The gates shook again.

The commotion distracted the sentry. Fulke plunged the dagger into the unsuspecting man's kidney. He fell to his knees and looked in disbelief as he touched his side to see the blood on his hands.

Fulke stepped towards the other sentry. 'You're next.'

He fled. Fulke laughed.

He kicked the injured sentry over and picked up his hand axe. He would be dead in no time. Fulke went into the gatehouse and found the key hanging on a hook by the door. He unlocked the doors and removed the bolt, lifted the catch and let the rebels in.

*

The cook scurried into Steward's dining room with a pewter plate in each hand and a third balanced on his arm. He put the plates of roasted partridges down in front of each of them. Steward leant across the table and filled the goblets with the wine left by Fulke.

Steward raised his glass. 'Gentleman, welcome. Let us toast to your victory, and Norwich's safe return to law and order.' They clinked glasses. 'Let's eat.'

Steward was glad he'd had the foresight to send his cook out to replace the tableware stolen by the rebels, paid for from the funds embezzled from the treasury. If they won't pay to help us to protect ourselves then they can at least suffer the cost of my reparations, Steward reasoned. Dudley and Parr tucked into their meal with the appetite of men who hadn't eaten in weeks. Before Steward's fork had touched his lips there was a furious banging on his front door. This could only be trouble. Conscious of his own safety and fearing if he left the table for a moment, Dudley and Parr may conceivably finish his partridge for him, he shouted for cook to show the visitor in.

The floor shook to the heavy footsteps of Sir Thomas Paston in a silk-lined, sky-blue doublet. He looked more like a man headed for a party than one involved in the defence of a city. Despite appearances, Paston lived in Norfolk and therefore had a greater stake than most in what was happening.

'Rebels have entered the city to the south.'

'And?' said Dudley.

His manner confused Steward, surely this was concerning?

'Well, they're in the city. Our defences are breached.'

'Of course. What did you expect to happen?' asked Dudley.

'They have set fire to the warehouses and buildings on King Street.'

Steward noticed Paston looked confused too.

'Thank you, Paston. That will be all.'

'What should we do, sir?'

'Nothing. Wait for them to come to us. Then slaughter the lot of them.'

Steward interrupted. 'Earl, let me explain. That is our warehouse district. It's a vital part of the city's trading network. Its destruction,' Steward hesitated because the thought was unthinkable, 'would set us back a generation.'

'I'm sorry to hear that,' replied Dudley. 'Paston, you're dismissed. Stand to and don't go chasing about in the dark looking for trouble. Let the trouble find you.'

Paston nodded and left the building.

'But, sir,' continued Steward, fighting to control his temper, 'the city's grain store is in that area. If it were to burn then we could not guarantee we could feed ourselves.'

Dudley nodded and resumed tackling his partridge. He finished his mouthful and washed it down with some wine. 'Look on the bright side, Steward. If there is no grain, then there's no reason for the rebels to recapture Norwich.'

Parr grinned, and Steward squirmed in his seat.

'No. In fact there'd be no reason for the place to exist at all,' he said, staring at his host.

Steward felt a new contempt for the man sitting, enjoying his hospitality, with his oiled beard and his receding dark hair. In his finery, he was every inch the courtier, and his disdain for others was distasteful even by Steward's standards.

Dudley put his cutlery down and looked Steward in the eye. 'My orders, no,' he corrected himself, 'my *aim*, is to put down this rebellion.'

'What about the king's subjects who live here?'

'It's a pity, I agree, but what better way to deter rebellions elsewhere is there than for the news of Norwich's annihilation to spread?'

'Everybody must make sacrifices for the good of the realm,' said Parr.

There were a dozen things Steward wanted to say, but nothing was to be gained by falling foul of the nobility.

'What would it take for you to see things differently?'

Dudley grinned. 'Something you can't afford.'

'Try me.'

'Seymour is a fool, and even a well-intended fool cannot be allowed to ruin our country. Once I have quelled this disturbance,' Dudley turned his attention to Parr, 'I will return to London and take the protectorship for myself.'

Steward saw Parr's eyebrows rise. 'And William here will support my coup. If he wants to recover his reputation from his disastrous attempt to recover this city that cost Lord Sheffield his life.'

Parr put his fork down. 'You can count on my support, John.'

Dudley smiled. 'Thank you. I'm glad we understand one another.'

Steward put down his cutlery.

He'd lost his appetite.

*

Robert stood on the edge of the escarpment outside Surrey House. Beneath him, the darkness of the night sky was interrupted by the orange glow of burning buildings in the distance.

'I'm not sure what's worse,' said William. 'Being up here, unaware and out of control, or down there amongst the chaos.'

'Do you think we'd be in control if we were down there?' asked Robert.

He was certain he preferred the view from the safety of the heath. Behind them, the rest of his rebels waited patiently amongst the shelters. Once Robert knew the flanking manoeuvre had worked and drawn troops to the flames, he'd send the rest of his men over the river. Under cover of darkness, Miles was positioning their cannon opposite the bridge, ready to batter the gatehouse doors down.

Robert knew he must face trial by battle, again.

Behind them, there was a rustling. Luke Miller appeared, breathless, carrying a burning torch.

'Robert. They've blocked the end of King Street, and despite our efforts to harry them, they won't put one foot in our direction.'

'Thank you, Luke,' said Robert. 'William, stand the men down. There'll be no attack tonight.'

*

Tiniker woke to the sound of people outside. It took her a moment to remember where she was. She realised the air was thick with a smell. She lifted her head from Alfred's chest. The building was on fire.

48

Sunday 25th August, Norwich

Tiniker wished it were warmer as they huddled together against the wall of the church. Churches were supposed to offer refuge, but this one had locked its doors. They must have feared it becoming a rebel dormitory, like many of the other churches. It wasn't a very Christian thing to do, she thought; surely the church should practice what it readily preaches?

She felt flat today; she was tired and cold. They had narrowly escaped being roasted alive as the wool warehouse was enveloped in flames. Alfred had managed to break open the doors that opened onto the jetty over the river, but there were no boats, so they had to wade into the water away from the flames. Her smock and red kirtle were wet, and her leather shoes were sodden and caked in mud. They'd escaped the attentions of the rebels who were busily setting fire to anything that didn't move, but they couldn't afford to be found wandering at night after the curfew, so they'd found shelter in the nearest churchyard.

Alfred returned from emptying his bladder. Margreet was still asleep, her head resting in Tiniker's lap.

'You should see the damage they've done. There's only the merchant's hall left.'

Tiniker wasn't interested. She'd seen what rampaging men were capable of. Why hadn't Alfred kissed her this morning? Now he'd taken what he'd wanted, she worried she was going to be tossed aside or taken for granted. She kept having flashbacks to what they'd done last night. At the time, it had been the most intensely pleasurable thing, if a little uncomfortable. In the cold light of day, she began to regret it. She had thrown away the one thing that she'd kept sacred all her life. She wondered if he would stand by her. Would he be bragging to his mates about what they'd done together?

'What's the matter?' asked Alfred.

I would have thought it was obvious, thought Tiniker. 'What are we going to do?'

'I'd suggest we go and see what's left of your house.'

She woke up Margreet, and they walked back to their house on Bishopsgate. Tiniker was sore, and the walk was uncomfortable. Margreet cried the whole way. It was some relief to see her house still standing. It didn't look like any fighting had taken place. Alfred went to check and came back to confirm it was still occupied by soldiers. Seeing her upset, he did at least put his arms around her and hug her. He kissed her forehead.

'I want to go home,' said Margreet.

'We can't, Margreet,' snapped Tiniker.

'I'm hungry,' cried her sister.

'Alfred, we can't stand about here waiting for the day's fighting to begin,' said Tiniker.

The streets were all but deserted, bar the patrolling soldiers. They had no money and needed to find safety, so Tiniker considered their options. She could see only one, but it was not without risk. She suggested they walk back towards the cathedral. As they passed the burned-out houses, Tiniker turned over the arguments for and against in her mind: Had she Alfred's loyalty? However she looked at it, now was the time to test her alliance with Steward, even if it meant testing her relationship.

'I know somebody who will offer us sanctuary.'

'Who?' frowned Alfred.

'An important man,' said Tiniker.

'Who do you know who's important?' Alfred sounded disbelieving.

Tiniker smarted. 'Augustine Steward,' she said as casually as she was able.

'The deputy mayor?' scoffed Alfred.

'We sold him some weave.'

'Hang on.' Alfred grabbed her hand. 'Was it Steward who called at the house? I wondered how you could manage that house without your dad. You're rutting Steward, aren't you?'

'No!' protested Tiniker, 'How could you even think that?'

'Was that him; sliding paper messages under your door?' She hesitated. 'Margreet said he comes to the house regularly.'

'Alfred. It was him, but not in the way you think,'

'You spread your legs for him?'

She slapped him, and Margreet started to sob again. 'I am not laying with Steward.'

Tiniker couldn't bear to look at him. The truth was worse. Tears welled in her eyes. She couldn't face more lies. She'd lived a double life for weeks — it might even be a relief to have the truth out.

'Steward guaranteed my house if I spied on the Ketts.'

Alfred looked puzzled. She saw in his eyes the moment the penny dropped.

'I thought it was too good to be true. You befriended me to get close to Kett. You've lied to me. I thought you loved me. Now I see it's all a ruse.'

'I do love you.'

'People who love each don't do that.' Alfred turned and stormed off.

Then the cannons opened fire.

*

Parr entered Steward's dining room as Dudley was finishing his breakfast. Steward had invited some of the city's aldermen to join them. No sooner had the sun risen than the merchants had rushed to inspect the damage by the wharfs and estimate their losses. They'd arrived at Steward's front door shortly after. Rather than convey their concerns, he'd invited them to join the earl for breakfast.

'I can hear cannons. What's happening?' asked Dudley.

'They're firing at the north wall now, sir. Attempting to open a breach and force entry,' reported Parr.

Dudley nodded. 'Put three hundred men on our side of the wall and make sure they don't get through. Sound a trumpet if you're overrun, but don't retreat. Your country requires that you fight to the death.'

Parr looked ominous. That must be the worst type of order to receive, thought Steward, glad he'd never taken up soldiering.

'Steward, how many bridges cross the river in the city?'

'Four,' replied Steward, his heart sinking.

'Parr, have your men destroy the bridges.'

Steward leapt to his feet. 'Earl, I must protest. Your actions are putting us back into the dark ages.'

Dudley's face turned puce. He rose to his feet and with a look that would have terrified the devil, drew his sword. Steward's arse twitched as Dudley pointed his sword at him, raised the blade and kissed the hilt.

'I swear on my life and that of King Edward that I will not retreat from this city while blood flows in my veins. I would sooner lay down my life than retreat before that dog, Kett.'

Steward sunk back into his chair. There was nothing more to say.

*

Alfred was too angry to regret leaving Tiniker to fend for herself because quite frankly, he thought she deserved whatever befell her.

He wasn't sure he really meant that, but he felt too betrayed and wounded to see it any other way. He didn't know where he was walking to, but his back was turned to Tiniker, which was sufficient direction.

Why hadn't she come after him?

She really had used him, he thought, as the river curtailed his walk. He heard noises to his left and stopped on the riverbank to watch as a party of royal soldiers busied themselves on Whitefriars Bridge. They looked to be chiselling holes in the mortar and filling them with what he assumed was gunpowder.

'I don't think that bridge will be there for much longer.'

Alfred turned to find a familiar face.

Fulke.

He was smiling, which could mean a great many things.

'How are you, mate?' Fulke had on an expensive jacket.

'Not bad, thanks.' replied Alfred. It wasn't true, but it was what people normally said.

'Looks like we're in for a good old barney today, lad.'

'You and I?' asked Alfred.

'No, you fool. The rebels and the army.'

Alfred breathed a sigh of relief.

'I've no quarrel with you, Alfred. You were protecting your woman as any man should. I owe you for the back of my head though.' Fulke rubbed his head at the memory of being clubbed with a pan. 'So, you had her yet?' Alfred's face must have said what Fulke wanted to know: 'You have! You old swine. Good for you. I bet she puts out faster than Catherine Howard?' Fulke paused. 'Although, you don't look very happy about it. Where is she?'

'Gone,' replied Alfred. He would never see his Flemish beauty again.

'Well, least you had your way with her. Don't give her a second thought. What say you and I go for some drinks, and I'll tell you what Fulke's been up to these past days?'

'I don't have any money.'

'Don't worry about that. I've plenty. Let's go and get drunk.'

Fulke put his arm around Alfred's shoulder, and they began to walk. Alfred wasn't sure he should be going for a drink at this time in the morning, but it was hard to say no to Fulke.

Fulke roused the innkeeper of the Adam and Eve. He opened up for them, locking the doors behind them. 'He needs money the same anyone else,' said Fulke. Fulke ordered two strong ales, and they parked themselves in the corner of the tiny inn.

'I was working for the deputy mayor, Steward, but as soon as his new friends from London arrived, he closed the door in my face. He'll rue the day he made an enemy of me.' Fulke took a large swig.

'Huh, Steward.' That man had a lot to answer for, thought Alfred as Fulke continued to recount his grievances. Alfred swigged his ale while he listened to Fulke. 'Well, he's no friend of mine.'

'What's he done to you then?' said Fulke.

'He used Tiniker to spy on the Ketts.'

Alfred watched as Fulke's mind connected the rest. 'Ah, so that explains why she visited him at night. I was at his door one night when she stopped in.'

Night-time visits could only mean one thing, thought Alfred. Steward would never have protected her for no reason. She had to be giving him something. His heart felt like it was being squeezed.

'So she didn't like you, after all,' continued Fulke. 'Should have let me rape her! Women, mark my words, lad, they're all ugly on the inside.'

Fulke ordered two more drinks.

Alfred was only halfway through his first; he would have to quicken up. He thought about what Fulke said. He feared it was true. Lynn and now Tiniker, who he thought was to be his true love. She had given him the greatest night of his life last night and in an instant, taken it all away. He sunk the rest of his drink; doubtful he would ever understand.

'That Steward needs a slap,' continued Fulke. 'That's what this whole thing was about. People like him, twisting and manipulating the likes of us.'

'Seems a long time ago since you beat up Morris in Wymondham.'

Fulke smiled at the memory and polished off his second ale. He nodded to the innkeeper to bring more. 'I think you and I ought to help Kett whip these London scum and give them a lesson they won't forget.'

'I'm not much use with an injured shoulder.'

'Don't worry about that. Stick with me, and you'll be fine.'

Fulke had decided: he was going to fight, and Alfred was going to go with him.

Turns out not much has changed, thought Alfred as he swigged his third ale of the morning.

49

Monday 26th August, Mousehold Heath

Robert's foot trembled as he stepped up onto the dais under the oak tree. It was six weeks since he'd declared it his 'Oak of Reformation' at the centre of his camp on the heath. Gathered in front of him were his followers, over ten thousand, despite the loss of their fallen brethren and those that had abandoned the cause. Looking out at a sea of expectant faces, Robert knew he had to give the speech of his life, and if he did, he would succeed in achieving the outcome he wanted least of all.

He took a deep breath. 'My brothers and sisters, we have come far. Not one, but two royal armies have not been able to stop us.' There was a cheer from his audience, and he felt his nerves calm. 'We have brought to the king's attention and that of his council, the injustices that infect our land like a plague. Your bravery and your efforts will ensure that never again will the gentry take for granted the loyalty of the common man.' He paused to let the cheers subside. 'We seek simple demands: to sleep in our beds free from worry that when we wake in the morning our farmland will be there to feed our families, that our lord will treat us fairly and respect our customs.' He was struggling to be heard, so he summarised. 'We seek nothing more than the way of life of our forebears before us and that this way of life is there for our children after us. But,' he paused, 'to preserve this way of life, God in his wisdom has decided we must fight for it, and we will!' He raised his arm above his head and drank in the roars of the crowd.

'For two days we have fought bravely for control of Norwich. Whilst we have infiltrated the northern part of the city, we have not succeeded in pushing the royal army out. Our stalemate is threatened by the arrival today of fourteen hundred mounted German mercenaries.'

Boos rang out across the heath.

The easy part of his speech was over.

'With these reinforcements, I can no longer guarantee our safety on the heath. The city's grain reserves have either been destroyed or are in royal hands.' There was total silence across the heath. 'So tonight, under the cover our darkness, we shall say goodbye to our home on the heath and withdraw. Tomorrow, we will offer Dudley battle, and a bloody nose he shall never forget. If God demands we fight, then we shall, and we shall prevail.' Robert could sense nervousness. 'We shall prevail!' he shouted. 'We are undefeated. We have their cannon and more men, we also have two things on our side with which they cannot compete: What we seek is right and just, and men will fight with more strength in their hearts for something they believe in and know to be right than any man who fights at the whim of another's orders. We must trust in the Lord's guidance. He will deliver us.'

Finally, Robert got the cheers he needed.

'We have come so far, and we will journey on together, in the name of what is right, and in the memory of those that have already forsaken their lives for our noble cause. Gather up your weapons and ready yourselves to leave.'

Robert stepped down and made his way to Surrey House. He hoped he could make it back before he was sick.

*

Alfred saw the first of the royal army's infantry appear along the hedge line at the bottom of the field. He jumped to his feet and grabbed his sword. The rest of the rebels followed suit and raised themselves from their various slumbers on the ground. Alfred had mistakenly thought the waiting was finally over, but as more of them slowly filed in, he realised it would be at least an hour while they lined up for battle. He felt impatient to get on with it. Since leaving the heath last night they'd positioned themselves in an open grass field at the top of a gentle slope. They'd spent the rest of the night digging a ditch to slow an enemy advance, cutting and burying stakes to protect their cannon.

With their preparations finished shortly after sunrise, they formed into ranks and attempted to get some rest. Alfred hadn't slept. Nervous men chatted to take their minds off what was to come. Brave men gave rousing talks, and angry men vented their spleens. As every hour passed, they grew hungrier and thirstier. No doubt the army had enjoyed a good breakfast and deliberately taken their time to sap the strength of the rebels.

Alfred lay thinking how he came to find himself here. He'd escaped the Ketts, and yet now he was about to fight for them, again. He'd been angry at Tiniker's betrayal. He still hadn't forgiven her, but had memories of her laugh, her voice, the touch of her skin: he missed her. He loved her. However, that was irrelevant now, he told himself for the umpteenth time. Alfred had opted to fight, and that was that.

Some rebels had vanished during the course of the night, but Fulke had made a case for fighting and persuaded a great many to stay. Perhaps Master Peter was right, and Fulke's thirst for fighting came from his father.

Wherever it came from, Alfred knew he'd once again fallen under his friend's influence. He hoped it wasn't going to be a lesson that cost him his life. He yawned and willed them to start. Gripping his sword to stop his hand from trembling, he took a moment appreciate the sight.

The flags of the army fluttered gently in the breeze. He reckoned there couldn't be more than seven thousand. Maybe the earl had left the rest to guard Norwich in his absence? They outnumbered the enemy and the less of them they had to fight, the better. The cavalry was at each flank with arquebusiers and pikemen alternating across the centre in front of the earl and his generals on horseback.

Alfred supposed every man wanted the same thing: to fight bravely and lay his head down this evening, certain they would wake in the morning. Luke Miller was an excellent fighter and Alfred had hoped to be next to him in the lines, but he must be elsewhere. He still had Fulke, whom anyone would have him fight for them, rather than against. Alfred watched The Earl of Warwick ride in front of his men, cantering the length of his front line.

Alfred presumed he was addressing his men to prepare them for battle.

Apparently, there were procedures for how such things were done. Would the Earl of Warwick be held captive by nightfall, he wondered, or would Mr Kett be alive? They would soon find out. The thought of it made the hairs on Alfred's neck bristle.

Between the two forces was a ditch, and a line of the

gentlemen prisoners held captive by the rebels. They were chained together and stretched out across the battleground to form a human shield.

'Look lively, Alfred,' said Fulke. 'Miles is about to light his cannon.' Alfred turned to see what was going on. On either side of him extended a tightly packed line of rebels, armed with pitchforks, axes, clubs, swords, bows and arrows.

Behind him, the Kett brothers were both mounted on horseback. Robert wore his leather jerkin and felt hat.

Alfred thought he looked tired.

Robert's hand was raised in the air. He brought it down, and moments later the sky was filled with the deafening blast of rebel cannon fire.

Hearing the blast, the prisoners fell to the ground. Some of the shot fell short and thudded harmlessly into the earth. Others found their target and skittled soldiers like bowling pins. The rebels cheered, and a waft of gunpowder smoke carried past them on the breeze. Once the rebel cheers faded, you could make out the screams. Alfred watched Miles commanding his novice team of artillerymen. He rushed to reposition the cannons that had missed, while the others cleaned out their barrels to reload. Then came another bang. This time screams from the rebel lines. The royal cannons hadn't fired, but there was no smoke. Alfred looked along the rebel line and saw a cloud of smoke about the rebel cannon. Men lay on the floor screaming. Miles was shouting at them furiously.

'They must have forgotten to swab the barrel with water,' said Fulke. 'The burning embers must have ignited the powder. He's blown off his hand and injured his mates. Idiot.'

It didn't inspire confidence.

The four royal cannon fired, and each found their target.

Two rebel cannons were crippled, felling the crews with shrapnel, and another two men suffered direct hits and were killed outright. Miles shouted at his terrified crew to return and finish reloading. Alfred watched the royal gunners busily reloading. The earl had been wise to spread his cannon. The rebel cannon were grouped together and presented a temptingly large target. Miles shouted the order to fire. The ground shook, and the air cracked. Either side of the earl, men fell. His own horse startled, but he regained control of it, though the royal standard dropped to the ground. The rebels cheered this good omen. All the shot had been pointed at the earl. Presumably, thought Alfred, if they could kill the earl, the army were leaderless and may fall into disarray.

Miles and his crews were reloading when the next volley clattered into their ranks. Another cannon was felled. Kett shouted for his archers to fire. The thwack of bowstrings and the whoosh of arrows brought courage back to the rebel lines. There was more cheering as they watched the infantry felled.

Then the royal trumpeters sounded their horns.

*

Robert glanced at William. He could not understand how his brother could look at ease. Perhaps it was resignation. He had no family and often remarked that at his age, every day was a bonus.

Robert felt exhausted. His neck and shoulders were set so rigidly there had been no point in him carrying a weapon. At his age, he couldn't make a difference, and if it was so close that he was required to carry arms, then the day was already lost. All the women had left camp to return to their homes. There had been many a tearful goodbye, praying they would see their husbands again. Alice too. Robert was glad she was gone. He couldn't bear for her to see him like this. With so much resting on his shoulders, she was worried sick, which only made it worse for him. He'd sent some riders with her, and they had reported on their return that she was home safely. He'd prayed he would take her in his arms again.

The cavalry charged and the bowman released another volley of arrows into the sky. The ground shook as the horses got up to a gallop. His cannon took another pounding, leaving only two operational. The air filled with blood-curdling battle cries as the royal troops broke into a steady jog, their pikes lowering to protect the gunners that accompanied them. Should they run to meet them? Robert had no idea. He had never felt so ill-equipped for a task in his life. They stood their ground and waited for the clash of steel.

The cavalry arrived first. A few had fallen prey to his arrows, the rest lowered their lances at the final moment and slammed into his lines, skewering the poor devils and trampling their neighbours. They dropped their lances and began wildly swinging their swords and axes, scything down men around them. Robert watched as one man drove his pitchfork into the belly of a horse, causing it to rear and unseat its rider.

The cavalry finished off the cannon crews and pushed inwards on the rebel flanks. The infantry crossed the ditch, and the arquebusiers fired their first volley. Together they were louder than the cannon. Robert felt a shot whizz past his ear. He crouched in his saddle and held onto his horse's neck. It never occurred to him they would target him. What if they shot his horse from under him?

As the smoke cleared, the rebel archers fired arrow after arrow into the enemy ranks. Robert knew they didn't have enough arrows for a sustained effort as they hadn't had time to rearm overnight, but if they could make every arrow count, then they could blunt the advance. Dudley, however, remained just out of range.

The arquebusiers had reloaded and charged alongside their pikemen to avoid more rebel arrows. The lethal pikes resembled a weathervane: a long, wooden pole, with a twin axe blade for chopping and slicing combined with a spear tip for stabbing. The pikes pierced the rebel frontlines, and Robert felt his gut twist at the sound of the screams of his injured men. He saw the hatred in the eyes of the enemy — men driven delirious with bloodlust. The pike handles were twenty-foot long and held his men at bay. Any that did wriggle past their injured comrades were picked off by the arquebusiers in between. The pikemen leaned forward and began to push, driving the rebels back. Only the rebel arrows were effective at softening the royal lines. A few pockets of rebels made it within arm's reach of the enemy.

Hand to hand fighting followed. The gap between the lines filled with smoke and the grass turned slippery with blood.

He heard William shout. His brother was clutching his arm. A shot had clipped him.

To his front, Robert saw Fulke bringing his meat cleaver down to knock out a pike blade. He stamped it into the ground, forcing the soldier to drop the weapon. Alfred fought shoulder-to-shoulder with Fulke. Together they hacked at the defenceless pikeman.

If they could break through, they could start to surround them and attack from the rear.

Robert ducked as more shot narrowly missed him.

He turned his horse to retreat a few yards and get a view of what was happening. Now the battle was underway he had forgotten his aches and pains, but his mouth was dry, and he was short of breath. He looked down his lines. Through the gaps in the smoke he saw the cavalry had rounded each flank and were cutting down his men from behind. His line was being encircled. Unless they could punch through, they would be surrounded. There were shouts to his left.

He saw a party of rebels fleeing the field.

The troops had broken his line. Robert didn't need experience in warfare to see what was about to happen. The end of his left flank was isolated. They would be worn down, and then the troops would overwhelm his flank.

William pulled back and joined his brother. 'We're holding them in the middle.'

Robert pointed to the left flank.

He knew for certain they were done for.

'Maybe we can regroup?'

More shouts on the right, and Robert saw more of his men running from the field. They had dropped their weapons.

'We're routed.'

The line was collapsing. It was only a question of time now.

William gripped his arm. 'Robert, it's pointless both of us dying. Flee now. Save yourself.'

'How can I? These men followed me. If I desert them…'

'Then you'll die too, and this whole thing will be futile. Save yourself. I'll see this through.'

'I can't,' pleaded Robert.

'Brother, kings do it all the time. Get to the coast. Board a boat. Just go.'

Robert hesitated. Could he live with his conscience if he left? He heard the screams of dying men all around him.

'Think of Alice,' barked William.

'What about you?'

'I'm old, brother. My time has come. Maybe they'll be happy with my head.' William moved his horse alongside Robert's. He leaned over and hugged him. Robert kissed him.

'Go!'

Robert kicked his horse. It took all his concentration to stay in the seat. He squeezed the reins between his fingers as hard as he could. He was beaten. He had failed. Thousands had died because of him, and he was going to survive. He knew it wasn't right. He left the field overtaking rebels fleeing and crossed a hedge into an open field. He picked a path through the crops and rode to the highest point, relieved to be clear of the shouts of dying men. He turned to take one last look at the battle. The last of his forces were being corralled into a ball and enveloped by the troops.

They were finished.

Uncertain what he should do, he decided to pick a direction and see what fate brought. He chose north.

50

Fulke shouted, 'Fight us, you cowards!'

A pike point was pressed against his chest and quelled his snarl.

The clash of steel was replaced by the groans of the dying.

Alfred struggled to stay upright. The pain in his injured shoulder had returned with a vengeance. Alfred glanced down at his blood-spattered torso but couldn't see any wounds.

The royal standard appeared over the heads of the enemy. Underneath it, the earl kept at a safe distance.

'You are defeated,' he announced. 'Drop your weapons.'

'Do as he says, lads.' Alfred recognised the voice of William Kett. He couldn't see Robert. He must have been killed?

The gentlemen prisoners were freed from their chains, and the remaining rebels were marched back in two lines to the heath, enclosed on either side by the royal troops. One man had made a dash for it, only to be cut down by a pursuing cavalryman. Thereafter, nobody else tried. Alfred overheard some rebels grumbling that the king had used the Italians and Germans against them, so they'd showed no mercy. Alfred couldn't see what difference it made who pointed a pike at you. He fought to keep his eyes open with every step of the walk. He was so tired he barely cared what the earl had in store for them.

They stopped near Mr Kett's oak tree. Alfred watched the earl talking to William Kett, who'd had his horse taken from him and his hands tied together. While they waited, Alfred had a look around to see whom he recognised amongst the remaining rebels. It was hard to tell who was who beneath the masks of blood and dirt. Geoffrey Lincoln held his hand over a slash on his arm that was dripping blood. Miles, the gunner had survived too. Luke Miller must have perished, as he was nowhere to be seen. The earl finished with William Kett and issued orders to one of his soldiers who dashed off.

'What's happening, Fulke?'

Fulke's jaw was clenched shut, and he shook his head. Alfred thought Fulke would have preferred to die fighting than be captured.

Soldiers busied themselves with the earl's orders. Three returned with lengths of rope. One counted out fifty rebels, touching Alfred and Fulke on the arm as he passed. They were separated from the rest.

'Take these men to be hung from their so-called Oak of Reformation,' said the earl as casually as if he were ordering a plate of food from a tavern.

Alfred's head slumped. He was about to die.

'You will be hung from the boughs of this tree until you are nearly dead,' continued the Earl. 'Then your bellies will be slashed and your innards removed. Your heads will be cut from your bodies and placed as a warning to others of the penalty for uprising.'

Alfred felt sick.

The man behind him was splattering the back of his heels with vomit. Fulke cursed the earl out loud. Those separated shouted protests, 'Why us? What about them?'

'They will return home. They deserve to die like yourselves, and I would have no hesitation in dispatching them had it not been for the harvest that needs gathering,' said the earl.

There was uproar amongst the condemned men, but Alfred was too tired to protest. He'd chosen to fight. He had little left to live for. Tiniker was gone. Mr Kett was gone and with it most likely his job. Fulke was his only friend, and he'd led him to a battle he shouldn't have joined. It wasn't a pleasant way to die, but it would be over quickly, and he could join his parents in heaven — if there were such a place. As he looked about landscape, he could see nothing that he would miss. Alfred felt strangely calm. Perhaps his next life would be more generous. Death would offer him a chance to close his eyes and sleep for eternity.

Two soldiers pointed at the boughs of the oak and debated how best to hang so many rebels from just one tree. The condemned men sat on the ground, guarded closely by soldiers. The other captured rebels, including William Kett, were made to stay and watch the executions. As word spread, people ventured up from Norwich to see the spectacle. No one wanted to miss a good hanging.

The soldiers tested a rope on the tree. Satisfied, they came and took the first ten rebels. The earl was deaf to their protests and pleas for mercy. They were lined up, and one-by-one hoisted by their necks on a rope hung over the largest bow and held aloft by a soldier standing behind. A foot clear of the earth, their legs flayed back and forth, and their hands grasped at the rope around their necks. The spectators recently arrived from the city cheered and clapped their approval at the swift justice being dispensed to those that had plagued their city.

Satisfied that they'd danced the hangman's jig for long enough, the earl nodded. A soldier walked along the line of men dangling from the tree and with his knife, cut a slit across the underside of their bellies. Their screams were stifled by the rope around their throats. Another soldier followed and inserted a hook into the cut and drew out their intestines. A mass of steaming entrails slopped onto the floor at their feet. One-by-one, the men stopped wriggling and began to sway gently, their lives over. The earl nodded as they were dropped to the ground without ceremony. They landed like sacks of grain thrown from a cart. The soldiers loosened the nooses and carried the bodies away to be decapitated.

A soldier counted out the next ten men, Alfred amongst them. Having witnessed the fate of those before him, his calm evaporated. He retched, and his hands trembled. He told himself to be brave and face death like a man, as they lined up as instructed under the tree. The stinking entrails of the previous victims at their feet made Alfred retch again. He had Fulke to his right and Geoffrey Lincoln to his left. Neither man said anything. The nooses were placed around their necks. The first man was hoisted. Next up was Geoffrey. He rose and began his fight for air. Alfred felt the rope tighten and the fibres press into his neck. His throat was squeezed, and his head felt like it was about to detach as his feet left the ground. His eyes bulged, and his sight went. All he could think of was the last thing he would ever see was the view across the heath. He fought for air as his body used up the last of its reserve. Everything went black.

*

Steward regretted his charity. Whilst her sister slept, the Flemish girl had done nothing but cry. He'd shut them in a guest bedroom, but no matter where he went in his house, he heard her sobs. At noon he decided to fetch her a cup of wine and water, hoping it would numb her sadness. They'd arrived on Sunday, destitute. In a moment of weakness, he'd agreed to house them. It may yet prove worthwhile, Steward told himself as his carved wooden staircase creaked when he made his way upstairs. If she could weave the bombazine cloth she and her father had shown him, Steward could have a monopoly on the fabric. Whatever the outcome, the rebellion had nearly run its course and life would soon return to normal.

He knew he had become too preoccupied with the commotions caused by the Ketts, but the chaos they had brought now presented opportunities for those that were awake to them. As the country continued its switch to Protestantism under Edward VI there would be a growing demand for the dark and sober clothing favoured by the reformers. It would pay to keep the elder girl on his terms.

'Here, take this.' He passed the wine to Tiniker, perched at the end of the bed.

Her younger sister was under the covers but awake, staring blankly out of the window.

She thanked him and took a sip.

'You should eat something.'

She shook her head.

'What has got you so upset?' asked Steward as he leant against the window frame of his small guest room on the second floor. Her father had been dead for weeks, and he didn't believe anybody could be so upset over a house.

She looked at him through bloodshot eyes.

'It's a man, isn't it?'

Young women were prone to such lovesickness. Had he left her? It didn't fit. She was pretty and intelligent — not a woman that any man would likely walk away from. Besides, ordinary people's lives had been on hold during the rebellion. There was too much uncertainty for people to address their own affairs when the threat of violence hung over them. Then it dawned on him, 'Ah, he's a rebel, isn't he?'

She shook her head.

'He was helping her spy on Kett,' said the younger girl.

'Quiet, Margreet.'

'What became of him? Is he dead?'

'I don't know.' She took another swig of wine.

Steward cleared his throat. She'd get over him.

He heard shouting outside. He cast his sight out of the window and saw people running in the street below. He opened the window. They were shouting between them. He heard something about the rebels being defeated. It must be over. He'd better go and see what was happening.

'It sounds like it might finally be over,' he announced. She looked pained at the news. 'Come with me then. Some fresh air will do you good. You can't spend your life hiding in here. Besides, they might have finished with your house, and, as fabulous company as you have been, people will talk if they believe I am harbouring young girls in my spare room.' Steward grinned at his own joke.

'We might even find out what befell this man of yours.'

The younger girl wanted to stay indoors, but Tiniker heaved herself up and followed Steward outside. They walked in silence towards the heath. They passed returning cavalrymen, their armour splattered with blood and their faces portraying jubilant exhaustion. They relayed to Steward how the rebels had been slaughtered and that Dudley was hanging the ringleaders up in the heath. One of the Ketts had been captured, the other unaccounted for.

If justice was being dispensed, Steward must show his

face. He was curious to see how Mayor Codd would respond given his association with the Ketts. Again, it presented another opportunity for Steward to oust his rival for good. He hurried on towards the heath with the foreign girl in tow.

Surrounding the oak tree was a curious crowd.

The earl was mounted on horseback and looked to be directing proceedings. Steward looked about and saw William Kett.

'What happened to Robert?' he asked a nearby spectator.

Steward pushed through the crowd, eager to find the earl. There was a cheer. A handful of rebels were hoisted up on a tree branch and began to swing by their necks. Their fellow captives looked on with foreboding.

Serve them right, thought Steward as he moved round to the earl.

'Stop, Augustine, it's him,' said Tiniker pointing to a man in the group of men waiting to be hung.

'Who, your man? Looks like he's about to pay the price for his poor company.'

There was another cheer as the rebels had their innards drawn out, a practice Steward had always found distasteful and unnecessarily violent.

She tugged his sleeve. 'We must save him.'

'What's he doing here with the rebels?'

'He's not a rebel,' she insisted, her feet planted firmly to the ground.

A soldier came over to the condemned men and pointed at ten of them. The girl's boy was one of them. They made their way over to the tree.

'He looks like one from where I'm standing.'

'If it weren't for him, you'd have known nothing about Kett's movements. We have to save him,' she demanded.

Steward shook his head. He hadn't come up here to act as

an ambassador for some peasant boy.

Tiniker pummelled him in the chest with surprising force. He was lost for words. Her cheeks flared red, and her gaze pierced his skull. 'Help me save my man, or you'll not get one yard of cloth from me.'

Steward paused. 'You'd lose your house.'

'Keep your bloody house. Save him, or I go home.'

The noose was placed around the boy's neck.

Steward groaned. 'I'll speak to the earl.'

'I'm coming too,' she declared as she followed him.

Her boy was hoisted off the ground.

'Earl, good day to you. May I be the first to offer my congratulations.'

Dudley looked down from his horse. 'Not now, Steward. I'm busy.' The earl gave the nod, signalling the knifeman to slit their bellies.

'I'd like to discuss something with you, your grace. It concerns one of the men hanging from that branch,' said Steward.

'I think they have more pressing concerns just now, Steward.'

'Stop! Stop! Everybody stop what you're doing,' shouted Tiniker as she ran out from the crowd.

The knifeman paused as he looked up. Alfred was next. His face had turned purple.

'What's the meaning of this, young woman? Do you want to be strung up with them?' asked the indignant-looking Dudley.

Steward cringed. That wasn't the way to endear the earl.

'Let him down. I'll explain. You're about to kill a man who has helped you more than you know.'

Dudley frowned.

'Please!' she shouted. Steward flinched. She was on thin

ice herself now.

Dudley squinted at her. He looked over at the men holding the ropes. 'Let them down. You might need to make room for a woman in a moment.'

He turned his attention back to Tiniker. 'This better be good, young woman.'

One man, with a branding on his forehead, relieved of his guts, remained hanging; the rest slumped to the ground falling in the entrails of those before them. Together, they coughed and spluttered as they writhed on the ground, pulling at the rope around their necks. Alfred wasn't moving. Maybe it was already too late for him. Starve a man of air, and they could be driven mad. Steward had witnessed botched executions in his career.

Tiniker strode up to the Earl. 'I spied for him,' she said, pointing at Steward. 'The only reason I got any information was because Alfred Carter betrayed the Ketts.'

There was an intake of breath from the on-looking rebels, shocked that there should be a traitor amongst them.

'So why was he on the battlefield today?' asked the Earl.

Steward shook his head. He couldn't see how she could answer that satisfactorily.

'We certainly can't even ask him when he's dead.' Her anger was turning to desperation.

Dudley looked to Steward. 'Is this true, deputy?'

Steward looked at Tiniker and nodded. 'Very much so, your grace. He was an integral link in my intelligence gathering.'

The creases in her forehead softened as a glimmer of hope was given.

Dudley sighed, 'Very well, bring him to me.'

Tiniker ran to Alfred.

Steward walked over to see if the boy had regained

consciousness. Tiniker shook him as he lay on the ground.

'Alfred, wake up, it's me.'

*

The world came back into view. Was that Tiniker kneeling in front of him? Am I dead and gone to heaven, he thought? His neck burned, and his brain throbbed. The floor was moist. He was lying on something warm that smelt of offal. He checked his guts, they were still intact. What had happened? He looked around, Geoffrey Lincoln hung over him, blood dripping from a gash to his belly — his eyes were vacant.

Fulke lay on the ground. He was breathing. So were the other men.

Tiniker hugged him.

'What happened?'

'You're alive!' She kissed him. 'You have to tell the earl that you helped me spy on the Ketts. Come on.'

The earl, looking impatient seated on his horse, beckoned him over. Tiniker put her arm around him to help him up, and he groaned as he struggled to his feet and hobbled over to the earl. Steward followed him. The captured rebels booed him as he walked, and he was spat at. William Kett, his hands tied, also made his way to the earl. As Alfred's confusion began to clear, it dawned on him what must have happened: Tiniker had given him a second chance, but he would have to admit to betraying Kett. His reputation would be ruined.

'State your claim, boy,' demanded the earl, irritated that his proceedings had been interrupted.

'He worked for the Ketts,' said Tiniker.

'I'll hear it from him, if you don't mind. Did you?'

Alfred nodded. The earl glanced at William Kett, and he

confirmed it.

'Why do you deserve to live?'

Tiniker implored him with her eyes. Alfred was unsure. Any help he'd given the authorities was inadvertent. He'd never intended to pass on information. He'd been stupid. She had duped him. He looked around. Every rebel's face wore a venomous expression. They would most likely lynch him themselves. William Kett's expression was stern.

'Speak up, lad,' demanded the earl, growing impatient.

'I was Mr Kett's page. I told her everything I knew about Mr Kett's plans.'

Alfred cringed at the boos and hisses and shouts of traitor.

'And yet you were on the battlefield alongside the Ketts and their rebels?'

Alfred didn't know what to say. Usually in these situations he said too much and made matters worse.

'He lived with me,' said Tiniker. 'Your troops commandeered my house. We had nowhere to go. He left me to find out what the rebels were doing and report back. He must have been swept up.'

'What do you think, Steward?' asked the Earl.

Steward tilted his head.

'Tell him,' demanded Tiniker.

He nodded. 'It's true, my lord. There is reason this boy should be spared, and there are others more worthy of execution.'

Dudley summoned a soldier. 'Replace this one with one from the shelf.'

Alfred shivered. His life had been exchanged for another. He'd just been handed back his future. He should have felt like a man reborn. Instead, he felt sick. Tiniker hugged him.

A commotion broke out over by the oak tree. Fulke had

removed his noose and broken free from his guard. He dashed over to where they stood.

'Steward, what about me?' asked Fulke. 'Tell them I work for you? Dudley, you remember me? I unlocked the gates and let you into the city.'

'Very well, fetch another rebel,' sighed the earl.

Fulke winked at Alfred.

'Thank you, your grace.'

Alfred scowled at his friend.

How typical of Fulke. He was the sort to fall in shit and come up smelling of roses. Alfred looked at the faces of the condemned men. Each one, a life cut short. Every dead man left a family condemned to hardship. How had he and Fulke escaped with their heads? Alfred thought back to Wymondham. If Fulke hadn't beat up the constable, he wouldn't have led the riots to Morley and Hethersett. He'd taken Flowerdew's bribe to involve Mr Kett's enclosures. Without Fulke, none of this would have happened. He tried to rape Tiniker and then pulled Alfred back into harm's way. The only reason Alfred was standing here was because of Fulke.

'He killed Lord Sheffield.'

There was a stunned silence.

'Who did?' demanded the earl.

Fulke's mouth fell open.

'He did.' Alfred pointed at his friend. 'In cold blood.'

Fulke lunged forward, head-butting Alfred. Alfred collapsed on the ground, and Fulke kicked him, called him obscenities. Tiniker screamed as Alfred lay prone, suffering the blows until two soldiers dragged Fulke away.

'You swear it?' asked the earl.

Alfred couldn't move. He lay on the ground, blood streaming from his nose. He nodded. 'I was there.'

'String him up!' shouted the earl.

Fulke wrestled against his captors, but more soldiers surrounded him. He cursed and spat as they dragged him to the gallows. He wriggled to the last as the men fought to put the noose over his head. He shouted as two soldiers hoisted him up. Wasting no time, the knifeman slit his belly and emptied his guts on the floor. Everywhere fell silent. Fulke was dead.

Alfred closed his eyes. Whatever the rights and wrongs of recent weeks, there was now one measure of evil less in the world.

51

Robert slid from his horse, fell to the ground, and his legs gave way beneath him. His beast was blowing and in need of water. They had ridden near fourteen miles at full gallop in an effort to put as much ground between themselves and the army. Robert could barely recall the countryside and villages he'd passed through. His mind had been dominated by thoughts of his children, Alice, William and the men he'd led to death. He'd cried for much of the journey, lamenting the hundreds of chance occurrences that had led him to this point. The boy defecating at the herald's feet. Cooper's intervention in stopping him speaking to Dudley. Flowerdew's bribe. Alfred arriving at his house to warn him. As a gambling man, the odds of it all conspiring seemed like a one in a hundred thousand chance, and yet, here he was, collapsed on the verge of the road, fleeing for his life.

His body wanted nothing but to fall asleep, but he couldn't stop in plain sight. He was the most infamous man in Norfolk and news of his disappearance would spread through the villages like wildfire. He'd already attracted enough unwanted attention; a lone horseman galloping through the villages had not gone unnoticed by local people. Even if they were sympathetic to his actions, they would not resist the opportunity for gossip a sighting of him afforded.

No doubt the crown would offer a reward for him.

He dragged himself up and led his horse to the nearby pond that had caused him to stop. The horse drank the stagnant green water, and Robert looked through the hedges and spied a barn. The sun neared the western horizon. If he could rest there he could continue his journey in darkness. He could be in the small port of Wells on the north coast by mid-morning. From there, he intended to board the first boat leaving the country.

As the horse drank, Robert heard a creak.

A heavy draught horse pulled a laden hay cart out from behind the barn. It was accompanied by two men and a boy. Robert contemplated making a dash for it, but his legs were like goose fat, he wasn't sure he could mount his horse from the floor. Better to stay and act innocently, he concluded.

He bid them good evening as they approached. He felt their eyes boring into the back of his head.

'What's your business taking from my master's pond?' asked the cart driver.

'My mount was blowing. She needed a drink. Thank your master most kindly for me.'

'Who should I say thanks him?'

Robert's tired mind couldn't think of any name other than his own. 'A man in a hurry.'

'What's got you in a rush then?'

Robert cursed. The leisurely routine of farming life meant that those involved always had time to poke their noses into the business of others. To commoners, the small innocuous goings on of others was the wood that fired their daily gossip in the alehouse. Robert ignored them, hoping they would get the message.

They did.

The driver mumbled an insult and slapped the horse's reins. Once they had moved on, Robert led his horse behind the pond to the barn. Like all farm buildings, the doors were unlocked. To pilfer a meaningful quantity of a crop required too many accomplices, took too long and was too hard to be transported and hidden, all under too many watchful eyes. Robert knew well that this apparent casualness with their supplies didn't mean that farming people were trusting of one another — they were ever suspicious. He led the horse in and closed the doors. The evening light seeped in through the gaps in the old timbers, casting rays of shining dust like silver needles across the gloom. Robert tethered the horse to an eyelet on the wall. He couldn't conceal the animal, so there was little to be gained by fashioning a hidey-hole for himself. It would be dark soon. He slumped onto the hay and was asleep before his head fell still.

He woke to a prod in his chest. Robert knew instantly where he was. Two candles interrupted the darkness. He could see the moonlit sky through the open doors of the barn. A pitchfork pressed against his chest.

'Who the hell are you?'

Robert's mind was ill-prepared. He felt the tines of the fork press harder.

'I'll save you the trouble of lying to me,' said the man. 'My money says you're Kett?'

Robert sighed. 'I am.'

'Ride to Norwich, boy,' said the man with the pitchfork. He was speaking to a younger lad whose face was lit by the glow of the candlelight. 'Tell them we've got Captain Mischief.'

52

14th October, The Tower of London

Seymour slumped onto the bed in his new quarters. He stared at the cell's stone wall. How many before me have stared at this wall, he wondered: Anne Boleyn, Thomas Cromwell perhaps? How many of them, like him, were related to the king.

He was Edward VI's uncle, residing in the tower at his nephew's pleasure, and at the behest of the insufferable Dudley.

That whole business in Norfolk was what had landed him here. If only they could have waited, his enclosure commission was set up to achieve the very thing the rebels claimed to want. All the troubles had filled Dudley's sails with wind.

Once Dudley had returned from quelling the rebellion, he'd requested a dukedom. Seymour had refused him. Why should a man expect such a reward just for performing his duty to his country? Especially a man who had helped precipitate matters by holding enclosures of his own. Dudley's motivations were too selfish to see the logic in

Seymour's method. Instead, Dudley had set about forming a rival council in London whilst Seymour was at Hampton Court.

Behind closed eyes, Seymour saw an image of Edinburgh. It was a month since his Scottish campaign of eight years had collapsed. He'd been denied the gift of finishing what Edward Longshanks had started centuries before, all because the people in command lacked the wherewithal to run the Scots through once and for all. On top of that, the French, who'd been in cahoots with the Scots all along, had declared war. The French were laying siege to the English town of Boulogne.

Those territories were rightfully English titles, why could the garlic-ridden French not respect that?

Seymour was too tired to sleep.

He had retired to Windsor for the king's safety. He'd issued letters to the common people, requiring them to stand up in protest against Dudley's behaviour and protect their king. None had answered his call to set up camp in Windsor. It seemed the English people were willing to rise and be led by a provisional nobody like Kett, but not willing to take up arms and protect their king and his administration.

Recalcitrants, the lot of them.

Instead, Dudley had arrived and persuaded the king to let him assume the protectorate. Seymour had been led through London to the tower.

At least he'd kept his head.

Seymour woke the next morning and cleaned his face in the water bowl on the table beside his bed. His door was unlocked, so he went in search of something to eat and drink. He was lucky to enjoy some privileges: he was allowed to freely move around the communal areas and corridors at will, provided he was in his cell by sunset. There was no chance of escape as all the staircases leading up to the cells were locked and guarded by two men. He helped himself to a beaker of rainwater from the butt that stood in the middle of the hall.

Then he sat down on the bench next to an elderly gentleman and engaged him in conversation.

*

Robert watched the glistening waters of the Thames from his cell window. He'd never seen a river so wide, teeming with so many types of boats. He passed the time by counting the boats and categorising them according to the purpose for which they were designed; transport, trade, defence, pleasure and so on.

He'd been held captive here since the ninth of September. Having been captured in the village of Swannington, he'd been presented to the Earl of Warwick, who'd been enjoying a thanksgiving service at St Peter Mancroft church in the marketplace when he'd heard of Robert's capture. Robert had joined William in the dungeons of the guildhall.

At least here he had daylight and a view.

They'd been tied to a cart and driven through the streets of London. Robert had never been to London, and now he'd seen it for himself, he regretted not having visited prior to now, with Alice. The streets thronged with people in a desperate hurry, rushing to get from place to place. He saw men with skin as dark as the night, others in clothes the like of which he'd never seen before. Carts and drays moved about the town, bringing goods to the houses that lined the streets. The air was alive with voices.

He could have made money here, of that he was sure. He understood why his son had wanted to come.

Capture had proved, in a way, a relief. He knew, barring a miracle, it was the end for him, but he realised now what a toll the rebellion had taken on him. Despite the prison food, the knot in gut had passed, and he felt like a weight had been lifted. He tended not to dwell on his fate or that of the men he'd led. He'd striven to give his best and only acted with the best of intentions. Nor had he demanded anything of anyone that they hadn't been willing to freely give. Even the gentlemen he'd imprisoned and used as human shields at the battle had been unharmed, if not a little inconvenienced.

So it seemed to Robert that God had other plans for him.

His regrets were reserved for Alice who he hadn't seen and was denied the opportunity to say goodbye to. It pained him to think of her going to bed at night on her own.

William returned to the cell.

Robert, as the principal troublemaker, was chained to the wall by his ankle.

'I have somebody to see you, brother.' William was followed in by a finely dressed man in a white ruff beneath a purple jacket, the sleeves of which had been slashed to show off the yellow silk lining.

'Robert Kett?' said the man.

'Yes.'

Robert looked at William. 'This is Edward Seymour, until yesterday, the Lord Protector of the Realm.'

Robert heaved himself to his feet.

'Mr Kett, you and your brother are the reason that I am in here,' said Seymour.

'We could say the same of you, sir,' said Robert. The man didn't smile, and Robert detected contempt. 'Or we could agree that we've all been brought here by the same man, John Dudley?'

'You'll both hang, you know.'

'I've made my peace with that, sir,' said Robert. 'Please, there is little to be gained by us rowing. Given our surroundings, it seems the time for arguing has passed. Will you take a seat and join us? I'm afraid I can't extend you much hospitality.'

Robert pulled out the chair from the writing desk in the corner of the cell. 'Have you somewhere else you need to be?' asked Robert with a smile.

The duke acquiesced. 'What did you hope to gain by your rebellion?'

Robert now moved to his mattress, dragging the chain across the stone floor. 'You saw our demands, a simple promise to end enclosure would have done it.'

Seymour grunted.

'But alas, you and your people had other ideas, so here we are.'

William sat down on his own bed. 'Are you angry with us, my lord?'

'Yes. Your actions brought my reign to an end. I was dealing with enclosure. People understood I was against the practice, did they not?'

'Yes. But people didn't believe that anyone in your government would comply, all of them being the beneficiaries of the practice.'

'Did you not enclose commons yourself?' asked Seymour.

'Oh yes.'

'Then what on earth possessed you to do what you did?'

'Because it was wrong, what I was doing. I saw every day the consequences of my actions, and I wanted to recount for it. I never intended for things to develop how they did.'

'Are you angry with me?' asked Seymour.

Robert looked at the duke. 'I'd have preferred it if you'd agreed to our demands, of course, and we could have all gone home, but,' Robert couldn't resist a smile, 'I'm not angry with you, nor do I wish you any harm. For my part, I am sorry that I have played some small role in bringing you to this place with me.'

'Some small role?' replied Seymour indignantly.

Robert interrupted. 'When you get to my age, your grace, you come to learn that the only person responsible for wherever you find yourself, is yourself. Where you are now is the consequence of every thought and decision you have taken.'

'I disagree, Mr Kett,' countered Seymour before Robert could finish. 'I alone knew what was needed for this country, and I was well on my way to enacting it. If it were not for the greed and incompetence of others, I would have gone down in history as The Good Duke.'

'You may blame others, sir, and you may believe yourself right, but ask yourself, where has that got you?' Robert opened his palms.

'Do you not blame others then, for by your own account, your deeds were noble and well-meaning, and yet you too are here.' Seymour looked at the ceiling of the cell.

'What good would it do me if I did? In the time I have spent at his majesty's pleasure, I have come to see that blaming others for your own situation, whilst understandable, is the same for one's soul as drinking poison and hoping that it is the other person who gets sick. I hope I don't die, but if I should, then I aim to meet God with a clear conscience, having forgiven everyone who has ever done wrong by me. As is the Christian way.'

The duke nodded.

'In which case, Robert Kett, I concede you are a bigger man than me, and I fear history will judge you more kindly than it will me.

'Thank you.'

Robert and William spent a further six weeks at the tower before being taken to trial at Westminster.

The good and the great were assembled in the courtroom. The two brothers were manacled together in front of six judges appointed to oversee the proceedings. Twelve men, good and true, sat in the jury box. The charges were read out.

The lead judge asked them how they pleaded.

'Guilty. On all counts,' said Robert.

There was a stunned intake of breath across the courtroom.

'To save the court's time, we offer no defence to our actions,' said Robert.

'Very well,' replied the judge. 'You shall be taken to Tyburn where you will be hung, your guts drawn and burned before your eyes. Your heads placed on London Bridge and your bodies quartered and displayed on the city gates.

'Thank you, your grace,' said Robert. 'In light of our cooperation, may you permit me just one suggestion for the court's consideration?'

53

20th October, Kenninghall, Norfolk.

Luke Miller removed his hood and waited as instructed in the hallway. His heart pumped a little faster, and his palms were clammy. Sometime later, Princess Mary arrived, accompanied by three ladies in waiting. Her legs were shrouded by the plumpness of her dress, making her petite frame appear to float as she walked over the coloured floor tiles. Behind her pale skin and sombre expression lurked the only traces of her Spanish lineage: thin lips, dark eyebrows and eyes that squinted at Luke. He fell to one knee and bowed his head. Mary offered her hand, her fingers warm and soft. He kissed the back of her hand, savouring her scent before rising to his feet.

Her legal status may have ebbed and flowed since her late father, King Henry VIII, divorced her mother, but irrespective of her standing, Mary's veins carried royal blood. She was descended from God; in Luke's mind, she personified perfection. A notion that left him both inspired and a little aroused. Whilst he may have been from good stock himself, he fell a long way short of royalty, so such occurrences to meet the princess were to be savoured.

'Mr Miller, let us take in the last of this year's clement weather.'

Mary dismissed her ladies in waiting, and Luke followed her to the back of the house. Mary stopped so he could open the door to the garden for her.

'It's so nice to be back home in Norfolk. We may not have the roses for many more days, so we must enjoy the last of them while we still can.'

Luke followed her outside. The afternoon sun was low, but bright and warm, casting long shadows over the garden.

'Thank heavens for the recent rain, Mr Miller, for without it the garden would look even more dishevelled.'

Luke agreed, and they exchanged small talk as they walked between the manicured beds of neatly arranged plants and herbs. When they were clear of earshot from the house, Princess Mary turned to meet Luke's gaze.

'You may have heard that our new friend, John Dudley, has deposed Seymour?'

'Indeed, I have. Do you expect him to be named lord protector? Will he honour his promise of loyalty to you?'

A brief smile flashed across Mary's face. 'We'll have to see, but by all accounts, Dudley is a man beset by his own self-importance. Once men like him taste power, they'll do whatever they can to keep it for themselves.'

'Then why back him?'

'There is no one on the council willing to challenge him, which makes him the heir apparent until King Edward comes of age. But, unlike Seymour, Dudley has no blood ties to the king. His loyalty will be no more to Edward than it will me, which is at least a step in the right direction, is it not?'

Luke nodded. 'Loyalty is precarious in such ambitious men it seems, Princess Mary?'

Mary nodded. 'Indeed. Now speaking of loyalty, I must

thank you for yours throughout this, *difficult*, summer.'

'Not at all,' said Luke, feigning modesty. 'I merely greased the wheels, a little encouragement to the right people here and there. I fought when I needed to, and neglected my duties when it served your interest to do so.'

Mary smirked. 'What's he like, Kett?'

'Well, if I have one regret, ma'am, it is that the cost of our efforts to restore this realm to Catholicism should be borne by Robert and William Kett. They may have been fools, with delusions of grandeur, ignorant of the game they were really caught up in, but for all that, they were decent men, with honourable intentions to better the lot of their fellow man.'

'They were Protestants though, were they not?'

'Indeed…'

'God will forgive them. For they have been unwittingly doing his work,' interrupted Mary, placing her hand on Luke's arm.

'I had persuaded them to negotiate a peace with Dudley, but events rather overtook them.'

'All actors in the Lord's divine plan.' Mary stopped to admire a rose, leaning over to smell the flowers' perfume. 'Tell me, Luke, have you seen anything as ridiculous as our Tudor rose, with its bastardisation of red and white petals?'

'I fear for me to make such a comment might be considered treason.'

Princess Mary laughed. 'Not to my ears, Luke.'

'Your grandfather created to it symbolise the compromise required to bring peace to the warring factions that divided the country.'

Princess Mary resumed walking. 'Maybe. But there can only be one faith, one true God. On that we must never compromise. We must continue to agitate.'

'I agree. Cranmer and his poisonous book of common

prayer should not be allowed free reign to pollute people's souls.'

Mary stopped and turned to Luke. 'Your father would be very proud of you, Luke Miller.'

Luke nodded. He preferred not to talk openly about his late father, a staunch catholic, for fear of becoming emotional. 'It is my pleasure to serve you, Lady Mary. I will forever do your bidding, in whatever small way I can.'

'He was a noble man, your father, a great comfort to my mother and I. A true believer.' Mary started walking again, running her fingers across the top of the rosemary bush that bordered the lawn. 'I so wish to right the wrongs of my father, Luke. We must do whatever it takes to bring about the demise of his wicked Church of *England*, and restore our links with Rome.'

'Let me know how I can assist.'

'Our hopes are in Dudley's hands, for now.'

'Well my lady, if Dudley gives them any provocation, there is no shortage of people around here, protestant and catholic alike, that would want to give him a bloody nose, for what he did to the Ketts and their rebels.'

Mary nodded. 'For now, do what you must to keep it that way. We shall have to wait and see what God has planned next for my little brat of a half-brother. I believe with all my heart, God will punish Edward for his crimes against the true religion.'

Mary plucked a sprig of rosemary and tossed in into the air. 'Luke, come pray with me.'

A beaming smile spread across Luke's face and his skin prickled with excitement. His small acts of service had led him to the intimacy of sharing prayers, and common cause, with the Princess Mary.

54

7th December, Tiniker's house

Alfred groaned in pleasure. Tiniker climbed out from under the bed covers and peed in the pot they kept under their bed.

'Do you want a drink, lover?' she asked. Tiniker ran downstairs to fetch some small beer. Alfred loved nothing more than watching her naked. She looked more beautiful every day. This past week her eyes sparkled, her cheeks glowed, even her breasts appeared to have swelled. She climbed back into snuggled up to his warmth.

'I need a drink after that,' grinned Alfred. They only ever had sex in the mornings. Tiniker worked hard all day, so she was too tired come nightfall. Alfred was happy either way. She passed him the beaker of ale. He took a sip and sighed.

'Let me have some. We are celebrating after all.'

Alfred frowned, 'Celebrating? What, it being a Saturday?'

'That too.'

What was she talking about?

Tiniker propped herself on her elbow. She looked him in the eye. 'Alfred, I'm pregnant.'

Alfred's mouth fell open. No words came out. Unsure what to say, he put some ale in. Tiniker was looking at him expectantly. He recovered from his shock, and a broad smile crept across his face. 'That's the best news I've heard. Ever.'

Tiniker looked relieved, excited and little nervous all at once. He leant over and kissed her. She returned his kiss with interest.

They made love again.

Alfred felt like the happiest man in England. He could never have known that the rebellion would prove to be the turning point of his life. After everything he'd endured, before it and during it, it had delivered him from Lynn and life in Hethersett. It had brought Tiniker into his life. It had taken him to the verge of death, and since then, Alfred vowed never to waste another day to drunkenness and idleness. He endured a brief ignominy after admitting a treachery that he'd never committed. Despite what others said, his conscience was clear as far as the Ketts were concerned. But it had meant, with nowhere else to go, he been forced to forgive Tiniker. She'd welcomed him into her home. Margreet too.

Alfred had grown fond of Tiniker's younger sister. She was simple-minded, but she laughed at his jokes and had a good heart. Tiniker had taught him how to weave, and together they made a new cloth called bombazine. Steward bought everything they could make. They would never be rich, but they didn't want for anything. They had bread in their bellies, a roof over their head and a warm bed. It felt like nothing could go wrong.

'Alfred?' Tiniker propped herself up on her elbow again.

'Yes, Tiniker,' said Alfred laying on his back with eyes closed and his mind numb.

'You do know what this means?'

'What?' he mumbled.

'We have to get married.'

Alfred nodded. He hoped he appeared calm, but inside he was in turmoil: he was already married. Bigamy was an offence, that if discovered, people never recovered from. Alfred pictured himself in church, gazing into Tiniker's eyes, the pastor reading the bands: 'Does anybody here know of any reason why these two should not be legally married?' Alfred shuddered and cleared the thought from his mind. It was too dreadful to contemplate.

'We've lived together for three months, and people are starting to talk.'

'Who?'

'The butcher, Steward, old Elsie next door.'

She was right.

They couldn't go on like this. To be unmarried and living together as man and women, they risked being ostracised. Once it became known they had a child, people could refuse to sell their wares to sinners. What if Steward stopped buying their cloth?

'We must,' said Alfred, quickly settling on the lesser of the evils. All their parents were dead, so they need not seek any permission. They were free to choose one another.

'I love you, Alfred.'

Something in her voice suggested there was more to follow that statement. 'I love you too, Tiniker.'

'If we get married, I will become your property and would be required to obey you in all matters.'

Alfred smiled, 'Good isn't it?'

'Alfred, I'm serious. We may not be equal in the eyes of the land, but under this roof, I never want to be treated as property. I may need your protection, but you will need my love. Margreet and I have had to overcome too much to submit ourselves to become beholden to the whim of a man.'

Alfred pulled her tight against his ribs. 'My love, if I'm

under this roof with you, that is more than I could ever wish for.'

She kissed him, letting her lips linger on his. 'Are you going to ask me then?'

'Oh yes!' Alfred hesitated. Still, what could he do?

'Tiniker, will you marry me?'

'I will.'

After breakfast they walked up Bishopsgate, past the burned-out houses, into the marketplace. They planned to roast a cut of beef that afternoon to celebrate their engagement.

Despite it being a Saturday, the market was busier than usual. The church bells rang ten. There was a commotion over by the guildhall. Two horse and carts waited by the door. Alfred held Tiniker's hand, and they followed the crowds to see what was happening. Mayor Codd and Steward emerged from the guildhall, followed by the Kett brothers, shuffling, their feet in irons and their hands chained together. William was helped into one cart, Robert the other.

'What's happening?' Alfred asked the man stood next to him.

'They're off to meet their makers. Poor bastards. They deserve to be knighted if you ask me. They're taking William to be hung from Wymondham Abbey.'

'They're executing him at a church?'

'I know. It's wrong, but what do you expect from those half-wits in London? Mark my words, lad, they'll be trouble to come. Maybe not today, but people around here have long memories.'

'What about Robert?'

'They're taking him to the castle. Doing him here as a reminder to warn people off causing mischief. If you ask me, making a martyr of those boys will have the opposite effect.

Those toffs haven't heard the last of us.'

They followed the procession to the castle. Robert was helped off the cart and positioned against the cream stone of the castle keep.

Alfred pushed their way to the front.

There was a shout from the top of the castle, and a length of rope fell to the ground. Alfred assumed the other end was tied to something on the battlements.

Tiniker gasped. 'Look there's a noose at the end.'

Alfred put his arm around her, as Robert shivered in the winter cold. A woman ran from the crowd, but she was halted by the justice of the peace.

It was Alice.

*

Robert had promised himself he wouldn't cry, but his resolve burst. He lifted his manacled hands over her head, and they embraced. He squeezed her so tightly that his hands stopped their trembling. She smelt of herbs, the most heavenly scent he'd experienced in months. Her body shook in his arms, and tears streamed down Robert's cheeks.

He'd hugged her at will all his life, but this time she felt as if she were slipping through his fingers. Alice leaned back so their eyes would meet.

'I'm sorry,' said Robert. It sounded so feeble. He needed to be stronger for her. 'I'll miss you, old mare.'

Alice wiped the snot from Robert's nose.

'I love you, Robert Kett.' Alice gathered herself, but her face remained contorted with pain. 'I've been blessed to have you in my life, and as my husband.'

Robert squeezed her again. 'It's not the best of deaths, but it's not the worst. I'd choose this over being an aged man slowly succumbing to winter's freeze.'

Alice nodded. 'I'm so proud of you, Robert, for what you did.'

Robert smiled. 'But for this, losing you, I'd do it all again tomorrow. I don't regret any of it. It was the right thing to do, and I'll meet God with a clear conscience.'

They kissed, and their lips lingered for the final time.

'Send my love to the boys. Tell them their old man will be watching over them. Tell them to set a better example than I did. One of them should take over the property and look after you.'

Alice sniffed. 'They're taking the house, Robert. It's been confiscated by the crown.'

'Bastards, tell them...'

Alice pressed a finger to his lip. 'I'll manage, people in the town have offered me all the charity any widow could require.'

Mayor Codd arrived and put his hand on Alice's shoulder. Their time was up. The crowd were getting restless in the cold.

'I'm so proud to have been your wife, and history will never forget what you did for your fellow man.'

'I'll be waiting for you in heaven, old girl.'

*

Alice looked lost as she returned to the crowd. The sight of her crying set Tiniker sobbing, and she called to Alice. Alfred froze as Alice headed directly for them. Given the events of the morning, she was the last person he wanted to see, but Alice looked relieved to see some familiar faces.

Tiniker opened her arms and hugged her friend. Alfred rubbed her back with the palm of his hand as he hugged them both. Alice shook in Tiniker's arms and cried into her shoulder.

Mayor Codd held out his hand.

Robert shook it.

The two men nodded to one another. The mayor retired, and the justice of the peace fastened the noose around Robert's neck. He called up to the guards at the top of the castle. The crowd watched in respectful silence as the rope pulled tight. Robert gurgled as his feet left the ground. His legs thrashed against the castle wall. By the time he reached the top, he'd stopped moving.

His body, like the hopes of those that had followed him, was left hanging.

THE END

John 3:16
¹⁶ For God so loved the world that he gave his one and only Son, that whoever believes in him shall not perish but have eternal life.

Historical Note

In writing this book, I have attempted to offer a plausible theory for one of the unknown questions in English history: Why did Robert Kett, a wealthy man with much to lose, become the leader of the 1549 rebellion that bears his name? In attempting to answer this question, one of my greatest frustrations has been the certain knowledge that my theory will be and is, wrong.

At the same time, one of my greatest comforts has also been that the real reason for Kett's participation is long since lost to history. Whilst plenty is known about the events, precious little is known about the main characters responsible for the Norfolk components of this fabulous story. Only two contemporary accounts exist from within Norfolk, both of which take a view sympathetic to the establishment of the time. The absence of pro-rebel accounts has allowed me to take enormous license, as I attempted to explore why things might have arisen as they did.

I am no historian, and my writing should not be judged as such, I have however tried to remain as true to the recorded events as possible. All the dates are accurate or where conflicting accounts occur, they are within a day of their original occurrence.

Nonetheless, this remains a work of historical fiction, and below is a list of all the characters that I have invented. Some of the rebel names I have used are true, albeit no account beyond that of their participation exists. A butcher called Fulke did murder Lord Sheffield, and a plaque bears testimony to that at St Martin at Palace Plain in Norwich. Thereafter, I have exaggerated Fulke's involvement in the commotions. Lord Sheffield's involvement with Princess Mary is a figment of my imagination, although theories exist that her spies were within the rebel camp. I have also taken great liberty with Robert Kett and Mayor Codd's relationship. It is plausible that they could have been acquaintances, although I have seen no evidence to confirm this. What is clearer is that the working relationship that developed between the two men could be described as cosy. Codd signed the rebels' demands and opted to remain at the rebel camp after Kett captured Norwich. I have omitted the alderman Thomas Aldridge from my story as I felt his inclusion alongside Mayor Codd at camp added little extra to the course of events. John Bossell did participate in Kett's representatives, but his real role in the rebellion is unknown. I fear I have treated Augustine Steward harshly. The inhabitants of Norwich owe him a great debt, for he saved many of the fine medieval buildings, which stand in Norwich to this day, including his own house on Tombland.

At their camp, the Ketts did in fact operate from two buildings on the heath: St Michael's Chapel, where Robert is said to have addressed his followers, and Mount Surrey, a stately home built on the site of the former monastery St Leonard's, which Robert used as a prison. Neither building remains, but some ruins are visible.

Throughout the story, I have opted to use the modern street names in Norwich.

Robert was hung in chains from the top of Norwich castle. His body remained there as a reminder of the penalty of treason until it was removed the following summer following complaints from local residents. His body was buried in an unmarked grave. His brother William suffered a similar fate, being hung from Wymondham Abbey.

More surprising however, are the things I didn't make up: the act of the rebel children bearing their backsides at the Bishopsgate Bridge fight causing the defenders to flea and the unnamed boy defecating in front of the royal herald are recorded as having occurred. The evacuation of his bowels and subsequent execution turned the course of English history and sealed the fate of Robert and William Kett – you couldn't make that up!

Whatever the real events of this rebellion, and the myriad of environmental factors that provided such fertile ground from which discontent could flourish, I hope that in writing this novel, despite all its failings, I can draw into people's consciousness one of English history's most fabulously tragic romps. And that the current inhabitants and visitors to Norwich will find a renewed appreciation of the parts of our fine city that feature in this book, as they follow in the footsteps of the Kett brothers and their rabble army.

For those interested in the rebellion, I would recommend the following books, all of which were instrumental in helping me develop my own understanding of events. I am indebted to all the following for their research and writing:

- The Commoyson in Norfolk by Nicholas Sotherton
- An Unlikely Rebel by Adrian Hoare
- In search of Robert Kett by Adrian Hoare
- Kett's Rebellion 1549 by Matthew Champion

- Medieval Norwich by Carol Rawcliffe & Richard Wilson
- Edward Seymour Lord Protector by Margaret Scard
- John Dudley the Life of Lady Jane Grey's Father-in-law by Christine Hartweg
- The 1549 Rebellions and the Making of Early Modern England by Andy Wood

Fictitious characters:

Alfred Carter
Lynn Carter
Richard Smith
Master Peter
Anders Marshwell
Adam Catchpole
John Robertson
David Fisher
Geoffrey Lincoln
Luke Miller
Jan Vinck
Tiniker Vinck
Margreet Vinck

Acknowledgements

First of all, I must thank Mark Robinson, my history teacher at Framlingham College. He will have had no idea the impact his throwaway comment left on me during my GCSE history class, 'Holden I think you have a book in you one day.' Why he should have thought this and why his words should have resonated with me in the way did, I don't know. But they stuck, and some twenty-five years later, I am pleased to finally say he was right.

Thereafter Katherine Skala deserves my largest thanks of all, for teaching me to write. Re-reading my early attempts at this novel, it became clear how much her help improved the manuscript. If this book is anything, it will be due to her tutorship.

I would also like to thank Andrew Morris for encouraging me to believe in myself when others thought I was mad. To Vince Tickel for helping me to make it possible. Richard Beck for his advice on military matters. David Rees for lending me his dissertation on the rebellion. Caroline Farrow, for causing me to continue when I'd given up. Emily Richards, Sean Johnson, Terri Johnson, Cheryl Cooper and Richard Beck for reading the unedited manuscript and for their generous feedback and critique. Nathan Butcher and

Alex Pollard for their help with the website and video content. Claire Blackledge and Paul Strowger at Farrows for the beautiful book cover. Claire Allmendinger for her painstaking removal of all my errors. And to everyone at Holdens, whose combined capabilities enabled the business to prosper while I attended to this manuscript.

And lastly, to my wife, Heather, for her continued patience and tolerance of my writing, her love and support and all the various drafts she was subjected to.

If you've enjoyed this book and would be willing to help others to find it, please leave a review where you bought it.

For access to exclusive additional content, including a video of the actual scenes featured in the book, and very occasional offers and updates, please join the mailing list at:
www.timholden.com